SINCE FOREVER

Neither spoke as the song ended. They stood apart. Rendering silent expressions of pain and anguish, their eyes, fixed on each other, spoke volumes. She turned to walk away.

He grasped her upper arm, stepped closer and whispered in her ear, "You had your say earlier, now it's my turn." He led her through the throng of guests and out onto the secluded deck. "You and I are not over, Alex," he emphatically assured her. "We will never be over."

He released his hold, letting his fingers tingle down her bare arm until he grasped her hand. "I'm in your blood and you're in mine. That's just the way it is, and the way it will always be." He closed his eyes and longingly kissed each finger slowly, one at a time. "I love you, Alex. I've loved you since, since forever, since before we even met. I just didn't realize it until now."

SINCE FOREVER

Celeste O. Norfleet

BET Publications, LLC
http://www.bet.com
http://www.arabesquebooks.com

ARABESQUE BOOKS are published by

BET Publications, LLC
c/o BET BOOKS
One BET Plaza
1900 W Place NE
Washington, DC 20018-1211

All Kensington Titles, Imprints, and Distributed Lines are available at special quantity discounts for bulk purchases for sales promotions, premiums, fund-raising, and educational or institutional use. Special book excerpts or customized printings can also be created to fit specific needs. For details, write or phone the office of the Kensington special sales manager: Kensington Publishing Corp., 850 Third Avenue, New York, NY 10022, attn: Special Sales Department, Phone: 1-800-221-2647.

First Printing: April 2003
10 9 8 7 6 5 4 3 2 1

Printed in the United States of America

Dedicated to Fate and Fortune

ACKNOWLEDGMENTS

I'd like to thank my family and friends for their endless support. Your input, motivation, and contributions are invaluable.

I'd also like to give special thanks to the remarkable women in my life.

To my mom, Mable, and my two sisters Amanda and Karen. Your constant support is truly a blessing. Thank you for patiently listening and encouraging my wild imagination.

To Hattie, Roszine, and Judy, you are the best role models I could ask for. To Rose, Angie, Erica, Wendy, Karen, Kelly, Indera, and Zoë. Your well wishes remain near and dear to me. To Anne, Amanda, Helen, Florence, and Miriam, the past has brought me to the present and paved the way to the future.

And last, I'd like to give special thanks to my daughter and assistant, Jennifer; you are truly a gifted writer.

Prologue

The jangled sound of metal hitting metal broke into the black soundless night. Four stories up, two intruders looked anxiously across to each other as faint puffs of icy breath encircled them.

"Shh, if you don't be quiet we're going to get caught," the smaller intruder whispered into the attached communications headset.

"All right, just hurry up." The other looked down at his state-of-the-art incandescent watch. "We've got less than thirteen minutes to get out of here. Over."

"We have plenty of time. How does it look? Is it straight?"

The taller intruder looked down the side of the building. "Affirmative. Over."

"Would you please stop saying that? It drives me nuts."

"Saying what? Over."

"Saying that!"

"What? Over."

"Oh, never mind. Come on, we're done, let's get out of here."

Instantly they pulled the release pegs, letting the black ropes drop four floors to the frost-covered ground. With quick steadfast agility, the two intruders released the metal clips and slid silently down the nylon ropes, then landed gracefully on the cold hard dirt. They quickly released and removed their harnesses, gathered and wrapped their ropes, then hurriedly met at the appointed rendezvous, beneath the center window.

Simultaneously they knelt down, stored and secured their equipment, then checked their backpacks. Clad in black heated thermal jumpsuits and down jackets, they lowered and adjusted their night-vision goggles. A muted iridescent green glow illuminated the surrounding area. With another clandestine task complete, the two dark figures crept stealthily back into the surrounding bushes.

Adrenaline surging, they covertly circled to the front of the building, then eased toward the darkened parking lot. Hidden by a grouping of low-hanging trees they hurried along the hard grassy path just as a bright orb of light beamed in their direction. They immediately halted their movements and pressed their bodies firmly against the rough bark of the nearest tree.

"He's early!" the intruder whispered into the tiny attached microphone.

"I know."

The security guard grumbled as he hunched his shoulders, bracing against the icy-cold wind. He hated the graveyard shift. He pulled the flaps down from his fleece-lined hat, then shoved his gloved hands deeper into his pockets. The thin company jacket did little to protect him from the frosty arctic chill. His feet were frozen, his hands were frozen and his favorite show was on in ten minutes.

Having just awakened from a quick nap, he was in no mood to be out any longer than necessary. He looked down at his watch. He was early, he knew it, but figured who'd care? Fifteen minutes plus or minus wouldn't change the fact that it was twelve degrees outside. And nobody in their right mind would be out here at this hour. His intention was to zip through his outside rounds, then return to the warmth of the building's lobby as soon as possible. So, at 3:45 A.M. he bundled up and with keys jingling on his hip, began his rounds.

The bright flashlight made low sweeping circles as the unknowing guard swiftly passed the trespassers, oblivious of their presence. The two figures slowly peered around the tree watching as the guard continued another twenty yards, then stopped and turned.

"Damn, he saw us," one of the intruders said as he slipped back behind the tree.

"No, I don't think so," the other said, following his lead and easing back.

Anxiously they waited a few moments. When the guard didn't retrace his steps they grew curious. One of the intruders peered around the tree trunk again.

The other whispered into the microphone, "Is he gone yet?" His partner smiled broadly and chuckled. "What? What is it? What's he doing?"

"He's still by the tree. But I think he's almost done." A few moments later the guard moved on. "He's done. He's leaving." Together they eased around the perimeter while staying hidden in the darkness. They watched as the guard quickly moved toward the back of the building.

The once stilled flashlight returned to the sweeping circular movements as the jingle of keys returned. Minutes later the guard disappeared.

"Let's go." Adrenaline-pumped, the two hastily slid down the embankment, then dashed across the dark empty parking lot. Mounds of plowed snow and ice obscured them from sight. They ran down the street, around the corner, then into a side alley.

Once safely inside the car, they removed their backpacks, goggles and earpieces. "That was close," one said as he inserted the key into the ignition.

"Hardly," came the confident response from his partner as the tight-fitted cap was pulled off. "This caper was planned perfectly and executed with impeccable precision." Looking at the iridescent dots on the wristwatch the passenger smiled proudly, then smugly added, "As a matter of fact, we still have two minutes and fifty-two seconds."

"What are you talking about? The security guard stopped at a tree not fifteen feet from us. He just as easily could have stopped at the tree where we stood."

"But he didn't."

"That was still too close." The car went silent as the driver backed out of the dark alley. He kept the headlights off until reaching the main street. "Why did he stop?"

"I believe he had to go."

"Go? Go where?"

"Not go as in go someplace. Go."

"What?"

"You know, like in relieve himself, take a leak, visit the john, shake the snake." The passenger laughed loudly.

"All right, I get it. I can't believe this, the guy was standing at the next tree and you're laughing. That's it, this was positively the last time! I'm not doing this again. It's too risky. I have a reputation to protect. How would it look if a person of my standing was hauled into jail on trespassing, breaking and entering and vandalism charges?"

Ignoring the usual tirade and threats, his partner finger-combed his mass of thick hair. "You have to admit, that guard showing up gave tonight an added thrill, didn't it?" They looked at each other. The rush of accomplishment was exhilarating. Laughter began slowly, then erupted in a full-blown spasm of relief, excitement and satisfaction.

The small dark sports car pulled unnoticed around the front of the four-story building. From a distance they could just make out the result of the night's escapade. "We do good work," the driver proclaimed with a sigh of self-satisfaction.

"Indeed we do."

Chapter One

Newly padded brakes choked the white-rimmed tires.

"Idiot! Are you crazy?" Alex Price screamed. The loud screeching of brakes sent the front end pivoting downward slightly and to the left. She turned the steering wheel to quickly compensate. Missing by inches, the car finally halted and jerked back into place.

He came out of nowhere. Like a streak of hot lightning, he deliberately aimed his car right for her front bumper. Had she not spotted the red blur a scant second earlier, they'd still be scrapping small bits of metal and glass off the icy black asphalt.

With her hands still trembling and her heart pounding fearfully in her chest, Alex laid her head on the steering wheel and offered a silent prayer. "Thank you, God." She sat motionless trying desperately to calm her frayed nerves. The mere mention of snow made people drive like nuts, so to actually see two flakes together turned them into lunatics.

"Hey, Miss Price, how about an exclusive?" he shouted as he jumped out of his car and dashed over to her window with flashing camera in hand. He rapped repeatedly on the glass. "Miss Price."

Alex turned and stared at him completely bewildered. Why would anyone put their life in jeopardy for a tabloid article and a few blurred photos? She pondered the question, then closed her eyes again to offer a second prayer. "God, please make him go away."

"Miss Price, Alexandra, why'd you really quit the business?" the pesky man continued. "Did you hear Shawn Anderson and his wife have broken up? Rumor has it he's still in love with you." He knocked on the window with his camera poised for a frontal shot. "Any comment, Miss Price? Miss Price?"

Alex shifted her car into gear as the reporter knocked on her window again. She maneuvered the small sports car around the yelling man and drove cautiously away. "Miss Price! Miss Price," he continued yelling as she turned the car around. She saw his frustrated stance as she eyed him in her rearview mirror. She immediately retreated to the solitude of her sanctuary as tears welled in her eyes.

Within minutes she exchanged vehicles. Calmed and undaunted, she refused to be intimidated. This time the drive was uneventful. She passed the small red car as she pulled from her driveway and glared at the ill-mannered reporter. He leaned relaxed against his car door with a telephone to his ear. Unlike his earlier insanity, he made no attempt to confront her oversize truck. Thirty minutes later she had arrived at her friend's house.

Special effects had nothing on Mother Nature. Lacy crystals drifted gently down, covering the surrounding countryside in a glowing pristine white. Mountain firs and spruce shed the white flakes easily, while pines stooped over heavily by the added weight. The quiet serenity of the scene was picture-perfect. Even Hollywood would approve.

It began slowly, just a few icy flakes for the first hour or so. Now the accumulation was close to three inches and the frigid wind had increased. The weatherman had predicted a major storm. It seemed for once he just might be right.

The hushed stillness of the outside world was a stark contrast to the loud laughter and shouting voices ringing out constantly inside. Alex stood in solitude in a room filled with people. The oversize picture window afforded her the perfect distraction from the overpopulated soiree.

"Is it that time already?" Alex groaned when she'd received the hand-scripted invitation three weeks earlier. Every year Victoria and Ted Reese threw a major affair celebrating the winter solstice and the vernal equinox. The party, falling exactly between the two celestial occurrences, was one of the major East Coast functions on the Hollywood cocktail circuit. This year's gala fell on the eve of the biggest forecasted snowstorm in twenty-five years. Adding to the wintry theme, the snow was the perfect backdrop. Victoria Reese was elated.

When the forecasted snow finally arrived the guests came in droves. No one would dare miss attending the event of the season. No one except Alex. After she had begged off the last two years, Victoria made a point of insisting she show this time. She did, but only to please her friend. In all honesty, she would much rather have stayed in St. Croix with a rum punch, a good book and the incredible view of the Caribbean Sea.

"You've been in seclusion long enough," Victoria asserted when Alex tried to beg off again. "It's high time you got out and started living again." Alex didn't argue, she knew it was the truth. She was by far the most famous and elusive recluse since Howard Huges. So she came, and here she stood watching the snow fall while the revelers enjoyed themselves.

Victoria Reese's solstice party was a resounding success, as usual. Beluga caviar and Russian vodka flowed like water, and everyone who was anyone showed up. Actors, agents, businessmen, models, studio moguls, they all came. The champagne was endless and the buffet tables overflowed. The soft, subdued lighting, crackling fireplace and continuous Russian classics added to the backdrop of the cozy cottage atmosphere.

The cottage being a twenty-two-bedroom mansion loaded with every conceivable amenity. The building itself was once a lakefront hotel, then a bed-and-breakfast and finally this magnificent private home. Victoria had hired the best architects, decorators and designers to convert the impersonal structure into a warm, comfortable home. The end result was magnificent. The centerpiece being the great room.

Tonight, that room had been transformed into a sparkling winter wonderland. The usual elegant furniture was removed and replaced with numerous oversize white ottomans and white-velvet-covered benches. The seating was arranged in small groupings around an inch-thick plush white carpet. Thirty ten-foot glittering birch trees with tiny sparkling white lights were hauled in for the evening. There was even a full-size stuffed white wolf with three cubs lounging beneath the white baby grand piano.

The forty or so assembled guests serenely walked through the snow-covered forest in lavish wonder. They were amazed at the transformation. Victoria had done it again.

With a fluted glass in hand, Alex watched the reflection of her friend as she mingled with her guests. Victoria was the embodiment of class and style. Alex almost envied her. She was perfectly comfortable in any setting. She had a unique ability to make anyone feel special.

Dressed in a cranberry silk jumpsuit with a three-inch gold belt that hugged her tiny waist like a clamp, Victoria was the perfect hostess. She visited each grouping of guests, added just a small remark to the conversation, then traveled to the next grouping. She never tarried too long with any one group or guest, as not to slight anyone. She insisted there was an art to entertaining. Her sparkling conversation never included politics, religion or sports and she would always leave the group with some humorous parting remark.

At that moment Victoria looked up and spotted her friend standing alone by the front window. Alex smiled as she winked and headed toward her. *Here we go again,* she mused to herself, then looked innocently to the ceiling.

"I should have known you'd be standing off by yourself in a room filled with interesting people," Victoria said as she walked up behind Alex and laid her head on her shoulder. "Well, I'm glad at least you decided to come this year."

"So, do I get bonus points for showing up?"

"We'll see." She raised her head and looked out at the snow-covered landscape. "I really missed you, seems like you've been gone for ages."

Alex smiled. "I haven't been away that long."

Victoria grinned. "You've been down there for more than half the year."

"Don't exaggerate, Vic, it's only been four months."

"It's been six months, and it seems like forever," Victoria said while glancing around the room, ever mindful of her guests.

"I missed you too. But not as much as some of my neighbors apparently. It seems that half of the male population have been asking about you. How could you break so many hearts in just one short two-week visit?"

"It's a talent." Victoria smiled, remembering happily. "They were gorgeous, weren't they?"

Alex opened her mouth in astonishment. "You are completely incorrigible," she honestly proclaimed of her friend.

"So I've been told." Victoria's hopeless addiction to handsome young men was legendary. She left a trail of broken hearts wherever she went.

"You outdid yourself, Vic. The party is delightful and the room is phenomenal." Both women looked around at the elegantly designed room.

"I'm pleased. It came out well. I was going for a Russian winter, or Dr. Zhivago atmosphere."

Alex looked around the huge room again. "It's perfect."

"We originally had six-inch icicles hanging from the trees but the room started to look too much like Siberia so we pulled them at the last minute." Victoria's expression changed as she turned to Alex. "Ted just told me about the incident with the reporter outside your home this evening. Are you okay?" she questioned her friend with genuine concern.

"Yes, of course, I'm fine. If nothing else, after all these years I've finally learned to feel sorry for that type."

"You've got to be kidding. Feel sorry for that leech? His only existence is to pick at your life like a vulture. Then expose any- and everything to the world."

"True. But still, look at him, he has nothing. His whole world revolves around someone else's life. He's always on the outside looking in. That's pathetic," Alex mused.

"Well, as long as you're all right, that's all that matters," Victoria said happily.

Alex smiled. "I'm fine."

"Good, because I had a fabulous idea a few minutes ago." Alex rolled her eyes to the ceiling thinking, *Here it comes.* Victoria continued, "I thought since you are my cause of the week that I'd get you to try something a little different this evening." Alex stubbornly turned away as Victoria continued. "You walk up to someone, stick out your hand and say, 'Hi, I'm Alexandra Price, pleased to meet you.'" Sarcasm dripped from each word. "It's called mingling, Alex. You really should try it sometime."

Alex turned to her friend and smiled. "Yes, I believe I have heard of the concept."

"Good, so you shouldn't have too much trouble performing it," Victoria said, smiling mischievously. "Come on, let's get started," Victoria prodded pointedly as she intertwined her arm around Alex's and half pulled her toward one of the louder groupings of guests. Alex went halfheartedly with her friend.

"Why do I let you talk me into these things?" she groaned.

Victoria smiled cheerfully at the group they approached. "Because you adore me, and you know I'm right," she whispered. Then aloud, she addressed her guests. "Is everyone having a good time?" she asked, still holding on to her friend. Alex smiled, recognizing a few familiar faces. "You all know my dear friend Alexandra Price." Most nodded and shook hands or kissed cheeks, greeting her warmly. Ted introduced her to those she didn't already know.

"So," Victoria began, "what are we talking about?"

"The night prowler's most recent escapade," a guest relayed excitedly.

"Really, what was it?" Victoria asked curiously.

"He climbed up and hung a twenty-foot banner from the top of the Central Library Building."

"When?" someone questioned.

"Last week."

"This is so exciting," someone else spoke up.

"So, who is this night prowler person? What's his story?" several West Coast guests asked.

"Nobody knows."

"He's like a Robin Hood for New Jersey."

"Really? Has anyone ever seen him?"

"No. I don't think so."

"Whoever it is must have considerable means."

"What makes you think that?" someone queried.

"It costs money to do some of the things he does."

"That would narrow it down to a little more than half of the Stoneridge population." The locals laughed.

"I don't get it. He climbs up the building and hangs a sign. What's the big deal?" one of the West Coast producers asked.

"He did more than just hang a sign. The whole thing was sentimental. The sign was for a retiring librarian. She had been there for fifty years and the powers that be are kicking her out because she's over seventy. Apparently the insurance company thinks she's old and too much of a risk."

"Aw, that's so sad."

"I'd love to meet this guy."

"What a minute, what makes everyone think that the night prowler is a man?"

"Yeah, and for that matter maybe it's more than one person. It could be like a whole group of people."

"That's a good point, it probably took at least two people to hang that banner."

"This sounds so exciting."

"Oh no, I think you just gave Mandy an idea for a new television drama." The gathering laughed at the mocking remark. "I'm not joking. Don't be surprised when you see the promotions next fall."

"I don't know, the whole thing sounds so dangerous. Climbing up and down buildings just to hang a sign."

"That's the easy part. When I was into rock climbing a few years back we scaled high walls all the time. All you need is the right equipment."

"I could never rock climb. The vertigo would drive me crazy."

The conversation eased gradually away from the night prowler's recent caper to rock climbing, then to the latest thrill sport of choice. "David, your glass is empty," Victoria said. She reached out for the empty tumbler. "I'll freshen it for you."

Within minutes Victoria was off again to the next grouping, leaving Alex to enjoy the conversation.

By the second hour Alex found herself back at the living room's large picture window. She continued to sip her champagne as she again distanced herself from the joyful surroundings. Hoping not to be noticed, she gazed out at the snow. Eventually, she lost herself in her thoughts as she watched the thick curtain fall.

"Alex, Alexandra Price?" She turned around.

A man smiled warmly. "I spent my entire puberty in love with you," he began. "As a matter of fact I had one of your posters plastered above my bed so that when I went to bed, yours would be the last face I saw at night and the first I'd see when I awoke."

Alex smiled graciously. "Aw, thank you, that's very flattering," she stated for the zillionth time in her career. She'd heard this same line so many times she lost count after the first million declarations of devotion. But, she realized each faithful fan deserved the same grateful expression and touched demeanor. Hence, all walked away thinking that it was the first time she'd ever heard the tender remark.

"Time hasn't changed you one bit," he continued. "You're still just as beautiful as ever."

"That's very sweet, thank you again," she said while turning slightly back to the window. *Now go away,* she thought to herself but to no avail. He remained next to her in silence and watched the snow. *Probably trying to figure out what to say next. Your name, tell the movie star your name,* she mused to herself, mentally cuing him his lines. Then, sure enough, it came.

"My name's Jasper Wells," he finally stated, extending his hand.

They shook hands. "Nice to meet you, Jasper Wells." She smiled pleasantly. Again they slipped into silence. Apparently he had no intention of leaving any time soon. "So, Jasper, what do you do?" she asked.

"I'm in public relations. I'm working with Ted on his current project."

"Oh." She faked interest. "That's wonderful. You must be very good. Ted only works with the best." He beamed at the compliment.

"So, Alex, why'd you quit the business?" he asked, still facing the window.

Her heart skipped a beat. Wow, she didn't expect that. She remained silent for a few moments. When she felt him turn to face her she simply answered, "It was time, the lure of Hollywood had run its course."

"But you were so good. I saw everything you ever did, from modeling, television, Broadway and then finally films. I know everything there is to know about you. You won three Emmys total, one before your tenth birthday. You received a slew of People's Choice awards and just about every other award imaginable. You got a Tony Award at nineteen and an Oscar at twenty."

Alex tried to look impressed, but the last thing she wanted to hear was her biography. "Wow, Jasper, you really do know a lot about my previous career. But I really don't—" she began.

He interrupted, continuing his comments. "Your fans were stunned when you quit and disappeared." He turned to her almost pleading. "I was stunned. I never understood why you quit like that. I always wanted to know why." He turned, waiting patiently for her response.

"There you are, darling." Victoria appeared out of nowhere. "Alex, shame on you. Stop hogging my most attractive male guest. Come along, Jasper, I have someone who's dying to meet you." She took his hand in hers. Alex mouthed the words *thank you,* as Victoria winked and steered Jasper toward two young women reclining casually in front of the large marble fireplace.

Alex turned back to the window. *This was a mistake,* she thought. *I never should have come here tonight.* She sensed from the beginning that this evening would be like none other. She lowered her eyes solemnly, then looked up at the snow. Suddenly she felt so small. Absently she focused back on the room's reflection. A familiar face broke through the crowd and was looking directly at her.

Hoping to avoid the inevitable, she averted her gaze and moved to the buffet table. She picked up a small china plate and began filling it with various edibles. From the corner of her eye she saw him peruse the room again. She squirmed as he began walking in her direction.

"Ciao belladonna, you've been avoiding me," he said smoothly as he eased up behind her.

"You're right. I have," she acknowledged honestly. But of course she couldn't avoid him all night. No one could. This was Chasano D'Lucchia, Italy's famed leading man. His thespian talent was unparalleled and often compared to a young Rudolph Valentinó. Known primarily in Europe, he was only just now attaining recognition as Hollywood's latest leading man.

Chase, to those who knew him well, was a notorious womanizer whose reputation was completely founded. For years he'd had a crush on Alex. Although she constantly discouraged his romantic advances, he invariably persisted. Theirs was a relationship of roguish proposals and playful banter.

He leaned in closer to Alex's ear. "I see you're still playing hard to get, Alexandra." He curled her name around his tongue, giving it a thick Italian flair. He often used his now faint accent as part of his arsenal of seduction weapons.

"More like impossible to get, Chasano Rafael D'Lucchia," she answered sweetly, mimicking his thick Italian accent precisely. He smiled adoringly, removing the small plate and grasping her hand. He eased closer, encircling her waist, then began dancing smoothly.

He placed her hand over his heart. "Alexandra, you wound me deeply when you doubt my affection." She rolled her eyes, then removed her hand and stepped back. "Ciao Chasano," she added laughingly, then walked away.

She moved back to the window and noticed that the snow had begun falling with a vengeance. The last thirty minutes had seen another few inches. The grounds were completely covered and the roads, though thickly cov-

ered, seemed still passable. Alex decided to look for
Victoria and Ted, then make her way home before the
roads were completely impassable.

She found Ted in the center of a group of men discussing his latest film. She walked over, air-kissed each
cheek and bade her good-byes.

She found Victoria surrounded by a group of adoring
men, as usual. She excused herself, pulling Victoria with
her, then led her friend toward the foyer informing her
of her departure.

"Don't be ridiculous, this is a huge house, with zillions
of bedrooms already made up for my overnight guests.
You absolutely can't leave, I just won't hear of it," she
protested adamantly.

"Drop the dramatics, Victoria, I'm just thirty minutes
away. I hardly think there'll be an avalanche between
here and home." She laughed, at her attempt at humor
and at her friend's pouting expression. "Seriously, Vic,
the storm is getting worse, and I don't want to get stuck
out in it, so it's now or never." Alex retrieved her black
sable coat, kissed and hugged her friend, then headed
for the front doors. Victoria followed dutifully.

"All right, all right, if you must go, then fine, but I
insist on having someone drive you home. I'll get Chase
to do it."

"That won't be necessary. I drove the four-wheel-
drive truck, so I'll be fine. Go back to your guests, I'll
call you when I get home."

"Leaving so soon, Alexandra?" Chase said as he
walked up to the two women. "Pity," he lamented disap-
pointedly while helping her with her coat, "I thought
we might spend more time together."

"Sorry, Chase, I don't have time to play games right
now," Alex said while slipping on her leather gloves.

"Drive carefully, darling," Victoria said, air-kissing
Alex again. "Don't forget to call and let me know you
got home safely." She smiled, then walked away calling
to a guest across the room.

Chase leaned closer to Alex and whispered, "Umm, playing games, that sounds delightful. I'm going to hold you to that. I know a few games that I'd enjoy teaching you." She felt his warm breath disturb the sable fur and tickle the loose hair curled at her neck.

"You need to cool off, Chase," she said while opening the door. As if on cue, a crisp, biting blast of arctic air blew in at them. The brittle icy chill stung her nostrils as she took a deep breath. She was invigorated. Her heavy fur flapped like tissue paper against her long stockinged legs. Chase uselessly gathered his suede jacket against the wintry cold, then extended an arm. Alex intertwined her gloved hand and together they walked to her truck.

"Has everything been arranged for the festival?" he asked, bristling against the cold.

"Yes, as far as I know. Although there are a few more details to work out, I foresee no problems. I'll be in Miami to finalize everything next month."

"Good, I'm looking forward to having you all to myself. I understand the vessel is enormous. We will have to find a cozy cabin for just the two of us."

"I've decided not to attend."

"But you must," he contended sternly.

"Captain Graham is very capable. He'll take care of everything in my absence." Walking quickly they finally arrived at her truck.

Chase dipped his head into the frigid wind as he took the key and opened the door. "Alex, you must reconsider and meet me in France, we could be so good together," he began, smiling the teasing boyish grin that weakened so many knees. "Why do you not take me seriously, is it my cologne, my money, my fame? The sexual tension between us is obvious. I can feel the love you have for me."

Alex lowered her head, grinning, humored by his arrogance. "Yes, Chase, you're right, that's exactly it," she admitted, gathering her dress and coat together and climbing into the elevated seat.

"Alex, our love has transcended all boundaries, the world will be ours." She closed the door, started the engine and lowered the side window. One swipe of the windshield wiper cleared the thick soft snow away. He reached his head into the open window. "Together, heart and heart, we will conquer the universe."

She put the truck into gear. "Chase, I said you were right. But I was referring to your cologne." She grimaced and waved her hand in front of her nose, then winked. "Now get inside before you freeze to death. Then I have every lovesick female on Earth after me. Arrivederci." She backed up, hearing Chase's boisterous laughter.

"Touché. Arrivederci, bella." He waved and blew her a kiss. His laughter continued as he hurried back to the house.

After five minutes on the road, the truck was bathed in comforting warmth. Alex relaxed back as fat snowflakes quickly melted on the toasty defrosting windows. She was relieved she left the party when she did. The dark icy streets had gotten pretty bad by this time. Feeling content once more, she smiled, knowing her sole aspiration, solitude, was hers again.

Years in the public eye had left her jaded and cynical. She frowned remembering the earlier conversation. Being reminded of her once coveted career was always unsettling. Thankfully, the multitude of questions had diminished over the years. But to her regret, so had her existence. She considered it a small penance to pay for cherished anonymity.

Wearied by the sullen thoughts she turned on the radio, adjusting the dial to a news and weather station. The announcer reported that smaller access roads leading into and out of the immediate area were completely impassible. All the major roads and highways were either closed or closing, including the expressway and parkway. He suggested either staying where you were or getting inside as soon as possible.

Alex cautiously eased along the dark deserted streets. Apparently the announcer's request was well heeded, because the center of town was completely abandoned.

Stoneridge was a small secluded community where everybody knew everybody else. The residents, mostly an affluent populace, enjoyed its unique proximity to New York and other major East Coast cities. Alex enjoyed it because it was as far away as possible from Los Angeles without actually crossing the Atlantic.

The main section of town was a cluster of stores and businesses spanning twenty square blocks while the residential areas surrounded a private man-made lake.

Although her home was just a few miles from Victoria's, there was no direct route. She lived on one end of the lake and Victoria lived on the other.

Alex crept along tentatively, then slowly turned a corner and swerved to avoid hitting a fishtailing car barreling through an intersection with the traffic light blinking red. The driver blew his horn and spun around aimlessly. He jumped out with arms waving frantically.

"Oh, no, you don't, buster, not this time," she said as she continued driving through the deep snow. Although she didn't recognized the car as the one earlier, she decided not to take any chances. She was so weary of reporters' tricks.

Several obscure turns later a familiar glow peeked through the darkened distant trees. She drove up the front road leading to the isolated safety of her home. The soft glow of the first-floor lights beckoned to her warmly.

Chapter Two

Lance Morgan ranted for twenty minutes. The weatherman had changed his prediction again. The initial passing snow flurry changed into a minor Alberta clipper, then into "the Blizzard of the Century" within two hours' time. Lance was furious. He blasted his impatience for driving to New Jersey in the middle of a winter storm. But, he was so excited to get back to the States after four long months on location in London that he had grabbed the first available seat.

That seat was coach, an unlikely choice given his fame. But, wearing a heavy parka, dark glasses and a very uncharacteristic five o'clock shadow he was virtually unnoticed. It seemed that almost everyone eagerly anticipated another passenger.

Rumor circulated at Heathrow Airport that Lance Morgan's friend and bodyguard Charles Taylor waited in the first-class section preparing to board the Concorde to Los Angeles. Everyone knew that wherever Charles was, Lance wouldn't be far behind. The media, paparazzi and hordes of fans also waited. They all anxiously expected to see the mega-superstar arrive. In the excitement Lance slipped by completely unrecognized.

Everyone waited, all wanting to know about his future plans after his startling press conference announcement. His hotel room's phone rang nonstop and his cell phone rang unanswered for eight hours straight.

Then, somewhere over the mid-Atlantic, he finally called his manager. "I know you're not still in London, so where the hell are you?" his irate manager bellowed through the receiver.

Lance looked out of the small round window. "I honestly have no idea," he confessed truthfully.

"Are you trying to give me a heart attack?" Franklin yelled after popping another two antacid tablets into his mouth. " 'Cause if you are, you're doing a damn good job." Lance chuckled.

Franklin Moore was impossible. He was Lance's manager, confidant and friend. But not even Franklin knew his plans for the next few weeks. In all actuality, Lance wasn't sure he himself knew. The only thing he was sure of was that he could no longer stand by waiting helplessly.

Lance picked up the foreign-edition New York newspaper lying on his lowered food tray. "Have you seen the newspaper this morning?"

"Of course I've seen the newspaper," Franklin grumbled. "How could you just dump your agent in one sentence and blatantly announce you're searching for another and not think of the consequences? The phones have been ringing off the hook all morning. Every agent, wanna-be agent and half-wit agent has called here at least twenty times every hour. There's a horde of reporters camped out in the lobby and we won't even get into the fact that Bob Burke's called over fifty times," Franklin went on.

"That's not the article I was referring to. Did you see the piece on Mason Turner? He donated one million dollars to the African-American Children's Relief Fund yesterday. The money was donated through Lillian Turner-Price."

Exasperated, Franklin answered, "Yeah, I saw it."

"We've got to find out who this guy is. Have you heard anything new from the investigator?"

"Nothing. Turner is too elusive, he's like a shadow.

I've got my best man on the job and so far he's come up with zilch."

"Well, keep trying. I need to talk to Turner in person."

"I told you before, he doesn't work like that. We've got to go through his attorney."

"Yeah, yeah, I know. I'd still like to meet the man." Lance observed the curious look the attendant gave him as she passed. He pulled his hat down lower and angled his back away from the aisle. "What did Burke want?"

"What do you think? He wants you to reconsider and sign. He's driving us nuts over here with his calls."

Lance felt a touch of remorse. But he knew Franklin was resourceful, he'd handle everything as usual. "Franklin, it was time for a change. You know I haven't been happy with Burke's work for some time. The contract expired so I let him go. It happens every day, no big deal," Lance stated calmly.

"No big deal! No big deal, he says," Franklin shouted to the empty office. "I've had to hire five new people just to handle the phones. The press is in a frenzy and my blood pressure is through the roof. Now, where the hell are you?" Franklin demanded for the second time.

Lance peered down at the blue water below the aircraft. "Somewhere over the Atlantic, I would presume," he said.

"Good, I'll send a car to pick you up at LAX." Franklin reached over and grabbed a piece of paper from his messy desk. "What's the flight number and arrival time?" Franklin dropped two white disks into a glass of water. The mixture immediately began to bubble and fizz.

Lance looked at the Concorde's boarding pass and connecting flight to LA. The seat adjacent to Charles was vacant. "Flight number forty-one arriving at 9:10 P.M. But—"

"Got it," Franklin confirmed, jotting the information down on a yellow legal pad. "I'll see you when you land." Franklin downed the effervescent drink in one huge gulp.

"Wait!" Lance caught him just before he hung up. "Franklin, Charles will be landing at LAX, I'm on a different flight to New York."

"What!"

Lance held the phone away from his ear, and the passenger seated next to him grimaced at the bellowing yell coming from the small device. "You've got a meeting in less than a week to finalize your bid for the Turner book and I just received another updated script change on your last movie. Not to mention Burke just sent four boxes over here, per your request."

"No problem. I'll be there in a few days." Lance looked up. The attendant was signaling the start of the landing procedure. "Franklin, I've got to go, I'll call you later." He flipped the phone closed and turned off the ringer.

"Lance! Lance!" Click.

By the time the flight landed, several passengers had finally recognized him and a small crowd gathered at the gate. Eventually airport security arrived, freeing him just as several news vans pulled up. Aided by security he caught a cab to his apartment, then picked up his car. Everything had gone smoothly until he got thirty miles outside of New York.

The weather had changed drastically and the road conditions became impossible. He was beginning to wish he'd taken the Concorde to Los Angeles.

Lance slammed his fist against the padded steering wheel angrily. First the blizzard, then three jackknifed tractor trailers on the interstate and now a detour to no-man's land. Not having much choice, he decided to take his chances and go for it.

What was he thinking? He had to be out of his mind. But, when Jake had suggested the alliance he jumped at it. The plan was harmless enough, he concluded. And since his hired detectives offered little information, it seemed like the only solution. All he had to do in return was sign for one year. Lance grimaced. If everything was so simple, why did he have the feeling he'd just sold his soul to the devil?

An hour later he was still driving around in circles and hopelessly lost. Then he finally saw the sign, WELCOME TO STONERIDGE.

Once there, he followed the directions he'd received. Unfortunately, the heavy snow and darkness made it impossible to locate the landmarks and street signs. With one eye on the road and the other deciphering the directions, he drove through an intersection and was almost blindsided by a truck.

He flashed his lights and blew his horn. "Great," he said sarcastically. The driver of the truck kept going. He jumped out of the car waving his hands but the truck's driver ignored him. "Fine, I'll follow you. Maybe you can lead me out of here."

He lost sight of the large truck several times in the blinding snow and high winds. Then eventually he saw faint red lights up ahead. He flashed his lights again and blew his horn. This time the driver stopped.

Alex continued driving until she heard a car horn blaring and saw white flashing headlights in the side mirror. "What now?" she muttered but kept going. The persistent car continued blasting the horn and flashing its lights until she veered off to the side of the road and stopped. The car pulled up behind. The sole passenger dashed toward the side of her truck.

She lowered the window. The cold, arctic wind immediately iced her face, matching the glacial scowl she gave him. He, on the other hand, was immediately awestruck. The classic beauty of her warm gentle features and the icy chill behind her soft brown eyes made him shudder. She clasped her fur collar together with her soft leather glove. "Yes?"

"Thanks for stopping. I could use some help. I'm lost," the stranger said, catching his breath. "I need directions. How do I get back to the parkway, going north?" he asked.

"The parkway's closed," she answered impatiently.

The man looked crestfallen. "Okay, how do I get to the expressway then?" he asked.

"The expressway's closed also."

"Damn." He slapped the side of her truck, then looked up into her annoyed face. "Sorry, well, how do I get out of this town?"

"Getting out of Stoneridge is no problem, finding someplace to go is. Everything's pretty much closed because of the snowstorm," she added. A gust of wind blew snow into the man's eyes and he shielded his face.

"Is there a hotel or motel somewhere around here, maybe in town?"

"I just drove through town, everything's closed."

"Okay, thanks." The man turned and walked back to his car pondering his luck.

Relieved, Alex raised her window. But pangs of guilt tugged at her heart. She couldn't just leave someone stranded out in the middle of this storm. She reasoned, *What if he's another reporter and this was a trick to get an interview?* She weighed the consequences briefly, then blew her horn.

The man looked up, turned, then came trotting back to her open window. "Do you know anyone in Stoneridge?" she asked hopefully.

"No," he answered.

Alex decided. "You can't drive around in this weather much longer. You'll freeze. You can stay the night at my house, then get back on the road tomorrow morning."

"Thank you, I really appreciate it," he said, smiling gleefully, then hurried back to the car. He was right! He'd have recognized her anywhere. It was Alexander Price. He couldn't believe his luck.

Flawless cinnamon complexion, long thick lashes and

the most exquisitely almond shaped eyes imaginable. Her staggering beauty was so unbelievably perfect she appeared almost unreal. A broad smile widened across his face. Alex Price. Even the icy-cold arctic wind couldn't penetrate the warmth he felt at seeing her hidden behind the dark brown fur. He got into his car and followed as she pulled out. Lance smiled to himself. She looked exactly the same. "Alex Price." His smile broadened. "It's now or never."

Alex waited until he got back into his car, then slowly pulled off. "God, that man could melt Antarctica with his smile. "I sure hope you know what you're doing, girl," she said aloud to the empty truck. Moments later the two snow-covered vehicles came to the forbidding ten-foot iron gate. Alex pressed the remote-control button on her dashboard and the gates slid back into the double-stacked stone wall entrance. She continued through followed closely by her unexpected overnight guest.

She pulled into the four-stall garage and parked next to the fire-engine-red convertible Corvette she had bought as a lark. A snow-covered black Mercedes sedan pulled in next to her. She got out and circled the front of the truck. "Please tell me you're not a nut or worse yet, a tabloid reporter," she said as the man popped the trunk and stepped out of the car.

"No. I'm not a nut. And I'm certainly not a reporter," he assured her while walking to the trunk of his car. She followed.

"Good." She peeked in the trunk. It was filled with a large duffel bag, a briefcase and a carry-on. "Traveling or visiting?" she asked.

He reached in and grabbed his briefcase and carry-on bag. "Something like that." He closed the car's trunk.

"I see," she said, turning away, thinking to herself,

It's really none of your business, girl, he'll be out of here by morning.

The stranger rearranged his load, then extended his hand. "I really appreciate your hospitality." He beamed a familiar sexy smile. "My name is Lance, Lance Morgan."

Alex nodded. "The actor," she said, surprised by not recognizing him earlier.

"Guilty." The awesome smile appeared again.

"I'm Alexandra Price," she said and removed her glove.

"The actress."

She nodded and grasped his cold hand.

He smiled as they shook hands. "Oh, your hands are freezing. Come on. Let's go upstairs and get you warm."

Lance smiled. This was going to be easier than he had thought.

Chapter Three

They climbed the spiral staircase to the enormous galley kitchen. Alex opened the door and was greeted by a jubilant shiny black Labrador. The dog barked once, then jumped up to Alex wagging his tail nonstop. "Hey, Coal, did you miss me?" she said, rubbing him gently behind his ears. The dog was obviously pleased to see her. Eventually he lowered himself and shifted his attention to the stranger behind her. He padded over curiously.

Lance put the bags and briefcase down. Then he held out his hand, palm open. Coal sniffed approvingly, then padded back to Alex's side. She absently rubbed his head. "This is Coal."

Lance walked over to the two. He bent down. "Hello, Coal," he said while patting his head generously. "He's beautiful. Labrador?"

"Yes," she said, watching as the two got aquatinted. "If you'll follow me, I'll show you to your room."

Lance gave Coal one last pat, then picked up his bags and followed Alex through the large kitchen. They went up the rear staircase to the second floor. The two walked silently down the plush carpeted hall and came to the first room by the front stairs. She opened the double doors and ushered him inside.

The cozy elegance of the bedroom revealed her apparent excellent design sense. The centerpiece wrought-iron canopy bed drew his attention immediately. The dramatically draped burgundy material was a waterfall of silk. Lance walked over and dropped his bags beside the bed. "This is very nice. I hope I'm not putting you out?" he asked.

"Not at all," she answered. "I'm sure you'll be comfortable here tonight."

Absently he stroked the silky fabric, then turned and froze. He watched hypnotically as she peeled off her coat and casually tossed it on the settee. His thoughts evaporated after seeing her slim sexy body in the shimmering emerald dress. She walked over to an adjacent door, reached in and turned on the lights. As a soft, loose curly tendril of hair fell down her bare back, his mouth dried and his pulse quickened. "The bathroom is in here," she continued. "I'll get you some fresh towels." She walked over to the king-size bed and picked up several of the many pillows and tossed them on the chair, then looked over to an admiring Lance. "Are you hungry?"

Stymied, Lance just smiled. "Yes, as a matter of fact I am." His coughed. His mouth was bone dry.

"Hot beef stew or cold turkey sandwich?" she asked as she walked back to the double doors.

"I think I'll go with the hot beef stew, if it's not too much trouble."

"No trouble at all. Why don't you freshen up and come down when you're done? I'll get your food started." She disappeared through the double doors. The scent of her delicate perfume lingered in the room. Lance walked over to the coat still tossed across the settee and picked it up. He fondled the soft brown fur, raising it to his nostrils. He inhaled her arousing scent again. One night with Alex was defiantly not going to be enough.

Lance pulled out the directions and his cellular phone, then called the Los Angeles number written on the top of the paper. The phone was answered on the second ring. "Did you find the house?"

"After driving around in a blizzard for hours, yes, I eventually found it. This place is so remote I would never have found it even with the map and directions. I get the feeling Alex Price doesn't want to be found. There's no street sign within five miles, the road leading here doesn't have a name and there's no actual street address. How did you find this place?"

"I have a friend at Celebrity Tracers," Jake lied.

"I don't think so. This place is too isolated and Celebrity Tracers aren't that good. Where'd you get the directions, Jake?"

Jake chuckled at Lance's astute perception. "You're right, I confess. Let's just say I know a guy who keeps close tabs on Ms. Price's whereabouts. So, after a recent business transaction I was able to persuade him to share the information with me."

"I see," Lance yielded, finding the scenario more plausible.

"Have you figured out a way to get inside?" Jake asked, dropping the subject.

"That's already handled."

"So, what's the great Alexandra Price like?"

Lance picked up the sable fur still lying across his lap. "She's . . ." He fanned the soft fur with his fingers, searching for the appropriate word. "Proper."

"Proper?" Jake repeated, slightly perplexed.

"Yes, proper. She's reserved."

Jake chuckled. "A real party animal," he said sarcastically.

"Nothing I can't handle," Lance said, beginning to get annoyed. "Did you find out anything else that might be useful?" he asked.

"Nah, nothing, other than what I've already told you. She's reclusive, so all information is over five years old. But I'm sure she couldn't have changed that much."

"What's she been doing all this time?"

"I don't know, she moves around a lot. I just found out she was back in the States a few days ago."

"Where's she been?"

"St. Croix."

"Alone?"

"Yeah, alone. I hear she still gets flustered around men. I'd work the seduction angle. You being America's sex symbol, you should have no problem persuading her to give it up." Jake chuckled at the double meaning, "I was referring to Turner, of course." He laughed again.

"Yeah, whatever. Talk to you later." Lance frowned as he hung up. This whole thing with Jake was beginning to reek. The idea of seducing someone for personal gain disturbed him. But if he wanted Turner this was the only way to get him, he maintained. And if Alex's mother knows him, surely she does too. Since Lillian won't talk and Mark Summers won't talk, maybe Alex will, with the right incentive. He smiled to himself. "The end justifies the means," he rationalized. He needed to think of this as just another acting role.

After freshening up, Lance picked up the coat and curiously walked to the front wall of accordion doors. He pulled back the center panels to reveal a comfortable seating area and balcony. He stepped closer to the arced glass and wooden rail, then looked out onto the splendor of the great room. The view was exquisite.

The architectural design of the enormous room was magnificent. Every surface plane was curved smoothly into another rounded form and all of them dramatically flowed around the contour of the sunken living room.

Lance slowly walked down the spacious spiral staircase. Each step turned him in a different direction revealing another splendid sight. The final step landed him at the base of a bare floor-to-ceiling window. The large windows lined evenly across the front and back of the room, providing an incredible view of the snow-covered landscape.

He stood by the front windows for a moment admiring the awesome splendor of nature. When he turned back to the beautifully adorned room, he smiled. The surrounding walls of glass reminded him more of being inside an enormous fish tank.

The demure lighting from above and the rich shades of green, blue and salmon added to the amusing sensation. He stepped down into the sunken living room area and placed the coat on the sofa. A small cozy fire was burning in the slate fireplace giving the room a warm cozy feel. Above, in place of a mantel, was an enormous tropical-reef aquarium. Amazed, Lance stepped closer.

Exotic fish swam and drifted easily among the vast natural vegetation. An array of blue-, green- and salmon-hued coral sat atop a bed of white sand, crystal pebbles and marble stones. He smiled as the small fish darted in and out of their underwater environment. Quizzically he squinted beyond the tank. There was something odd about the glass's reflection. He leaned in closer, barely able to make out various shapes, but stopped when he heard glass shatter.

Alex poured a glass of red wine and turned on the television in the den. The dismal weather report confirmed her apprehension. The storm's aftereffect would last at least a few days. Coal padded up next to her and lay down. She smiled down at him. "So, what do you think about our house guest?" Coal sat up and began panting. "Yeah, I totally agree." She walked back to the kitchen and began heating the beef stew.

As the beef stew warmed, Alex sipped the last of her wine while watching the weatherman continue spouting warnings of blackouts, power outages and the onset of scattered frozen rain. Everything was closed and presumed closed for the next few days. Electricity was out all over the county. The phone lines were a disaster and there were traffic accidents everywhere. She shook her head sadly and sympathetically, then got up and went to the stove.

The beef stew was simmering when she turned the gas down low. She reached over for the warmed plate and knocked the wineglass onto the floor, shattering the crystal goblet.

Lance burst into the kitchen as Alex bent down to pick up the larger pieces of glass. Startled at his sudden appearance, she jumped, cutting her finger on a small glass fragment. A thin line of blood ran down her finger. Lance came up behind her and ushered her to the sink. She tensed as his arms wrapped around her shoulders.

"I'm fine," she assured him, "it's just a small cut."

Ignoring her protests, he instructed her to rinse her finger in the cool water. She did, watching as he picked up the last of the broken glass. With his task completed, he moved back to the sink and stood behind her massaging her wet hand beneath the warm water. He frowned as he dried and examined her finger, then gave his diagnosis. "I think you'll live." She remained silent. "First-aid kit?" he inquired.

She pointed to the lower drawer beneath the sink. He retrieved the kit and returned to her side. As she watched him, an odd sensation overwhelmed her. His masculine nearness set butterflies fluttering in her stomach. Reflexively she pulled her hand away. "I'll put that on," she said, apprehensive of the feel of his strong hands on hers.

He smiled, feeling her tense again, then retook her hand. "I'll be happy to." Without further debate he sprayed on an antiseptic and covered the cut with a small bandage. He stepped back to observe his handiwork.

She looked at her finger approvingly. "Thank you."

"My pleasure, Ms. Price," he whispered seductively. Then, as if suspended in time, the moment held as Lance peered into her soft brown eyes. Her body tensed and her hand began to tremble. Her heart pounded wildly within her chest. She pulled her hand away apprehensively and took a step back.

He smiled knowingly. He'd heard rumors of Alex's wide-eyed vulnerability over the years. Apparently they were well founded. Much to his delight Jake was right, it seemed Alexandra Price truly was intimidated by men. "Do I make you nervous, Alex?"

"No," she responded too quickly.

He eased closer, never taking his eyes from her face. "I think I do." His victory was evident.

She glared back at him, allowing her jittery nervousness to wash away. Then, as if taking on an altered persona, she grinned smugly. "Then you'd be wrong."

"Would I?" he queried disbelievingly.

"Yes, you would." She smiled brightly. "You mistake nervousness for caution. I'm not accustomed to having strangers in my home," she added smoothly.

He eased closer still in an attempt to keep her off guard. "Strangers, Alex, or men?"

She boldly held her ground, then tipped her chin upward in defiance. "Strangers," she stated emphatically, then offhandedly asked, "Why should men make me nervous?"

Lance tilted his head quizzically and chuckled openly. She was a paradox. "You are an extraordinary actress," he boasted. "I can't tell if you've just stepped into character." He paused for one last affirmation, then continued, "or just stepped out."

The openly provocative way she gazed at him was arousing. "Does it matter?"

Lance was intrigued as he gazed into her unwavering eyes. Apparently her quiet, sedate demeanor was a defense. He smiled. It seemed Alexandra Price would be more of a challenge than he had originally anticipated. She was beautiful, smart and sexy. A lethal combination in all respects. He found himself emotionally drawn to her, but resisted. This wasn't supposed to happen, he admonished himself. This was just another role, playacting, no emotion. So why was he feeling the stir of attraction? "Umm, that smells delicious." He looked over to the covered pot still on the stove. "Is it ready?"

"Yes." She motioned to the plate on the counter. "Help yourself." He began heaping large spoonfuls of stew onto the warm plate. "I'll get the bread out of the oven."

Lance sat down at the center counter as Alex placed several slices of Italian bread and a glass of wine near his plate. He put a large spoonful of stew into his mouth. "Umm, this is delicious," he said, relishing every bite. Moments later the plate was empty, so he helped himself to a second and third helping.

Coal came up beside Lance and laid his head on his knee. "No, you don't, go back to your pillow," Alex said. Coal got up and moved back to the warm fleecy pillow beside the hearth. Lance smiled at his obedience.

"He's a good dog," he said. She nodded her agreement.

Lance finished eating and helped Alex clear his glass and plate. The lights flickered just as they finished. Lance looked to Alex. "Think they'll go out?"

"Probably. But it shouldn't be a problem," she answered.

"I guess the rest of the county is having the same problems. Snow and ice on tree limbs usually add up to downed lines and power failures."

"We should be okay," she reiterated. Lance nodded, half disappointed. He and Alex in a blackout seemed too perfect.

"Thank you for the meal. It was delicious."

"You're welcome."

An awkward silence was broken by another flickering of the lights. Alex glanced at her watch. It was 12:30. "It's getting late. Is there anything else you need tonight?"

He thought of a number of things but answered no. Alex went into the den to turn off the television. When she returned she saw Lance standing by the back stairs. "Shall I walk you upstairs?"

She shook her head no and said good night.

"Good night, Alex, I'll see you in the morning." Lance hoped the disappointment in his voice wasn't as obvious as he felt. As he climbed the stairs he heard Alex call for Coal and saw the bright kitchen lights fade.

Alex walked into the living room with Coal padding along behind her. Using the remote control, she dimmed the soft lights, then walked over to the large front windows. She stood and watched as the slow curtain of white powdery flakes continued to fall. Then she pressed another button, lowering thin row after row of blind panels between the thick outside and inside glass.

Slowly she turned away, picked up her coat, took a last glance at the balcony, then pressed the mahogany panel and entered her bedroom.

After crawling into her warm bed, she lay staring at the ceiling for some time. Sleep eluded her as thoughts of Lance Morgan drifting wistfully through her mind. She wasn't quite sure what to make of him. Smiling, she wondered if he flirted with every woman he met. Probably, she surmised as she snuggled deeper beneath the silken sheets. She was well aware of his highly acclaimed professional credentials, as well as his other more debonair reputation.

Lance Morgan was an internationally known screen actor whose career had exploded within the last seven years. His blockbuster action films grossed billions worldwide and his handsome face beamed from every popular magazine cover imaginable.

She had always considered him a handsome man but he was magnificent in person. His flawless mocha complexion, his strong angular chin and his sparkling eyes were irresistible. Everything about the man was devastatingly handsome. She even liked the wispy beard he'd apparently begun growing. She smiled in the cover of darkness. She could see how millions of woman threw themselves at his feet.

Suddenly she remembered one woman in particular, Amber Hall. Amber was a six-foot-tall supermodel whose name had been linked to Lance's for the past four months. She was his costar and love interest in a film, and rumor had it they'd also become an offscreen couple. Alex wondered just how serious their relationship was until she eventually drifted off to a restful slumber with mingled thoughts of her upstairs house guest.

Upstairs, Lance twisted restlessly in the bed for hours. Finally, he sat up and turned on the side lamp. The low glow enabled him to see the time. It was close to five o'clock in the morning. Frustrated, he lay back down.

"Who is Alexandra Price?" he asked himself in the muted darkness. "The soft-spoken, timid woman who barely speaks two words or"—he grinned in obvious fascination—"the sassy vixen who held her ground when provoked?" The enigma was too tempting.

Still restless, he got up and walked to the window. Pulling the heavy velvet drapery back, he looked out at the approaching dawn. The snow had finally tapered to flurries. As he turned to go back to bed he glanced down and spotted two figures outside. They frolicked and played in the deep snow.

He smiled recognizing Alex and Coal. Alex tossed a disk and Coal ran to retrieve it. When he returned with the disk in his mouth, he refused to let go. Alex pulled on the disk until he let go and she plopped down into the deep snow. Covered from head to foot with powdery flakes, she got up laughing heartily. Coal jumped up on her and she fell back down still laughing. When she finally regained her balance she tossed the disk again. Together the two raced to get it.

"So, Ms. Price," he pondered aloud, "it seems you can let your guard down." Lance stood at the window watching the two until they eventually moved from view. Smiling knowingly, he returned to bed. In a few hours he'd embark on a more direct approach.

Chapter Four

"Well, good morning," the pleasant voice greeted Lance as he came into the kitchen.

He smiled awkwardly, baffled. "Good morning," he said, holding his hand out to the tiny middle-aged woman. Her bright cheerful smile was contagious. "I'm—"

"Lance Morgan. Yes, I know. When Alex told me we had a guest I just couldn't believe my ears. How do you do, Mr. Morgan? I'm Hazel Fletcher." She took his hand and pumped vigorously. "I'm a huge fan of yours. And my Kenneth, oh, he's just going to bust a seam when I tell him I met you." She leaned closer and whispered, "But don't worry about us telling anyone that you're here, we're very good at . . . keeping secrets." She acted out placing a key to her lips, turning it, then tossing it over her shoulder.

Lance grinned and chuckled, nodding his understanding. "Thank you. The pleasure is mine, Mrs. Fletcher." The smell of something cooking wafted past his nose. "Umm . . ." He looked around the empty kitchen. ". . . That smells heavenly. What is it?"

"Sit down," she commanded. "Breakfast is just finishing up." She opened the oven and pulled out several covered dishes. Lance walked trancelike to the counter stool. He sat down as Mrs. Fletcher placed a plate of

food in front of him. He lowered his face into the plate
and inhaled the aroma of the succulent edibles.

"Oh . . ." His mouth watered. "This looks fabulous."
He rubbed his hands together and picked up the linen
napkin. He looked around the kitchen and den areas.
"Where's Alex, won't she be joining us?" He put a
forkful of food in his mouth and chewed heartily.

Mrs. Fletcher returned with a cup of hot steaming
coffee. "Oh, she's already eaten, she's around someplace," she answered evasively. "Cream and sugar?" she
offered.

Lance nodded as he placed another forkful of food in
his mouth. Mrs. Fletcher obliged, pouring an abundant
amount of each into his cup. He continued eating as
she chatted endlessly about his career and all of the
movies she'd seen. He smiled, laughed and answered
her questions, giving the appropriate responses yet ever
mindful of Alex's obvious absence.

Jake Marrows sat across from his boss's desk and listened to him belittle, berate and degrade him for over
thirty-five minutes. Outwardly, he seemed placid
enough but inside he seethed. He was furious. He didn't
need this crap. Robert Burke was the last person to
lecture him on ethics. He was a two-bit hoodlum who'd
been lucky enough to be in the right place at the right
time. His name was connected to some of the biggest,
highest paid names on the Hollywood scene and also
the lowest ethically. He was a superagent who'd do anything for a buck.

Burke jeered at his associate in frustration, then ran
his hand through his oil-lacquered salt-and-pepper hair.
When he was angry his wide mouth and enlarged front
teeth increased his usual Cheshire Cat likeness. Jake
almost laughed aloud when he snarled at him again.

Burke tossed the folder on the desk. Exasperated, he
leaned in on his bony elbow, pushed the intercom but-

ton and bellowed, "Get Lance Morgan on the phone, now."

"Yes, sir," his secretary stammered.

"Burke, I've talked to him until I'm blue in the face. He's not budging on this," Jake stated truthfully. "He's made up his mind. He had a five-year contract that expired on January first. You have to face it, it's over, he's not coming back."

"It's over when I say it's over!" Burke yelled and slammed his fist down on the desk. "Do you know how much money he brought into this office last year? I can't believe you let his contract run out without telling me or any attempt on your part to resign him."

Jake prided himself inwardly. He knew exactly what he was doing. Once Lance's contract was up he'd be free to sign with anyone. "Burke, I did. I tried everything. He's not signing. He doesn't want anything to do with this agency. Besides, by now every agency between New York and L.A. is after him."

"That"—he held his finger up for emphasis—"I will not accept. Find something, somewhere, somehow, just get his signature on an extended contract. I don't care how you do it, just do it."

"Burke, you're being unreasonable."

"Do it!" he thundered. His pale face reddened with rage. "Either you sign Lance Morgan or start looking for another job. Do I make myself clear?"

Jake smiled nodding his head. "Yeah, crystal clear."

Below freezing temperatures and another daylong snowstorm completely paralyzed the East Coast. The news anchors continued long listings of canceled schools, closed roads and hints of power outages. The weatherman warned of continued frigid temperatures, freezing wind-chill factors and increased icing conditions. Everyone was warned to remain inside.

Salt-laden trucks plowed through four- and five-foot

snow drifts in a futile attempt to clear the main highways. Abandoned cars were pushed aside like Matchbox toys. Rooftops and trees sagged, dangerously weakened under the added weight. Branches snapped like twigs, and power lines were downed in most areas. The dazzling display of nature's fury and the crystal fantasylike beauty of the world outside was unimaginable. Lance was ecstatic.

Unfortunately, Alex's absence the remainder of the weekend was blatantly obvious. Yet, the ever attentive Mrs. Fletcher kept him company and fed him heartily. He found that if he asked the right questions, Mrs. Fletcher was a wealth of interesting information about the last ten years with Alex. Unfortunately, she never spoke of Alex's current whereabouts. Moreover, when Alex's relationship with author Mason Turner was broached, she completely changed the subject.

Very late Sunday evening, after Mrs. Fletcher had gone home, Lance noticed a dim glow in the living room. He stepped out onto the balcony. There, for the first time in two days, he saw Alex. She stood staring out of the rear window. After a few moments he watched as she disappeared into the kitchen.

He followed. Hurrying down the front staircase, he heard the sound of a door closing. Quickly he entered the kitchen and looked around. She wasn't there. He checked the den, butler's panty, wine cellar, then glanced down the back stairs to the garage. There was no sign of her. As he walked to the den he noticed a paneled door ajar. He walked over and pushed it open. A cold wind chilled his bare chest. Curious, he stepped inside the glass-enclosed walkway.

A wide windowed path led along the back and sides of the house. He began walking; then hearing an unusual sound, he turned and went in the opposite direction. When he reached the entrance of the conservatory he stopped in his tracks. There, surrounded by vast greenery and a cloud of mist, Alex sat submerged in a steaming Jacuzzi. He stood and stared for a few moments, then awkwardly cleared his throat. Startled, she turned and glared at him.

"I'm sorry," he began, "I couldn't sleep. I saw you at the window and wanted to thank you for your extended hospitality." He shivered and looked to the open frosted windows. Icy-cold air continuously blew in.

They stared at each other until she finally responded, "I see." He shivered again. "Well, Mr. Morgan, you can either go back the way you came, stand there and freeze to death or join me." Her peculiar smile took him off guard momentarily. Then he grinned, stepped closer and snapped the band of his sweatpants.

"Buff?" he asked with a raised brow.

She politely turned her back as he removed his pants, stepped up onto the platform, then dropped into the hot water. "Umm . . . this feels great," he purred. Alex turned and greeted him with a breathtaking smile.

"So," he began, "do you come here often?" Unable to hold back, she burst out laughing at the corny pickup line. From that moment on, Lance was sure he'd finally seen a glimmer of hope for his plan. For the next two hours they sat in the heated water talking about everything and nothing in particular.

Alex awoke the following morning exhilarated. She wasn't exactly sure when the idea came to her, but it was perfect. Delighted, she picked up the bedside telephone and punched in the speed-dial number. The phone on the other end began to ring as Coal hopped up on the bed.

A sleepy Lillian Turner-Price picked up the receiver and heard her daughter's cheerful voice. "Hi, Mom. How are you?" Alex said as she rubbed Coal's stomach, then shooed him down from the bed.

"Alex?" Lillian muttered as she focused on the bedside clock. "It's four o'clock in the morning. Why are you calling this early?" Then she sat up, becoming more alert. "Is everything all right?"

"Yes, of course, everything's fine. I just called to chat. Also I had a wonderful idea for the business."

Lillian yawned. "What about the business?"

Alex sat up excitedly. "I know the business has been a little slow lately, and I think I have a possible solution. What you need is a big-name draw."

"Don't tell me you're ready to come back to work again?"

"No, not me. You need someone more current. Someone with a recognizable name. I'm afraid that's just not me anymore."

Lillian relaxed back against the cluster of satin pillows. "I have a few interesting feelers out. But don't worry about the business, Alex. It's doing just fine."

"But it could be better, right?" Alex reasoned.

"What are you up to, Alex?"

"Just a few thoughts, that's all," she said cryptically. Alex intended to tell her mother about Lance, then decided against it. She didn't want to get her hopes up.

"Alex . . ." Lillian admonished.

"I'll let you know more when things are more concrete." She quickly changed the subject. "Did you hear about our blizzard this weekend? It's crippled the entire area. Nothing's been able to move for the last three days. They're only just beginning to dig out."

"I heard. It was all over the news. I was going to call you later. Is it still coming down?"

"No. The weatherman said we're over the worst of it."

"Are you okay there by yourself?"

"I'm fine, I've just been stuck in the house for a few days. Hazel's been around, thankfully. How's the weather out there? Bright, sunny and seventy degrees, I bet."

"Hardly, it's four o'clock in the morning, Alex, it's still dark outside," Lillian said sarcastically. "How's work?" she asked. Alex complained about a particularly frustrating dilemma as the conversation continued for another half hour.

After hanging up, Alex stretched lazily, then looked over to the clock on her nightstand. Suddenly she was energized and starving. She hopped out of bed and turned on the speakers. Latin rhythms pulsated through the bedroom's sound system. Gyrating along with the beat, she grabbed her robe and headed for the bathroom.

By 9:30, Alex, dressed in a silk sweater and jeans, stood at the kitchen counter cutting an array of citrus fruits for breakfast. Coal was stationed at her feet as usual. She bumped into him each time she turned to the sink. "Coal," she complained, "come on, move it." She nudged him lightly with her socked toe. The dog stood and lumbered off to the den and lay in front of the frosted window. Moments later he returned to his previous position just beneath her feet. Stumbling over his large body, she complained again, "Coal, move." He sat up, ears perked.

Dressed in white drawstring sweatpants, a large studio T-shirt and white socks, Lance walked into the kitchen. He stood and watched Alex for a few moments. Her humorous antics with the large dog were comical. Coal lobbed over to him wagging his tail excitedly. "Good morning, Alex," Lance said, greeting his hostess with his usual debonair smile. He reached down and rubbed Coal's midnight fur. "Hey, boy."

Alex turned around. Lance's thousand-watt smile was radiant. "Good morning, Lance, what would you like for breakfast?" she asked.

"I'll just have whatever you're having." He knelt down to roughhouse with Coal. "Where's Mrs. Fletcher?"

"She's at home. Did you sleep well?" she asked.

"Great," he lied. Thoughts of the time spent in the Jacuzzi with this woman had kept him up until dawn. She was so different than he'd imagined. He sauntered over to the counter, picked up a slice of apple and popped it into his mouth. "Umm, what smells so good, you?" He dipped his face into the crook of her neck and shoulder and inhaled perfumed soap and lavender.

Alex giggled nervously and moved away. "No, I made banana-nut muffins. They're still in the oven."

Lance turned and leaned against the counter. "The muffins smell great but you smell better." He reached and grabbed another apple slice, then helped himself to a mug of hot coffee. "Have the roads been cleared yet?" he asked.

"No, not yet."

He walked to the connecting den area and stood in front of the television. The station showed the paralyzing effect of the storm on the entire East Coast. Families were stranded at airport terminals, grocery-store shelves were picked bare and cars were stranded in five-foot snowdrifts along the highway.

Alex came up behind him and leaned against the side of an overstuffed sofa. Lance turned to her. "Would you mind having a house guest for a few more days?"

"No, not at all." She looked at him, then quickly back at the screen. "I see the roads haven't gotten much better," she said, frowning at the devastating sight.

"It looks pretty bad out there. I'm sure glad I ran into you the other night."

Alex sipped from her mug. "You're welcome to stay as long as you'd like."

Lance walked over to her. His sensual smile was unmistakable. "Thank you, Alex, but be warned, you may never get rid of me." She looked into his dark smoldering eyes. There was something there, something she couldn't quite discern. He reached for her hand and they instinctively drew closer. He leaned forward as she tilted her head back, her eyes widened amid the tender touch of his soft lips. The kiss was chaste, but what reflected in his eyes was anything but virtuous. They stood looking into each other's eyes. Alex's heart pounded as Lance bent down to her again.

Suddenly the oven alarm sounded, startling them apart. "Muffins are ready," she rasped breathlessly as she quickly scurried to the kitchen. Lance smiled, applauding his initial performance as he watched Alex's panicked retreat. The moment was not lost, he affirmed reflectively. This was merely the opening act.

Alex dumped the tin of warm nutty bread into a warming basket while quietly muttering to herself, "I hope you know what you're doing, girl."

The baked aroma of bananas and pecans was mouth-watering. It drew Lance into the kitchen like a moth to a flame. "Did you say something?"

"No," she lied guiltily.

He picked up a hot muffin and bit into the warm nutty bread. "Umm, these are delicious," he praised. He was about to continue when the faint sound of his cell phone rang upstairs. "I'll be right back," he said, heading for the stairs.

Alex blew a sigh of relief when Lance reached the top step. Her heart had been pounding so rapidly she was afraid it was going to jump right out of her chest. She fanned her flustered face. That man sure knew how to kiss. And if that was what he considered just a friendly thank-you peck, she wasn't sure she was able to handle an intimate embrace.

"Alex," Lance called down from the upstairs landing, "I need to have some papers sent to me. What's your fax number?"

She gave him the number and he repeated it into the receiver. Coal dashed up the steps and followed Lance back to his bedroom.

"Who's Alex?" Franklin questioned from the other end of the phone.

"A friend," Lance confessed. "Soon to be a very good friend, if all goes well." He sat heavily on the side of the bed absently rubbing Coal's thick neck and shoulders.

"I don't recall your ever mentioning anyone named Alex," Franklin said, openly fishing for more information. He could always tell when Lance was up to something. "I hope you're considering him as your new agent."

"Alex isn't an agent. She's more of a new friend whom I'd like to know better."

"Ahh, I see. Alex is a she. Give me her full name. I'll have Charles run a check on her."

"No need. Not this time. I've known Alex Price all my life. I know everything there is to know about her, even things she doesn't realize I know." Coal yawned, then settled down at his feet.

"Alex Price, *the* Alex Price?"

"The one and only."

"So, can I assume things have cooled between you and Amber? If not, I hope you know what you're doing, Lance. You don't need bad press reviews before the summer openings."

"Amber and I are fine, and yes, I know exactly what I'm doing," he said. Whatever Lance went after he got, including career, fame and women; nothing eluded him for long. Smiling, he thought of the woman down in the kitchen. She was still as beautiful as he remembered. Seeing her brought back the intense longing and desire he had felt for her as a young man. She was the key to the one goal he had yet to achieve. "Anything new from the investigator?" he asked.

"Nah, same as before, more dead ends. Although he said he might have a lead in a few days. His associate was just hired by Mark Summers's law office."

"Tell him to make sure to keep it legal."

"Oh, he will. The job is on the up and up. His associate has been hired as a file clerk. She'll be in Mark's files all day, so if she happens to see something on Turner, so be it. But so far she hasn't come across anything."

"Summers probably keeps the Turner file in his office."

"That's what we figured too. If that's the case, she'll have to use other means."

"All right, just make sure he keeps it legal. I'll talk to you later." Lance closed the small phone and dropped it into his pants pocket. He sat pondering his actions as Franklin's words of concern echoed in his ear, "I hope you know what you're doing."

Lance looked down at Coal and shook his head. He had no choice. Alex was his only connection to Lillian and she was connected to Turner. Coal's ears perked up as he tilted his head from side to side. "Come on, boy, let's get something to eat."

Alex sat at the counter eating mixed fruit, a warm muffin with honey and hot tea. She looked up as Lance and Coal returned to the kitchen. He sat down across from her and helped himself to breakfast. A telephone rang in the distance. "That's probably my manager. He's faxing some papers over."

Alex stood. "The machine is in my office." She led him through the dining room, and around the side of the sunken living room. When she reached the side of the giant aquarium she pushed a concealed mahogany panel. The door swung open easily.

As with the living room, the office was submerged two steps lower than the main level. "Watch your step," she said as she entered the room bathed in bright sunshine by the enormous window.

Lance stood in the entranceway while Alex stepped down and crossed the room to the machine. Instead of following her, he walked around the raised perimeter in the opposite direction. A wall of books stretched across the entire length of the room. He moved closer and ran his fingers over the leather bindings. The titles ranged from the Shakespearean classics and Greek mythology to Freudian theories on personality disorders.

He smiled. The perfect opening had just presented itself. He pulled a book down from the shelf. "I see you're a Mason Turner fan." She remained silent. "I am too. *A Pilgrimage to Heaven,*" he read the book's title aloud. "I loved this one." Alex lowered her head and concentrated on the machine. "I understand that your mother is Mason's agent." He waited for a response.

"Yes, I think she is."

"Have you ever met him?"

Seemingly engrossed with the emerging papers, she said, "Who?"

"Mason Turner, have you ever met him?"

She nodded. "Kind of."

"Kind of?" he asked as he returned the book and moved to the large windowed wall. "What does that mean?" She shrugged her shoulders but remained silent. "What's he like?"

"Turner's just like anybody else."

"I doubt that. The man is a genius. His books are phenomenal. He has to be incredibly intuitive. Is he?"

Alex turned and looked at Lance for the first time since the conversation began. "Why are you so curious about Mason?"

"The man is an enigma. He writes million-dollar stories and screenplays and no one has ever seen him. I think just about everybody is curious about him."

"I don't know what all the fuss is about," she quipped. "Mason is just an ordinary writer. No big deal."

"Hardly, the man is a genius with words." Alex turned her back again to end the discussion. Lance decided to drop the questions for now. He didn't want to tip his hand. He turned and looked out the window to the sparkling lake, then smiled to himself. Alex did indeed know Mason Turner, but she was apparently not willing to talk about him, at least for now.

Eventually Lance turned back to face the room. As he looked around, he smiled. It wasn't at all what he'd expected. He continued walking around the perimeter. The opposite wall was lined with file cabinets and more built-in bookshelves. He turned to the back wall, a display showcase of awards and statuettes.

"I wondered where these were." He stood humbled before the wall of honor. Alex turned but didn't reply. Every conceivable award was represented. Golden Globes, Emmy statuettes, a Tony and numerous others lined the backlit shelves. Then, situated prominently alone on the center shelf, the ultimate prize, the Oscar.

He picked it up gingerly. "This is beautiful." He shook his head in awed astonishment of her achievements. "I always wanted one of these," he admitted while turning the heavy statuette to read the inscription. "The ultimate statement of fame and success."

Alex stood at the credenza looking up at him against the backdrop of her lustrous career. Answering him slowly, she quoted, "Fame is something the public gives you, success is something you earn." She smiled up at him. "I don't remember who told me that, but it always seemed to apply."

Silence stood between then as they contemplated her words. She held up the first few pages and offered them to him. He returned the golden icon and paused in thought. After one last glance at the display case he approached, saying, "You're right, success is something you earn."

Taking the papers from her, he looked at them briefly. "Looks good," he proclaimed as he walked to the desk. Alex turned back to check the next page emerging from the open slot.

He sat down in her plush leather seat and laid the papers on the surface of the desk. Two darkened computer monitors sat on either side of a large glass-topped table. An open operating laptop sat between them showing a number of program files. A stack of books and a script lay beside the monitors. Lance looked quizzically at the pile as the machine beeped, signaling the end of the transmission.

"All done," Alex announced. She carried the remaining papers to the desk and handed them to him.

"Thank you," he said. She nodded. "Where's the music coming from?"

"What music?" she asked.

They listened together. "That music. Where's it coming from?" Lance asked again.

"Oh . . . my bedroom." She motioned toward a closed door by the file cabinets. "I must have left the music on," she answered as he walked toward the door.

"Your bedroom's through here? I thought . . ." He smiled at his assumption and shook his head. "I thought you gave me the master bedroom, your bedroom."

"No. Well, yes, technically you do have the master bedroom for the original structure. This . . ."—she waved her arms wide—". . . was added later."

"I see," he began, but a muffled ring interrupted this thought. The cellular phone in his pants pocket rang. He opened it and answered as Alex excused herself and left the room.

"Did you get everything?" Franklin asked.

Lance walked over to the neat pile of papers Alex had stacked on the desk. He flipped through them briefly. "Yes, looks like they're all here."

"Good, read them through and we'll discuss it when you get back tomorrow. Remember, you have a studio appointment Thursday afternoon."

"That may be a problem. I'm pretty much snowed in for a few more days. Is there any way to postpone the meeting?"

"Until when?"

Lance looked at the tiny date display on his watch. "Today's Tuesday, let's see, try to make it for Friday." I need to take care of some business before we meet.

"I'll see what I can do. Read the revisions and call me later." They hung up. Lance shifted through the papers in his hand as he headed to the living room. As he walked toward the door he paused and glanced across the room. A dramatic beam of light illuminated the solitary golden statuette. He smiled. If all went well he'd have his own to display very soon.

Chapter Five

Snow covered, the countryside resembled a white fluffy cloud over a cozy bed. Coal dashed out as soon as Alex opened the door. His shiny black fur contrasted with the stark brightness of the brilliant white snow. Alex and Lance ventured out on the premise of clearing the walk and driveway. They'd long since abandoned the snow blower and shovels since the war began.

Alex packed a soft snowball and threw it, just missing Lance's face by inches. With astute reflexes, he dodged the snowball, then turned to her. "Oops," she giggled, then backed up, holding both arms out to keep her distance. Lance quickened his pace. "No!" she squealed as he lunged for her. He tackled her around the waist, then pulled her down gently on top of his six-foot frame, taking the brunt of the fall. Coal circled, barking loudly at the playful pair.

Lance maneuvered until he straddled her hips keeping her secure with his long legs. Distracted, he looked down into her perfect face. Her white fur hat and jacket collar blended perfectly against the snow-covered ground. She shifted her body, then twisted. He lost his balance, and together they rolled several times ending with her giggling and him looming above her. He scooped up a large handful of snow and held it threateningly above her head. "Surrender, infidel," he demanded dramatically in his best English accent.

"Never!" she proclaimed nobly, then swung at the glob of snow, sending white powder flying over both of them. He grabbed her cashmere-covered hands and held them securely above her head. He bent down to just inches from her smiling face. "Surrender, infidel," he repeated in a whispered tone as his face continued to descend.

"You don't give up easily, do you?" she said while laughing.

Just inches from her mouth he vowed, "I never give up, Alex. Not when I find something I want."

"That's good to know, because neither do I." Alex tucked in both knees and twisted her hips. The action sent the two rolling down a steep decline and into a five-foot snowdrift. They were completely covered with glistening white flakes. Concerned for her safety, Lance immediately jumped up, pulling her with him. He swooped her up into his arms and carried her up the slope and away from the drift.

"Are you all right?" he asked as she wrapped her arms around his neck. Her heart pounded in excitement. Breathlessly she answered, "I'm fine, you can put me down now." He did, reluctantly. They stood staring into each other's eyes. Then, with his arm protectively around her waist, he pulled her closer. Coal began barked feverishly behind them.

"Hey, Miss Price, who's your new friend?" A man's loud voice broke the silent spell they were under. Alex whirled around. "Damn," she muttered. They had gone too near her property's edge. She saw the snow-covered red car parked on a mound of unshoveled snow. "Miss Price, who's the guy? Hey, turn around, is that you, Shawn?"

Lance never turned, but instead he eased her body closer, tighter, safely within his embrace. "Did I mention I make the best hot chocolate in the Northern Hemisphere?" he said, distracting her.

Alex leaned into him. "Really? That's funny, 'cause

it's been said that I make the best hot chocolate in the Northern Hemisphere."

"Interesting, we'll have to compare recipes one day," he said. "But seeing as how the spoils of war usually go to the victor, I think you should serve hot chocolate to me in front of the fireplace."

"What?" She pushed her hip at his thigh, moving him away from her side. "Spoils of war? Who said you were the victor?" she demanded.

"It's obvious, you surrendered. That would make me the victor," he rationalized.

"I did not surrender!"

"Yes, you did." He laughed in response.

"Why would I surrender when I was winning?" She stood in front of him with both hands planted on her hips. "So, as I see it, I'm the victor and you owe me chocolate in front of the fireplace."

He calmly stepped around her and continued walking. "I beg to differ. I distantly remember your pleading for mercy. I, on the other hand, had just—"

Alex scooped up a huge snowball and tossed it at Lance. She hit her target, then laughed hysterically at his expression. Icy-cold snow penetrated his coat, freezing his neck and shoulders. Turning, he yelled menacingly, "Alex!" Sensing imminent and mortal danger she squealed, darted past him and ran for her life. "Alex!" Lance yelled again and lit out after her. Coal barked noisily at the distant intruder as the man continued shouting personal questions. Eventually, his voice faded on the wind as the couple walked toward the house still debating the victor.

They compromised. Lance made a fire in the den's fireplace and Alex made the hot chocolate. "How about some music?" he asked as he stacked split logs into the soot-charred cavern. He lit the kindling and rearranged the logs. Within moments, a warm blazing fire loomed.

"Good idea," Alex said as she walked over to the wall

and turned a knob on the panel. An easy flow of rhythmic jazz piped into the room.

Lance came over to the stove and peeked at the slow-simmering brew. "Do you want marshmallows?" Alex asked as she slowly whisked the cocoa powder into the hot frothy milk.

"Naturally," he answered, opening the bag of soft spongy orbs and popping one in his mouth. "Where are the cups?"

"Over there," she said, pointing to the top cabinet. Lance pulled out two large mugs and placed them on the counter next to the stove. "Are you hungry?"

"No. You?" he asked.

"No, not really." She turned the burner off. "Ready for the best hot chocolate in the world?" Lance smiled, nodding eagerly like a small child. Alex poured while Lance held the cups. He plopped in several marshmallows, then took them into the den. He sat down in front of the blazing fire. Alex followed and settled on the sofa across the room.

There was an uncomfortable silence as they sipped the hot drinks and stared at the crackling embers. "You can come closer, Alex, I don't bite," Lance said.

She lowered her head feeling somewhat silly about being halfway across the room. She got up and moved closer to the fire. He got up and moved closer to her.

Lance took another sip of his chocolate. "This is pretty good," he admitted.

Alex smiled and sipped the drink. "Thanks. So, Lance," she began, "tell me about your next project. Comedy, drama or action?"

"It's an action adventure. I just finished shooting in London a few days ago. I still have voice-overs to do but the project's pretty much in the can."

"When's it scheduled for release?"

"This summer, tentatively the first weekend of July," he said.

"A summer blockbuster?"

"Something like that."

Solemnly she looked out at the wind blowing snow from the roof. "Summer seems so far away." She looked back at him. "What's after that? Another film?"

"I'm taking a break for a few months." He paused thoughtfully. "Actually, I'm thinking about taking my career in another direction."

"Really? I presume you mean going on the other side of the camera?"

"Possibly."

Coal came up and lay by Lance's side. He rubbed the now dry black fur. "Hey, where've you been?"

"Probably downstairs in his room."

"He's got his own room?"

"Of course," she said. Coal rolled over as Lance scratched him behind the ears. "It's right off the garage with all the comforts of home." Lance smiled, remembering the scene of the two playing in the snow his first day here.

"Who was your agent when you were in the business?" he asked nonchalantly. Alex froze.

"Excuse me?" she asked.

"I mean when you were working, who was your agent?"

Alex's stomach lurched. "My mother, Lillian Turner-Price, is my agent." Using her finger, she batted at a marshmallow floating in the cup. "Why do you ask?"

"I'm looking for representation," he confessed.

"Really?" she said, trying to sound composed. "Who do you have now?"

"Up until a few days ago, Robert Burke." Alex bristled. Lance noticed her agitated expression. He chuckled. "I gather you're acquainted with Burke."

She nodded. "Yes, I'm well acquainted with Robert Burke." She stared at the dwindling flames.

Lance stood, took the iron poker and stoked the fire, then added another log to the pile. He closed the mesh screen, then turned back to her. "Is?" She looked up.

He clarified, "You said *is*, your mother is your agent. I didn't realize you were still in the business."

"I'm not, technically, but I still have my card."

"I see. So I presume by your success she's pretty good."

Alex smiled. This was too perfect. "Definitely. She's very good. Tenacious without being obnoxious, persistent, focused, diligent, I could go on, but I think you get the idea."

"That good, huh?" he said, sounding skeptical.

"I have a wall of shiny statues to prove it," she stated proudly.

"All because of Mom, I suppose."

"That's right, all because of Mom. She got me started in modeling when I was two years old. It was something my father always wanted. He died when I was three. After a few years of modeling, I started acting. I did some commercials and local jobs. Then I started getting national spots; then before I knew it I had the television sitcom, a play on Broadway and the Oscar. It happened so fast."

She smiled, remembering. "It never seemed like acting to me, it felt more like I was just growing up. At one point I even thought that all kids had their own television show." She suddenly stopped talking. "I'm sorry, here I am droning on about me." She got up and went into the kitchen.

"No." He stood and followed. "Don't stop. I love to hear you talk," he confessed.

Alex blushed. "To answer your question, yes, my mother is very good. I have her card if you're interested."

He nodded. "I am." Alex opened a side door. Inside was a mini workstation complete with computer, desk and file. She opened the desk drawer and handed him a card.

"Lillian Turner-Price, Los Angeles." He read the name on the card. "Thanks. I'll give her a call when I get to the coast." Alex smiled, pleased by his interest. Chimes began to ring.

"Excuse me," she said. Curious, Lance followed her into the living room. She stood at a small security panel near the front door and pushed a button. "Yes?" she said into the intercom.

"Hey, Alex, welcome home. It's Matt Hughes from the garage. I'll make a quick pass around your property before I hit the main roads again." Alex pushed another button on the panel to activate and open the iron gate.

"Thanks, Matt. How are Rhoda and the kids?" Alex asked into the screened box.

"Driving me nuts. Why else would I be out here in this weather? Give her a call, she'd love to hear from you."

She laughed. "I'll do that." She released the button. Seconds later a huge plow truck came barreling down her road and driveway. She waved through the window and the driver blew the horn. After several passes around the perimeter of the house the truck backtracked through the front gate.

Alex pushed the button on the panel again. The front gate closed and locked. She walked back to the window. Lance came up behind her. He sighed heavily at the cleared snow. "Looks like my last excuse to hang around just got pushed to the side of the road." He looked down at his hostess. "I hope you're going to miss having me around." Alex smiled but remained silent. "Well, are you?" he prodded.

She turned to face him. He was much closer than she realized. He reached down and took her hand, raised it to his lips. Then, with whisper-soft kisses he memorized every inch. He bent down to just inches from her mouth. "Will you?" He lightly kissed the corner of her lips. "Miss me?" He kissed the opposite corner of her lips. His dark intense eyes never left hers.

Hypnotically she nodded her head. "Yes, I will."

"Good." He beamed triumphantly, then added, "Maybe I'll come back."

"You're welcome any time."

He smiled, playfully taking her into his arms. The open invitation was just what he wanted to hear. "Good. Then I'll definitely be back."

Chapter Six

The dark overcast sky belied the early hour. It was midafternoon but it seemed much later. Two days of bright sunshine and above-freezing temperatures had quickly melted most of the remaining snow. Coal dashed past Alex as they entered the side door. He shook the dampness from his black fur and hurried over to his water bowl.

Alex slowly walked up the back stairs to the empty kitchen. She had never realized how quiet and empty her home was until she watched Lance's black Mercedes drive away Thursday morning. Their time together was like a dream. After ten years, suddenly she felt vital and alive again. Their late-night talks and long walks in the snow-covered woods stimulated a part of her she'd long since repressed. She realized that the barren existence she learned to accept was no longer enough. She wanted more, she deserved more.

Alex made a steaming pot of honey-and-lemon tea. She carried the hot liquid into her office and sat down behind her desk. Sipping the tea, she spun her chair to look up at the statuette Lance coveted. The majestic golden figure stood stoic amid her many awards. "One day, Lance," she promised, "one day." She turned and clicked the television remote. Flipping through the various stations, she stopped at an old black-and-white 1940s film. She muted the sound, turned on the monitors and began working.

Amid several unanswered telephone interruptions, she worked diligently all afternoon and into late evening. The phone rang again. Recognizing the New York extension she tapped the phone key on the computer keyboard. "Hello?" she said into the attached microphone.

"Alex, it's Mark. I'm sending the proposal over now. Read it carefully and call me tomorrow. We'll discuss it then. I think you're going to be pleased with the offer."

"Mark, can't you at least say hello before you jump right into business?" she said with her eyes still glued to the monitor.

"Hello, Alex," he said weakly.

She stopped typing and began scanning the screen. "Hello, Mark, how are you? I'm fine. We had a major snowstorm a few days ago, but don't worry, I survived. How did you make out?"

He laughed. "All right, I get the point, how are you?" he said with more sincerity.

She laughed along. "Fine, thanks for asking. I'll read the contract and call you tomorrow."

"Make it late," he suggested. "I have a two-P.M. meeting with Moore and his people. I should have their final proposal by then."

"Okay, talk to you tomorrow," she said, disconnecting with a push of a key. Within minutes the fax machine rang out.

Lance strutted into Franklin Moore's personal office unannounced. His secretary said he was on the telephone and to go right in. He grimaced. The room smelled of stale cigar smoke and spaghetti sauce.

Lance casually moved to one of the two fat leather chairs facing Franklin's desk and sat down, resting his briefcase against the chair's leg. He grimaced when he saw a half-eaten mozzarella, green pepper and sausage sandwich leaking oil onto the wrapped paper beneath it.

Franklin sat behind his cluttered wooden desk barking orders to the unfortunate person on the other end of the receiver. He frowned at Lance and stubbed his cigar into the already overflowing ashtray. The computer monitor suddenly blinked to black and then transformed into a soothing fish-tank screen saver. Lance's thoughts immediately went to Alex.

"So, the prodigal son finally returns," Franklin said sarcastically as he dropped the receiver into the cradle.

Lance grinned the smile that won him so many fans and broke so many hearts. "Hello, Franklin, nice to see you too."

"Don't give me that bull. Where the hell have you been?" he growled, looking curiously at his half-eaten sandwich.

"New Jersey."

"New Jersey, my ass, nobody lives in New Jersey," Franklin contended. "I called you twenty times Tuesday, no answer." He lit a cigar, puffed a few times, then blew out the smoke and coughed. "I called you another twenty times on Wednesday, again no answer. So here it is Thursday afternoon and you finally decide to make an appearance."

Lance smiled again. This gruff man was the reason he was such a big star and enjoyed the pampered life he had. Franklin Moore was the best celebrity manager in the business. He handled everything from paying monthly bills to hiring domestic help. He only had a few clients, and those lucky enough to acquire his services understood his special charm.

"Ah, but that's where you're wrong, my friend. Someone very definitely lives in New Jersey," Lance said.

"Alex?" Franklin inquired after another puff.

"Alex," Lance confirmed.

Franklin just shook his head. "Did you read the contract I sent you?"

"Yes, it looks fine. I made a few changes in the wording on the second page, nothing drastic." He reached into his briefcase and pulled out the stapled fax pages. "Also I thought we could pass on the last amendment. It doesn't seem necessary." He reached over and handed the papers across the desk.

Franklin scanned the corrections and changes. He nodded his head. "I didn't think you'd agree to this last one, but they wanted it in. I'll rework a final draft and submit it. I'm sure they'll sign off on it." He pointed to a manila envelope on the corner of his desk. "Don't forget to take that, it's the updated script changes on the last film. They're still working on the junkets and promotional schedule."

Lance dropped the packet into his case. "Good. Have you heard anything new from Mason Turner's people?"

"No, too soon. I understand they have a few studio offers on the table as well." He looked up from the contracts. "With the success of his last four projects—" Franklin shook his head. "I'm not going to lie to you, Lance, your chances of getting the rights to this script are slim. The studios have deep pockets. Turner could write his own ticket on this one."

Lance nodded his agreement. "The meeting is still on for tomorrow?" he asked.

"Two P.M.," Franklin confirmed.

"Will Mason actually be there?"

"I doubt it. He usually lets the suits do the grunt work. I hear he's a creative recluse, just sits and writes, churning out blockbuster scripts and million-dollar hits."

"So it's true, no one's ever actually met him?" Lance wondered.

"Not to my knowledge. He's strictly by the book and goes through his lawyer and agent. That reminds me." Franklin leaned up to search his messy desk. Finally he pulled out a folder with Lance's name on it. He tossed it across to him. "Take a look at these proposals. We've narrowed them down to six."

Lance flipped through the folder indifferently. "Ever heard of an agent named Lillian Price? She works here in Los Angeles."

"Lillian Turner-Price, yeah, I know Lillian. She's good, very good. Her agency might be a bit small for your needs. She usually only handles beginners, but if you're interested, I'll give her a call."

"Don't bother, I'll call her personally," Lance said. Franklin removed the cigar from his gaping mouth. Shock registered on his face. Lance stood to conclude their business. "Shut your mouth, Franklin. I'll see you tomorrow." Lance paused before opening the office door. "By the way, I'll be returning to New Jersey in a few days."

"For how long this time?"

"I'm not sure yet." He smiled. "I'll let you know."

"By the look on your face I assume you enjoyed yourself." Lance winked his answer and closed the door.

Once in the outer office he paused at the nearest desk. Franklin's secretary looked up. "Hello, Lance. What can I do for you?"

Exhibiting his trademark devastating smile, Lance turned on the charm. "I'd like to send a fax."

"Sure." She stood and walked over to the small, barely noticeable machine in the corner of the room. "What's the fax number?"

Lance reached into his briefcase and pulled out the cover sheet from the contract Franklin had sent him in New Jersey. Alex's fax number was on the top. He looked at the machine mysteriously.

"I'll take care of that for you." The phone began to ring. She looked over to her desk. Her excessive efficiency wouldn't permit her to leave a telephone unanswered any more than she would send an envelope out unstamped.

"You go ahead and get that," Lance said, "I'll figure this out."

"It's simple, put the paper in here, dial the number on this panel, then push this green button to send. Everything else is automatic," she said, hurrying to the ringing phone.

Lance looked over the high-tech machine. He scribbled a few words on a piece of paper, eased it into the open slot, dialed the number, then pushed the green button. The paper slid through just as Franklin called out, "Hey, I thought I got rid of you." Lance chuckled as he retrieved the sent paper.

"You did, see you later." He opened the door to leave.

"Hey," Franklin called out after his secretary reminded him by shaking the invitation under his nose. "Don't forget you're getting an NAACP Image Award tonight! And before you ask, yes, you have to be there. You're also one of the main presenters."

"I remember. Black tie, seated at eight, bring a date and don't be late," he repeated the rhyme Franklin had taught him years ago.

"See that you're not," Franklin yelled at the closing door.

The bright glow of the television screen illuminated the darkened room. A loud ring startled Alex to look up from the monitor as a page slid from the fax machine. It was late and as usual she had worked far into the night.

Alex glanced up at the television screen. A close-up of Lance's smiling face beamed back at her. The camera panned back. She immediately recognized the young beautiful woman standing by his side, Amber Hall. Alex quickly grabbed the remote and pushed the mute button just as the announcer concluded his report. She frowned and watched the remainder of the broadcast waiting for a follow-up report. When it didn't come she went back to the keyboard. After a struggling and unproductive half hour, she realized her concentration was lost.

An hour later she pulled the covers back and crawled into her bed. She sat up surrounded by her ritual late-night reading: mail, contracts, proposals, articles and research. She flipped through the stack of papers Mark had faxed her. The last one gave her pause. She picked it out of the pile and read the quickly scrawled writing aloud. "I miss hearing your voice, call me." She smiled.

She picked up the receiver and punched in the numbers scrawled on the paper. Lance answered on the second ring. "Hello."

"Hello, Lance," she said.

"Hi, beautiful." She could hear the smile in his voice. He continued, "I was beginning to worry about you."

"Really?"

"Yes, really. How's the snow?"

"As a mater of fact the snow's almost gone."

"Already?" He sounded surprised. "That was quick."

The obvious background noise drew Alex's attention. "Sounds like you're at a party."

"I am."

"Oh," she said uneasily, "I'll let you go then."

"No, don't hang up." The loud talking and laugher slowly diminished as Lance stepped onto the terrace. "I'm glad you called. I missed hearing your voice," he admitted.

Alex's thoughts immediately went to the beautiful actress on his arm. "Really?" she replied skeptically.

"Really," he confirmed without a doubt.

She sighed and snuggled deeper into the warmth of her bed and closed her tired eyes as he told her just how much.

Chapter Seven

The door burst open. "Mrs. Turner-Price, you're never gonna guess who just walked into the office," Linda squealed hysterically, gasping for breath. She held both hands protectively over her heart. "I can't believe it, it's just like my horoscope said last week, *Life holds surprises for you . . . be prepared.*"

Lillian continued reading the contract she was holding. "Not now, Linda. If they don't have an appointment, I can't see them today. I'm swamped." She looked up curiously. "Where's Helen?"

"She's running an errand and Mavis is at lunch. They told me to watch the office."

"Fine," she said patiently, "give my apologies to whoever it is and ask them politely to make an appointment. I just don't have time today."

"I think you're gonna want to see this person," Linda insisted, still breathless.

Lillian looked up. "Who is it?"

"Lance Morgan!" Linda uttered reverently.

"Lance Morgan?" Lillian was stunned. She knew Lance was in the market for a new agent but never in her wildest dreams had she even presumed to offer her services. He was a superstar. Every agent in the States and most of Europe was after his contract. And since she usually only handled new talent, she hadn't given his announcement a second thought, until now. "Send him in."

Linda stepped aside and ushered Lance into Lillian's private office. She melted when Lance thanked her with his thousand-watt smile. "I'll bring in refreshments, Mrs. Turner-Price," she whimpered, closing the door quietly behind her.

Lillian came around to the front of her desk and greeted Lance warmly. "Well, Mr. Morgan, this is a pleasant and unexpected surprise." She held out her hand to shake.

Lance clasped her small hand in his. "Mrs. Turner-Price, it's an honor to finally meet you." Lillian was immediately struck by Lance's obvious charm and good looks. She could definitely see why he was so sought after. This man was impressive.

"Please." She motioned to a soft fabric office chair. "Have a seat." He did. She sat in the matching chair next to his. After a timid knock on the door, Linda stepped in carrying a full service china tea set. "Tea, Mr. Morgan?" Lillian asked.

He gleefully accepted. "Yes, please, two sugars with lemon, if you have it." Lillian smiled, nodded, then prepared his tea. His mind immediately went to Alex. She was the spitting image of her mother. Lillian's determined chin reminded him of Alex's stubborn refusal to admit defeat when they played checkers, and her twinkling almond-shaped eyes, of the mischievous glint he loved to see each time Alex had tossed a snowball at him.

"Now, Mr. Morgan." Lillian handed him the delicate cup of tea. "What can I do for you?"

"First of all, you can call me Lance."

She nodded. "Of course, please call me Lillian."

Lance smiled. "Okay, Lillian, for starters, I'm looking for new representation."

* * *

"Okay, what do you think of this one?" Victoria asked as she stepped out of her dressing room smiling radiantly. Alex looked up. Victoria glittered from head to toe in a dazzling fire-engine-red see-through beaded gown. Reminiscent of her New York runway model career, she glided gracefully around the room. She paused, leaned against one of the bed's four towering posts, then struck a dramatic pose.

At five feet nine, Victoria was a glamorous woman. Her dark complexion, keen Italian features and long jet-black hair added to her exotic beauty. Men usually dropped to their knees when she walked into a room.

Coal raised his large head and yawned loudly. Alex sighed. Several fashion designers had lent Victoria their designs in hopes of enticing her to wear their creation to the upcoming Golden Globe Awards ceremony. Victoria had modeled each one in hopes of choosing the perfect outfit. This was her tenth gown so far.

"Wow! That's . . . ah . . . really red," Alex said as she sat up and stopped flipping through one of the many fashion magazines scattered across Victoria's oversize bed.

"Alex, I know the color." She turned around slowly and eyed herself in the three-way mirror, then pulled her hair up and then let it fall loose down her back. "What I want you to tell me is if it's sexy enough. I have to look drop-dead gorgeous. I want to wow Hollywood." She looked over to the bed. "Well?" Alex crinkled her nose and shook her head no. Coal got up from his resting place and trudged over to the base of the bed.

Victoria sucked her teeth and marched back to the bedpost. "You haven't stepped foot in Hollywood in five years." She bent down to Coal and scratched his back. He immediately lifted his head to acknowledged the attention. "Look, Coal likes it, don't you, boy?" She scratched his ears, then bent down.

"What would he know?" Coal barked loudly in response.

Victoria stood up and snorted. "See? He agrees with me."

"Victoria, Coal's a dog. I wouldn't take his opinion too seriously."

"So, you're saying you don't like it?"

"That's exactly what I'm saying," Alex retorted.

Victoria glanced back at her reflection. "Why?" she moaned.

"Because the dress makes you look like a floozy," Alex said. Victoria smiled mischievously in the mirror. "Victoria D'Lucchia Reese, that was not meant as a compliment!" Alex said pointedly.

Victoria stopped primping. "A floozy? No one uses the word floozy, Alex." She laughed as she sashayed back into the dressing room.

"Although," Alex began, then paused, waiting for Victoria to reappear. "I bet Ted would get a kick out of seeing you in it."

Victoria stuck her head around the door frame. She raised her eyebrow curiously. "You think so?" Alex nodded. Victoria smiled happily as she slipped into another borrowed gown. "Why don't you come with us, Alex? You can stay with me and Ted and go to the movie premiere and then attend the awards ceremony."

Victoria left the dressing room and stepped in front of the mirror. The gown, a deep chocolate brown, accentuated every curve and flowed on her body like liquid silk. It was a sweeping waterfall of satin fabric with thin gold-link straps. A short train dipped just long enough to emphasize her tall, slender frame. The look was classic and Victoria was exquisite. Alex smiled and whistled a wolf's call. "Hubba, hubba! Va-va-va-voom!"

Victoria placed her hand on her hip and caught Alex's eye in the mirror. "Honestly, Alex, you really must get

out more. You're starting to talk like a 1920s film clip."
She turned around. "I gather you like this one?"

Alex nodded eagerly. "You look magnificent. The
color and material are perfect. Who's the designer?"

Victoria turned and walked a few paces, letting the
short train trial behind her. "It's a Suzi Banks."

"She's talented, I like her work. That's the one, it
looks spectacular on you."

"All right then, this is the one," she decided while
eyeing herself in the mirror again. "We missed you at
dinner last night. Chase was still in town. He asked about
you, as usual."

Alex went back to flipping through the magazine. "I
can't believe he hasn't gotten tired of this game yet.
There are thousands of women all around the world
just dying for his attention."

Victoria went back into the dressing room. "Because,
dear friend, you're the first woman ever to say no to
him. He's intrigued. You've become a challenge. It's
that ego thing. You're the one who got away. You broke
his perfect record."

"That's ridiculous," Alex scoffed.

Victoria peeked around the corner. "Trust me, I know
my brother too well. He's a typical male." She ducked
her head back into the dressing room. "That, and the
fact that he's been in love with you ever since he first
met you." Alex mused, that was probably true.

Alex and Chase had met when she was on location
in Italy. Victoria, who was dating the director at the
time, invited Alex to spend a long weekend in her home-
town of Chirro, Italy. The weekend was unforgettable.
Everyone immediately fell in love with Alex, including
Victoria's younger brother, Chasano.

As descriptive of his name, Chase pursued a conquest
with a relentless passion until eventually he succeeded.
Once a woman was seduced by his charms, he'd eventually get bored and move on to his next goal. Sending,

of course, an expensive bauble with an appropriate note to ease his conscience.

Victoria came out of the dressing room wearing jeans and a blue cashmere sweater. She had the brown satin and red-beaded gowns draped over her arm. "You know, I really liked this red gown too. I think I'll keep it and wear it for Ted. He'll get a kick out of it." She moved in front of the mirror and checked her hair and makeup, then looked over to the bed. Alex was engrossed in the magazine article. "The roof is on fire, Alex," Victoria said to get her attention.

"Uh-huh," Alex mumbled, still reading, then suddenly looked up. "What?"

Victoria sat down on the bed. "What's so interesting?" She peered at the entertainment magazine cover in Alex's hand. "Oh, Lance Morgan."

In the cover photo, Lance stood in an open doorway leaning against an iron gate. He was casually dressed in jeans. They were zipped but unsnapped at the waistband. He also wore an open denim shirt, a backward baseball cap and his feet were bare. His easy smile and relaxed posture hinted at the playful direction of the article. The caption read AMERICA'S INFATUATION WITH LANCE MORGAN. The article relayed how Lance's enduring fame transcended his fifteen years in the business. It went on to boast resounding accolades about his latest eagerly anticipated action film.

"Believe it or not he's a really nice guy," Victoria said. "He's got real movie-star panache." She picked up a magazine and flipped through the pages.

"I didn't know you knew Lance Morgan," Alex stated, then as casually as possible added, "How do you know him?"

"I met him about five years ago. Ted was doing a film and he wanted Lance to star. The timing wasn't right and Lance had to pass because of other commitments." Victoria grabbed another magazine and pulled her hair up, imitating the cover model. She nudged closer. "You know, he's up for a Globe and I hear he's practically a shoo-in to win." She winked. "Why don't you come to the coast with me? I'll introduce you."

"No. Thanks anyway. I'm still trying to catch up on things after being in St. Croix for the last few months."

"Well, the offer remains open as usual," Victoria promised.

"Is this thing with Amber Hall for real?"

"Who knows?" Victoria remarked, still primping with her hair. "Personally I think it's just for show. I've met her, she's like the biggest valley girl airhead. Holding a conversation with her is like talking to broccoli. I can't imagine anyone actually taking her seriously."

"I'm sure most men couldn't care less what comes out of her mouth. Look at her, she's gorgeous."

"Oh, please," Victoria protested, "you're a thousand times more attractive than her, and, you can actually hold an intelligent conversation."

Before Alex could reply, the telephone rang. Both women looked at the phone sitting on the large pillow sham. Alex glanced at her watch. "It's getting late, I need to get home." She hopped off of the raised bed, grabbed her coat and purse, then headed for the door. Coal followed. "Call me when you get back from the coast." Victoria nodded and waved as Alex closed the door. As Alex walked down the hall she realized she was still holding the magazine with Lance's picture on the cover.

On the way home she stopped at the market to pick up a few things for dinner. As she loaded the brown bags in the car, Coal barked wildly inside. Curious, she looked up seeing the tabloid reporter walking over.

Leery of provoking Coal, the reporter stood back several feet. "Ms. Price," he yelled, "rumor has it that Shawn Anderson has been spending his time here in Stoneridge, any comment?" She ignored him. "Are you and Shawn getting back together after all these years?"

She got into the car, locked the door and drove off. The reporter hopped in his car and followed.

Alex tensed, knowing the lengths this man would go to for a story. As soon as she approached the safety of her property she relaxed, seeing him stop just beyond the iron gates.

Safely in the garage, she opened her car door and heard the telephone ringing. Her first thought was Lance. She rushed to answer it as Coal went bounding up the back stairs to the kitchen. As she opened the door she heard the familiar beep of the answering machine ending the call.

Disappointed, she hurried to the office and listened to the five messages. The first call was from Mark. He reported that the meeting went well and he'd faxed over notes. Alex saw a stack of papers sitting in the receiving bin. She leafed through them while the second message played.

"Alex, pick up." The caller paused for an answer. Then concluding that she wasn't at home she continued, "You'll never guess who came to my office this morning." Her mother's usual calm voice radiated excitement. "Lance Morgan! He wants me to put together a proposal. Can you believe it? He's seriously considering me as his agent. Call me back. Bye."

Alex smiled happily. Apparently her boasting about her mother worked better than she thought. Lance had actually contacted her mother. Alex listened to the third call. It was from Lance. "Alex, I need a favor." His melodious voice penetrated the room. "Call me when you get a chance." She reached for the phone just as it began ringing. "Hello?"

"Alex?"

"Hello, Lance."

She recognized his voice, he thought, smiling, to himself. "Hello Alex," he began. "I was just thinking about you."

"Really?" she said.

"Really. Believe it or not I've been thinking about you a lot these past few days. Are you busy?"

"No," she said, "I just walked in the door."

"How's Coal?"

"He's good. I just heard your message. What's the favor?"

"I wonder if I could impose on our friendship to finagle an invitation."

"An invitation?" she asked, somewhat confused. "An invitation to where?"

"Well." He took a deep breath. "You said I'd be welcome there any time, so I'd like to take you up on that offer.

"Here? With me?" she questioned. "Won't it be a little too quiet for you? I mean you're Lance Morgan, and Stoneridge isn't exactly a whirl of excitement. As a matter of fact it's practically deserted this time of year."

"That's exactly what I'm looking for, peace and quiet. I've been working on this new project and I need someplace where I can concentrate."

"Sure, I'd love to have you. But, I seem to have attracted an annoying tabloid reporter. He's staked out just down the road. There's no way to get in unnoticed. So, if you want solitude I doubt you'll get it once he sees you."

"No problem. I'll take care of that. I'll see you in a few days."

Alex hung up the phone. She was ecstatic. Lance was actually coming back to see her. She smiled. "Sorry, Amber, may the best woman win."

Chapter Eight

Burke slammed his drink down in disgust. He was fed up with Jake's lame excuses and lackadaisical attitude. So as soon as Jake sat down he lit into him.

Jake seethed. *This is bull,* he thought as he sat listening to another one of Burke's tirades. He needed to start his own agency. All he needed was a couple of big-name talents to draw the others in. And those talents would be Lance Morgan and Mason Turner. The rest would be a breeze. Actors and actresses would be begging for him to represent them.

The console on Burke's desk beeped once and a pleasant voice cut through the tense room. "What?" Burke barked.

"Lance Morgan on line one."

Burke reached over and grabbed the receiver. Miraculously his demeanor transformed. "Lance, it's Burke," he announced happily.

"Hello, Burke," Lance responded.

"We need to talk, Lance," Burke began. Lance listened patiently as Bob Burke expounded their long, lucrative history together. He pleaded his case masterfully. Jake sat smirking in silence. Burke's pathetic pleading and begging were demeaning. Suddenly noticing Jake's disgusted expression, Burke waved his hand dismissively. Jake smiled as he strutted from the office.

"Mr. Morgan," Lance's assistant whispered an interruption. Lance looked up, still half listening to Burke as she continued talking. The whisper continued, "Mr. Moore is waiting in the library. Shall I bring him out here or would you care to eat elsewhere?"

Lance placed his hand over the mouthpiece. "Have him join me out here. You can serve lunch any time. Thanks," Lance answered. "Burke, I have to get with you later." Burke continued to state his case. "I'll stop by next week and we'll talk." Lance ended the conversation, then closed the script he'd been reading. He gathered the contracts and notes he'd made into a neat pile.

Waiting patiently for his guest, Lance removed his dark sunglasses and looked out over the rolling hills beyond his home. It was a beautiful day and he felt energized. All it had taken was a brief conversation with Alex. In another two days he'd be with her again. He smiled to himself, satisfied with his progress.

"You look like the cat that just swallowed a rat," Franklin said as he removed his sunglasses and ducked his six-foot bulky frame beneath the large umbrella. He had his cellular phone to his ear. "Yeah, that's the one. Send it out this afternoon," he commanded into the receiver, then closed and slipped the small device into his shirt pocket and sat down.

A silver-trayed dome was placed in front of Lance. "These are for you," he said, handing Franklin several signed contracts. Lance lifted the silver cover. A delectable garden salad greeted him. Franklin glanced over the papers, then nodded. "I'll have copies of these delivered to you later today." He leaned back to allow a silver dome to be placed in front of him. He rubbed his hands together eagerly, then looked over to Lance's plate. His jaw dropped open. "Rabbit food again!" He blew out in exasperation. "Man, sometimes I really hate eating here, you're always on that health food kick," Franklin grumbled in disgust.

"I'm not on a health food kick. I simply eat well-balanced meals," Lance said as Franklin removed his plate's cover.

Lance grinned at Franklin's obvious surprise. "Never let it be said that I am not an accommodating host," Lance proclaimed as Franklin gleefully smiled at the four-inch-thick Reuben sandwich in front of him. He rubbed his large hands together again, removed the toothpick and bit into the sloppy, towering sandwich.

"Now, that's more like it," he commented happily with his mouth filled with corned beef, coleslaw and Russian dressing. "So, how long are you going to be in Jersey?"

Lance leaned back in the cushioned lounge chair and sipped from a tall glass of sparkling water. "That depends."

"On what?"

Lance toyed with a speared tomato as he stared at the shimmering blue pool of water reflecting in the bright sunlight. "On how far I get."

Franklin wiped his mouth on the white linen napkin and bit into the fat kosher pickle. "Does she have any idea how you feel?"

"What do you mean, how I feel?" Lance said as he bit down, letting a juicy cherry tomato explode in his mouth.

"Could you be any less obvious?" Franklin admitted with a slight chuckle. He grabbed several potato chips and dumped them in his mouth. Between crispy crunches he continued, "Remember, Lance, you and I go way back. There's not too much I don't know. You've loved Alexandra Price since forever."

Lance smiled and nodded knowingly. Franklin was right. They did go back a ways.

Franklin Moore was Lance's father's manager for years. So, when he decided to go into the business, Franklin became his manager also. He was there when Lance got his first commercial, his first walk-on and then finally his first major role. He was also there when Lance had first met Alex.

Lance had leaned nervously against the wall waiting impatiently for his turn to audition. This was his fourth call-back. Today he actually would read with her. The coveted role he was going for was television boyfriend opposite Alexandra Price and he really wanted this part. He even considered revealing his legal name to get it.

If the casting director knew he was Patrick Anderson's son he'd have the role in a second. But he wanted to do this on his own terms, without his father's famous name.

The door opened and a cocky Shawn Anderson strutted out. Lately, it seemed he and Lance vied for the same roles. They had the look, style and talent that most casting directors coveted. The two glared at each other as Shawn walked to the elevator. "Go home, Lance. I just aced the part," he scoffed with a belligerent grin as the elevator doors closed. Before Lance could respond, his name was called. Lance turned. Franklin exited a nearby office. He eyed the script pages in Lance's hand. "Aren't you supposed to be in New York with your mother?" he asked.

"It's spring break. I'm visiting the old man." He smiled broadly. "I have a call-back."

Franklin looked at the closed door with the paper sign indicating AUDITIONS. *"Does your dad know you want this part?" he asked.*

"No. And I'd rather you not tell him. I want to get this on my own. As a matter of fact I'm going by the name Lance Morgan instead of Lance Anderson. I don't want Patrick calling in favors for me."

Franklin laid his hand on Lance's shoulder. "Lance, this is show business. It's all about who you know. Nepotism is done without even thinking twice."

"I know . . ." Lance admitted ruefully.

"Lance Morgan," the casting assistant called out, then stepped back into the room.

". . . but not this time," Lance had said and headed to the open door. Franklin called out, "Break a leg." Lance spun around, beamed brightly and gave Franklin a thumbs-up signal before disappearing behind the closed door.

"That reminds me," Franklin said now after sipping his cold drink. "I need Alex Price's home phone number and address."

Lance reached over and handed Franklin a folded piece of paper he'd written out earlier. Franklin unfolded it and nodded. "What did you think of Mark Summers the other day?"

"He's a bit stiff. He could definitely use a night out on the town." Franklin laughed and nodded his agreement. "I noticed he didn't seem fazed by the offer," Lance continued.

"He's a lawyer. He gets paid not to be impressed. Remember, Lance, just because you've got your mind set on Turner's book doesn't necessarily mean you'll get it. This book is even hotter than his last one. Everybody and his brother wants it. Eighty-two weeks on the *New York Times* best-sellers' list, and still at the top . . ." Franklin didn't finish, he just shook his head in amazement.

"I'm working on a venue that might just get us directly in touch with Turner," he suggested hopefully.

"Summers will never go for that. The last time someone made that attempt, they were booted out of contention. Face it, Lance, Mason Turner won't meet with anyone face-to-face."

Lance shook his head in annoyance and threw his napkin down on the table. He hated having so little control over situations involving his career. The helpless feeling was totally unacceptable. "I really want this, Franklin," he pressed emphatically.

"I know, I know. But this time there's nothing you

can do to manipulate the outcome. You just have to be patient and hope for the best."

"I'm not used to operating like that and you know it. Patience has never been one of my stronger virtues."

"And you're telling me something I don't already know?" Franklin shook his head. "Careful, you're starting to sound like your old man."

"Hardly. I'm nothing like Patrick."

"On the contrary. You're more and more like him the older you get."

Lance looked at Franklin with a fierce chilled expression that would have made a lesser man cringe. It made Franklin chuckle. He continued, "You're both aggressive, bullheaded, stubborn and determined to get everything you go after. Which isn't always a good idea sometimes."

Lance chuckled. "Sounds more like you're describing Shawn, not me."

"Oh, he's also got a touch of the Anderson charm. He's just too obvious with it. Whereas you and Patrick are more conservative about your indulgences, Shawn, on the other hand, tends to be spoiled and obsessively domineering."

"Well, at least I'm not spoiled and domineering too."

"I wouldn't go that far, but let's just say you're not exactly a happy camper when you don't get what you go after. Luckily for everyone around you, that's a rarity."

"Let's see, so far I'm aggressive, bullheaded, domineering and a spoiled brat. Anything else?"

"Yeah, you procrastinate."

Lance smiled at the sudden change of subject. Franklin could always get under his skin with his little pearls of wisdom. Usually he was right on the money when it came to character analysis but this time he was dead wrong. Lance didn't see himself as Franklin described him. And he certainly was nothing like Patrick or Shawn. He would admit he was aggressive when it came to something he wanted but he'd never resorted to unscrupulous means to get it. That was more for his father, Shawn and Burke.

"Have you decided on an agent yet?"

"Not yet. Although I met with Lillian Turner-Price a few days ago. I like her style. But she might be a bit too laid-back for me. I'm still considering the list you gave me."

"Don't underestimate Lillian. She's a lot tougher than she looks. Just ask your previous agent. He made the mistake of thinking she was a pushover. She had him so whipped he didn't know if he was coming or going."

Holding his fork speared with endive suspended in the air, Lance looked up from his meal in shock. "Burke? Bob Burke."

Franklin nodded with his mouth filled with the last of the sandwich. He chewed patiently, then added, "Yes, Bob Burke. Years ago he and Lillian had some kind of a relationship. Rumor had it he tried to use her to get to Alex's contract. But she found out and hit the ceiling. They say that's why Alexandra Price quit the business." He took a long sip of his drink.

"Wait a minute, I though Lillian was Alex's agent. How did Burke get in the picture?" Lance asked.

"Lillian was her agent. At least in the beginning when Alex was a kid doing that television series. She was an overnight phenomenon."

Lance nodded. "So, what happened after the series?"

Franklin continued eating his pickle. "Don't know. She disappeared for a while. I think maybe she stepped back and reinvented herself or something like that. But, whatever she did, it worked. As a teenager she came back and her career was stronger than ever. She had a new comedy series on television. And the fans loved her. After that, she went to Broadway. The following year she won the Oscar. After that her career really exploded. Everybody wanted a piece of her."

"So basically Alex's career got too big for Lillian to handle?" Lance theorized.

"Yeah. Anyway, that's when Burke stepped into the picture. He hired Lillian as a top associate. Therefore, Alex technically worked under his agency."

Lance sat quiet and thoughtful while Franklin savored the last of his drink. "I remember Alex from the sitcom and that movie," Lance said in a dreamlike state. Franklin looked up from his empty plate.

"Man, I remember you had it bad for her," Franklin added after assessing the abundant fruit cup placed before him. He began picking at the cut morsels. "All I heard for months was, 'Do you know Alexandra Price? I want to meet Alexandra Price! I love Alexandra Price.' You were relentless."

Yeah, I guess I was, Lance mused to himself. "So what exactly happened to make her quit?" he asked aloud.

Franklin shrugged his thick shoulders. "I don't really know. I don't think anybody really does. Except of course for Lillian, Alex and Burke. But rumor had it that after Lillian went to work for Burke, all hell broke loose."

"Figures," Lance put in sarcastically.

Franklin chuckled, then continued, "Alex was a huge star by then. The sitcom, the Tony and the Oscar catapulted her to major stardom. Lillian became really popular with the studio executives. She of course had Alex as her client and everybody wanted Alex. Then, somehow Burke found out that Alex and Lillian never had a contract. It was just a mother, daughter thing. So, he tried to get Alex away from Lillian and under contact with him exclusively. There was a big mess. It eventually went to court. I think the ruling was in Burke's favor as the agency's owner. But if you ask me, I think he paid off the judge." Franklin took another sip of his refilled drink. "Alex quit the business shortly after that. She retired, saying that she wanted to explore other artistic endeavors. So technically, at least for a while, Burke was her agent, although she never actually worked with him." Franklin began laughing. "The funny thing is after all that drama, Burke never saw a penny of Alex's worth. She retired before he had a chance to exploit her."

Lance nodded absently. He realized that living in New York at the time, he had missed the whole story. After that he never really gave much thought to the reason Alex left Hollywood. He just remembered she disappeared from sight. By then his own career had taken off.

"So," Franklin began, "what's the deal with the two of you?"

"Who? Me and Alex?" Franklin gave him a *who else?* expression. "There is no deal, she was Shawn's lover. Everybody knows that. My taste and my half brother's tastes in woman are not exactly similar. For all I know they could still have a thing going on. The press seems to think so."

"The press? Oh, you mean the tabloid press. Oh, and we know how accurate their articles are."

Lance chuckled. "I have no real interest in Alex other than business," he assured Franklin.

"I'm your business manager, remember. What kind of business is there between the two of you?"

"Although I must admit," Lance stated, smiling thoughtfully and ignoring Franklin's question, "she does have a certain charm."

"Charm?"

Lance shrugged. "She's different."

"Different?"

"She's got the Greta Garbo 'I want to be alone' syndrome. I just need to draw her out."

"Why is it so important to get to her? What's the business deal?"

Lance didn't respond. He glanced out at the Hollywood Hills below his home. "Funny," he said more to himself than aloud, "after getting to know her, she's just not what I expected."

"What did you expect?"

"Truthfully, I really don't know." Lance paused for a moment, reflecting on thoughts of Alex. "Do you believe in destiny, Franklin?"

"I believe we make our own destiny."

"So given any arbitrary situation, there are any number of factors that will alter our destiny according to how we respond."

"Yeah, basically, it's cause and effect."

"Therefore, if we choose the wrong response to a situation, our destiny is forever irrevocably altered. And nothing we can ever do will modify the outcome. No second chances, no retakes, no hope. Every single second of our lives is a direct result of our past decisions. Right or wrong we are forced to live by our choices. Our destiny is completely fulfilled regardless of our growth process. The inevitability of our fate is decreed. We're predestined, forever doomed by our past." Lance closed his eyes and lowered his head.

"Damn." Franklin peered to the other side of the table. "What the hell was in that salad?"

Chapter Nine

The doorbell rang again. Alex stuck a pencil in her hair and frowned. At this rate she'd never get this done. She trudged begrudgingly to the front door with Coal on her heels. Angrily, she mashed the button and answered the second intercom buzz. "Yes?"

"I have a delivery for A.M. Price." Alex pressed the button to activate the gate's lock and opening mechanism. She watched as the small flowershop truck drove between the even mounds of melting snow. The driver stopped at the front steps and hopped down from the truck with a huge mound of flowers. Alex rolled her eyes to the ceiling in exasperation. *Again,* she thought.

The delivery man gave her three separate bouquets. "Sign here please," he instructed, handing her an electronic pad. She laid the flowers down and signed the dark strip. Coal sniffed at the large bunch, then sneezed. "Ms. Price, I'm a real big fan of yours. I was wondering, can I have your autograph?"

Alex smiled. "Sure." He produced a strip of paper and Alex wrote a short note. *To a man who always delivers. Love, Alex Price.*

He beamed as he read the note. "Thank you so much, Ms. Price." He walked down her front steps, then turned and waved. "Have a nice day." Alex waved and watched as he disappeared into his truck and then down the salt-covered road.

She locked the gate, then looked at the huge pile of long-stemmed roses on the floor. They were beautiful, as expected. After picking out and reading the card from the abundant spray, she took a handful of flowers into the kitchen. She inhaled the aromatic aroma, read the attached card, then stuffed the green stems into the garbage disposal and flipped the switch. The red buds whirled quickly as the stems were chewed up into digestible microscopic pieces.

Coal barked loudly and charged into the kitchen. Alex turned off the machine, hearing the doorbell ring a second time. She huffed and tramped back into the living room mumbling a number of expletives under her breath. "Yes?" she said, punching the wall intercom button again.

"World Express. I have a delivery for Ms. Alexandra Price."

"Fine." She repeated the previous action and watched a large blue truck drive up the road. A man got out and hurried up to her front door just as she opened it.

With his blue cap pulled down low over his eyes, the man shoved a clipboard into her hands. "Sign here please," he said. His voice was deep and somewhat familiar. She took the offered clipboard as he handed her a small, beautifully wrapped gift box, then returned to the truck.

The second delivery man, dressed in a matching company jacket and hat, began removing several large boxes from the back of the truck. He was a virtual mountain. He walked toward the open door effortlessly carrying two large boxes. After depositing them in the foyer, he returned to the truck and brought back another large box as the first delivery man approached again. Alex signed and returned the board as the man carried his box into her foyer. Coal moved to the man's side and sniffed at his hand. The man absently rubbed his furry ears.

After the four large boxes were neatly stacked, both

men smiled and looked around. The first delivery man removed his hat and turned to her. "Lance!" she exclaimed, laughing in astonishment, "what are you doing here?" The two delivery men chuckled at their charade. "Hello, beautiful." He grabbed her and spun her around, hugging her warmly. Still laughing, Alex looked over to the second delivery man. "And you are?" she asked.

"Alex, I'd like you to meet the head of my security team, Charles Taylor. Charles, this is Alexandra Price."

The two shook hands. "Hello, Ms. Price," he said. "Pleased to meet you."

"Hello, Mr. Taylor, it's a pleasure meeting you too. But please, call me Alex."

"If you'll call me Charles." She smiled and nodded. He turned briefly to glance out of the front window. "Lance, I'd better get going before our friend at the gate gets suspicious."

"All right, man, thanks again." They shook hands and Charles left carrying the clipboard. He tipped his hat. "Nice meeting you, Alex." He looked over to Lance. "I'll be at the apartment; call me if anything jumps off." Lance nodded and Charles left.

"I can't believe you did that," Alex said, still shaking her head.

"Well, you said that reporter had been camped out by your gate. He saw one delivery man arrive and one delivery man leave."

"So what's in the boxes?" she asked.

"What else, my clothes," he explained. She laughed at his ridiculous expression.

"Of course." She leaned down to pick up the nearest box. "Let's get your luggage up to your room."

Lance noticed a few roses strewed onto the carpet. He looked up at Alex. "Am I interrupting anything?"

Alex looked over at the red floral mass. "No." She reached to pick up one of the boxes.

"No, I'll take care of these."

Easily he picked up a box and headed for the stairs. "How about a cold drink?"

"Sure, what would you like?"

From the upstairs landing he called down, "Surprise me."

"Okay," she called up. "But remember, you asked for it."

Alex stooped down and gathered the last of the roses. Her thoughts lingered on Lance's comical entrance. She chuckled to herself as she walked into the kitchen.

Ten minutes later Lance stood on the last step and watched as Alex cautiously wiggled the cork from a bottle of champagne. She fearfully squinted one eye and hunched her shoulders. The inevitable pop sounded and she shrieked into giggles as the chilled liquid poured over her hand and onto the counter. Coal barked loudly and dashed after the cork, then padded over to Lance.

Alex turned and smiled. "Hey there, finished unpacking already? That was quick." She sensuously licked her wet fingers and poured the champagne into two crystal glasses.

"No. I decided to leave the unpacking until later. I'd much rather spend time with you." He walked over to her and took the offered glass. "Are we celebrating?"

"Yes. Definitely."

"Good. I feel like celebrating too." Lance smiled broadly. His white teeth and soft sexy lips made her stomach flutter. It was easy to see why this man was a heartthrob to half the women in the world. His exceptional good looks and easy demeanor only added to his appeal. He played the role of action hero in most of his films. A superman who rescued mankind, saved the world and always got the beautiful woman in the end. With a body like his, he could save her any time. Her mind began to wonder at the possibilities.

She asked innocently, "So, what are you celebrating, Lance?"

"Being here with you, naturally," he confessed honestly.

Oh, you are smooth, Mr. Morgan, she thought to herself, then said aloud, "Okay, to what shall we toast?"

Lance moved closer and captured her chin with his finger. Alex gazed deeply into his dark, penetrating eyes. The intense passion she sensed was overwhelming. She smiled awkwardly. *He's an actor,* she reminded herself. *He gets paid to make women feel this way.*

"To you, Alex Price," he whispered softly. "The woman of my dreams." Her stomach fluttered again. *This man is incredible,* she determined. *No wonder he's got half of Hollywood at his feet.* Their glasses clinked.

Lance's heart stirred when he looked at Alex. He was losing his prospective. He needed to pull back. He sipped his champagne, then glanced into the rose-strewn sink. "Having a problem with your disposal?"

Alex stood next to him. "No, why do you ask that?" She flipped the switch. The roses twirled chaotically, then finally disappeared down into the drain's abyss. Alex raised her glass. "*This* is what I'm celebrating."

Lance peered deep into the dark inner recesses of the drain. He saw blackness confettied with red velvet and shook his head. "Remind me never to get you angry with me." He picked up a lone straggling petal. "Did you open the box yet?"

"Oh," she declared, "I forgot all about it." She picked up the small festive box from the countertop and shook it gently. "What's in it?"

"Open it."

She did. Within the box, she found a small red velvet jewel case and opened it. "Oh, Lance, it's beautiful." She carefully pulled out an exquisite heart-shaped diamond surrounded by rubies set on a delicate gold chain. She held the elegant jewel in the palm of her hand admiring its sparkling luster. "What's the occasion?" She looked at him, questioning.

He leaned over and kissed her softly. "Happy Valentine's Day."

She smiled broadly. "Thank you, it's beautiful. But you really didn't have to do this."

"I wanted to." He took the gold chain and draped it around her slender neck. After fastening the clasp she turned around to face him.

"How does it look?"

He shook his head, speechless, then finally uttered, "Perfect."

The telephone rang.

She picked up the red velvet box and walked to the wall mount and answered the phone. "Hello." Lance and Coal discreetly moved to the adjoining den to give her privacy. "Hi, Mark, hold on a second." She covered the mouthpiece and turned to Lance, "I'll be a few minutes. Why don't you make yourself comfortable?" She picked up the flower's card from the counter and walked away.

Lance's determined frown creased his brow from the mention of the man's name. He studied the wall panel, then pressed a button he saw her use. Low jazz music flowed from the concealed speakers into the den.

"My, my, I am truly impressed. Your telephone etiquette has definitely improved." Alex stepped into the office as she continued the conversation.

"Thank you. I've been practicing," Mark said. She laughed. "Okay, now to business," he began and continued for the next fifteen minutes. Alex jotted down hurried notes, asked pertinent questions and agreed to most of his assessments and suggestions. "I should have the paperwork ready for you to sign within the next few days."

"Okay, I'll expect to see it then," she confirmed.

"Do you have a preference?" he asked.

"Not really, I just want someone who'll do justice to the work. The money really doesn't matter, you know that."

"Were you disappointed with the last contract?"

"No. No, of course not. As a matter of fact I want the exact same thing this time," she insisted. "Also, I'd like to suggest ideas for casting. Do you think that would be possible?"

"I don't see why not. I'll make sure to incorporate the stipulation in the contract," he promised.

"Thanks, Mark. I'll talk to you later." They hung up. Alex sat quietly for a few moments thinking about the conversation and adding to notes she'd written down.

Afterward she sat pensively at her desk and stared at the floral card sitting on the desk. She reread it. *With All My Love, Your Greatest Fan.* Memories of receiving dozens of roses with this same message every year annoyed her. Whoever sent them knew exactly where she was every Valentine's Day. London, St. Croix, Catalina Island, even on the yacht at port, she'd always got the same bouquet of red roses and same cryptic message. It was eerie to know someone out there knew every move she made.

She folded up the card several times, then tossed it across the room to the trash can. She missed. Lance reached down and picked it up and dropped it in the can. "Everything all right?"

She looked up, slightly startled to see him framing the open doorway. "What, huh?" she murmured as he eased farther into the room.

"Alex, are you all right?" She looked so fragile.

"Yes, of course. I'm fine." She smiled weakly and moved to the sofa.

"Alex," Lance began as he sat next to her, "if there's a problem, I'll be happy to help any way I can."

"It's nothing, really. Just trying to figure a few things out."

"Are you sure?" he asked.

She nodded and stood up. "Come on, I'm starved, let's eat."

* * *

After the filling meal they'd eaten and the bottle of champagne, his concentration was shot. "Better watch your queen," Alex warned, "she's in danger." Lance didn't really care anymore. Add that to Alex's sexy pouting mouth and her alluring fragrance. He was quickly losing all willpower.

For the past twenty-five minutes he had sat staring at the marble chessboard inhaling Alex's sweet exotic perfume. His mind was completely clouded.

The setting couldn't be more perfect. The lights were low. The music, soft and romantic. The fireplace ablaze. And they lay on the thick carpeting with just a few scattered marble game pieces between them. He looked up at her. "Yes," she said sweetly, assured of her victory. Lance flicked his king down with his finger, sending him down, thus conceding the game. Alex smiled triumphantly until Lance slowly leaned closer.

Alex anticipated the kiss that never came. He was just inches from her mouth when he paused. She looked into his searching eyes and responded by embracing his neck and pulling him to her lips. The sweet rapture of his kiss was exquisite. She moved closer, fusing her body to his; slowly they melted into one. She moaned. This man's mouth was designed for a woman's pleasure. Then suddenly she swayed away from his embrace. "Wait," she breathed, then pushed back.

He groaned as he pulled away and rolled over on his back. His mind whirled and his body yearned for her. But she was right, this wasn't the time.

"I'm sorry. I didn't mean to lead you on," Alex confessed in humiliating confusion. She sat up, drawing her knees to her chest and sinking her head low in embarrassment.

"No, it was me," he said without hesitation, suppressing the desire to hold her again. "I'll be honest with you, Alex, I want to be with you, but I need to know that this is also what you want." He rolled back over and sat up next to her. "Tell me, what do you want, Alex?"

She mulled the words over in her mind. What *did* she want? It was an easy enough question. But one she was unable to answer. All of her life her indulgences were consequential. As far back as she could remember, people depended on her. One small mistake, one thoughtless miscalculation in judgment, and hundreds of lives would be affected. The significance of that burden prevented her from experiencing many of life's pleasures.

She remained silent, then looked up out of the window. Ice crystal fingers laced the outside pane and the delicate rapping of sleet tapped at the glass. How could she possibly answer his question?

She turned to him. "My life has always been complicated. Simple questions like 'what do I want?' tend to unnerve me. I guess some habits are hard to break."

"What habits?"

"Caution. Discretion." Years of heartache and deception had taught her never to let her guard down.

"I see."

"I didn't have a life growing up, I had a schedule and every moment was accounted for. Don't get me wrong, I enjoyed every bit of my time in front of the camera and onstage. It's just that everything I did directly and indirectly influenced so many others. One slip on my part and, just like falling dominos, others would also be affected. I guess I simply got used to refraining." Lance sat quietly listening to her words. "As celebrities we're completely exposed. But you of all people know that," she said.

"To a certain extent, yes, I agree. Having sole responsibility for a series is definitely overwhelming. And living and working in a fishbowl is extreme. But with me it was different. The Hollywood publicity machine created the image, I merely went along for the ride."

"I find that hard to believe. You're a hot Hollywood property. Surely you abstain from certain situations because of potential ramifications."

"Where's the fun in that?"

She laughed, "Okay, I give up. Tell me, when did you get the acting bug?"

Lance smiled at the sudden change of topic. "Not until I was in my freshman year at Yale." He laughed at the thought. "I had all intentions of becoming a cardiologist."

"You? A doctor?" She laughed.

"What's so funny? You can't see me as a heart surgeon?"

Breaking hearts, she thought immediately but answered, "Sure, I guess." She laughed again, then crinkled her nose. "A cardiologist, who would have guessed?"

"Yes, a cardiologist. As a matter of fact I still have my nameplate from my high school graduation, *Lance Anderson, MD*.

"Lance Anderson?"

"Anderson is my legal name."

"So where did Morgan come from?"

"It's my mother's maiden name. She was in the business before she got married, she kept her maiden name.

"Would I have heard of her?"

"Definitely, she even did a few guest spots on your sitcom."

Alex's face brightened. Those were the best years of her life. She loved her days on the set. The show was a hit from the very beginning. The ensemble cast was like a real family. Her television mother and father were already well-known stage performers with several Tonys and Emmys between them.

She was signed to an extended contract and like many successful young performers, grew up on the screen. There, in front of millions of viewers, she experienced her first crush, her first boyfriend and first kiss. Consequently, her first heartbreak.

"Who? What's her name?" she blurted out anxiously.

"Faye Morgan."

"Faye Morgan is your mother! I love her. She's an incredible talent. I remember some of her earlier work." Alex shook her head slowly. "She's brilliant. She has the most uncanny comedic ability."

Lance nodded. "I think so too."

"You're right. She was on the show my last season. I remember I used to go into the set early just to sit and listen to her talk about some of the actors she worked with. She must have known them all." Alex suddenly stopped reminiscing. "I'm sorry, here I am talking about your mother as if you don't even know her. She must have told you those same stories a hundred times."

"A hundred and one." He smiled. "But each time it's like the first. She always made it new somehow."

"Yeah, I know what you mean. It must have been incredible to be an actor in those days."

"Not only did you have to compete with other actors but you also had to contend with racism and bigotry . . ."

". . . Jim Crow, segregation," she said, completing his thought. The two slipped into an easy silence mindfully respectful of those that had paved the way for them. "Your mom is an extraordinary woman." He nodded his agreement. "But I don't remember seeing you on the set."

"Oh, I was never allowed. My mother kept me as far away from the business as possible."

"To tell you the truth, I don't blame her. What is she doing now?"

"She's back to her first love, the stage. Actually she's in rehearsals for a Broadway production of *Hello, Dolly*. The show is scheduled to open this summer. You're welcome to join me for the opening night. I'm pretty sure I can get us a couple of seats right up front."

"Maybe." Alex took a deep nervous breath. She

wasn't sure she was ready to face the world on the arm of Lance Morgan. "So, what happened after Yale?"

"Julliard. I left Yale in my sophomore year for Julliard. I studied acting, landed my first role in a soap opera two months after graduation. From there I did television, some stage and then finally film."

"And you never wanted to act before college?" she asked, amazed.

Lance bowed his head. "Well," he began modestly, "there was this one time in high school. I was in L.A. visiting my father for spring break. I'd heard about this audition for a television sitcom. So I tried out."

"Which sitcom?" He looked at her and smiled shyly.

"Mine?" she questioned. He nodded yes. "Well, since I would have remembered meeting you, I assume you didn't get the part."

"No. But I did have several call-backs. The final outcome was between me and Shawn Anderson. Shawn got the part, obviously."

"Oh, that was for my character's first on-screen boyfriend. I remember," she said. "I bet your mom was thrilled."

"More like furious. My dad, on the other hand, was thrilled."

"Is he in the business too?"

"Yes, Patrick Anderson."

"That's right, Faye Morgan was married to Patrick Anderson. No wonder you're such a fabulous actor. You got it naturally."

"Well," he began modestly, "I wouldn't say I'm fabulous necessarily . . . maybe more like stupendous, brilliant, talented, gifted . . ." Lance continued jokingly.

Alex laughed. "What's he like?"

"Patrick?" She nodded. Lance shrugged. "He's exactly as he appears onstage, larger than life." Seeing the confused expression on her face, he continued, "Sir Patrick and I aren't as close as we once were. We enjoy a somewhat rebellious relationship. He's never forgiven me for taking my mother's maiden name professionally.''

She thought about his statement for a few moments, then began, "I always thought . . . no, never mind."

Lance leaned in closer. "No, tell me, what?"

Alex shyly continued, "I always thought your mom and dad were sort of an odd couple." Lance immediately began laughing. "No, wait, I don't mean that in a bad way. It's just that Faye is so down-to-earth and funny and your father is such a celebrated dramatic actor. I mean, he's the epitome of distinguished gentry. He's even been knighted by the Queen of England and has a 'Sir' before his name—"

Lance interrupted her. "It's merely an honorary title."

She continued, "I remember my mother and I went to see him in London years ago. He performed *Othello*. Talk about dramatic nobility, the man was masterful. I couldn't take my eyes off of him the entire time. The audience was spellbound. He had such a powerful connection with the dialogue."

Lance listened intently to her every word. He was genuinely touched by Alex's appreciation of his parents' abilities. As their son, he often took them for granted and saw them just in parental roles. Seldom did he have the opportunity to discuss them as skilled professionals.

Alex continued, "In their own right, they're at the pinnacle of their craft. You must be so proud. They're both so accomplished, and yet so different."

"Well, maybe that's why the marriage didn't work out. They were too different."

Alex shrugged her shoulders. "I always heard opposites attract."

"That would make you and me the perfect match."

Alex blushed slightly. Then, suddenly it dawned on her whom she was sitting here laughing and talking with. "Wait a minute, if Sir Patrick Anderson is your father. That means Shawn Anderson is your brother?"

"Half brother," he stated emphatically. "We have the same paternal parentage, that's all." His tone was brief and abrupt. Apparently there was no love lost between the two siblings.

Chapter Ten

The Pacific Coast Highway was jam-packed as usual.
Yet Burke still mashed down on the accelerator, inching
forward. His candy-apple-red Lamborghini Diablo Road-
ster convertible sped up and deliberately cut off a merg-
ing BMW. He looked over to the frustrated driver and
smiled with pleasure as he ranted into the mini cellular
phone. "Did you at least find out which agency he's
talking to?"

"Nobody knows," Jake insisted. "He's working with
Franklin Moore on this. Everything's tight-lipped over
there. I did find out he's got it down to a short list of
three agencies, CAA, Turner-Price and I don't know the
third one, I'm still trying to find out."

"Damn. Well, keep trying!" Burke snapped the telephone closed and beeped his horn as a black stretch
limo pushed in front of him. After giving the driver
an explicit hand signal he picked up his phone and
connected with his office. While the phone rang on the
other end, he changed lanes, sped past the limo at
breakneck speed, then cut in front of it and slowed
down.

He glanced in the rearview mirror at the irate chauffeur and grinned. He loved the PC Highway. A pleasant
voice answered, "Robert Burke Talent Agency, may I
help you?"

"What's taking so long to connect me with Lance?"

Burke demanded as he turned off the highway at the approaching exit. The car slowed to a stop. At a traffic light he looked over to the beautiful woman sitting next to him. Long red hair blew across her face. He shifted into gear, then released the stick shift and ran his skinny fingers up her left thigh. When he reached the top of her laced stockings she placed her soft hand onto his to halt his progress. He smirked behind his dark sunglasses.

The voice on the other end of the line continued, "I've tried Burke. I called his home in the Hills, and the apartment in New York. I even tried calling Faye's and Patrick's home. Either no one's talking or they really have no idea where he is. I can't figure it, he's not at the usual places."

Burke looked over to his attractive passenger. She was young enough to be his daughter and she wanted to be a star. She had the looks, the body and the ambition. Unfortunately, the only thing lacking was talent. Her screen test was disastrous. She read lines for a small part in a B movie as a favor from a friend. She had twelve lines. Half of which she screwed up, the other half she forgot. When she finally remembered them they were choppy and incoherent. She never hit her mark and her movements on camera was more like a walking zombie. Someone somewhere had old her she could be a star, so she came to Hollywood. They were wrong.

"Well then, look in the unusual places," Burke raged. "Just find him. Try Franklin Moore's office again. Somebody there must know something."

Burke removed his hand and turned the wheel to navigate the steep scenic hills. Looking hungrily from mansion to mansion, his companion gazed around in astonishment. Beverly Hills mansions were the homes that dreams were made of. Burke watched as she crossed and recrossed her long bronzed legs excitedly. She wanted to be a star, so he was going to teach her how to play the game. He smiled, anticipating the next few hours.

"Yes, Burke, I called Franklin Moore's office this afternoon. I left a message with his private secretary. He's been at the studio all morning."

"All right, keep looking." He closed the phone as he pulled up to his massive structure. He leaned out the side door and keyed in a security code. Iron gates opened instantly. The woman looked properly impressed. She lowered her sunglasses. Her eyes glistened as they approached the house. Whitewashed and surrounded by native palm trees, the house was very impressive. Slowly she put his hand back on her knee. He smiled and eased up her leg again. This time she let him proceed all the way up.

"This is delicious," Alex declared after putting another tender morsel of salmon into her mouth. The pungent lemon dill sauce molded with the flaky firm pink. "Where did you get this guy? He's fabulous," she said, referring to Victoria's new chef.

"Where else? Ted." Victoria remarked. "And he is actually a she."

"Well, she's wonderful."

"Yes, she is. Ted took me to some nouvelle cuisine restaurants while we were in L.A. She was the assistant chef. I remarked how wonderful the food was. He hired her on the spot."

"You two are the most married divorced couple I know. I have no idea why you wasted time getting a divorce."

"Simple, we can't live together without the services of a full-time referee. Divorce was our only option. Besides, it would be cruel to inflict our idiosyncrasies on the unsuspecting public, so there you have it. The perfect solution."

Alex giggled at the simplistic explanation. Victoria

sucked her teeth and laughed at her failed attempt to categorize the odd on-again, off-again relationship she enjoyed with her ex-husband. She changed the subject. "You look particularly radiant this afternoon, Alexandra. If I didn't know any better I'd say you've been seeing someone."

Alex gasped and choked on her fish. The maid, who was standing by, rushed over to quickly refill her water glass. Victoria calmly told her to raise her arms above her head. Tears streamed down Alex's cheeks as Victoria smiled suspiciously. After a few more sips of water, she slowly regained her composure. The maid refilled her water glass again. "Thank you," Alex croaked out, then sipped more water while nervously eyeing Victoria over the brim of the crystal goblet. "I'm fine." She coughed again, then placed her hand over her throat. "The fish must have gone down the wrong way or maybe I swallowed a bone."

Victoria nodded, then said dryly, "Yeah, you must have. What's going on, Alex? Who is he?"

Alex's mouth dropped open. "Excuse me?"

"You heard me. Who is he?"

Alex stared at Victoria, her eyes wide and innocent. "What are you talking about?"

"Alexandra Price, you know very well what I'm talking about," Victoria said as she sipped her wine.

"I do not," she stated, appalled by the implication.

Victoria looked at her slyly. "I bet you don't. Okay, have your secrets. Fine with me." She dropped the subject and continued eating her salmon.

Suddenly feeling silly, and behaving like a grade-school kid infatuated with her first love, she relented. "All right, I have been seeing someone, kind of." A barley suppressed grin burst through. "It's not serious," she cautioned. "As a matter of fact I have no idea what it is. We're just sort of together, sometimes."

Victoria smiled. "Together is good. Do I know him?"

"Actually yes, you do."

"Aha, so the plot thickens," Victoria said, then set her fork down and propped her elbows on top of the starched white linen. She folded her long manicured fingers under her chin and smiled. "Who is he?"

Victoria waited patiently as Alex hemmed and hawed for a few seconds, then finally decided to confess the name of her house guest. She opened her mouth to speak, but Victoria spoke up instead. "Alex, you don't have to tell me if it makes you uncomfortable."

"It's not that, it's just that we're really not together. I mean as a couple. Actually, there is another woman in the picture." Victoria's brow raised in surprise. "They're not married or engaged or anything," Alex immediately added. "What I mean is . . ." She paused. "I have no idea what I mean."

"Whoever he is, it sounds like you really like him."

Alex smiled at the thought of Lance. "I do."

Victoria picked up her fork again. "Well, that's enough for me. As long as you're happy."

Alex nodded and smiled broadly. "I am. I'm very happy."

Victoria went on to relay the latest news and gossip from Los Angeles. The Globe Awards were wonderful but too long, the various parties afterward were boring and typical. The women were all scantily dressed and the men were all balding. Alex nodded dutifully and smiled at the appropriate comments but her mind was still on their earlier conversation. She hadn't really thought about it, but yes, she was happy. And Lance was definitely the reason.

The past few days with him had been wonderful. Despite occupying the same house, they only saw each other over meals. During the day he'd study his script and she'd work in her office. They'd meet for a quick afternoon meal and then again for a late dinner. Afterward they would play chess, watch television or a movie or battle aliens on one of her game systems. But more often than not they'd just sit up and talk into the early morning.

"Excuse me, Mrs. Reese." Victoria looked up at the approaching maid. "Mr. Reese is on the telephone."

Victoria stood. "I'll be right back," she said as she disappeared from the dining room.

Alex sipped her wine. She was actually delighted for the reprieve. There was nothing more exhausting than hearing about the beautiful people in Hollywood. She'd put that life behind her over ten years ago and never looked back. Victoria, on the other hand, thrived on the energy of Hollywood and the intensity of Manhattan. She soaked up everything she could on the hottest people, places and things. She prided herself on knowing anyone worth knowing on both coasts.

The maid took Victoria's and Alex's empty plates and replaced them with creamy tarts piled high with fresh berries. Alex speared a raspberry with her fork. Thoughtfully, she popped it into her mouth.

Victoria returned. "Ted says to give you his love."

Alex smiled. "How's he doing?"

"Working too hard, as usual. He had his assistant fax us something, special delivery." Victoria shook her head, then handed the pages to Alex. She sat down and picked up her wineglass. "Sometimes I really can't believe these people."

A grainy photo of a mascara-running, tearful woman was on the reduced first page. The headline read SHE BROKE UP MY MARRIAGE. Then underneath was an inset grainy photo of Alex and an unidentified man walking in the snow. Alex read the caption aloud, *"Alexandra Price breaks up happy home vowing to finally get the man of her dreams, Shawn Anderson."* Alex shook her head. "I expected something like this."

Victoria looked surprised. "Well, I'm pleased that you're taking this so well. The last time this rag insinuated a relationship between you and Shawn you threatened to sue them and cut off the reporter's head. At least this time you're handling it more ..." Victoria paused in midsentence and glared at Alex.

Alex looked up from the article she'd been reading and seeing her friend's concerned expression began to laugh.

"I'm glad you find something funny about this."

Alex stopped laughing long enough to sip her drink. "You're right, it's not funny. And no, before you even attempt to ask such a ridiculous question, the man in the photo is definitely not Shawn Anderson."

"Well, thank God for that," Victoria said, finishing the last of her wine. Alex continued reading the rest of the article aloud. "This publicity is always a boost for Shawn's career. He could definitely use it after his last three movies bombed so badly," Victoria admitted.

"That's probably why he won't come right out and say it wasn't him in the photo. He's the only one I've ever known to actually agree to be interviewed in a tabloid magazine. He lives for this stuff," Alex concluded.

"I'm not surprised. He always had a thing for you."

"It'll never happen."

"I know, but the possibility of the two of you together would be worth a week or two of free publicity in most rags." Alex handed Victoria a few pages to read.

They enjoyed their dessert while entertained by a five-year-old boy who ate a mattress and a natural rock formation that resembled the Last Supper. "I can't believe people actually buy and read this thing."

"It's part of our culture, like television trash talk shows and shock radio. Nobody wants to admit they buy it but the paper's circulation is through the roof. The public feeds on gossip, the sleazier the better, and this rag feeds that need. It's a vicious cycle."

Alex nodded her head sadly. "Meanwhile, you and I just spent half the afternoon laughing at these imbecilic articles. Some of them are just so moronic."

"And others are just plain mean."

They sat in silence for a few moments until Victoria decided, "Let's get out of here, I feel like shopping."

Alex stood and followed Victoria into the great room. The two women gathered their coats and headed for the front door. "What kind of shopping are we doing today, groceries, clothes or men?"

Victoria smiled mischievously. "You know me, it doesn't matter, I'm not particular."

Coal watched Lance pace the den anxiously. He gripped the script in his hands, read a few lines, then closed his eyes and imagined the scene. The lines faded as soon as he opened his eyes. It was no use, he couldn't concentrate since his phone conversation with Franklin earlier that afternoon. He tossed the rolled script on the counter and paced again.

He still couldn't believe his brother could be so contemptuous. He'd use anybody to further his career. Lance picked up the article Franklin had faxed him. Shawn was asked several times if he was the man in the photo and whether he and Alex were back together. Instead of refuting the rumors he smiled his familiar boyish grin and said, "Sorry, no comment, this affair is between Alex and myself."

Lance fumed. Could he be any more blatant? He all but gave credence to the allegations and admitted that he and Alex were having an affair. It was so typical of Shawn. He was a firstrate publicity hound. Whenever there was a camera you'd find him posed and ready for the shot.

Coal barked, drawing Lance's attention. He barked again, then trotted down the stairs to the back door. Lance stood at the kitchen landing and listened as the garage door closed. A few minutes later Coal came bounding up the steps followed by Alex.

She noticed the peculiar expression on Lance's face.

She greeted him with a beautiful bright smile. "Well, hello there," she said, delighted to see him. He relieved her of the two cumbersome grocery bags.

"Hi, yourself," he said, carrying the two brown bags to the center counter. "Any more bags in the car?"

"No, that's it." She followed him to the counter and began putting the groceries away as he emptied the bags. Afterward she picked up his script and flipped through the many pages. "Studying hard?"

"No, not really."

"Why not?"

"I have some bad news."

Alex frowned, then leaned back against the counter, bracing herself for the worst.

Lance picked up the faxed papers and handed her the tabloid article. She took the papers and read the bold-print headline. She shrugged her shoulders and took a deep breath. "Oh yes, I just saw these." She laid the pages down on the counter. "Was that the bad news?"

Lance was surprised by her unconcerned reaction. "Apparently not," he remarked. "I assumed you'd be livid. I know how well you guard your privacy. And apparently my being here prompted this new interest in the relationship between you and Shawn."

"There is no relationship between me and Shawn. There never was." Then as an afterthought she added, "Not *that* kind anyway."

"What do you mean?" he pried further.

"Years ago when Shawn first started on the set we were good friends." She smiled, remembering the days fondly. "Actually, we were inseparable, we talked constantly, about his mother, growing up, things like that. He seldom talked about his father and he never mentioned you at all."

"I'm not surprised."

"He was cool then. I really liked him. He was like my best friend. He understood me. Anyway after a while

things began to change. He started with the drugs and
alcohol. He'd stay out all night and usually came onto
the set wasted. We had to shoot around him so many
times." She shook her head, remembering sadly. "I
wish . . ." She paused. "I wish he'd get himself together
and go to rehab or something. He used to be such a
great guy. We had a really special friendship. Sometimes
I miss that."

"But I thought . . ."

"What? That we were romantically involved?" He
nodded.

"Everyone did," she continued. "That was the whole
idea. The producers planted the bogus relationship
rumors to boost ratings. Before the show's final year I
waived a new contract. I didn't want to return. So the
producers decided to play up Shawn's character. They
were going to phase my character out and he was supposed to take the lead."

"That's right. You were in college at that time."

"Right. Anyway, the fall season went okay. So I was
completely written out of the spring season with one
provision. They wanted me to do guest appearances. I
agreed. A few weeks into the spring season the show's
ratings plunged. The advertisers were livid so the net-
work threatened to pull the plug if I didn't go back.
By then I was full-time at school and in rehearsals for
Broadway. I couldn't just leave and go back to L.A."

"So they canceled the show?"

"No, not right away. The producers came up with
the publicity stunt. They leaked word that Shawn and
I were having a relationship off-screen." She laughed.
"The funny thing was that at that time Shawn and I
were barely civil. He blamed me for the show's low
ratings. We didn't see each other a lot after that. Occa-
sionally, my character did guest appearances. The writers wrote more provocative dialogue in keeping with
the rumor. The ratings eventually went up again."

"So, whenever Shawn wants publicity, word leaks out

that you two are together again and he's back in the spotlight."

Alex nodded. "Something like that. Although, I have to admit"—she smiled—"Shawn and I haven't been particularly close since then, but I've always admired his drive."

"I know what you mean, Shawn lives by his impulses."

"I envied that at times. In Hollywood every mistake, every slip is recorded for posterity thanks to the tabloids. That never bothered Shawn. After years I finally understood why. It was so simple. He didn't care what the reporters said or wrote about him. And he never concerned himself about other people's opinions. It just didn't matter to him."

"Nothing matters to Shawn," Lance stated with annoyance.

"Not true. There is one thing that will always matter to him. And I hope one day for his sake it happens for him."

Lance stared at her, touched by her concern. "The business is filled with schemers and charlatans. They spend all of their time coming up with intrigue to add drama to their lives. Los Angeles is filled with them. I bet you're glad you moved away from all that."

"I don't know about that. We have our little dramas here too. Of course ours aren't nearly as extreme."

"What kind of dramas could this little town have?"

"We have a mysterious night prowler."

"A what?"

"A night prowler?"

"What's a night prowler?"

"It's a person or persons who perform Robin Hood stunts."

"You mean rob from the rich and give to the poor, wearing green tights."

"No, it's more like innocent practical jokes. For instance, last March someone dumped green food coloring in the City Hall Center Fountain for Saint Patrick's

Day." Lance laughed. "And three years ago persons unknown borrowed the police chief's official car. It was found parked on a small wooden barge in the middle of the lake. Photos of that were on the front page for weeks and eventually went national. And the ultimate scandal, about five years ago there was a huge snowstorm on Valentine's Day."

Lance looked at her, questioning. "So what's so scandalous about that?"

"Well, first of all, the temperature was around sixty degrees and the only place there was snow was on Main Street."

"What?"

"Apparently someone used a snow blower and covered one city block with two inches of snow. They also made a huge red watercolor heart in the center with words underneath saying *Happy Valentine's Day*. It was great." They laughed as she continued. "Then there was the thousand mylar balloons at the high school, the giant seven-foot sunflowers blooming down the center of town and the ever-popular Noah scare of ninety-nine."

Lance looked at her. "The Noah scare?"

"Noah, as in rain for forty days and forty nights, inside the ark."

"You mean to tell me someone actually built an ark and got it to rain for forty days and forty nights?"

"No, of course not. It didn't actually rain and no one built an ark. It was more like some animals penned up in the front of the zoo one morning."

"So someone just got a couple of animals and put them in front of the zoo. What was the big deal?"

"Not exactly. It was more like two lambs, two goats, two chickens, two geese, two ponies and two pigs, you get the idea."

He looked perplexed. "What?"

"Then a few hours later a paid construction crew arrived at the front gate. They had lumber, supplies and the specs to build a petting zoo for the younger children. The town had been debating about building it for some time. I guess our prowler got tired of all the political red tape.''

Lance laughed hysterically. "I think I'm safer in L.A. At least the people there *look* nuts.''

Chapter Eleven

Robert Burke leaned back in his cushioned office chair. He drew a deep toke from the fat marijuana cigarette he'd been smoking. He watched the lazy veiled smoke rise above his head, then slowly dissipate into the cool air. The air-conditioning was on full blast but he was still sweating. He looked at the man seated in front of him, then loosened his knotted tie more and said, "I've been trying to get in touch with your big brother."

Shawn blew smoke out through his nose, coughed, then rasped out huskily, "I'm an only child, I don't have a big brother." He cleared his throat, then leaned over a small oval mirror and vacuumed the remains of the powdery substance with his nose.

Burke looked at the smug actor with annoyance. His agency handled some of Hollywood's top talent and hottest new names. Unfortunately, along with the popular young talent often came huge egos and childish tantrums. Burke referred to them as expendable talent. Given their unlikelihood for longevity and their limited range of ability, most of them rarely lasted more than a few seasons.

Shawn Anderson was the exception. After years in the business he still had the cocky attitude and huge ego. But, to his credit, he'd stuck faithfully with Burke the entire time. He was a valuable client and an excellent drawing name now that Lance had gone. Burke realized that. He also knew he had to tread lightly.

Shawn was by no means the draw his brother was but he had a healthy enough following that kept him working. That's when and if he wanted to work. Shawn had gotten lazy. He was a good actor, even talented, but he didn't have that natural gift seldom seen in Hollywood anymore. Burke assumed it was because he never really had to work at it. He got by on his good looks and his father's name.

Patrick Anderson was notably a phenomenal English talent. He had that natural spark that drew an audience in. Lance had it too. But Lance not only drew the audience in, he submerged them in his character. They felt what he felt. He was the quintessential talent, he engaged pure emotion. Shawn would never achieve that level.

Burke sucked his teeth in disgust. Just his luck to have chosen the wrong brother. Although he'd met Lance first, at the time he had no idea who his father was. Burke assigned Lance to one of his new associates, Jake Marrows.

Shortly thereafter, Shawn, who was already a well-known name, expressed interest in representation with his agency. Burke jumped at the opportunity and decided to handle his career personally. Then a few years later Lance's career took off. Eventually Burke relieved Jake of the burden of representing Lance.

Jake was furious at first. Burke still smiled remembering his face when he told him of the switch. He was mad, but what could he do? Nothing. After that, Burke made a mental note to keep an eye on Jake. Jake was too much like himself. He had big dreams and didn't mind taking the shortcut over someone else's career. He was a dangerous man and that's why Burke kept him close. His motto being "keep your friends close and your enemies even closer." He lived by that rule.

But whether or not Burke liked Jake was arbitrary. At

the moment he needed Jake just as much as Jake needed him. Burke wanted a man like Jake at the helm when he expanded the business into film distribution. That's where the real money was. And that was Burke's future draw. Wherever the cash flowed he followed. And right now there was big money to be made in distribution. Burke puffed the thickly rolled cigarette again. "You know who I'm talking about, Shawn. Where's Lance?"

"How the hell do I know where Lance is? Am I my brother's keeper?" The statement struck Shawn as extremely humorous. He laughed so hard he choked on the smoke he'd just inhaled. His red eyes watered profusely and he gasped for air. Burke looked over to him, not particularly concerned. Shawn would never change. He would always despise Lance.

The intercom rang through. "Burke, Jake's here."

Burke pressed the button on the phone. "Send him in."

Jake opened the door to the smoke-filled room. The pungent odor of stale cigarettes, cannabis smoke and abrasive cologne repulsed him. Both men looked totally wasted. He grimaced in utter disdain.

Indulgence in a vice was a luxury Jake didn't allow himself. Be it alcohol, drugs or women, they were all mortal failings as far as he was concerned. They could be perceived as a weakness to be manipulated by an adversary. Jake considered himself above such flaws of imperfection. He shook his head in a mixture of pity and disgust as he stepped farther into the room.

Burke sat behind his desk while Shawn sat facing him with his loafered feet propped up on the opposite chair. Jake walked over to the chair and stopped, looking down at Shawn's feet. Shawn didn't move. Jake thought of several things he could say at this moment. But, he settled for the least damaging to his career.

"Hello, Shawn, you look great," he lied and held his hand out to shake.

Shawn looked up at Jake and nodded through half-closed eyes. The haze in his head didn't allow him to speak. His limp, sweaty palm left a residue of moisture as Jake withdrew his hand.

Burke took another drag from the dwindling cigarette. "What did you find out?" he asked, exhaling smoke.

"Not a whole lot. I still don't know where he is," Jake admitted truthfully. He was just about to continue when Burke went on a verbal rampage. The tiny rolled cigarette was crushed out as Burke ranted about firing employees and finding more competent help. Jake looked down to Shawn. He had suddenly grown a great interest in the lines on the back of his hand.

The loud yelling didn't faze Jake. He expected it. "What are you standing there for? Get out of here. Find him!" Jake smiled, then strutted out of the office. Outwardly he was calm and collected. But inside he was furious.

He'd long had enough of Burke's abusive behavior, but he couldn't afford to anger him, at least not yet. Burke was still too powerful in Tinseltown. He instilled fear and panic in most studio executives. They practically cowered at the mention of his name. Whispered rumors were that Burke gained power the old-fashioned way, he bribed, bullied and blackmailed his way to the top. It was said that he had something damaging on just about every top studio executive in the industry.

Jake slammed into his office and picked up the phone. He punched in Linda's number and waited for the phone to be picked up. Her voice-mail message came on. He left a brief message regarding drinks after work. Forty minutes later he sat in the Beverly Plaza Hotel sipping a club soda and jotted down notes in his notebook.

As soon as the door closed, Shawn began laughing and coughing uncontrollably. His eyes watered as he tried to regain control. Burke reached over and tossed the box of tissues across the desk. Shawn grabbed one and held it up to his face. He wiped the dampness from his cheeks. "Did you see his face? He looked like he was ready to kill."

Burke swiveled his chair to the side. Shawn was beginning to get on his nerves. He'd been in the office all afternoon and Burke was growing increasingly bored with supplying his habits. He pointed to the papers still lying on his desk. "Don't forget to read over the contracts, Shawn. I want to sign off on this project before I go to New York this weekend."

Shawn nodded his head wearily and asked, "So, what's the big deal with finding Lance?"

Burke put fingers tip to tip making a triangle beneath his clean-shaven chin. He studied the wasted actor sitting across from him. "I'm sure you've heard that Lance left the agency."

"Yeah, so?" Shawn grumbled.

"So, his contract was extremely lucrative to this agency, to me. It would be in everyone's best interest if he returned."

Shawn sucked his teeth childishly. "Everybody makes such a big deal about Lance." He stood and steadied himself against the back of the chair. "Personally I don't see the big deal."

"He's a superstar. He's huge right now and his popularity isn't showing any signs of ebbing any time soon."

Shawn jeered, "He's no bigger than I am. Yeah, he's had a few more breaks, so what? He used the old man's name just like I did."

It was the perfect opening. "Actually, I believe he goes by his mother's name, but you already know that, don't you, Shawn?" Burke smiled wryly as Shawn cringed openly at the mention of Lance's mother. Burke knew Shawn's Achilles' heel, and delighted in rubbing salt into the festered wound every chance he got.

He knew of the hatred Shawn had for Faye Morgan and her son. After all these years he still blamed them for denying him Patrick's attention. If it wasn't for Patrick

Anderson's obsession and relentless pursuit of Faye, Shawn felt he would have lived the perfect Hollywood childhood. Instead, he tolerated his existence at the hands of an alcoholic mother who never got over her brief affair with Sir Anderson.

Although Patrick had paid thousands of dollars each month in child support, he never actually gave Shawn the attention he yearned for. As was his fatherly duty, he saw to it that Shawn attended the best prep and boarding schools in the country and made sure he enjoyed a life of comfort envied by most. From the outside looking in, Shawn had it all, a beautiful home, cars, money, everything a young man would desire, everything except a father. In Shawn's eyes, that love was always reserved for Lance, and he hated him for it.

"Whatever," Shawn said, waving his hand to dismiss the subject. "So when are you gonna get me another gig, or do I have to slip over to United Talent?" He attempted a cocky strut around the office.

Patiently, Burke watched Shawn. He despised it when he threw his weight around. "Hollywood is a fickle town, Shawn, you know that. The bottom line is the only determining factor and you're just not pulling them in like you used to."

Shawn balked, glaring at Burke smugly seated behind the desk. "What are you talking about? I'm still a hot commodity in this town. I just got my star put on the Boulevard walk. I have over twenty films out there. What about a sequel?"

Burke shook his head no. "A sequel has to show definite profit possibilities. The studio execs will never buy it. You know as well as I that an actor is only as good as his last project. Three of your last five films barely pulled the production costs. The good thing is you still have the potential earning power and the talent, not to mention the name. It's just that profit margins are more important these days."

"All right, then find me something onstage or on television."

"Guest appearances?"

"Hell no, I don't do guest appearances. My career ain't in the toilet. Find me a television series. Get me something with teeth. I need to show the studio I can stretch as an actor. Find a drama, maybe something like a New York detective or an L.A. doctor. But no more comedies, I don't want to do a comedy."

Bored with the conversation, Burke stood and walked over to Shawn. "I'll tell you what, give me a few weeks to find the right script. I'll talk to a few writers I know and see if I can come up with something." He moved Shawn toward the office door. "In the meantime, I suggest you go someplace and dry out. Booze, drugs and a weekly gig don't mix."

Lance rapped lightly on the open office door. It was late and the room was cast in deep shadows. Alex sat at her desk, busily typing. She looked up, pleasantly surprised. "Hello, Lance."

He stood in the open door frame dressed in denim jeans and a crisp white shirt buttoned low. His bright white socks gleamed in the bluish glow of the muted television screen. His smile reminded her of the many photos she'd seen. Sexy would be an understatement.

"Are you extremely busy?" he asked, curious as to what kept her in here all day typing on the computer. She pressed several keys, turning both screens black.

She looked down at her watch. It was a few minutes before eleven o'clock. "No, not really. Come on in. What's up?" The muted television drew his attention for a second. Then he walked farther into the room and stood next to her desk. The small lamp illuminated the papers he held in his hand.

He smiled down at her as he casually leaned against the desk. "I could use your professional expertise."

"My professional expertise. Which professional expertise?"

"How many professions do you have?" he asked.

"At the moment, several," she answered cryptically.

He handed her the rolled papers. She uncurled them and glanced at the title page. It was a film script. She'd recognize rewrites from a script anywhere. She stood, leaned back on her desk and flipped through the papers.

"They're called rewrites," she said, offering the pages back to him.

He smiled but didn't take the pages. "Yes, I know what they're called. I'd like you to read them. I want to get your opinion."

Alex shook her head from side to side. She had no desire to act again. When she first retired she had received an average of fifty scripts a day. Broadway, television and movies, they all came pouring in. She always sent them back with a polite note declining the project and offering the writer the best of luck. She never even read the titles or cracked the binders open.

"Sorry." She pushed the pages back into his hands. "Acting is not one of my current professions." She absently picked up the remote and clicked the off button. The room immediately darkened. The only light was the low glow from the dim desk lamp. Lance reached out and took her hand, then pulled her closer. His long legs straddled her body.

The feel of him pressed against her staggered her senses. She inhaled his clean masculinity. He smelled so good, felt so good. Yielding to temptation, she reached up and rubbed her hand against his jaw.

"You need a shave."

He pulled her even closer. "You think so?"

She smiled mischievously. "Yeah, I think so. Shall I do the honors?"

His eyes sparked in delight. "Are you any good?"

She smiled, then added seriously, "I haven't had any

complaints. Of course, dead men tell no tales." She ran
her manicured finger tracing the line beneath his throat
from ear to ear.

Lance's whole body vibrated with hearty laughter.
Dead Men Tell No Tales was his biggest blockbuster film
to date. There was a shaving scene in the film in which
he was being shaved by a psychotic homicidal female.
She tried to slit his throat while in the process of shaving
his face.

He reached up and took her finger from his throat.
"I think I've had my fill of female barbers, thank you."
He pressed her finger to his lips and kissed it gently.
He looked longingly at her hand after the kiss. Then
he raised his eyes to her. Alex's stomach fluttered at his
piercing gaze.

The room swirled and the temperature escalated. She
was sure he could hear her heart pounding. How could
this man make her feel so alive by just holding her
hand?

Lance felt his body respond to the nearness of Alex.
This was like a dream come true. For years he had
fantasized about being with Alexandra Price. Now, here
he was.

"Seriously, Lance." She stepped out of his embrace.
"I really don't perform any longer." She walked over
to the end table and turned on the two lamps on either
side of the sofa. The room brightened instantly. Lance
winced at the sudden illumination. She turned to him
sadly. "I'm sorry," she said, then left the room.

Lance followed her to the kitchen. "Alex, I didn't
ask you to perform, I just asked you to read with me. I
just need another voice for this scene." Coal's head
popped up as they entered the kitchen. He padded over
to Lance and stood by his side as he leaned against the
counter. Alex opened the refrigerator and pulled out
two small blue bottles of natural spring water. She
handed one to Lance.

"You're a professional actor, Lance. You read dozens

of scripts every day. What's so special about these few pages?''

He took a deep sip of the water. "It's a good script but, to tell you the truth, I don't think these rewrites read well.'' She looked at him suspiciously. "What I mean is, I don't think the average woman would say the new lines. They just don't flow naturally in the scene.''

Alex took a deep breath, then held her hand out for the pages. Lance smiled and graciously placed them in her hand. She flipped through the papers as he stooped down to rub Coal's back. Delighted with the attention, Coal responded to Lance's playfulness. They romped in the den while Alex read through the script.

Twenty minutes later a flushed Alex joined Lance. Coal had retreated to his usual spot in front of the fireplace. Alex plopped down on the sofa next to him and watched the last few minutes of local news.

"Looks like another storm is headed this way,'' Lance said.

"Terrific,'' Alex said sarcastically. "It's the beginning of March. I can't believe they're predicting another winter storm.''

He looked at the pages in her hand. "Well, what do you think?''

She couldn't look at him. "It's a very interesting script, at least the few pages I've read. I think you'll be great in the part.''

"What do you think about the last scene?'' He referred to the very sensuous love scene between the two key characters. Alex blushed. There was no way she could tell him that the scene really took her breath away. The thought of Lance in the lead role was too arousing.

She shrugged her shoulders nervously. "It's fine.'' She looked at the television, at Coal, at anywhere, but at him.

"Fine? That's all you're going to say?'' Lance frowned, frustrated. He'd specifically given Alex the script in hopes of arousing her. But apparently it didn't work. He was no closer to finding out about Mason Turner than he was weeks earlier. "Do you think that a woman would find the character appealing?"

"Sure, why not?" she said flippantly while fidgeting uncomfortably.

Lance nodded, finding her composed response too indifferent. He moved closer and took the script from her hands. "So, if I were to do this . . ." He reached for her hand and pulled her closer. Instantly her body obliged, colliding with his hard frame. ". . . would you come willingly?"

Alex looked into his smoldering eyes. "Yes."

"And if I were to touch you here, like this . . ." He ran his fingers lightly down her cheek and neck, then across her shoulder. ". . . would you feel the sensations that the character would feel?"

Alex closed her eyes, relishing the feeling his touch inspired. "Yes," she muttered.

"And, if I were to kiss here, like this . . ." He pressed his lips just below her ear. "And here . . ." He nibbled her neck, kissing his way to her shoulder. Alex rolled her head back, a natural response to his sensuous assault. "And, if I were to do this . . ." He began unbuttoning the front of her sweater. She swayed closer to him, allowing his hand to tantalize her breasts as they worked their way downward. Her eyes fluttered open.

Then suddenly she jerked back, clearing her foggy emotions. She said, peering over his shoulder, "You're on television." The opening credits of one of his action films was beginning. They looked at each other. "I've never seen this one before," she said, "let's watch it."

"Now?" he asked, grimacing. "You really want to watch this, now?"

"Sure, why not? I'll make popcorn, you get the drinks." She backed up, putting distance between them. "Come on. It'll be fun." She pulled him into the kitchen. Together they made a huge bowl of buttered popcorn and carried it into the den.

Alex dipped her face to the brim of the bowl. "Umm, this smells heavenly." She grabbed a handful of popped corn and dropped them into her mouth. Disappointed, Lance grabbed a few popped kernels and followed suit.

The movie was fantastic. The high action had Alex dodging and weaving behind a cushioned pillow as Lance laughed, smiling at her antics. "You know, I've seen this movie before. I can tell you how it comes out to save you the stress and anxiety." She tossed a pillow at him. He easily deflected it with his arm and laughed.

Her responses to the film delighted him. She seemed to really enjoy it. One hundred twenty minutes later the film ended in an explosive spectacle of high action. Alex squealed, sighed, laughed and shrieked. She was exhausted. "That was great! You were really good! I can't believe how physical that was. You must have prepped for weeks," she blurted out, still excited.

"You sound surprised."

"I am. It was so exciting. I can't imagine being on a set like that." She stood, picked up the empty bowl and headed for the kitchen. He followed carrying their two empty glasses.

"You mean you've really never seen that film?" Lance moved to the large kitchen window and gazed out. The earlier downpour of rain had turned into slow, steady sleet.

"Never." She put the bowl and glasses in the dishwasher. "It's nothing personal. I just don't get out to the theaters often."

He nodded his head. "I bet you like those intense dramas like the kind Mason Turner writes." He walked back to the sofa and sat down.

"Sometimes. I enjoy all types, comedies, musicals. Anything but horror."

He smiled. "I can't wait to see *A Pilgrimage to Heaven*." He paused for a reaction as she followed him into the den. "Tell me honestly, what's Turner like?"

She shrugged. "Like anyone else, like you, like me, anyone."

"I suspect he lives alone on an island in the South Pacific."

She laughed at his theory. "Actually, you're not too far off. It's in the Caribbean."

"You've been to his home?" She nodded yes. Cautious of his next move, Lance added, "Would you introduce me to him sometime? I'd really love to meet him."

"Sometime."

"When?" he pressed.

She smiled gently. "Soon." An uncomfortable feeling gripped her. This was the second time Lance asked questions about Mason Turner. His interest seemed more than mere curiosity. She glanced back at the television. "Have you ever seen this one?" she asked. "It's *Carmen Jones,* with Harry Belafonte and Dorothy Dandridge."

They moved back to the den. "Yes." He smiled. "It's one of my favorites."

They sat in silence as the movie began. Lance looked over to Alex. "Come here," he whispered smoothly. She did. He wrapped his arm around her shoulder and pulled her close. She cuddled comfortable to his side, molding her body to his. Halfway through the movie they drifted off to sleep listening to the harmonious voice of Harry Belafonte and the constant rapping of the icy sleet against the glass.

A few hours later Alex snuggled deeper into his protective embrace. He tightened his arms around her. Smiling, she turned to face his hooded eyes. "I think we fell asleep," she whispered. The television was off and the last golden glowing embers burned in the fireplace.

"Uh-huh," he murmured and held tight.

"Uh-huh," she answered and cuddled back down, drifting into a warm, soothing sleep.

They slept soundly in each other's arms until morning.

Chapter Twelve

"You're gonna wake up the whole town," she whispered over the hood. "We're almost done."

"I can't believe you've got me out here on a night like this. If I catch pneumonia you'd better nurse me back to health," he murmured. "Here, catch." He tossed the sticky paper.

She leaned over and caught the roll just as it unraveled across the top. Their eyes met through a thin sheet of icy mist. She smiled mischievously. "I'll take good care of you when we get home," she promised. "I still have that skimpy little nurse uniform you got me a while back. White lace-topped stockings, three-inch spiked heels and a cute little stethoscope."

His amorous eyes clung to her bright red lipstick. She was so beautiful and alive while on an escapade. He remembered their very first caper. The one thousand purple and gold mylar *you're still winners to us* balloons would always be his favorite. Each balloon was weighted down by four quarters. The exact amount needed to send the local football team to the championship game in Cherry Hill. The team didn't win but after seeing the mass of mylar on the front lawn of the high school upon their return, no one seemed to care anymore.

After each stunt they'd gone home and celebrated. Tonight promised to be no different. Something about the very real possibility of getting caught was always exciting.

They stepped back, standing next to each other, admiring their handiwork. She tilted her head from side to side. "I think it looks fabulous," she admitted, looking to her cohort. He smiled, shaking his head shamefully. She always came up with the wildest ideas. He confirmed with a nod. "It looks"—he began to chuckle, then sneezed—"great."

"Come on, partner, let's get you home and into a nice hot shower, then a warm bed." He smiled knowingly as she intertwined her gloved hand with his dark rain slicker. They leisurely strolled back to their car several blocks away. The rain came down harder as the engine roared to life.

"You know, of course, we're gonna get caught one of these days," he said as the car eased by their latest creation.

"Maybe. Think they'll put us in connecting cells for conjugal visits?" They laughed as the car disappeared into the cold icy darkness.

Coal's loud barking brought the sound sleepers suddenly awake. Alex's head popped up with a start. She looked over to Coal, then back to the now awake Lance. A bell sound chimed. "It's the doorbell."

Lance looked at her, confused. "That's your doorbell? How could someone get past the security gate?"

"It's probably Victoria. She and my mom are the only ones who know the security code." The bell rang again. "I'd better open the door before she uses her key and comes in." Alex eased up raggedly and ran her fingers through her limp curls. She stretched her arms above her head and leaned back loosening her stiff muscles. Lance sat up and rolled his neck.

She headed to the living room with Lance following closely. She continued fluffing her hair and straightening her rumpled clothing. Lance watched her hopeless modesty. "Don't bother," he joked, "you still look like you've slept in them."

"Thanks a lot," she grumbled and waited for him to climb the front stairs to the second floor. When he disappeared into the bedroom she unlocked and opened the door. Coal barked again, his tail wagged feverishly as Victoria crossed the threshold.

"Well, it's about time. Good morning, don't you look a mess," Victoria snorted cheerfully as she breezed in. She rubbed her burgundy gloved hand over Coal's ears. "Hello, darling." He circled her excitedly, jumping happily. She removed her white fur jacket and casually tossed it across the sofa as she passed.

"Don't start with me," Alex warned, closing and locking the door. "I had a long hard night. So leave me alone."

"It couldn't have been that hard, you're alone," Victoria remarked just as the faint sound of shower water running came from the upstairs bedroom. Victoria looked suspiciously at her friend and smiled wickedly. "Company, Alexandra?"

Alex looked at Victoria and groaned inwardly, holding her hand to her head. She continued walking to the kitchen followed by Victoria's laughter. Alex fixed coffee and popped two slices of bread into the toaster. Victoria, perched on the stool, laughed each time Alex looked at her. "Go home, Victoria, you're giving me a headache."

Victoria rubbed her chilled hands together, then sipped her hot coffee. "Not on your life, darling. I'm not moving until your friend comes down here."

"He's not coming down with you here."

"Oh, so it is a *he*." She giggled knowingly. "It's cold in here. Turn the heat up."

Alex looked at her friend oddly. "Victoria, it's seventy-five degrees and roasting in here. If you're cold, go home."

Victoria stood and walked over to the back stairs. "No way, I've got all day. I'm staying right here." She looked up the carpeted steps and hollered, "Good morning up there."

"Victoria, would you please stop that? Sit down and eat your toast."

Victoria turned with her most innocent expression. "What? I'm not doing anything. I merely greeted your guest." Slowly she walked back to the counter and sat down. Alex glared at her. "All right. The reason I'm here is that Ted and I are throwing a small last-minute pre-Oscar dinner party tonight. Dress is casual, cocktails are at six and dinner's at seven. We'll be showing a film around nine-thirty or ten. So you shouldn't be out too late."

Still perturbed, Alex grumbled, "I'll try to make it, no promises."

"Good, and feel free to bring your upstairs guest."

Alex looked at her persistently irritating friend. She opened her mouth to rebuke her when a deep masculine voice chimed in. "Good morning, ladies," Lance said as he stood on the last step of the back stair. He'd showered, shaved and changed into jeans and a T-shirt. He strolled over to the counter. Victoria's mouth dropped open, in total surprise.

"Lance? Lance Morgan?" Victoria smiled wryly, then looked at Alex and began laughing. "Oh, this is *too* rich." Lance moved to Alex's side and sipped coffee from her cup. "You and Alex." She laughed again. "I never would have guessed."

Alex looked to the ceiling and blew out an exasperated breath. She was never going to live this down. Victoria would hold this over her head indefinitely. Lance moved to Victoria and kissed each cheek. The two of them began talking as if they'd just met at a neighborhood pub.

"So, how've you been, Victoria?"

"Wonderful, and yourself?"

"Great. How's Ted these days?" Lance took another sip from Alex's cup. She got up and made herself another cup of coffee.

"Oh, you know Ted. He works too hard and plays too little. We missed you last month in L.A."

"I had another engagement, my apologies."

Victoria smiled gleefully. "You can make it up to me by attending a gathering this evening. Alex has already agreed to come."

Alex spoke up finally. "I didn't agree, Victoria, I said I'd try."

Victoria waved her hand nonchalantly and stood. "You'll be there," she retorted knowingly. "I've got to be off now. I still have a million things to do before this evening." She headed for the living room. "Lance, dear, do make sure Alex attends this evening." He nodded and smiled his famous thousand-watt smile.

"I'll do my best," he assured her.

Alex glanced to Lance after closing the front door. "Don't encourage her."

"Actually, a party sounds like a great idea." Lance eased closer to Alex. "You and me on the dance floor." He smiled seductively. "I can hardly wait."

The evening couldn't have been more perfect. Unfortunately, the small informal dinner party turned out to be anything but. Still, within a mere twelve hours, Victoria had put together a spectacular catered dinner that would rival her most elaborately planned gathering.

Apparently word had gotten out earlier that Lance would be attending the gathering. Victoria's telephone had rung nonstop for hours. Reporters, agents and acquaintances begged, implored and cajoled for an invitation to the evening's function. Victoria finally limited the guest list to twenty for the dinner, then another twenty or so for the movie and late cocktails. Thankfully she called Alex to forewarn Lance about the change in plans and that the press had assembled at her driveway's entrance. As usual, he took all the adorned attention in stride.

The sit-down dinner for twenty seemed more cozy than cluttered. The meal was delicious and the conversation sparkled with interesting stories and witty anecdotes of Hollywood past and present.

After coffee and dessert, the guests adjourned to the projection room on the lower level. True to their motto, "Why not bigger?" the Reeses' massive eighty-seat theater was equipped with screening room, projection booth, film library, popcorn cart and glass-enclosed candy stand.

Ted's latest release, a romantic comedy, was destined to be another winner. After the movie a series of ten or twelve Oscar-nominated film trailers dominated the large screen. Following the trailers Victoria showed scenes from Lance's latest film. The room went wild at the high-action stunts and heated love scenes.

Lance sat sandwiched between Alex and an overly adoring young female starlet who was obviously a huge fan. The woman held her hand firmly on his thigh the entire evening. Each time he shifted in the red velvet seat she dutifully returned her hand to its previous position.

After the movie and screening, all the guests went back into the great room for cocktails and dancing. Alex sat with Lance until he stood and took her hand. "Dance with me."

Alex sighed happily as Lance held her close within the circle of his body. This was sheer bliss. "Have I told you how beautiful you look this evening?" he whispered, after humming softly in her ear. She smiled and eased farther into his embrace.

"Yes," she murmured wistfully, "about twenty times so far." She loved the feel of being wrapped in his arms.

Several heavily mascaraed eyes bore enviously into her back, but she didn't care. She closed her eyes and enjoyed the glorious feeling of being held by Lance. For this dance at least, he was all hers.

"I want to make love to you, Alex," he whispered softly, allowing his words to hang between them. She tensed. The magnetic pull of his desire was arousing. Wide eyed, she reluctantly pulled back as the song ended. Looking up into his perfect dark eyes, she saw the reflection of raw passion. Her mind screamed *Stop, slow down,* but she couldn't. Not now, not ever. The stark reality of his appeal mirrored her own. She wanted him too.

A female guest came up and interrupted the moment. "Lance?" He turned his attention to the woman. She smiled brightly. "I'm one of your biggest fans. I was wondering," she cooed, batting her long thick lashes, "would you like to dance?"

He turned back to Alex, smiled and replied, "Sure." With his eyes still locked on Alex, he stepped back. The young woman grasped his hand firmly and pulled him across the room to a more secluded locale.

Alex never moved. Her eyes were still riveted on Lance and his eyes still on her. The hushed sound of his tender plea still reverberated in her ear. She watched as the two danced. From over the woman's head he continued to stare. She smiled, unaware of the man approaching.

Burke had arrived late, missing most of the evening's activities. But as soon as he stepped into the great room he spotted his query immediately. He beamed his usual smirk. Black turtleneck sweater, black slacks and black leather jacket, Lance Morgan was unmistakable. He exuded power, control and success, and the women flocked to him in droves.

Burke watched as Lance danced with a luscious female. Her tender body was molded to his. From the angle he could only see her profile, but what he saw

intrigued him. The sensuously deliberate way she moved
with Lance's body was enticing to watch.

Burke assumed she was some starstruck wanna-be
actress fan. He decided he'd give her the "I'll make
you a star" routine. It always worked, and he knew Lance
never availed himself of overly enthused fans.

When Lance stepped away to dance with another fan,
Burke moved in to make his offer. But, surprise gripped
him. The song ended and the woman turned slightly.
"Alexandra Price," he muttered aloud.

He stood behind Alexandra as she continued to stare
at Lance. "Hello, Alexandra." His raspy voice interrupted her wayward thoughts.

She turned, stunned, then quickly regaining her composure. Nodding a condescending acknowledgment,
she walked casually to the bar.

She looks good, Burke mused as his shifty eyes watched
the slow sexy sway of her hips moving against the silky
material of her skirt. She'd been a young child when
they first met. Now, every bit of her was a woman. A
very desirable woman.

He followed her to the bar. "Alexandra," he said.
She picked up a glass of champagne, then turned to
face him wordlessly. The soft welcoming gloss on her
full mouth drew his immediate attention. "I hope you
and I can come to terms with our past," he began.
She parted her mouth slightly. The tip of her tongue
playfully eased out as she moistened her lips. He
watched hypnotically as he continued his offer of peace.
"After all, it's been over ten years since . . ." He trailed
the statement off. He'd been distracted by her actions
and said more than he meant to reveal.

Her piercing stare never strayed from his dark cold
eyes. He could tell she wasn't the same little girl that
ran away and hid years ago. She stood haughty, with her
chest protruding proudly. He liked the metamorphosis.
"Since what, Burke?" she asserted boldly. "Since you

maneuvered me out of the business?" Acidic contempt dripped from each word.

He winced defensively. "That's not what I was going to say, Alexandra," he whispered as he stepped closer to her side. Again, she surprised him, she didn't move away. Had she budged even an inch he would have known she hadn't changed. But, instead, she stood her ground. "I was going to say since you left Hollywood." She didn't reply. So he openly looked her up and down and continued, "You look ravishing." Surprising himself, he meant every word. He smiled greedily. "The past few years have been extremely good to you, I see." Again, she remained silent. She just stared at him as if he were some repugnant foreign object scraped from the bottom of her shoe. She slowly sipped her wine. "How's Lillian?"

"My mother is fine," she finally responded.

"Good. I must drop her a note sometime. By the way, a very interesting script crossed my desk the other day. I thought of you immediately, I think you'd be perfect for the lead." He reached into his jacket pocket and pulled out a card. "If you're interested or suddenly find yourself looking for representation, give me a call. I'd be delighted to add you to my client list once again." He held the card out between his two fingers.

She stared at the card venomously. "Excuse me," she sneered dismissively, then strolled away.

This was a very different Alexandra, he concluded. He liked it. As far as he was concerned this was just the beginning of their new relationship. She'd eventually come to terms with their past. He chuckled to himself thinking of a time long ago. If things had worked out differently, she'd be his stepdaughter. Burke continued watching, amazed by the ten-year transformation. She looked so much like her mother.

Eventually Burke looked back over to Lance. He had finished his dance with the lovely young lady and was now surrounded by a number of admiring fans. Burke smiled. He couldn't believe his luck when Ted had mentioned that Lance would be attending the party that evening. He leaned back against the bar and picked up a glass of champagne. There'd be plenty of time to approach Lance. Might as well relax and enjoy the scenery, he decided.

Alex angrily stalked into the kitchen. Seeing the expression on her face, Victoria stepped away from the small group she'd been entertaining and followed. The kitchen was bustling with activity. "Alex," Victoria called with concern, "you look like you've seen a ghost." She took her friend's hand and moved to the wine cellar. Alex immediately began pacing the room. "What is it?" Victoria questioned. "What happened?"

Alex took a deep cleansing breath and mouthed slowly, "Robert Burke is here." Her angry, shaky voice matched the tremors of fury she felt. She stopped pacing and sat down.

"Robert Burke? Oh no, Ted." Victoria sat down next to Alex. "Ted was in Manhattan this morning, he must have invited Burke. Did he say anything to you?"

Alex chuckled sarcastically. "Same old Burke, he thinks flattery can whitewash anything. He actually had the nerve to offer me a script, telling me that he'd be delighted to add me to his client list again. Can you believe that?"

"Just ignore him," Victoria advised.

"I wish I could. But every time I see him I want to put my hands around his scrawny little neck and choke him until his eyes bulge out."

"Assault and battery is punishable with up to ten years. Ignore him, he's not worth it. There's nothing else you can do."

"I know, you're right." Alex sighed heavily. They sat in silence until she chuckled. "What I need is a mercenary," she said mischievously, "or, I guess I could always call the night prowler?"

"The night prowler, how, check the yellow pages?" Victoria snickered. "Or maybe you can shine a light in the sky like the bat signal."

"Yeah, why not? I'll put an add in the local newspaper. Night prowler wanted to do whitewash job on asshole agent, call immediately."

"You'll have to be more specific, Alex. Do you know how many asshole agents are out there? Half the population of L.A. would look like Casper." The two laughed at the visual image.

"Speaking of the night prowler, you'd be interested to hear about his latest caper."

"What'd he do?" Alex asked.

"He wallpapered that tabloid reporter's car."

"He did what?"

"You heard me. Apparently, late one night the prowler plastered his car with pink- and blue-striped wallpaper. I even heard there were tiny little cut out dolls and trucks parading across the front and back windshields."

"The whole car?" Alex asked as tears streamed down her face.

"The whole car," Victoria confirmed, "windshield wipers, tires, even the antenna."

"I wish I could have seen that," Alex said, dabbing her moist eyes.

"You can." Victoria grinned. "They towed it to Matt's repair shop. I hear Rhoda and Matt are still trying to figure out what to do with it."

"I can't believe he did that."

"Well, serves him right. That photo he took of you and . . ." She looked cautiously around the empty room. "You know who, was totally out of line."

"I agree," Alex scoffed. "He's been a real menace around here lately. But since he hadn't broken any laws, there wasn't anything legally the sheriff could do."

"So looks like the night prowler took care of him. Can you imagine trying to explain that to your insurance company?" The two woman laughed again. Victoria grabbed her arm. "Wait, how much would you give to have seen his face when he first saw the car?" The laughter accelerated. "Can't you just see the stunned expression? He must have been shocked."

"Dazed," Alex reiterated. The two laughed again.

When the chuckles finally eased, Victoria looked over to Alex and asked, "Are you ready to get back out there?"

Alex smiled easily. "I still remember a few things from years of acting." She stood. "Let's do it." Together they pranced back into the midst of the party. Alex was more lively and entertaining than she'd been in years. Lance marveled at the vivacious woman in the center of the room. Both men and women gathered around, drawn by her magnetic personality. She was remarkable. Victoria glanced at the small crowd surrounding her friend. She could definitely see why Alex had received the small coveted statuette named Oscar.

Chapter Thirteen

The party ended just as it had begun, in a flurry of excitement. The overnight guests were settling into their respective rooms, others had already departed while several more headed for their cars. Ted and Victoria held each other and waved at the bright red lights driving down the path. Inconspicuously, the catering truck was being loaded in the rear as the first remnants of dawn crept over the horizon.

"You were fabulous," Ted said as he held Victoria close. She smiled up at her companion.

"Let's go to bed," she whispered seductively. Ted followed without a word. He'd follow her anywhere.

Alex dimmed the houselights. She stood alone at the wall of windows in semidarkness. A box-shaped catering truck pulled into her dark driveway and a lone shadowy figure disembarked and hurried up her front steps. She waved as Victoria's chauffeur flashed the truck's lights, turned and headed back through the iron security gates. Coal barked once and nudged his nose into the opening of the cracked door. Alex smiled as the figure approached.

Lance stepped inside and secured the front door. He walked over to Alex. Dipping his head to nuzzle her sensitive ear, he murmured, "Have I told you how beautiful you are this evening?"

The deep masculine rumble of his voice, the arousing scent of his cologne and the heat of his touch sent shivers through her body. "Umm-hmm . . ." She tilted her head back and sighed sheepishly. "I seem to remember you mentioning something like that earlier."

Lance wrapped his arms around her narrow waist and slowly began moving to the soft melody of their shared hearts. He nibbled down Alex's neck, making love to every inch of her bare skin. She moaned inwardly. The intensity of his touch was intoxicating.

"I want to make love to you, Alex," he repeated softly. She felt the sincerity of his words as she turned to him. "Not Alexandra Price the star, but Alexandra the woman. Yes, I know the conflict. You wonder, does this person really see me or the character I've played?" He took her hand and continued, "I don't want to pressure you. I just want you to know how I feel."

She looked into his eyes. "Why did you come back again, Lance? I know it wasn't the need for solitude as you claimed. You could have gotten that anywhere. Why here? Why now?"

Lance thought silently for a moment. "I came back because for the first time in a long time I enjoyed spending time with someone. I liked the way we are together. I can let my guard down. There's something special between us, Alex. I guess I need to know if there was more. I need to know if you were feeling what I was feeling. Do you?" he asked hopefully.

"Make love to me, Lance," she whispered. He stepped back from the embrace. She took his hand and led him to the hidden panel along the side wall. She pushed at the molding, and the tall door swung open.

Lance stopped just inside the room. "Are you sure?"

She smiled as they continued walking. "Yes." With her hand gently planted on his chest, she eased him down onto her bed. He reached up to touch her, she stepped back. Slowly, she unbuttoned the jacket of her suit letting the skimpy lace bra peek through. She stepped closer, removing his jacket and slowly pulling the cashmere sweater from his pants and over his head.

His body was magnificent. Tight muscles rippled across his chest and stomach. Deep-defined biceps danced around his powerful arms. He reached for her again, she pushed his hands away. Capturing his face with her hands, she leaned in and kissed the smooth caramel skin covering his neck. Descending slowly, he moaned through the passion of his desire.

Encircling her waist beneath the open jacket he removed it, then pulled her down onto the bed next to him. She rolled onto her back. Hovering above, he kissed, nibbled and caressed every part of her visible body. Leaning back, he unzipped the side of her skirt and pulled it down from her hips. The matching lace panties and garterless stockings were his undoing. Within seconds he tore away his remaining clothing and stood completely naked before her. Hot blinding waves of passion erupted as she gasped for breath. Her chest heaved as he inched slowly up her body, licking, tasting, savoring, pausing first at her lace-covered thigh, then at her lace panties and finally at the patches of lace covering her breasts.

His hot mouth enveloped the skimpy lace material while his hands roamed her body. Using his teeth, he pulled at the lace cup until the dark orb was exposed. Delighted with his found treasure he relished her, then moving over to bite away the second hindering obstacle.

Passionately he kissed her lips, her neck, her stomach, her breasts, her navel, then lower and lower until madness overtook all reasoning. She squirmed beneath his skillful touch. As he hovered teasingly above, impatience gnawed at her. Drawing her legs up around his hips, she prompted him to continue. His powerful need raged. He secured a condom from his wallet and protected them. "Lance!" Her pleas drove him quick and deep, filling her completely. He tensed, but it was too late. The barrier had been penetrated. The stinging pain of her nails bit into his shoulders as she called out his name again. "Lance."

He looked down into her wanton eyes finding only passion. Her hips arched up urging him to continue. He did. This time more slowly, gently, then gradually he increased the speed and depth.

Plunging again and again, deeper and deeper until their union exploded and wave after wave of ecstasy crested, throwing them onto a plain only God could create. He collapsed, weak in her arms. He rolled until the weight of her body molded on top of his. Holding him tightly, she sighed, then happily drifted into a deep, satisfied slumber.

Lance stared off into the dimness after she rolled from his body. Even with the comforting sounds of her restful breathing he chided himself. He got up and walked around the spacious chamber of her sanctuary. He'd been living here for days, yet this was the only room he'd never seen. It was large and exotically adorned with velvets and satins.

His bare feet left solid indentations in the thick dark carpeting. He turned and looked back to the bed. Resisting the urge to return to Alex's arms, he moved farther into the shadows of the darkened room until he came to the muted light.

He stood before the enormous aquarium nestled above the slate fireplace. Colorful fish swam delicately through the live coral reef. Their ease and grace did little to lull his anguish. His troubled reflection stared back at him in the crystal waters. Then, out of the dim shadows, Alex appeared.

She came up behind him and placed a loving kiss on his bare shoulder. Slowly she snaked her hand around the narrow of his waist. "Come back to bed," she commanded softly. Then spread her fingers wide, feeling the soft curly hairs gradating downward from his chest to his stomach. She felt his lower muscles tense, then curiously peered around his arm. His expression was dim. "Lance, what's wrong?" Her hand quivered. "Did I do something wrong?"

"My dad loves reef aquariums. This reminds me of him." Lance ran his hand along a section of the protruding circular bend of the glass. "I've never seen aquarium glass curved like this." He looked at the shadowed living room. "Two-way glass. I never even noticed."

"Lance?" She eyed his reflection in the glass.

Finally, he looked into her eyes. "No, Alex, you . . ." He blew out in exasperation. "You were . . . incredible." He averted his eyes from her again, focusing fully on the colorful swimmers. "Why didn't you tell me?"

"Tell you what?" She continued to purposely play with the delicate hairs. "That I'm a virgin?"

He stilled her hand and looked into her eyes, correcting her. "Was a virgin."

"Was a virgin." She smiled inwardly. He didn't. "Exactly when does one broach the subject of virginity, Lance? Over lunch? Dinner? Cocktails maybe? Or how about, 'Please pass the mashed potatoes, oh, and by the way, I'm a virgin'?" she joked easily.

Taking her off guard, he spun quickly and took her hands. "This is serious, Alex." His heart pounded rapidly. "Do you realize I could have seriously hurt you tonight?" He looked down at her naked body. Immediately his arousal resurfaced.

"You didn't," she whispered, moving closer, feeling his quivering spasms of desire. She kissed his chest and bit at his pebbling nipples softly, contending, "Nothing happened that I didn't want to happen."

He laid his chin on top of her tousled hair and kissed the loose curls. "You should have told me, Alex," he chastised. Her love bites drew a gasp, then a low groan of pleasure from deep in his throat. "Your first time shouldn't have been so . . ." He searched for the appropriate word. "Intense." She grasped and massaged his firm buttocks while her mouth continued the gentle torture. "I should have been more gentle, more patient," he mumbled incoherently.

"More gentle, more patient," she repeated, looking up into his glazed eyes. "Show me."

"What?" The haze in his mind refused to clear.

"Show me, more gentle, more patient," she whispered.

"Later, your body needs to rest."

"I've rested all my life." She pulled him back to the bed and cleared away the rumpled sheets. "What my body needs now is you." She traced her finger around his navel. He smiled at her teasing touch.

"Oh yeah?" he muttered, kissing her gently.

"Oh yeah," she repeated, savoring his slow gentle caress. He showed her more gentle, more patient.

Saturday brunch at the Reese household was filled with excitement. Overnight house guests rambled in silken pajamas, kimonos and designer sweats. The new chef and kitchen crew prepared a virtual banquet of appetizing edibles. The cozy solarium was set up buffet style with numerous linen-topped circular tables and chairs informally scattered amid the lush greenery.

The host and hostess finally appeared. "Ted," Burke called out as he approached the loving couple. "Good morning." He shook Ted's hand, then turned to Victoria. "Good morning, Victoria." He kissed both cheeks. "You look as beautiful as ever."

She smiled graciously. "Ted, I was wondering, have you seen Lance this morning?"

Ted smiled happily. "No, I haven't." Burke looked at Victoria. She smiled. "If I'm not mistaken, I believe he left earlier this morning."

A tense nerve twitched in Burke's neck. He frowned. He'd assumed as much when he knocked earlier on Lance's door. There was no answer. He'd just wasted the entire morning waiting for Lance to exit an empty room. The nerve twitched again as he held tight to the twisted smile plastered on his face. "That is unfortunate," he said aloud as Ted and Victoria watched with curious expressions. "I wanted to say good-bye to him before I took off. Well, I'll catch up with him in New York." He shook Ted's hand and kissed Victoria on the cheek. "I had a wonderful time, I'll see you two Monday night, right?"

Ted smiled. "We wouldn't miss it."

The constant rapping increased in volume and the bell rang repeatedly. Annoyed, Charles Taylor snatched up his towel and headed for the front door. He mumbled a few obscenities, then yanked on the brass knob.

Burke's eyes flew open. He didn't expect to see Lance's personal bodyguard standing before him in sweatpants and a towel. "Good afternoon, Charles," Burke said, recovering quickly, and attempted to proceed into the apartment. Charles stood blocking his entrance. "Are you going to step aside and let me in?"

Annoyed about his interrupted workout, Charles frowned, causing deep-burrowed ridges to crease his smooth forehead. "No." His menacing tone froze Burke in midstride. He stepped back, surprised by the one-word answer. He knew this mountain of a man didn't approve of him, that was always obvious, but to refuse his entrance was blatant insubordination as far as he was concerned.

"Charles, I suggest you move aside and let me pass." He smiled his warning. "I'm sure you wouldn't want me to discuss your rudeness with your employer. Or, might I venture to correct myself? Your former employer," he threatened ineffectively.

Charles let the corner of his mouth curl up slowly into what might pass on someone less intimidating as a sly grin. He removed the crisp white towel from his neck and stepped aside.

Pleased with his handling of the situation, Burke strutted haughtily into Lance's Upper West Side apartment. He removed his outer jacket and draped it neatly across the sofa as he entered the lavish living room. Charles followed him, smiling to himself. Burke turned around. "Don't just stand there, tell Lance I'm here." Charles clenched his massive fists, nodded and backed out of the room.

Twenty-five minutes and eight phone calls later Burke found Charles seated on a low bench briskly curling massive weights with his powerfully meaty arm. Burke watched silently from the doorway at Charles's reflection in the mirror. The man's strength was unbelievable. The power he exuded as his biceps and triceps flexed and released was impressive. He was as solid as a brick wall and just as large.

Apparently Lance knew what he was doing when he had hired Charles for the position. No one in their right mind would dare touch him with this giant around. Burke announced his presence by clearing his throat. Charles changed arms but never looked up. "Did you inform Lance of my arrival?"

"No." Charles performed several more curls, then let the weight fall heavily onto the floor. Burke frowned as the floor seemingly vibrated beneath his loafered feet.

He rolled his eyes to the ceiling. "This is like communicating with a two-year-old," he mumbled under his breath. Charles stood and with the swiftness of a panther crossed the room in seconds and glared down at the scrawny man. Burke's legs jellied as he eased to the side.

Charles breezed past him and continued down the hall. Burke yelled out when Charles was safely thirty feet ahead, "Well, why not?" Charles responded with his usual silence. Burke followed him into the kitchen. After several gulps of orange juice Charles locked his black, piercing eyes on Burke. Burke instinctively took a step back. "Is Lance here, Charles?"

"No."

Burke began laughing, slowly at first, then louder as he threw his head back. Charles poured another glass of juice and watched the little man. When Burke settled down he asked, "Why didn't you tell me that a half hour ago?"

Bright white teeth parted Charles's full lips into a wide grin. "You didn't ask." Burke began chuckling again. This was the oldest joke in the book and he fell for it. He shook his head. "Pour me one of those," he instructed casually. Charles ignored the request. Burke added, "Please." Charles still didn't move. Burke took a deep, aggravated breath, then asked, "When will Lance be back?"

Charles shrugged his mighty shoulders. "Soon." He shrugged again. "Later."

"What time did he get in this morning?"

"He didn't."

"I was at a party with him last night. He left first thing this morning heading home." Charles shrugged his shoulders again. Anger prompted Burke to take a menacing step forward. When Charles looked up from his glass, Burke sank back against the counter.

"Look, Charles, this Abbott and Costello routine is starting to wear on my nerves. Just give me a straight answer to the question, where is Lance?"

Charles looked at Burke, unbelieving. Did this puny little man really expect him to divulge his friend's whereabouts? After everything his boss had done for him he'd gladly kill for Lance, starting with this little piece of crap.

Seeing he was getting nowhere fast, Burke shook his head in disgust and walked out of the kitchen. Joyous laughter roared throughout the spacious duplex apartment as the front door slammed loudly. It was the best laugh Charles had had in a long time. He chuckled the rest of the afternoon.

Soft melodious music lulled Lance from his light slumber. With his eyes still closed, he laid his hand on the flat of his stomach. He was still stuffed from the heavy meal of scrambled eggs, pancakes, bacon and sausage. Afterward he and Alex had crawled back into bed and made love, again. He smiled. She was insatiable and he savored every delectable minute.

His arm reached out to a cold empty bed. Puzzled, he sat up and looked around. Bright sunshine blanketed the empty bedroom. He got out of bed and curiously followed the sound of violins, cellos and harps. He opened the cracked door and peered inside.

His eyes quickly adjusted to the dim lighting. The room glowed with the low blaze from a white marble fireplace and dozens of candles. The scene was enchanting. Glowing candles everywhere, on the sink, the floor, lining the shelves and counters and surrounding the sunken tub. The tub, on a raised platform of glass blocks, reflected the flicker of dozens of tiny flames.

Alex, lying back in the midst of the dream spectacle, was covered with tiny iridescent bubbles. She picked up a large sea sponge and lazily drizzled scented water onto her neck and shoulders. She turned, a mellow smile greeted him as he approached. "Hello," she uttered sensuously, then leaned up, putting the glass of liquid on the marble-tiled floor.

He moved farther to the warmth of her smile. His eyes never left the swell of cleavage just above the mass of foam and froth. "You look comfortable," he observed.

She leaned back and raised her hand, beckoning innocently. "Join me." A lustful smile brightened his strained expression. He picked up the bottle of champagne from the floor and poured himself a tall fluted glass. He sipped as she leaned up again. "I meant in here," she teased while moving forward into the large mass of bubbles.

"I thought you'd never ask," he replied, easing down into the deep accommodating tub. He wrapped his moistened arms around her shoulders and drew her back closer to his broad chest. She cuddled back comfortably against him. "Umm," she moaned, "this feels wonderful."

He smiled as his playful hands began massaging her shoulders, arms, then breasts. Involuntarily Alex rolled her head back as he nibbled her ear, causing a deep rasping groan to escape from deep within. His nimble fingers dipped beneath the surface of the water until reaching her delicate curls. She gasped and instinctively grabbed to stop his probing hand. "Shh." He held her still, soothing and comforting her with tender passionate whispers. "Lie back, close your eyes and relax." Her strained breathing accelerated immediately. Her mind and body were a shattered mass of sensations.

She squirmed beneath his masterful fingers, then rocked her hips to the slow rhythm of his sweet relentless torment. Again and again she writhed in swelling ecstasy. She cried out as her hips arched near the water's surface. Then slowly the rippling waters stilled as her mind, awash with rapture's pleasure, returned to her blissful reality. She lay wrapped in his caress, embraced by the strength of his arms. There she stayed until the sun's deep shadows were chased away by the awakening moon.

Alex stopped brushing her drying hair and watched as Lance moved around the bedroom. *He is truly a magnificent sight,* she thought, smiling wickedly. Dressed in a thick white towel wrapped low around his narrow hips, Lance gathered their tossed clothing. His smooth caramel skin glistened with each step. Sensing her attention, he turned. She blushed, embarrassed by her obvious gawking.

"See something you like?" he queried.

"Possibly," she answered with a lingering smile.

"Possibly?" he disputed.

Their eyes met in knowing pleasure shared until her attention was drawn to a commercial advertising the upcoming Oscar Awards ceremony. Her smiled faded. "When do you have to go back?" she asked, well aware of the inevitable.

He paused. "Soon."

She turned around to face him. "How soon?

He walked over and knelt down in front of her. His soft hands lovingly stroked her face. "In the next day or so." She nodded. "Why don't you come with me?" he said temptingly. "You can stay at my home in the Hills. It's very secluded," he enticed. The hopeful offer surprised him. But he meant every word. He'd grown extremely fond of Alex. More than fond.

She crinkled her nose. "No, I don't think so. The last thing you need before your next film opens is a scandal."

"A scandal?"

She squared her fingers in the air, presenting a headline. *"Alexandra Price Has Ménage À Trois with Anderson Brothers, Shawn and Lance!"*

He laughed. "That's hardly the truth and I don't think they'll go that far."

"Somehow I don't think most tabloids reporters are overly concerned about accuracy."

He leaned his arms on the padded chair and held her hips. His serious expression concerned her. "So, do you want to tell me why?" She looked at him, confused, so he clarified the question. "Why'd you choose last night? Why with me?"

Her heart raced. How could she dare tell him that

she'd fallen in love with him? She gently rubbed the tiny bristled hairs on his jaw. "It was time."

Two days later she stood at her door watching Lance and Charles in the delivery truck as it drove away. Sadness and longing gripped her heart instantly.

Chapter Fourteen

Giddy with excitement and anticipation, Alex muttered to herself, "I can't believe I'm doing this."

She pulled up at the front gate of Lance's Beverly Hills estate. His home was massive. She waited her turn for admittance behind two other cars, a Bentley and a Porsche. Evidently Lance was hosting some kind of party. Upon her turn, she proceeded slowly to the front gate.

A uniformed guard eyed the vintage two-seater convertible admiringly, then came around to the driver's side on the right. "I love these old cars," he declared, grinning broadly. "A 1960 Bugeye Austin-Healey 100, right?"

She smiled. "Close enough, although I think it's a fifty-four, and slightly before the Bugeye series."

"It's gorgeous, and in mint condition," he exclaimed admiringly, then chuckled. "I love this wild color, what's it called?"

"Marmalade," she said humorously, crinkling her nose at the absurd color name. "Sounds like you really know your marque automobiles."

"Actually, my older brother started me on model kits when I was a kid. This was the first model," he said, still eyeing the car. "It took me almost two months to put this baby together."

"It is pretty neat. Although driving it takes a little

getting used to. But after a while it feels like driving any other car. Except of course I want to drive on the other side of the road.''

The guard laughed. Then, for the first time he took his eyes off of the car and looked at the driver. ''Oh man.'' He grinned down at her. ''Alexandra Price! I can't believe my luck today. First the Austin-Healy and now you.''

She returned his cheerful acknowledgment with her famous bright smile. ''You weren't supposed to recognize me in this disguise.''

''Miss Price, I'd recognize you in a monkey suit.'' His soft brown eyes brightened. ''No offense,'' he quickly apologized.

She laughed, removing her dark shades, and squinted at his name badge. ''None taken, Mr. Taylor.''

''Greg,'' he corrected immediately.

She nodded. ''Alex,'' she added, then noticed the clipboard in his hand. ''Greg, I don't have an appointment and I know Lance wasn't expecting me. I doubt seriously that I'm on any kind of list, but I think Lance would be happy to see me. Do you think you could let me in?''

He beamed again. ''This will probably mean my job, but I'd do anything for you.'' He handed her a pen and the clipboard. ''You'll still have to sign in, I'm afraid.''

Alex took the clipboard from him and quickly scrolled her famous name. The guard looked down at the initials and signature, then back to her questioningly. ''A.M.T. Price?'' She winked at him. He grinned and nodded. ''Hold on one second.'' He hurried around to the guard's booth and quickly returned with a crossword puzzle booklet.

Giving her his best puppy dog eyes he handed the pages to her. ''Believe me, I don't usually do this, but, Miss Price, you are my biggest fan.'' He laughed, then corrected himself. ''I mean I am your biggest fan.'' They laughed as she took the book.

"Actually, my dream is to sign with you mother's agency someday."

"You're an actor?" she asked. He nodded proudly. "Are you any good?"

"I'm very good. If you get a chance, stop by the Hills Playhouse this evening. I'll be there the next two weeks. I've gotten wonderful reviews."

She nodded and continued writing. "I just might do that." She finished scripting the note and handed the book back. He looked at the message curiously.

"It's my mother's private office line. Give her a call when you're ready."

"Thank you," he exclaimed happily while hurrying to the guard's booth. He pressing a button and the iron bars slowly parted. She replaced her glasses and waved at him. His smile was worth the trip.

Alex pulled up along the side of the immense lawn and parked the car. She walked the short distance to the magnificent home. Several guests were out in front talking on the marble steps. Others strolled the neatly cut lawn carrying drinks and talking quietly. She adjusted her hat, lowered her head and walked through the open doors. As she stepped inside a young woman greeted her with a small notebook. "Good afternoon." She smiled brightly. "May I have your invitation please?"

Alex returned her greeting. "Good afternoon. I'm afraid I don't have an invitation."

The woman opened the notebook filled with names. "That's okay, your name?"

"I doubt I'm on that list."

The woman grimaced, looking overly concerned. Alex stepped closer and leaned down to her side. She lowered her voice to a bare whisper. "My name is Alex-andra Price." The young woman seemed oblivious of her famous name. Alex smiled and thought, *At least this part won't make the tabloids.*

The petite woman motioned behind her. "I'm sorry,

miss. But this is a private party by invitation only and I don't see your name on the permanent guest list. I'm not sure how you got through the front gate but you'll have to leave, now."

Alex smiled outwardly but she was crestfallen. She'd come so far to see Lance only to be turned down at the door. "If you'll just call Lance over . . ." she said as she began scanning the faces in the crowded room. "I'm sure once he realizes I'm here he'll be . . ."

She never finished her statement. Two large neatly dressed men stood on either side of her. "We're sorry, miss. We're going to have to escort you to the front gate." Alex was mortified.

"Don't bother, that won't be necessary," she stammered after spotting Lance. He was dancing with Amber Hall, the woman to whom he'd been linked romantically for months. His arms snaked around her tiny waist just as he'd held her just a few nights earlier. She muttered, "How soon they forget," turned, then tramped back to the car completely humiliated.

The guard at the gate waved but she didn't see him through her wet tearful eyes. He frowned as the yellow sports car sped recklessly down the steep hills.

Two of Greg's associates arrived at the front gate. They looked after the car. "Man, I can't believe you let a strange woman in here, this could mean your job." The other man added, "Brother or not, you know the rules." Taylor sighed an exasperated breath. That's all he needed, for his brother to hear about this.

"Back so soon?" Victoria said, surprised to see her friend park the car in the extended row of occupied garages. One look at Alex and Victoria said consolingly, "Come on, let's shop!"

* * *

"What's the problem?" Charles asked as his younger brother walked into his office. "I heard you let a strange woman through the gates." He never raised his head from the paperwork.

Taylor bowed his head. "I know. I messed up. But when she said she knew Lance, I figured it was okay."

"Man, I told you before, these fanatics will try any- and everything in the book to get next to Lance. It's our job to protect him from that."

"I know, I know, I messed up. It's just that when Alex smiled at me, I guess I kind of lost it."

Charles Taylor suddenly stopped writing and looked up. "Who did you say?"

"Alex, Alexandra Price, the movie star. You probably don't remember her. She was famous a while back."

Charles picked up and pressed a button in his phone panel. Lance's rich voice returned. "Yeah." Charles spoke softer. "Lance, was Miss Price supposed to meet with you this afternoon?"

"Miss Price?"

"Yes, Alex."

Lance's heart leaped. "Alex is here! Where is she? Send her up. No, wait, I'll be right down." Before Charles could say another word the phone clicked.

Lance charged into Charles's office moments later. The two Taylor brothers greeted him sheepishly. Lance looked around the office. "Where is she?" he demanded.

"She's not here," Charles said. Lance's eyes narrowed as Charles continued. "Apparently she came by earlier and my brother was at the gate. He let her in but when she got to the front door, Macy had Parker and James escort her out."

The deafening "What!" echoed throughout the lower level. Franklin rushed into Charles's office. "Fire them," Lance bellowed, "fire all of them!" He paced the room rapidly. "Never mind, where are they? I'll fire them myself." Franklin quietly questioned Greg, then picked up the clipboard.

Charles stood up. "Lance, calm down. They were only doing their jobs. She didn't have an invitation and she wasn't on the admittance list. I'm sure she'll be back later."

Greg shook his head and blew out loudly. "I doubt it, not the way she sped down that hill. Man, she looked pissed. She tore out of here like a bat out . . ." He didn't finish as all eyes angrily turned at him.

Lance sank into the leather chair and put his head in his hands. He groaned and muttered to himself.

"Did she sign the clipboard?" Franklin asked, looking at the two brothers.

Greg moved beside him, flipped several pages, then pointed to the scrolled signature. "There, she signed her initials. A.M.T. Price."

Franklin looked at the signature. "A.M.T?" he questioned.

"Yeah, Alexandra Mason, I don't know what the T stands for."

Franklin's mouth dropped. "I think I do." He dashed over to Charles's phone. He barked a few orders, then hung up. Then turning to Greg he questioned, "Are you sure this woman was Alexandra Price? *The* Alexandra Price? Have you ever met her or seen her before?"

"No," Greg replied, "but I know it was Alexandra Price." He pulled the puzzle book from his back pocket. "See, she signed my book and gave me her mother's phone number," he insisted emphatically. Franklin blew out a heavy sigh and began chuckling.

Charles spoke up, "We'll find her, Lance. We'll start with the car rentals. Do you have any idea where she might have gone? Or where she might be staying, a hotel, with friends, maybe family?"

Lance looked up. "I have no idea if Lillian lives in L.A. But I know she's close friends with Ted and Victoria Reese."

"Yeah," Greg exclaimed. "That's it, Ted Reese." Everyone looked up at him, stunned by the sudden outburst. They gave him a *how do you know?* look. "I knew I saw that car before. She was driving a vintage Austin-Healey sports car. You know the kind, the ones with the steering wheel on the right side." He stopped and considered, "Ah, the left side, no, the right side." He shrugged. "Whatever, I remember because she talked about how easy they are to drive once you get used to it. It was a bright orange color, marmalade actually." He smiled, remembering. "With overseas tags."

Franklin nodded. "Sounds like one of Ted Reese's cars. He ships those British models over from his estate in England."

Charles nodded and jotted down the name. He flipped through his Rolodex and wrote the address. "Come on, Greg, we have work to do."

"Charles." Lance stopped him at the door as Greg continued down the hall. "Find her." Charles nodded his understanding. "Oh, and forget what I said about firing the three stooges. I'll talk to them later." He nodded again, then turned to go. "Oh, and, Charles, make damn sure Alex's name is on every entrance list from now on." Charles nodded his complete understanding. As he walked down the hall he shook his head knowingly. His boss had a serious love jones.

Franklin handed Lance the clipboard. "You'll want to see this." Lance looked down at the page of inked names. He glanced over several pages. Franklin's assistant burst through the office door, breathless. "Sorry it took so long," he apologized, handing Franklin a book, then left. Franklin nodded and opened to the title page.

The book, a rare author-signed edition of *A Pilgrimage to Heaven,* was auctioned a year ago to raise funds for the African-American Children's Relief Fund. Lance won the bid at ten thousand dollars. Franklin held the clipboard and book together. He chuckled.

Lance handed the clipboard back to him. "So, these are the people that attended this afternoon." Franklin, still laughing, leaned over and pointed out one signature in particular. "Look familiar?" He placed the book on the clipboard. "Look at the initials, The A.M. Turner and the A.M.T. Price. The initials and signatures match perfectly."

Lance was stunned. "No, it can't be that simple."

Franklin smiled. "Sometimes the simplest solution is the one most overlooked."

"Turner was here? If those three knuckleheads didn't let him in either I'll personally murder them."

"We'd better start raising bail money. 'Cause if I'm not mistaken, Alexandra Price is Mason Turner."

Lance's jaw slackened and fell open. He stared blankly at Franklin, trying desperately to comprehend his words. Slowly he eased into the nearest chair. Lance had known Franklin too well and too long. He wasn't one to openly speculate without a lot of forethought. "What makes you think Alex is Mason Turner?"

"Same exact initials and signature, A.M.T., on the clipboard and signed book jacket."

"So? I'm sure there are hundreds of thousands of people with the same initials." Lance waved his hand nonchalantly.

Franklin continued, "Look at the similarities in the signatures."

Lance studied the book and clipboard again. "The signatures look alike. But it's probably a coincidence, you'd need an expert to prove anything."

"Okay, how about this for coincidence? After you accidentally ran into Ms. Price I did a little checking around."

Lance frowned, disapproving. Franklin immediately

held his hand up to delay any objections. "Before you say anything, I routinely do background checks. It's part of my job, remember, I get paid to be cautious. Better safe than sorry." Lance nodded his reluctant agreement.

"Alexandra Price, age thirty, was named after her father, Mason Alexander Price. Her mother's maiden name is Lillian Turner. Alex's full name is Alexandra Mason Price. Another thing, Mason Turner only goes through a management attorney, Mark Summers." Lance nodded. "Guess who was also Alexandra Price's management attorney."

Lance threw his head back and started laughing. Remembering the day he overheard her speaking on the phone to someone named Mark. "Of course, Mark Summers."

Lance smiled broadly. "Circumstantial. I think you've been working too hard on this Turner thing. You're grasping at straws."

"Maybe, maybe not. You said yourself she works on the computer all the time, sometimes nonstop late into the night. Tell me, what's she writing? Her memoirs? She's been a virtual recluse for ten years. What's she been doing all that time? I know she made a lot of money in the business but even that runs out eventually." Lance frowned. "One more minor point, Mason Turner's first book gained raved reviews. It was published just a few years after she quit the business."

The idea was starting to take hold of Lance. The possibility was intriguing. Alex Price as Mason Turner. Yet threads of doubt still tugged at his mind. "She could be writing anything."

"True," Franklin agreed. "But what if she's not just writing anything?"

"It's still all circumstantial," Lance slowly added.

Franklin nodded. "Did you know that Alex attended Harvard and graduated summa cum laude with a master's degree in English literature? That's where she and Mark Summers met. Seems she was a very promising writer. As a matter of fact her final thesis was remarkably similar to Mason's first published novel.''

Lance's thought's whirled. ''As I see it,'' Franklin continued, ''there are several ways to find out for sure.'' Lance looked up, very interested. ''You could come right out and ask her or . . .'' He let the statement lie.

''Or what?'' Lance prompted.

''Mason Turner has been writing the screenplay for the book, correct?'' Lance nodded. ''Mark Summers said that the script was almost complete. That means that if Alex is Mason Turner she's been working on it, and the screenplay is somewhere in her house.''

Lance eyed Franklin. It was a stretch but the coincidences were mounting. If Alex was Mason Turner, then the screenplay would definitely be in her home office. A place to which he had total access. Lance stood and took the book from Franklin. He eyed the signatures again. Smiling, he mused, ''This is too good to be true.''

Robert Burke watched as Alexandra and Victoria put their numerous bags on the empty chairs and sat down laughing. After almost ten years, this was the second time he'd seen Alexandra Price in two weeks. He took this as a sign. She was emerging from her self-imposed exile. He was sure she was about to reenter the business. If she did, he'd be there poised with pen and contract.

He smiled knowingly. Her strategy was flawless. Just as before, she had positioned herself brilliantly. After an absence of several years she reinvented herself into a teen idol and returned to the business. A few years later she went on to superstardom drawing in millions of dollars. Now, he was positive, she was about to do it again.

* * *

"Shopping with you is truly an experience," Alex lamented before scanning the extensive menu. "My feet are killing me."

"Now, now, let's not be disagreeable," Victoria returned as she scrutinized the entire Four Seasons Restaurant in a single glance. "Shopping on Rodeo is a spiritual regenerator. No matter how dismal the day the Drive has the power to rejuvenate you."

Alex held her menu aside, pondering aloud, "I still don't know about that gold pantsuit and matching bustier."

"Are you kidding? You looked marvelous." Victoria complimented. "That golden shade made your complexion radiant. It's perfect for you." The waiter introduced himself and placed lemon-garnished bottled water in front of them. He recited the day's specials and promised to be right back. "I'm glad you decided to visit for a few days."

"Me too. My mother's delirious. She and I are driving up the coast this weekend. Just the two of us. I'm really looking forward to it." The waiter returned with a bottle of Dom Perignon champagne and two glasses. Alex looked up, perplexed. The waiter relayed the message, "Compliments of Mr. Robert Burke." He nodded toward the table in the corner. Burke raised his glass to salute. "Alex frowned. "I don't think . . ."

Victoria laid her newly manicured fingers on Alex's hand. "This is Tinseltown, darling, just smile and toast." Reluctantly Alex complied.

The waiter wrote down their dinner choices, then disappeared into the back. He appeared seconds later at Burke's table. "Here's my photo and résumé, Mr. Burke." Burke took the young man's credentials and carefully placed them in his briefcase. "Make sure the ladies' meal is on my tab."

"Yes, sir," the overzealous waiter pledged faithfully. Burke stood and strolled over to the two women. "Good evening, ladies." Alex twitched her nose; the odorous scent of his strong cologne had arrived moments before he did. Burke leaned down and air-kissed Victoria's cheek, then grasped Alex's tense hand and kissed it.

"You two are definitely a breath of fresh air," he vowed.

Victoria smiled easily. "You always know just the right thing to say, Burke, thank you for the champagne. It was very thoughtful of you." Alex also mumbled her gratitude.

"Alex, you look especially lovely. I wonder if I might venture to invite you both for late cocktails this evening, if you're not otherwise engaged, that is."

"I'm busy, Burke," Alex snapped.

"We already have plans this evening. But thank you for the invitation," Victoria added diplomatically.

"All right, maybe another time then." He nodded and dipped his head. "Have a good evening."

After he walked away, pausing several times to chat with other restaurant patrons, Alex glared at Victoria. "I can't believe the audacity of that man."

"Remember, dear, this is Tinseltown, no one is what they seem and nothing is ever real," Victoria said as their meal arrived. Alex shook her head disgustedly. Truer words had never been uttered. Except Burke was and would always be a real snake.

By the time dessert arrived, Alex and Victoria had returned to their jovial spirits. They chatted endlessly about their shopping spree. Two men approached their table. "Alex, Mrs. Reese." The women looked up. Charles Taylor and his brother stood patiently beside the table.

"Charles?" Alex said, raising her head up to look at the mountainous man. Then peering around his side, she smiled. "Hello again, Greg."

Greg beamed with admiration. "Hi, Alex." Charles looked at his brother in annoyance.

"Alex, I would personally like to extend my sincere apologies for this afternoon's misunderstanding. Had we been informed of your arrival, I would have personally picked you up at the airport and delivered you to your destination."

She smiled at his graciousness. "Thank you, Charles. That's very kind of you. I appreciate your coming down here to tell me that."

"Also," he added, lowering his voice several octaves, "my employer would like you to join him for"—he looked down at the dessert plates—"cocktails this evening."

She smiled pleasantly. "That's very inviting, Charles, but I already have plans this evening. Maybe the next time I'm in town."

Charles Taylor's frown was deep and unsettling. "I see. If you should change you mind"—he handed her his card—"please contact me directly. Again my apologies. Good evening, Mrs. Reese, Alex." Greg waved and followed his brother out of the restaurant.

"Somebody wants to see you, real bad," Victoria teased.

Alex pushed her half-eaten mango-mousse tart away. "Let's get out of here." She looked around for their waiter. He promptly appeared. "Our check please." She grabbed her purse.

He smiled at the pending message. "Mr. Robert Burke has already taken care of the tab, Ms. Price, Mrs. Reese." The two woman looked at each other. Alex fumed and Victoria chuckled. "Welcome back to Hollywood, darling."

Alex rolled her eyes and grabbed her packages. "Come on, I need to do more shopping." Victoria smiled in agreement; nothing eased a broken heart like shopping. She picked up her bags and followed.

Daylong shopping was strenuous enough, but daylong

shopping with Victoria was suicide. By the time they drove back to the Reese estate there was literally no room left in the Rolls Royce. An exhausted Alex collapsed in the library as Ted and Victoria attended a party. Alex begged off, pleading total exhaustion vowing to spend the evening with a good book.

"I heard you had plans this evening." The deep voice was unmistakable. Alex looked over the top of her book. Lance stood at the entrance of the library. He stepped inside and closed the double doors behind him. The thought of Alex as Mason Turner ran through his mind. He grinned.

"Hello, Lance." She looked back down and continued reading. "I do have plans."

"You're right," he confirmed. "Get your things."

She looked up again. "Excuse me?"

"I said, get your things."

She laughed. "Do you seriously expect me to drop everything because you say so?"

A knee-melting, toe-curling grin spread across his face as he walked closer. "Yes, as a matter of fact I do." He took her hand and gently pulled her up. The book dropped to the floor. He bent down to pick it up. It was a signed edition of Mason Turner's first book. Lance smiled mindfully and placed the book on the side table.

His eyes focused on her tender lips. They begged to be kissed. He complied, kissing her passionately. "I'm sorry about the misunderstanding this afternoon. My assistant had no idea who you were." The memory of seeing him with the young model in his arms stiffened her. He felt her withdrawal. "What is it?"

"What are we really doing here, Lance?"

"What do you mean?"

"I mean us, you and me, together. I don't like wasting my time. What exactly do you want?" Wordlessly he smiled his answer. She understood completely as she looked at him suspiciously. "And Amber? Do you want her too?"

"Not everything is as it seems."

"Meaning?"

"Meaning, Amber and I are friends. We're together from time to time because it benefits our careers mutually. She's my fallback date when needed and it's an advantage to her career to be seen with me."

She nodded her understanding. His explanation seemed plausible. Spin doctors and publicists constantly created sham relationships to benefit their clients. "I still can't go with you, Lance. I'm waiting for an important phone call," she said truthfully, expecting a call from her yacht's captain in Florida.

He looked into her soulful eyes for a sign. They betrayed nothing. But of course she was a consummate actress. "Fine, then I'll stay here. I'll have Victoria make up a guest bedroom." He turned to leave.

Her heart jumped from her chest. "No!" she blurted out quickly, then more sedately continued, "That's not a good idea."

Lance smiled to himself. *Score.* At that moment he knew he had her. He turned back to face her. The emotion on her face was obvious. "Why not, Alex?" His voice was soft and soothing. "I thought you wanted to see me. You did earlier."

Her stomach lurched and her heart pounded. "I changed my mind." He came closer. Her mouth still felt the arousing impact of his probing tongue. His finger touched her lips. She stepped back.

"What made you change your mind?" He stepped closer.

"It didn't occur to me that you might be seeing someone else, romantically." She stepped back again.

"I am," he confessed, stepping closer and taking her in his arms again. Her heart sank until he continued, "I'm seeing you."

Forty minutes later she walked into the foyer of his Beverly Hills mansion. The massive structure was deserted. There was no evidence of the earlier celebration. As soon as they stepped inside he pulled her firmly to his body. "Welcome home," he proclaimed as he looked at the soft planes of her face. His thumbs stroked the length of her back. "Alex, you are my treasure. You alone have fulfilled my every desire. Running into you in the middle of that snowstorm was the best thing that ever happened to me."

She sighed, letting herself be swept away by the feel of his loving embrace. "I love you, Lance," she announced.

I love you, too, he mouthed silently. The remorse of his dishonesty tightened in his throat. It would not allow him to return her tender words aloud. "Come on, it's late." He led her up the staircase. "We'll get the rest of your things tomorrow." He opened double doors to reveal the huge master suite. "As for tonight . . ." She smiled, knowing at that moment, she was hopelessly addicted to him. And he knew it.

Franklin Moore leaned over his desk showing concern. "I don't know, Lance, this doesn't sound like you. You should just tell her your suspicions and produce the film together. I don't trust Jake Marrows. He's too much like his boss. This whole thing sounds like trouble if you ask me."

The original plan was simple. Get next to Alex Price, seduce her, persuade her to find out Mason Turner's identity from Lillian, then find Turner and get the book rights. The revised plan was even simpler. All Lance had to do was pretend that nothing had changed. He'd get Alex to sign over the book rights to his production studio, then . . . then . . . what? He moved back to the office chair and sat down.

He ran his wavering hand over his thick black curly hair. "I know, I don't trust him either. At the time it seemed like the only way to get to Turner. I still can't believe I agreed to do this." He stretched his long legs out and sank deeper into the chair. Putting his hands behind his neck, he continued, "I don't want to hurt her. She's just . . . so . . ."

"Just so what?" Franklin asked.

"Captivating. Compelling. Exciting. Alluring." He smiled, remembering his time with her. "I don't know. That's just it. She's confusing as hell."

"Sounds more like you're the one that's confused. What were you looking for when you started this thing with her? Better yet, how did you think this was going to end once you got what you wanted?"

Lance sat up and seriously looked at him, long and hard. He began regretting his confession to Franklin. "I don't know. I guess, maybe I thought we'd just go our separate ways."

"So you didn't consider that one of you might become emotionally attached and actually fall in love?"

"No one's going to get hurt, Franklin. I'm just going to finish what I started."

"It's a little late for that, don't you think? You know it's not that simple anymore. What about Jake, are you going to tell him what you suspect?"

"No, of course not."

"Are you still going to sign with him?"

"What do you mean?"

"Technically Jake did as he promised, he put you in contact with Mason Turner. Whether he knew the identity or not is beside the point."

Lance lowered his head. "Yeah, I know. I have no choice. I promise you she'll never know what happened."

"So you still intend to get the book, how?"

He nodded. "I'll innocently mention that I'm interested in purchasing the book rights from Morgan Turner. And that I'm in negotiations with Mark Summers." He stood up. "This book is dynamite and in the right hands . . . who knows? It could be another *Citizen Cane* or *Gone With the Wind*. It just needs, no, it deserves the right production team and I can put that team together. I have the know-how, the experience, the connections." He collapsed back in the chair.

Franklin shook his head. "The best-laid plans seldom turn out as we expect."

"Nobody's going to get hurt, I promise."

"Are you trying to convince me, or yourself?" Lance looked at Franklin. "It still sounds to me like you're using her." Franklin lit a fat cigar. "You know what? This whole thing sounds like something your brother would have cooked up."

A fowl taste entered Lance's mouth. Franklin was right. This was something Shawn would cook up just to get what he wanted. But he was nothing like his half brother. He never used people, at least not until now. Lance sat looking dejected.

After brooding a few more minutes he stood and walked to the door. "I'll see you later, Franklin. I have a meeting with Burke in an hour; then I'm heading back to New York."

"If anything new develops give me a call. Good luck," Franklin called out just as the door was closing. "You're gonna need it this time."

Chapter Fifteen

Lillian was pleased to see a familiar face at the reception desk. It had been years since she'd last set foot in this place. The receptionist immediately recognized her and allowed her access to the private penthouse elevators. She stepped onto the elevator dreading the next half hour as the hushed soft music did little to calm her frayed nerves.

Lillian eyed herself in the elevator's surrounding mirrors. The charcoal-gray suit was classic Dior and tailored perfectly. She looked down the length of her slim body. A vibrantly colored scarf draped casually around her neck and flowing down her back completed her fashionable appearance. Impatiently, she stroked the back of her short stylish haircut and tapped the toe of her gray pumps. This was the last place she thought she'd ever come.

The elevator came to a halt and the doors finally slid open. The first thing she spotted was an enormous black-and-white photo of Lance Morgan. His smiling face beamed down at her from its lofty-positioned frame. Lillian walked down the corridor noting several more famous faces peering down, welcoming the viewer to a promising career in the performing arts. She continued down the hall of fame when she stopped, spotting a large black-and-white photo of her daughter. It was a candid shot from the set of her television series. Lillian shook her head in astonishment. "How typical."

Lillian's stomach twisted angrily as she entered the glass-enclosed private offices of the Robert Burke Talent Agency. She looked around. The room was crowded with beautiful young portfolio-toting men and women, all waiting anxiously for their bid for stardom. A young woman of about twenty looked up at her from behind a large wooded desk and smiled. She stopped filing her nails and with cherry-red lips puckered, she spoke. "Yes, may I help you?" Lillian acknowledged the woman's pleasant smile, replying, "Yes, my name is Lillian Turner-Price and I'd like to speak with Robert Burke please."

The receptionist looked down at her open calendar and traced her long bright red nail down the day's appointments page. Lillian's name was not there. "Mr. Burke is in conference at the moment and you don't appear to be on my list, Ms. Price. To what is this in reference?"

Lillian smiled graciously. "It's Ms. Turner-Price and this is a private matter."

"I see." The secretary's polite demeanor changed abruptly. "Well, why don't you tell me what it is and I'll decide whether or not it's a private matter? Or perhaps you'd like to speak with Mr. Burke's attorney. His office is just down the hall." She pointed the long nail file in the direction of the elevators.

"No. I'd like to speak with Mr. Burke directly."

The young woman looked down at the calendar again, then back at Lillian. "As I said before, Ms. Price, Mr. Burke is in an important conference at the moment and can't be disturbed. You don't seem to be on his calendar today; perhaps I can make an appointment for you. He's booked solid for the next few months, but I can pencil you down for—"

Lillian's precariously teetered temper spiked. "First of all, dear, and for the last time, my name is *Turner-*

Price, secondly I do not wish an appointment with Burke. I simply require a few moments of his time. I suggest you inform him that I'm waiting." Lillian turned on her heels and strolled over to the seating area.

Surprised by the older woman's sudden dismissal, the secretary sucked her teeth and rolled her eyes, then went back to her nail filing. Lillian picked up a trade magazine and angrily flipped through the pages. Five minutes later Burke's door swung open with loud exuberant laughter. All eyes glanced up as Lance Morgan stepped out of his office. Lillian's arched brow raised slightly in a curious expression of interest. Lance and Burke shook hands; then Burke went back into his office. Lance disappeared down the hall.

Lillian stood and walked back to the desk. The secretary stood as she approached, smoothed her microshort skirt and sauntered to the door of Burke's inner sanctum. She knocked once, then entered. "Burke, I'm sorry to disturb you but there's a woman outside that insists on seeing you."

Burke never looked up, he just absently waved his hand dismissingly. The receptionist was just about to exit when he called out stopping her, "Hold, what's this woman's name."

"Lillian Price."

Burke smiled his lopsided grin. "Lillian Turner-Price," he corrected. "Send her in."

Burke stood and walked to the office door. He'd been expecting her. He opened it and smiled as Lillian breezed in without a word. She stopped in front of his desk. "You look stunning, Lillian. But then you always were an incredibly sexy and attractive woman," he confessed truthfully. She remained silent. "Can I offer you a drink?"

"I'm sure you were expecting me so skip the pleasantries and get to the point, Burke."

He came closer and spoke softly in her ear. "What

do you mean, Lillian?" She stepped away in disgust. "I am genuinely delighted to see you."

"You know exactly what I'm talking about." She pulled a white envelope from her gray leather purse and held it out.

"Honestly, Lillian, I . . ." She tossed an open enveloped onto his desk. "Oh, that," he stated. "And here I was thinking this was a social call. I'd hoped you'd finally missed me and decided to come to your senses."

"Either get to the point or I'm leaving."

He went around to his desk and sat down. "Please." He gestured for her to have a seat. She remained standing. He shrugged. "As you wish. It has recently come to my attention that your daughter has been keeping herself very busy. I understand she's decided to return to her previous profession." Lillian glared at him. "And as for you, my dear, I merely sent the card to offer my most sincere congratulations."

Lillian crossed her arms over her chest. "That's it?" He nodded. She turned to leave.

"Oh, and, Lillian, one more thing. I'd also like to offer my services."

She turned back around. "I beg your pardon?"

"I received a script not too long ago. I think it would be the perfect venue for Alexandra's return to film. I'd like you to mention it to her. And since she's going to need more than you can possibly give her as an agent, I'd also like to offer my representative services."

Lillian laughed heartily. "I believe you've been smoking too many of your funny little cigarettes. Do you honestly believe that for one moment she'd actually consider you to represent her? With anything?"

"Why wouldn't she? I am the idea candidate. I have the connections, the know-how and the means. I can turn her back into the star she deserves to be. The money and offers will come pouring in. She'll be able to name her own price."

"Don't overstep your bounds, Burke. An agent can't

negotiate a deal without a client. You don't have a client."

"Think of the money."

"You still don't get it, do you? It's not about the money, Burke. It was never about the money. It's about the love of the craft. She loved acting and performing and you stripped that away from her."

"No!" he hollered. "You"—he pointed accusingly across the desk—"it was you and Alex who decided to quit the business. I had nothing to do with that press conference."

"Given our options, you gave us little choice in the matter."

"I wanted you here with me, by my side. All you had to do was accept my offer. Together we could have ruled this industry and Alexandra would have been immortalized as a cultural icon."

"This is getting us nowhere," Lillian said, turning to leave.

He stood, slamming his fist on the desk. "I gave you myself, Lillian! I gave you love!" He came around the front of the desk and softened. "I loved you, Lillian. I still do." He fingered the brightly colored scarf.

She snatched the chiffon material from his fingers. "You don't love me, Burke. You never did. You only loved yourself. You used me, just like you use everybody in you life."

Their heated uproar suddenly calmed, leaving the office blanketed in silence. The two glared at each other. Burke finally smiled. "Be that as it may, it's all water under the bridge. Ancient history, long forgotten as far as I'm concerned. By the way," he added casually, "I understand that Alexandra is seeing Lance Morgan."

"You shouldn't believe everything you hear."

"Tell me, Lillian, how did you acquire Lance Morgan's contract?" She looked into his eyes knowing exactly what he was implying. Her eyes filled with pain.

"You honestly believe I'd offer my daughter up for

an account?" Flabbergasted, Lillian turned to leave. When she got to the doorknob Burke put his hand on top of hers.

"Lillian, wait. I'm sorry. I didn't mean that. I hope you believe me."

She never responded, just walked out of his office. Burke watched as the delicate scarf fluttered in her wake. She was still the most perfect woman he'd ever met.

"Hey, Burke," Jake said, pivoting around from his seat on the secretary's desk. Burke eyed Jake angrily, took one last glance at the receding Lillian, then went back into his office and closed the door. Jake turned and watched Lillian walk down the long hall. He smiled menacingly. The look Burke gave Lillian was very interesting. He made a mental note to jot that information down in his book.

He hopped down for his perch and followed Burke. He knocked once, then opened the door and stuck his head in. "Hey, Burke." He strolled to a seat across from the desk. Burke looked up abruptly.

"What do you want?"

Jake grinned. "Wasn't that Lillian Turner-Price I just saw leaving here?"

Burke glared at him.

Jake continued grinning. "I was just curious, I hope we're not considering a merger, are we?"

"*We?* There is no *we!*" Burke thundered, pointing his finger across the desk. "What I do with my company is none of your damn business. I suggest you get out of here and sign Morgan."

Jake stood and strolled back to his tiny office still grinning. He sat at his desk, propped his feet up and pulled out him notebook. Toying with his pen, he drummed it several times, then began scribbling random thoughts. There was something going on. He could feel it. Lillian would never come to this office without good reason. Suddenly it was very important for him to know that reason. He picked up the phone and dialed the familiar number.

An hour later he sat in a heavily padded booth across the table from his friend at the eatery they'd frequented since their early high school days. The sassy waitress placed their food orders on the table and provocatively sashayed away. The two friends smiled at each other knowingly.

Some things never change. The place looked exactly the same, same tables, same dishes and same waitress. The overstuffed buxom blonde had been working there since the place opened over thirty years ago. She was a vision transfixed in time with her retro beehive hair and gum-popping attitude. Although twenty-five pounds heavier, she still squeezed into the same size uniform.

"God," Linda declared, lighting another cigarette, "I haven't been in this place in years." She took a deep drag from the tobacco stick, then blew the fumes across the table. "What made you decide to meet here?" She globbed half the bottle of ketchup onto her fries and burger.

Jake frowned, sickened by the sight of her hemorrhaging plate. He looked around the diner thoughtfully. "I don't know. I just felt like seeing some of the old haunts. Did you want to go someplace else?"

"No, no, this is great," Linda squeaked after another drag from the cigarette. Jake grimaced as she spoke with her filled mouth open. "It just feels kind of weird being back in the old neighborhood." She giggled excitedly, stamped out the butt in the ashtray, then leaning over to whisper, "I feel like I'm playing hooky again."

Jake looked around. The small diner was empty except for a few school-age teens sitting around just as they'd done almost ten years earlier. Reflecting inwardly, Jake summarized his life. How far had he really come? A smile slit his thin lips. In the span of eight years he was positioned and poised for his boldest move ever, his own talent agency.

After enduring two wasted years at community college he dropped out for the quick, easy money Tinseltown promised. He immediately went to work at the Robert Burke Agency as a gofer in the mailroom. Within three years he worked his way up the ladder to the assistant of Burke's highest paid associates. When he realized that there was no special training to be an agent, it was only a matter of time before he nudged his boss out and assumed his position. After all, an agent's life was wielding power and making deals. It wasn't rocket science. It was skill. Something he learned from the best.

Burke was Jake's mentor in the early years. Once considered one of the most powerful men in Tinseltown, Burke was his hero. Jake wanted to be just like him, ruthless and powerful. The mere mention of his name invoked grown men to sweat bullets. His Machiavellian power reached out in all directions. There wasn't a single part of the business he didn't dominate. But now, his adamant pursuit of Lance Morgan was pathetic. In Jake's eyes Burke had lost his edge. He had apparently forgotten the first rule of the game, that there are no rules. The killer instinct Burke once had was gone. He was an embarrassment to the entire profession.

Yeah, he thought to himself arrogantly. *Burke has grown old and gotten soft. It's time for younger, more aggressive blood to take over.* Jake smiled at the possibilities. The world would be at his feet.

"Jake!" Linda pouted in that annoying way that sent a cringe down Jake's back. "You're not even listening to me, are you? Here I've been telling you all the latest gossip and you've been ignoring me." She tossed a greasy ketchup-soaked french fry back onto the plate. "I have a good mind to get up and leave."

"No, baby," he cooed, placing his hand lovingly on top of hers to placate her irritation. He stopped speaking. Disgusted, he withdrew his ketchup-soiled hand. Linda noted Jake's expression of annoyance. She sucked her teeth, rolled her eyes and mumbled weakly, "Sorry."

Jake forced a smile, then grabbed several paper napkins. "Don't worry about it. I was just remembering how you and I used to sit here all day dreaming of the time when we'd rule this town together. Just you and me." Linda giggled loudly. He smiled brightly, then hardened his expression and saddened. "But, it looks like that's all it was, just a dream."

Linda immediately responded. "No, Jake, it will happen, you'll see. We can do it, just like we planned, the two of us together. Just like you promised. You'll be my agent and I'll be your number-one client. The name Linda Beale will be up in lights and you'll be right there beside me. After a few years in the spotlight we can be married, have a family, then live happily ever after. It'll be just like we dreamed."

Jake smiled as a tiny ember of remorse nipped at his frayed conscience. Linda was the least talented person he knew and she wasn't particularly pretty either. She was bone thin, flat chested and wore a ton of makeup to hide her bad skin. How she could conceivably believe that she could be a star was beyond him.

For years she begged him to introduce her to Burke. But Jake refused. He told her it would be a conflict of interest and too distracting for the two of them to be at the same agency. To get her off his back he suggested she go to Lillian Turner-Price since she handled new talent. So she did. To his surprise Lillian told her the unvarnished truth about her chances of making it in the business. Though extremely tactful, Lillian had still destroyed Linda's only dream. Disappointed, she cried on his shoulder for days.

Jake was surprised by Lillian's honesty. It wasn't the nature of his business as far as he was concerned. Hyping dreams, deluding fantasies and indulging egos, those were his strengths, and he was good at it. He was damn good. He made losers believe the impossible. They all trusted his assurances that all dreams could come true. Everyone had a dream based on their reality. He simply

exploited that dream, knowing that money was the only
true reality in Hollywood.

"I don't know, Linda." He lowered his head dramatically. "It looks like all our dreams will go up in smoke
if I can't get Lance Morgan to sign an exclusive contract.
If he goes with your boss, we're through."

"That's just it," she squealed excitedly. "That's what
I was telling you." Another cigarette went up in smoke.
"I overheard Lillian and Mavis talking in her office
earlier. Lillian plans to withdraw her proposal of representation." Jake looked stunned. That wasn't in the
plan. Lance was supposed to string Lillian along until
she gave up Turner's identity. Linda took his expression
for confusion. "That means that she no longer—"
Linda stated slowly as if speaking to a child.

Jake held up his hand to interrupt her. "I know what
the wording means, Linda. This *is* my business, remember," he stated emphatically. "My question is why?"

"Who cares why?" she said, blowing smoke across the
table. "The important thing is that Lance is still free to
sign with us." Jake looked at her crossly. "I mean sign
with you," she quickly corrected herself, nervously
fluffing her dull lifeless hair.

"No, no." Jake's mind buzzed with ideas, schemes
and scenarios. He muttered aloud, "Something's going
on. I can feel it. That's why Burke was so closemouthed
about Lillian's visit. There's something more happening
here. And if Burke's involved, that means it was an epic
deal and big money. The question is, what? What don't
I know?" He spoke rhetorically but Linda shrugged her
shoulders to answer anyway.

She watched Jake intently, then rolled her eyes to the
grease-caked ceiling and stamped out the cigarette. She
hated when Jake started acting like this. He totally forgot
she was in the room. He sat there like a dazed zombie
scribbling in his notebook acting as if he were trying to
figure out some great universal mystery. Linda sighed
remorsefully. She never should have told him about

Lillian's proposal. That would have fixed him good. Why should she keep helping him? What had he done for her?

For years he'd promised to sign her with Burke and make her a star. But there was always one excuse after another. Linda sucked her teeth loudly. Jake continued scrawling in his book. When he suggested she take the job with Lillian she should have been suspicious. But she was in love and they'd just returned from a fabulous weekend in Mexico. She knew he was using her. It's just that sometimes it hurt more than other times.

While absently drawing circles in the blob of ketchup with a french fry Linda wondered why she stayed with Jake. He wasn't all that good looking, at least by Hollywood standards, and he looked nothing like he did when they were in school. The once mousy hair was now thick, bleached blond, cut and perfectly styled. His crooked teeth were straightened, capped and polished monthly. His pale eyes were now sea-blue contact lenses. And his clothes were selected and tailored by a professional service. Nothing about him was genuine except his temper.

But he had money and he was smart, even if he didn't finish school. He had street smarts and always said that book smarts could only take you so far. To be rich, really rich, filthy, disgustingly rich, you had to have the kind of drive that growing up in the streets gives you.

Linda pulled out her favorite newspaper and scanned the pages for her horoscope. She read the smudged ink, ". . . *A new love one offers you adventure . . . seize the opportunity.*" She looked over to Jake, who was still engrossed with his book. Disappointed, she tossed the paper beside her and looked around the emptying diner again. Several patrons still lingered at the counter while others sat in nearby booths. She paused to smile at a young pimple-faced teen eyeing her as he stood by the bathroom doors. Linda smiled and blushed, then slyly looked down at her half-eaten burger and fries. She picked up her vanilla shake and slurped the last of it through the plastic straw. The sound made Jake scowl as he half turned his back to her.

Linda clumsily returned the glass to the table. "I'm going to the bathroom," she proclaimed.

Jake nodded and pulled out his phone. "Don't be too long, I need to get back up town."

Linda didn't say anything. She knew that once Jake began talking on the phone she had a good fifteen to twenty minutes before he missed her. She grabbed the shoulder strap of her purse and flounced toward the back of the diner. The infatuated teen leered at her as she passed. She winked and he followed. Jake watched the interaction between the two. He shook his head thinking, *Linda will never change. She was a tramp in high school and she always will be.*

Alex dropped her suitcases in the middle of the living room floor. She kicked off her shoes and padded barefoot to the fish tank. Watching the fish swim always raised her spirits. She was exhausted and glad to finally be home. She sprinkled flaked algae and shrimp into the tank and watched as the brightly colored fish eagerly swam to the surface to nibble at their evening meal.

She'd been gone longer than she anticipated. After spending time with Lance, she joined her mother on Santa Catalina Island, then flew to Miami to make arrangements for her trip to Italy. Thankfully she had arranged for Mrs. Fletcher to take Coal and stop by daily to feed the fish. Absently she watched as a brightly colored angelfish nibbled a large flake, then gobbled it up in one bite.

Alex smiled, remembering her first few days at her mother's home on Catalina. They took a private tour around the island in a glass-bottom boat. It was an incredible time. The colorful sea life was unforgettable.

Afterward they visited the Palomar Mountains and gazed through the world's largest telescope at the sunset.

The originally planned weekend turned into one week, then eventually into two weeks. During the weekdays Lillian drove into her Los Angeles office and Alex stayed home and wrote. On weekends the two spent most of the time shopping on Melrose or strolling down Wilshire, the Miracle Mile. For the first time in a long time she didn't regret traveling to the West Coast. She didn't even mind when several reporters cornered her and her mother outside a famous restaurant.

They questioned her about rumors linking her with Shawn Anderson and rumors about her return to acting. She easily rebuffed them as absurd. One reporter asked about her rumored relationship to Lance Morgan. The question caught her off guard. But forever the proficient actress, she gave an Oscar-caliber performance with her denial. The reporters believed her, Lillian didn't.

Their last evening together, the two sipped champagne and sat out on the verandah surrounded by age-old palm trees. It was a gorgeous peaceful night. Alex sighed happily gazing out at the marina; she always adored her mother's home. The 1920s four-bedroom Italian chateau was Old World elegance. The airy Mediterranean kitchen overlooked the open courtyard complete with Italian tiles, grapevine trellises and Tuscany-style fountains. "Lance Morgan?" her mother stated matter-of-factly. "Do you want to tell me about it?"

"Now don't you start," Alex warned jokingly.

"Darling, I'm your mother. I trained you. I know when you're acting. The other day, that one reporter hit on something, didn't he?"

Knowing it was impossible to fool her mother, she confessed. "Yes, he did."

"Is that why Lance is considering me as his agent?"

"No, of course not," she contended emphatically. "We talked about your agency long before things got . . ." She stopped.

"Before things got what, Alex?" Lillian questioned. She didn't answer right away. Her mother ventured to guess, "Before things got . . . serious?" Alex grimaced and lowered her head. She wasn't fooling her mother any more than she was fooling herself. She was serious about Lance. "Be careful, Alex, Lance is an incredible actor and a remarkable talent. And I'm sure he's a wonderful man, but he isn't exactly new at this, you are."

"I'll be careful, I promise." She knew it was already too late, her heart was already hurting. Lillian's heart went out to her daughter. She could see it in her eyes, it was already too late.

Alex watched the fish a few moments more, then turned, seeing a reflection in the glass. Lance stood at the top of the stairs staring down at her. "Hello," she said. His expression was unreadable.

She cocked her head to the side, resisting the over-whelming urge to run to him. "I suppose Victoria let you in."

He grinned seductively while demanding, "Come here."

She shook her head no, then stammered, "I . . . I don't think so."

"Come here," he repeated, taking a another step down.

She remained still but continued to shake her head no. "How about a game of chess?" He stepped down again and continued. "Checkers?" When he reached the bottom step she blurted out, "I know, how about a rousing game of charades?"

Ignoring her playful suggestions, he abruptly closed the distance between them. He captured her around the waist and drew her to his body. "You know what I want." His kiss was burning, meant to seer his passion forever on her lips. His tongue searched and demanded entrance to her moist domain.

She pulled back, breathless, evading his persistent advances. "When did you get here?"

He dipped to her lips again. "Yesterday," he muttered as she leaned back avoiding his kiss.

"You've been here all day!" He made another attempt to capture her mouth. "I thought you were supposed to be in New York."

"I was. But I left early, I needed to see you." He kissed her neck and shoulders, removing her light jacket.

"Why?" she asked.

He gave her a tremendous hug. "Umm, I just needed to feel your arms around me." Alex's long eyelashes fluttered, then closed. This man could sweet-talk a fish to walk the Sahara.

"Why, has something happened with the film's post-production?" she asked.

"No, that's in the can. I did the voice-overs and reshoots a few days before you arrived in L.A. I still have some junkets and promotional interviews to do but other than that, it's done." He released her and they sat down on the living room sofa.

"So? What is it then?"

He couldn't look at her when he did this so he turned her around and laid her back against his chest. "It's my next project. More accurately, I *hope* it'll be my next project. My production company is in the process of negotiating the purchase of a book and it's taking longer than I expected."

Alex picked up the Chinese silk pillow, fluffed it, then answered, "Really? What book?"

"A Pilgrimage to Heaven."

Alex gasped silently as her heart skipped a beat. She tensed, squeezed the pillow nervously, then sat up. Outwardly, seemingly unaware of her reaction, he added, "Have you read it?" She nodded. He continued nonchalantly. "Of course. I forgot," he lied, "you know Mason Turner, don't you?" Alex closed her eyes. Lance was negotiating for her book. She couldn't believe the coincidence. She didn't remember seeing his name on any of the paperwork she got from Mark.

"So," she began, prompted by ego, "I gather you liked the book?"

Lance laughed. "You could say that. Ever since my first reading I was hooked on the characters. The book was so visual I could actually see the action driven forward. I couldn't put it down. Ideas for the settings, the costumes, the score were instantaneous. After reading it again I immediately called my manager, Franklin Moore. He had the same reaction. I guess everybody did, that's why the book is so popular."

"Maybe, or maybe it's because nobody knows who really wrote it. You know, the mystery angle."

"I doubt it. Maybe that was true when the first Turner book came out years ago. But even then the story stood on its own, and the subsequent film merely cemented the work. After the first few pages of *A Pilgrimage to Heaven,* you're so absorbed in the story that the anonymity of the author doesn't matter. All you care about are the characters. That's what good writing is supposed to do."

Lance continued, "Anyway, Franklin and I are still negotiating even though the studios have offered bids." He waited for her to confess but she remained silent. "I guess I should look at it as a good sign that Turner hasn't just gone with the big money. The studio's pockets are much deeper than mine." Lance closed his eyes. He knew what he was doing was wrong.

Just as he knew it was wrong to knowingly arrive a day early and get Victoria to let him in. All this was so he could prove Mason Turner's identity and gain an edge in the bidding process. Franklin was right, his morals were beginning to break down. It did sound more like something Shawn would do. However, this time it wasn't Shawn manipulating people to get what he wanted, it was him.

As soon as Lance saw the book and partial script sitting on Alex's desk his qualms were silenced. Alex Price was the infamous Mason Turner.

It took less than an hour to read the screenplay. He was riveted, it was impossible to put the pages down. Although it wasn't quite finished, the part he had read was incredible. The words flowed from the pages and melted into his heart and mind. The visual imagery, the attention to detail and the intense dialogue were outstanding. This was an actor's fantasy role and a director's dream.

"I'm sure everything will work out, Lance," she offered, interrupting his wayward thoughts.

"The thing is, I really believe in this project. The concept is original, the story line is rich with interesting characters and the dialogue is moving. I know I can make a great film. I've already put together an award-winning preproduction team." He took a slowing breath after pleading his case. "I'm sorry, I don't know why I'm burdening you with all of this. I guess I just needed to get it off my chest."

She turned and placed her delicate hand on his cheek. "You really want this, don't you?" This was it. His last chance, he could turn back and stop this whole charade now. He wanted to but the thought of securing the book was too enticing. He smiled and nodded yes.

"Then you'll get it," she promised. Lance was stunned. Her statement was precisely what he wanted to hear. She'd just verbally agreed to sell him her book.

Chapter Sixteen

A sleek black chauffeured car slowly maneuvered its way up the long driveway, then pulled to a stop at the front walkway. From the open door, Alex anxiously watched as the sole passenger leaned over the seat to speak to the driver. Afterward the small stout driver got out, opened the trunk and pulled out a small paisley overnight bag. The lone passenger emerged from the car's backseat and looked up at Alex's sparkling eyes.

Alex hurried down the front steps to welcome her guest in a loving embrace. "Look at you, you look absolutely radiant. I guess this New Jersey weather really appeals to you."

"Thank you, so do you." They hugged again. "You look fabulous," Alex exclaimed. "Come on inside. I've got lunch all ready." Alex took the overnight bag and they walked arm in arm up the steps. The curious driver climbed back into the car and drove down the path. He watched in the rearview mirror as the two disappeared into the large home. He smiled to himself thinking about the long drive back to New York and the enormous tip he just received.

Alex poured cold tea into two iced glasses, then added a slice of lemon and a fresh mint sprig. She carried them to the den and sat down on the sofa. She offered the drink to her mother. "Here you go."

"Thank you." Lillian sipped her tea immediately. "Umm, this is really good. What's in here, seltzer?"

"Lemon seltzer, it gives the tea a little zing."

"I like it." She sighed heavily and reached out to hold her daughter's hand. "You really look great, Alex. You look contented."

"Umm, I don't know if that's a good thing or a bad thing."

Lillian smiled. "It's a very good thing." The conversation lapsed as the two sipped their tea. "Oh," Lillian added, "I went to the Hills Playhouse and saw the actor you told me about."

Alex crinkled her nose questioningly. "Greg Taylor, was he any good?"

"Actually he was very good. He was the best thing about the production. I plan to attend the show again when I get back to L.A. If I still think he looks good, and I'm sure I will, I'll give him a call."

"That's great, he seemed like a really nice guy. I'm happy for him." Alex went into the kitchen and cut two small slices of New York cheesecake. So, tell me, what brings you to my neck of the woods? I know it wasn't just to tell me about Greg Taylor."

"Work, what else?" Lillian called out behind her. "I have a few clients I need to see and I wanted to take in a couple of Off-Broadway shows. There's one in particular I'm interested in seeing. And I hoped I could talk my favorite daughter into going with me."

Alex grabbed a couple of napkins and returned to the den. "Your only daughter, unless you've also come to tell me I'm going to be a big sister."

Lillian gasped, drawing her hand to her heart. "Bite your tongue, child. Never, never say something like that about your mother." The two women laughed.

"All right, I apologize." Alex sat down cross-legged on the sofa next to her mom. "Rarely do you leave the coast, particularly since I just saw you a few days ago. Why the sudden trip east?"

"Well, dear, I could say the same about you until recently." Lillian looked toward the back stairs. "Is Lance here?"

"No, he's taping promotional interviews in New York. Why?"

"There's another reason I came to see you," Lillian confessed.

Alex took a forkful of cake. The luscious cream melted down her throat. She smiled in euphoria. "What other reason?"

"I went to see Robert Burke a few days ago." Alex's face soured. Lillian watched as she pushed the cake away, having suddenly lost her appetite. "I know, I know. But it was necessary. He sent me a congratulations card. Apparently he's under the impression that Lance has chosen me to represent him."

Alex grabbed her mother and hugged her. "I can't believe he didn't tell me. This is so wonderful. Congratulations!" Alex felt the stiffness in her mother's embrace. "What? What's wrong?" she asked, confused. "Aren't you happy?"

"I formally withdrew my proposal of representation."

"You what? Why?"

"Two reasons. First of all, I enjoy scouting new talent, like Greg Taylor. There are a lot of gifted performers out there waiting for their big chance, just like you were. But, you were lucky, you had a pushy mother with connections." Alex smiled, remembering her mother's steadfast diligence. "Most amateurs never get that chance to shine. They're hungry for that first shoot and I think of it as a challenge to get them out there. I delight in introducing the world to them."

"I understand." Alex was never so proud of her mother. She could have taken the easy way as most agents had done. The temptation to go for the big money by representing established artists was all too common. But, instead she remained true to herself. "What's the other reason?"

"I don't want it perceived that I got Lance's contract because of your relationship with him. That type of notoriety would nullify my credibility as an agent."

"Mom, it's not true. Who would think something like that? You're an incredible agent and Turner-Price Agency is famous for its integrity, something Burke is sorely lacking. He's just jealous you got the contact. Besides, nobody even suspects anything."

"Both the reporter and Burke brought up the question of a relationship. So, I withdrew my proposal. Plus after seeing him there . . ."

"Seeing who there?"

"Lance. I saw him when I went to Burke's office. It was the day after you left for Miami."

"Lance was with Burke? I don't understand," she said, bewildered.

"Well, he was there. I was sitting in the waiting area when he left Burke's office. They seemed very chummy."

Alex frowned. She wanted as little to do with Robert Burke as possible, and the thought that Lance was with him bothered her. "I wonder why," she said aloud.

"Well, Burke was his agent for the majority of his career. I'm sure they're still good friends."

"I didn't think so, at least that's not the impression I got." Alex looked troubled. "Speaking of Lance, his production company is bidding on *A Pilgrimage to Heaven*."

Lillian was curious. "How do you know that?"

"He told me."

"He told you?"

Alex nodded. "Yes. Then I confirmed it with Mark. Lance already has preproduction plans set up."

"He's obviously determined," Lillian surmised. "So much so that it sounds like he's positively assured he's getting the book rights." She paused, suddenly leery. "Alex, does Lance know about Mason Turner?"

"No, of course not."

"The public has always been curious about Turner's identity. Are you sure he doesn't know?"

"How could he? We've had our share of prying reporters and detectives for years. No one has ever even come close. They all presume Mason is male so they look for a man."

Lillian reached out and took Alex's hand, then gave a deep sigh. "Alex, if Lance knows, or even worse, if he knew all along, you know what that would mean."

Lillian watched as Alex drew the only logical conclusion. "Yes." She stood and walked to the den's bay window. Bright sunshine gleamed down as young birds flew from tree to budding spring tree. The lively scene blurred through her welling tears. Lillian stood behind her. "Do you think he's using me, Mom?"

Tears fell continually. "Sweetheart." Lillian put her arm around her daughter's waist as Alex laid her head on her mother's shoulder. "I don't know. I do know that his leaving Burke for me and his running into you in the middle of a snowstorm are curious, to say the least. But it could all be coincidence just as easily."

"Or he might have planned all this. But why, just to get the book rights?" She held her head up. "That doesn't make sense."

"Only he can answer that question. We know the book's worth millions after production, but I can't believe he'd go through all this just for the rights. To tell you the truth it sounds more like something Burke would engineer."

"Well, Burke was his agent up until a few months ago; they probably planned it together. The critics are right, Lance Morgan is a great actor. He really fooled me."

"Give him the benefit of the doubt, Alex. Nothing's been proven. All this is just speculation."

Alex shook her head. She couldn't deny the facts. The evidence was overwhelming. It was so clear, he was using her. All his sweet talk, his flattery and thoughtfulness were all lies carefully scripted for his performance. And what a performance, she completely fell for it. "He must be having a good laugh."

"We could be completely off base with this," Lillian warned.

Alex buried her head in her hands, oblivious of her mother's words. Every touch, every caress, every word, all lies. The question now was, what was she going to do about it?

"She did what?" Franklin blurted out, shocked by Lance's revelation. "Are you sure? Maybe you misunderstood."

"I didn't misunderstand a telegram, Franklin. Here, read it yourself." Lance slipped the yellow paper across the coffee table. Franklin picked it up and silently read the fuzzy carbon words. The message was clear. Lillian Turner-Price was withdrawing her proposal of representation. "What the . . ."

"Tell me about it." Lance scribbled his signature across the papers Franklin brought with him to New York.

"Let me get this straight, you told me your meeting with her went well and that Lillian was anxious to submit a proposal, right?" Lance nodded. "So what happened after that?"

"Nothing happened. She sent me the proposal, I looked it over, it looked fine, so I sent it to you. Her agency seemed a little small but that might actually work to my advantage. You saw the proposal, what did you think?"

"Just like you said, it looked fine, simple, straightforward, pretty standard wording. I didn't foresee any problems. My office set up an appointment with her for later this week. I was under the impression everything was going smoothly; now this." Franklin tossed the telegram back down onto the thick Italian marble table.

Lance slammed down the antique fountain pen. "So tell me what happened between now and then."

"I have no idea. Maybe she's menopausal." Lance frowned at him. "All right, I'll get on it. Somebody's got to know something. What about Alex? Maybe she can shed some light on this."

"I doubt it, but I do intend to mention it to her."

Franklin looked around the empty living room. "What about the other thing? Have you talked to her yet?" Lance ran his large hand over his hair. His frustration was obvious. "You couldn't do it, could you?" Franklin stated knowingly. "I knew you wouldn't be able to use her like that."

"I tried, Franklin, I really did. I went as far as to mention that you and I were bidding for the book and that I was worried about being outbid by the studios. She asked me if I really wanted it. I told her yes—"

Franklin interrupted. "Wait, did she admit she wrote the book?"

"No, of course not. But she did say that everything would work out and I'd get the book. After that I couldn't say any more. I just dropped the subject."

"I don't think it really matters. She practically gave you her word that you'd get the book."

"I should have told her what I suspected and that I read the script."

"Sure, now he listens to me," Franklin said, looking to the vaulted ceiling. "It doesn't matter now, Lance, she's giving you the book. You should be happy. This is what you've wanted, right? You worked hard for this moment."

"I know, I know, I really wanted the book. But . . ."

"So you got what you wanted, right? All's fair in love and war."

"I guess."

Chapter Seventeen

The houselights went up, exuberant applause rang out, lifting the rafters. The cast returned to the stage twice to accept their thunderous accolades. In a line, they held hands, bowed low and smiled, waving graciously at the audience. Opening night was a resounding success. Lillian leaned over to Alex, applauding madly. "So, are you ready to make a comeback?" she shouted above the thunderous applause.

Alex nodded and grinned. "Maybe," she answered. Stunned by Alex's remark, Lillian stopped clapping and opened her mouth in surprise. "I'm joking, it was a joke," Alex laughingly assured her.

When the applause finally died down Lillian and Alex slowly made their way through the crowded aisle toward the stage. They each greeted familiar faces and spoke with old friends. Lillian led Alex to the dressing rooms. Several well-wishers were already standing around drinking champagne. "Lillian! Lillian!" the lead actress, still in full makeup and costume, yelled out across the packed hall. "Lillian, you came," she screamed. "I'm so happy you could make it." They hugged when she finally reached them.

"You were wonderful!" Lillian exclaimed, beaming after the long embrace.

"Thank you, oh, my goodness, you brought Alex! Hi, I'm so happy to finally meet you. Lillian talks about you all the time. I've seen all your work, I feel like I already know you."

Alex smiled and held out her hand to shake. "Hello, I'm pleased to meet you too and congratulations, the play was phenomenal. And you were brilliant." The young actress smiled and hugged Alex.

"Thank you, thank you so much. I'm so glad you came. And, Lillian, thank you for getting me this part. You were right, it was made for me."

Lillian chuckled at the young woman's unbridled enthusiasm. "You got you this part. I merely informed you of the audition."

"Oh, please." She turned to Alex. "Your mother worked with me day in and day out to prepare for this role. There's no way I would have gotten the part if it weren't for her."

Alex smiled proudly. She knew the sacrifices her mother made for her clients. Lillian was totally committed to her talent agency and the people she represented.

"Good evening, Lillian, Alexandra." Both woman turned around. Burke stood stoically staring at mother and daughter. They looked at each other, then back at Burke. Lillian acknowledged him stiffly. "Good evening, Burke." Alex turned away. Lillian made introductions and Burke complimented the young actress on her performance.

She thanked him politely, then turned back to the two women as Burke turned to speak briefly with a passing actor. "Lillian, Alex, there's going to be a small get-together for the cast at the restaurant across the street. We're going to wait for the early reviews. Why don't you join us? Just give me a few minutes to get out of this makeup and I'll meet you there."

"Ohh, it sounds wonderful, but we've already made plans for the evening," Lillian said sadly.

Alex looked at her watch, continuing her mother's remark. "As a matter of fact, Mom, we'd better get going or we're going to be late." Lillian nodded her agreement.

"Well, maybe next time, thanks again for coming." The young actress hugged Lillian and Alex. "Alex, it was wonderful to finally meet you. Lillian, I'll call you tomorrow. Have a good night." She turned and was immediately absorbed by the multitude of backstage well-wishers.

"Let's go, Mom," Alex instructed.

Burke quickly finished his discussion and turned as the two women began to make their way down the hall to the rear stage door.

He caught up with them and held the heavy door. Burke looked up at the dark cloudly sky. A light drizzle fell. "Well, ladies, shall we have a late dinner?" The women kept walking. "One moment, Alexandra, Lillian, I'd like to speak to you for a minute," Burke said.

Lillian continued walking. "We have nothing to say to each other." He moved to stand blocking their path. Lillian brushed past him and he held on to her hand. She paused and glared at him.

"Lillian," he began.

"Good-bye, Burke," she reiterated. Burke stared after the two women. Alexandra was beautiful and an arousing woman but Lillian was elegant, classy and still the only woman to steal his heart.

Burke stood on the sidewalk and watched as the two disappeared into the back of a yellow cab. The driver made a U-turn and continued down the dark wet street. Burke turned and made his way back to the stage door. A young beautiful woman emerged. She winked and smiled as she slowly sauntered past him. He didn't even notice. His thoughts were still on Lillian Turner-Price.

The restaurant was packed with the usual after-theater clientele. The rich huddled together discussing mergers and deals, the famous sat basking in the limelight and the beautiful people sat just wanting to be seen. Alex and Lillian sat in the rear of the plush surroundings amid twinkling lights and abounding greenery.

They ate a late dessert, drank wine and talked about the play and Alex's upcoming trip to the Cannes Film Festival. The conversation finally got around to Burke. "If I didn't know any better I'd say the man was following me around. I've seen him three times in the last few weeks. That's three times more than I saw him in the past eight years."

"That's because you're starting to get out more." Lillian sipped her wine. "Let's face it, Alex, for the past ten years you've lived a life of a recluse in a gilded home, either on that boat of yours, in London, St. Croix or Stoneridge. You hardly ever stepped foot outside your door."

"I went out," she protested self-righteously.

"Catching a flight from house to house to boat and standing at the door watching Coal run around is not what I consider going out." Alex smiled at the truth in her mother's words. Lillian was right. This was the most she'd been out in years. The curious thing was, she was actually enjoying herself.

"Do you think Lance and Burke are cohorts?" Alex asked, sipping her drink.

"I really don't know, Alex. One thing is certain . . ." Lillian stopped speaking in midsentence and smiled wryly across the room. "Well, speak of the devil . . ." she said, looking over Alex's right shoulder. Alex turned casually. She immediately spotted Lance being seated at a table in the center of the restaurant. He was joined by a large entourage of actors and actresses. The model turned actress she'd once seen at Lance's home sat so close to him she practically perched in his lap. The last seat, at the table's head, was occupied by Robert Burke. ". . . and he shall appear." Lillian finished the old parable as she assessed her daughter's reaction.

Alex turned back to her mother and smiled. Lillian

began to chuckle, Alex joined in. Within seconds the two were laughing joyously. Tears rolled down Alex's cheek. When their laugher subsided, they hailed their waiter and requested the check. Lillian smiled at her daughter. "So, how are your acting skills these days?"

Alex winked. "Try me."

Lillian winked back. "All right, let's do it." The two women stood and walked casually toward the front door. The open aisle led them right past the attractive group. Burke was the first to notice their approach. He stood. Lillian moved slightly ahead of her daughter. "Good evening, all," she proclaimed. Lance stood, stunned to see Alex standing beside him.

He couldn't take his eyes off of her luminous face. She was exquisite. Her hair was pulled back in a loose French braid with wisps of hair delicately framing her face. She smiled graciously at the familiar faces as introductions were made. Polite greetings were echoed followed by brief casual conversation.

Burke snapped his fingers several times until a waiter hurried over. He motioned to add chairs to the already crowded table. "We'd be delighted if you'd join us," Burke insisted. Lance stepped aside to offer his chair.

"Thank you, but we're just on our way out," Lillian assured him. "Have a good evening."

"Good night," Alex added, following her mother.

The two continued through the crowded restaurant. Lance excused himself immediately and followed the women to the lobby. "Alex, Lillian," he called out just before they reached the front door. Both women turned. "Lillian, I received your telegram yesterday. I'm afraid I don't quite understand," he said, letting his eyes drift to Alex's beautiful face. Her blank expression was unsettling. She was aloof and distant. She looked away and he returned his attention to Lillian. "I was under the impression you were interested in representing me."

Lillian smiled. "I apologize for the inconvenience,

Mr. Morgan. Unfortunately I find that my agency is unable to adequately handle your interests at this time." Lance noticed she'd quoted the telegram's wording verbatim.

"I haven't made a final decision as yet. I hope you'll reconsider." She nodded her understanding. His eyes drifted back to Alex. Lillian looked on for a moment, then excused herself to hail a cab.

Lance took Alex's hand. He stared at her, observing everything. She had an astonishing natural radiance. She lit up the room with her beauty. The golden pantsuit reflected her rich skin tones and her open jacket exposed a sexy beaded lace bustier that had several men openly drooling. "Where are you staying?"

Alex smiled pleasantly. "Amber is very attractive."

He ignored her reference to his friend. "Where are you staying, Alex?" he repeated.

She peered around his shoulder. "I think your dining companions will be wondering about your prolonged absence. You'd better go," she chided sweetly. Her soft lilting voice was as pleasing as always but something in her eyes recanted her gentle words.

He inquired again, "Where are you staying?"

"Good night, Lance." She smiled cheerfully, turned and walk away.

Lance stood at the glass door and watched as she got into the waiting cab. "Damn," he thundered as he stormed back to the table.

Watchful eyes witnessed the intriguing interaction. If being an agent had taught him anything, it was that things are often just as they appear. Observing Lance closer, he realized he'd underestimated the appeal of Ms. Price. She was far more alluring and provocative than he'd first assumed. It also appeared that Lance had readily succumbed to her many charms.

Chapter Eighteen

New York was enchanting in early spring, and the view from Park Avenue's forty-second floor was spectacular. The trees of Central Park had filled in almost completely, and returning birds were busy preparing for the hot summer months to come. Alex hardly noticed as she anxiously waited in Mark Summers's private office.

She stood at the plate-glass window flipping through folders filled with legal documents. After checking the time again she closed the open folders. She'd been reading these same pages for a half hour with the same attention span and understanding of a two-year-old child. There was no use, concentration was impossible. Each time she read a paragraph her thoughts would inevitably wander to Lance.

Dozens of questions crossed her mind as she moved back to the comfortable couch. The first and foremost being Lance Morgan's true intentions. She laid the folders on the coffee table, then melted back into the soft leather sofa. How had her life become so complicated? For years it was simple, she wrote and someone else brokered. She never ventured far from the confines of her cocooned environment.

Mason Turner was her greatest invention. Through her pen name, she indulged her convictions and created her most exciting work. A multitude of fans adored her books, and Hollywood was just beginning to embrace her accomplishments through film.

Her fifth book, still on the paperback best-seller list, was a phenomenal success. It went to the top of the best-seller list and remained for months. When Mark informed her of the film industry's interest she was apprehensive. Suddenly, she was thrust back in the feigned world of Hollywood. Before long, proposals were tendered, offers negotiated, the screenplay was accepted; then finally contracts were signed.

Now, here she was again, braced for another round with Tinseltown. But unlike before, this time she was in the midst of a bidding war resulting in exorbitant assessments. She massaged her temples with the tips of her fingers. "I can't believe this," she mutter to herself aloud. The pending headache had arrived with a vengeance.

She got up and walked around the tastefully decorated office again. Deep shades of blue, burgundy and mahogany surrounded her. She'd been an edgy jumble of nerves all morning. Seeing Lance and Amber last night was disturbing. She sat back down and sipped from the cup of lukewarm herbal tea. It didn't help, the nervous feeling and endless butterflies continued in her stomach.

"Ms. Price?" Alex looked up at the smiling woman. "Mr. Summers informed me that he will be in shortly. His last appointment is just leaving. My I get you another cup of tea?"

"No, thank you. I'm fine." The secretary left just as quietly as she'd arrived, leaving her alone again. Alex picked up the papers and read through them quickly. She looked at her watch. It was getting late and she wanted to head back to Stoneridge before rush-hour traffic. Unfortunately she arrived at Mark's office much later than she anticipated. Lately she found it harder and harder to get herself together in the mornings. Not only did she oversleep this morning but she woke up sluggish and tired. Thoughts of Lance and Amber had kept her up most of the night.

The door burst open and a handsome man in his mid-thirties strolled in. He scanned the office, finally letting his eyes rest on Alex. "Good afternoon, Alex," he said brightly.

"Hi, Mark," Alex said as she sipped her cool tea again.

He moved over to the sofa and sat down next to her. "Sorry about the delay. I expected you earlier." He picked up the papers she'd signed. "Any questions?"

She quietly answered, "No."

"You didn't read them, did you?"

"No, how did you know?"

He smiled broadly. "You usually have questions." Mark turned to look directly into Alex's eyes, concern blanketing his face. "Are you okay? You look a little tired."

"Gee, thanks for the compliment, Mark. You really know how to make a girl feel special."

He smiled miserably and laid the papers back down on the coffee table. "You know that's not how I meant it, Alex. It's just that you look a little fatigued." He took her hand in his. "I'm not only your attorney, Alex, I'm also your friend. Don't tell me you and Lillian tripped the lights fantastic last night and overdid it."

"I'm just joking." She squeezed his hand. "I'm fine really. I just have a slight headache, that's all."

"What can I get you?" he inquired earnestly.

"Nothing. I'll be okay."

"Are you sure?" Concern shadowed his handsome features as he eyed her protectively.

She grimaced. "Positive." Then she reached for the teacup. "Come on, let's get this paperwork done." Mark didn't move. "What? What is it?" she asked.

"Humor me." He got up, crossed the room and pushed a button on his desk. His secretary's voice came through the speaker. "I need an ice pack, a glass of ice water and something for a headache."

Within moments the door opened and the requested items were deposited on the coffee table in front of them. Mark gently placed the ice pack on her forehead, then gave her the water. She sipped it as he opened the bottle of pain reliever. "Here, take these." He deposited two caplets into her hand. She swallowed the pills, sipped the cool water, then replaced the ice pack.

"Thank you, Mark."

He smiled as his assistant returned to the office with a fresh pot of hot tea. He nodded his thanks, poured the tea and handed Alex a cup. She took a slow, timid sip, letting the hot herbal brew soothe her. She removed the ice pack. "I feel much better."

"Are you sure?" She nodded and reached for the papers. Mark laid his hand on top of hers. "No, we can do this another time. It's not imperative that we do this today."

"I'm all right, Mark, really. I feel much better," Alex promised.

Mark looked at her skeptically. "Did you eat breakfast?" She nodded yes. "How about lunch, have you eaten yet?"

"No," she confessed. Mark looked at the gold Rolex on his arm. It was close to three o'clock.

"Well, why don't I treat you to an early dinner?"

"I can't this time. I've got to get back to Stoneridge. This was supposed to be just a quick overnight trip with my mom but it turned out to be three days so far."

"Well, one more day won't make that much difference. And I'd love to see Lillian again. You can join me for dinner tonight? I'll cook my specialty. I make the best stir-fry sesame chicken and vegetables outside of Chinatown." Mark smiled proudly.

"That sounds wonderful, Mark," she lied, "but I took Mom to Kennedy before I came here. She had to get back to Los Angeles. And if I remember correctly, your stir-fry specialty came from the NU Ming Chinese restaurant." Mark opened his mouth in astonishment. "Come on, Mark. Admit it."

"How did you know?"

"I saw the white boxes in your kitchen trash can the last time you cooked your specialty."

Mark chuckled. "All right, I confess. I'm a lousy cook. So why don't I take you to dinner? It's already late, you might as well stay over and get an early start tomorrow morning. Besides, we can get some work done on these tonight." He gestured to the papers in her hand. "I have an early morning flight to the coast tomorrow, so dinner with you this evening will be a perfect send-off."

"How long will you be on the coast?"

"I should be back in a few days. If anything comes up call me directly." He stood and reaching out his hand for her. "Come on, get out of here. Go home and take a nap. I have to get back to work." Alex took his offered hand and grabbed her purse and together they walked to the door. "I'll pick you up at eight." She nodded her acceptance.

Dutifully Alex went back to the apartment she and her mother shared. Before lying down for a short nap she called Stoneridge and listened to her messages. The first was from her mother confirming her safe arrival. The second was from Victoria. She was in town and wanted to meet for lunch. The last three messages were from Lance. She returned Victoria's call and left a message for her mother, then decided to contact Lance after she'd gotten some rest.

Alex awoke from her nap at 6:30. The thunderous pounding in her head was finally gone and she was starving. The refrigerator was bare so she nibbled on the box of stale crackers she found in the cupboard. By the time she showered and applied her makeup, half of a package of crackers had disappeared. She riffled through her mother's wardrobe and chose a low-cut black silk evening dress with black stockings and black spiked heels. After eyeing herself in the mirror she felt encouraged by her appearance. The outfit was sexy, sleek and elegant. She grabbed a colorful silken shawl just as the bell rang.

An evening out with Mark was just what she needed. He was charming, gallant and entertaining, and the restaurant he'd chosen was exquisite. The only drawback was the swarm of paparazzi stationed at the curb greeting patrons with bright flashes of light. But even that didn't dampen her mood. She felt fabulous.

The two ate heartily, drank champagne and talked nonstop. They joked about Mark's Casanova love life, the latest movies, plays, her expected trip to France and of course the book's bidding war. She questioned him about Lance's interest in *A Pilgrimage to Heaven* and verbally reviewed the papers she signed earlier. Alex informed Mark of her decision to have Lance's production company gain the rights to the book. He confirmed their steady interest and planned to draw up the necessary paperwork.

Over coffee and dessert they discussed several new projects of interest including her pet charity, the African-American Children's Relief Fund. He gave her an invitation addressed to Mason Turner in care of his office. She opened the hand-scripted envelope. The beautifully adorned card invited Mason Turner to an appreciation dinner in his honor in Los Angeles the following weekend. It was decided that either Mark or Lillian would attend with Mason's apologies.

"How's your meal, Lance?" Franklin asked. Charles looked at him, then back at his employer. Lance didn't answer. His eyes were glued to the far table where Alex and Mark sat. The cozy darkened booth was too secluded for his liking and Mark Summers sat much too close.

Lance seethed. He couldn't believe his eyes. He didn't

think it was possible for her to look even more sensuous than she had the night before. The low-cut black dress reeked of seduction. Her slim, curvy body caressed every inch of the dress. He yearned to touch the softly molded fabric.

"Lance? Lance?" Franklin called out just above a whisper.

Jerking quickly, Lance returned his focus to the table and the two men seated with him. Annoyed, he snapped, "Yeah, what?"

Charles placed his knife and fork down. "Why don't we go somewhere else?" Franklin quickly agreed.

"Why? We just got here," Lance snapped. "Finish your meal." He pointed to the inch-thick T-bone steak Charles had just cut into. Lance looked at Charles, then at Franklin. "What, you think I have a problem seeing her with Mark? I'm sure it's just a business dinner. They're friends. I don't have a problem seeing Alex with another man," he said emphatically, more to convince himself than the others. Franklin looked at Charles. The expression "yeah, right" was mirrored on both of their faces.

Charles, who was sitting facing the lobby door, rolled his eyes to the ceiling. "I hope you're right. 'Cause here comes your brother."

The three men watched as Shawn walked up to Alex's and Mark's booth and stopped. Mark stood protectively between Alex and Shawn. From a distance they seemed to exchanged pleasantries; then Shawn and his party quickly moved on to be seated. Lance watched Alex's face after Shawn walked away. He recognized the look, she was angry. He ached to go to her. Just then Mark leaned closer and whispered something into her ear. She smiled broadly, laughed, then reached over to hug him. Lance pushed his untouched plate back and placed his napkin on the table. He was done.

Charles remarked, "Well, looks like Mr. Summers handled that smoothly enough." With Lance stewing,

Franklin and Charles continued eating and enjoying the remainder of their meal.

Lilting laughter sang out as Mark told several amusing anecdotes about his unnamed clients. With the meal complete, the couple walked hand in hand to a waiting cab oblivious of Lance's stark grimace and Shawn's angry glare.

Chapter Nineteen

Lunch at the posh Central Park restaurant the following day with Victoria was as expected, gleefully distracting. Yet the bright cheerful room did little to lift Alex's spirits. Surrounded by a sea of Armani suits, stiletto heels, face-lifts and artificial tans, Alex enjoyed Victoria's usual exuberant self, which made the afternoon a true delight. She was the perfect remedy for even the most melancholy of moods. And that's just how Alex felt as she picked through her curried chicken salad and listened to Victoria talk.

"If you stab at the croissant one more time I'm gonna report you to the chef," Victoria declared after closely observing her friend's pensive demeanor.

Alex looked up and smiled at Victoria. "Sorry, I guess I'm not very good company this afternoon." She sighed heavily. "It's been a long morning and I'm beat. I'm really looking forward to going home today." She looked around the popular eatery. It was filled to capacity with late lunch patrons. All preoccupied in their own world, busily conversing on cellular phones, picking at tiny morsels of food, talking with companions or just posturing to being seen.

During the remainder of the meal Victoria chatted on incessantly about Ted's next project, Chase's newest love and her latest trip home to Italy. By the time coffee and dessert were served, Alex's mood had immeasurably lightened.

"Alexandra Price?" Both women looked at the pretty young woman dressed patriotically in blue slacks, white cotton T-shirt and red blazer. She resembled a walking American flag. Her blond ponytail draped over her left shoulder along with an oversize brown leather backpack.

"Yes?"

"This is for you. Sign here please."

Alex signed the small receipt pad, and took the offered manila envelope. The young woman bade the women good day and disappeared through the crystal-clear glass doors in the front of the restaurant. Alex opened the registered letter as Victoria picked at her fruit tart. When Alex laughed openly Victoria turned back to her curiously. "I'm being sued."

"You're what?"

Alex repeated, "I'm being sued."

"Sued? For what?" Victoria asked, pushing the dessert plate aside.

Alex continued laughing. "Alienation of affection." Victoria's mouth gaped open as Alex quickly scanned through the remaining papers. "It says here that Mrs. Shawn Anderson is suing me for alienation of affection. It seems I willfully destroyed her relationship with her husband. She cites the tabloid photo as proof of our affair."

"That's it, now I've heard everything." Victoria threw her hand in the air. "Do you mean to tell me that the courts are actually taking tabloid photos as proof positive these days?"

"Apparently so," Alex answered absently and continued reading. "It goes on to state that Shawn and I have been having an illicit affair throughout their entire relationship, including preceding, during and currently." She read further. "It also says that I willfully enticed and convinced him to leave her in December of last year."

"Now how is that possible when you were in St. Croix from July to the end of the year and only just returned in February? Besides, you started seeing . . ." Victoria paused, looked around the crowded restaurant and lowered her voice. "You started seeing Lance. Proof being the photo of him, not Shawn. So how could you have possibly been with Shawn?"

Alex shrugged her shoulders. "I have no idea what Shawn's wife is thinking." She folded and returned the papers to the manila envelope. "I'll call Mark and have him look at these."

"Oh, Mark," Victoria moaned, letting her long thick eyelashes flutter rapidly. "How is that gorgeous attorney of yours?" She paused to smile inwardly. "Now he is a perfect male specimen, tall, dark and handsome," Victoria crooned.

"You forgot wealthy," Alex added.

"That's right, he's filthy rich too. You two should have gotten together. Shame you're already seeing"— she lowered her voice again—"Lance," she whispered.

Alex looked up at the beautiful stained-glass lamp suspended low over the table. "Nah, Mark and I have been friends too long to suddenly begin a romantic relationship. Besides, I'd only jeopardize my friendship with him if it didn't work. Then I'd be out one incredible attorney."

"Well, sure you say that now that you have the most eligible bachelor in North America."

Alex sipped her drink. "Speaking of which, I've decided to throw him back."

"What? You can't be serious," Victoria said, astounded, as Alex nodded affirmatively.

"On the contrary, I'm very serious."

Victoria sat back shaking her head, unbelieving. "I'm speechless, and you know just how rarely that happens." She leaned closer and took Alex's hand preparing to convince her to reconsider. She stopped after seeing the unmistakable spark in her eye. "Wait a minute, there's more, isn't there?" Alex smiled and sipped her drink. "I know that look, Alex, I perfected it. Spill it," Victoria commanded.

Alex smiled calmly. "It seems Mr. Morgan has been pursuing our relationship for purely professional reasons."

Victoria's brow raised inquisitively. "Meaning?"

"Meaning, I'm being played. Everything from the very beginning had been carefully scripted. Every word, every touch, every kiss, all perfectly calculated to further his career."

"Using someone to further a career is like a game in this industry, it's standard practice."

"But I'm no longer in the industry, the games don't apply."

"Are you sure about this, Alex? Remember we live in a world of smoke and mirrors. Not everything is as it appears; you of all people should know that."

"I understand what you're saying, Victoria, but sometimes things are just as they appear."

"Okay, let's say you're correct in your suspicions. To what end? Lance Morgan is at the pinnacle of his career. He's got Hollywood groveling at his feet. And as you say, you're no longer in the business. So what can he possibly gain from an association with you? How can you further his career?"

"I have something he wants."

"I assume only you can provide this 'something.' "

"He wants the rights to *Pilgrimage*."

"I see." Victoria thought for a moment. "So he wants Mason Turner then. How did he find out?"

"I don't know." Alex ran her finger slowly around the rim of her glass. "To tell you the truth it's not that difficult to figure out once you know the players."

Victoria shook her head. "I don't agree. Mark and Lillian are the only visible players. The final connection isn't that obvious. Remember everyone assumes Mason is a male. If anything they think he and Lillian are an item." Victoria looked at Alex and smiled wryly. "Let me guess, the hunter has now become the unwitting quarry."

"Exactly."

"Are you sure you want to do this?"

"Positive."

"A word of caution, as you sow, so shall you reap. Be careful, Alex. A returning boomerang is impossible to elude and leaves a hell of a scar."

Alex nodded. "Understood."

"Does he suspect that you know?"

"No, not yet. I'll wait for the right opportunity."

Victoria looked around the restaurant, then whispered, "Tossing Lance Morgan superstar back is pretty significant. He's like a mythological god to some people. And I'm sure according to about a million women you should have your head examined, because he's damn near perfect. I actually thought you'd get the fairy-tale ending. You two were the perfect storybook couple."

"Well, the fairy tale is over. This time without the 'lived happily ever after' ending."

"That, my dear, is an oxymoron. There's no such thing as 'happily ever after.' "

"Oh, please. You and Ted are the most happily ever after, married, unmarried couple I know. You flirt like crazy but never see anyone other than Ted. And he doesn't even pretend to see anyone else. To top it all off, you still live together. I will never understand the two of you. How can a flimsy piece of paper change a relationship so much?"

"When Ted and I were married we were miserable. You remember, we were constantly arguing, fighting and at each other's throats. He was jealous, I was jealous, we were horrible together. The divorce gave us our space. Now he's free to go, do as he likes and so am I. Voilà, we have the perfect love affair."

Alex leaned her elbow on the table, exasperated, and put her hand to her head. "Why did I even ask?" she said rhetorically. "Come on, we'd better get on the road if we're going to be back before dark."

Jake sat in Lance's living room waiting patiently for him to hang up the telephone. He picked up his drink and looked around the elegant room. Aesthetically, it wasn't his taste, but he could see how some got into it. One day soon he'd have a million-dollar duplex apartment in New York too. He pulled out his notebook and began scribing ideas for house locations.

"Sorry about that," Lance said as he returned to the sofa.

"No problem, I know you're busy. I just stopped by to check on any progress you've made with Price."

Lance took a deep breath. "Things got more complicated than I intended."

"What do you mean?"

"Well, first of all I'm one hundred percent certain of Mason Turner's identity, but—"

"Yes!" Jake jumped up ecstatically, interrupting Lance. "I knew it, I knew it," he proclaimed. "Yes! So, Price led you to Lillian and Lillian gave Turner up. Excellent."

"No, that's not how it happened—"

Jake, still standing, interrupted again. "Of course." He snapped his fingers. "Price also knows Turner." He chided himself. "I didn't think about that." Finally he sat back down. "This calls for a celebration." He picked up the glass of club soda and toasted, "Here's to my first two clients."

Lance looked at him and frowned. "What do you mean, first two clients?"

Jake sipped heartily, then put the glass down. "Two, as in you and Mason Turner."

Lance stood. "Wait a minute, our bargain was for me

to sign with your agency. You never mentioned anything about Turner signing also."

"Come on, man, get real. This Mason Turner guy is a gold mine. With his signature on the dotted line the green will come pouring in. Everything the guy writes goes to the top."

Lance paced the floor. "Question," he put in, "what if this Mason guy already has an agent or what if he doesn't want to sign with an agent? What then?"

"He'll sign."

"But what if he doesn't?"

"Then I'll just have to make him." Lance frowned menacingly. "Naw, man, nothing like that, I don't do force. That's not my bag. If the guy doesn't want to sign I'll simply offer him a choice."

"Which is?"

"Sign, and keep things the way they are or else . . ." He let the statement linger.

"Or else what?" Lance inquired.

"Or else I'll hold a major press conference. In a matter of hours he'll have no less than a hundred reporters at his front door."

"Ah, but that way you both lose," Lance pointed out.

"Correction, if it plays that way it's still good. You see, I would have been the one to unmask superman. Everybody and their brother will be knocking down my door. So, technically, I still win. That's why Turner's got no choice but to sign." He smiled greedily. "As a matter of fact, I bet I'll be able to get him to sign for like forty-five percent commission. Hell, I'll be a sweetheart, I'll make it fifty percent."

Lance turned his back using everything within him to suppress the urge to jump across the room and strangle Marrows.

Jake stood and downed his club soda. "Look, man, I've got to blow. I'll talk to you later." He headed for the door, then turned to Lance. "By the way, who did Price tell you Turner was, and where do I find him?"

Lance smiled, suddenly found himself back in power. If Jake never found out Turner's identity, he couldn't take advantage of her. Lance silently shook his head from side to side. "She didn't," he reported truthfully.

Jake laughed loudly. "So you figured it out without her." Lance didn't respond. "Smart man." Jake started for the door, then paused and turned. "One more thing, Lance, I wouldn't try to double-cross me if I were you. I'm sure Ms. Price will be very interested to know the truth behind your accidental meeting." Lance didn't noticeably react to his threat. "I'll have the paperwork together and ready for you to sign by next week." He grinned the familiar cocky grin and continued to the front door.

Lance stared at the mahogany doors. He needed to talk to Alex.

Chapter Twenty

It felt good to be back home.

Spring was the rejuvenating season and after a good night's rest, Alex's energy abounded. She spent the next day working busily in her gardens. A parade of landscapers dutifully tended the surrounding grounds giving specific attention to the front entrance. There, she had several large trees planted to obstruct and discourage intruders and impede the view from the driveway. She helped the gardener plant hundreds of accent annuals to add to the large perennial beds scattered throughout the property. By evening she exhaustedly collapsed into bed.

The following day she was pleasantly surprised by an early morning visitor. "Mark! You didn't have to drive all the way here. I could have messengered the papers to you."

"Actually I did, I needed an excuse to get out of the city this morning," he said as he breezed across into the living room. He accepted Alex's hug and kiss on the cheek, then followed her into her office. "Besides, you know you're my favorite client. When you call I come running."

She smiled at the all too common statement, knowing that for her and Mark, it was very true. They had been friends and associates for over ten years. He'd been her lawyer, her friend and her confidant. A graduate of

Harvard Law School, his specialty was intellectual property law. But he'd always assisted her in all legal procedures.

Alex crossed the office to her desk. She riffled through a stack of papers and picked up an envelope. "Here it is." She handed him the registered letter she had received during her lunch with Victoria. He opened it and moved to sit down on the nearby sofa. Then, scanning it briefly, he took a pen and leather-bound note pad from his briefcase.

Alex leaned against the desk carefully studying his reaction. After jotting down a few notes he began asking a series of questions. "When was the last time you saw Shawn Anderson?"

"A few nights ago in New York. He came to our table during dinner." She moved to sit down on the sofa next to Mark.

He nodded. "How about before then?"

Alex thought back carefully. "I haven't actually seen him in five or six years." Mark nodded again as he wrote down more notes. Keeping his head down and writing steadily, he asked several more questions.

"Have you had any contact with him at all? Where were you on the date mentioned in the complaint? How long were you there? Could others testify to your whereabouts? Did he contact you in St. Croix? Have you ever met his wife? Is this him in the tabloid photo?"

Her answers were honest and precise. She'd had no contact with Shawn in years. She'd been in St. Croix for six months and before that she was in London, before that on her boat in the South Pacific. She'd never met Mrs. Anderson and the enclosed photos were definitely not Shawn. Mark nodded after each answer while continuing to write notes. He looked up at her. "It shouldn't come to this, but is the man in the photo available to confirm this if necessary?"

Alex took a deep breath. "I'm sure he wouldn't have a problem. The man in the photo is Lance Morgan,

Shawn's half brother." Mark nodded in typical lawyer fashion, zero reaction and recognition factor. "Well, what do you think? Should I start writing out a check to make this thing go away?"

Mark looked up as he closed the notepad. "No. There's no case here. I'm actually surprised that a judge let it get this far. I'll file the necessary motions tomorrow morning."

The relief on Alex's face was evident. Knowing that the charge was bogus was one thing; proving it in a court of law was another.

Mark refolded the letter and placed it and the notepad back in his briefcase. "I do have just one more question to ask you."

Knowing that her answers were critical to her defense, she eagerly leaned forward with great interest anticipating his final question. "Yes?" she asked, her face rigid with grave concern.

"What have you got around here to eat? I'm starved."

A lone glowing desk lamp illuminated the darkened office as Alex typed incessantly on the keyboard for the remains of the day. For hours the script had completely engrossed her. She didn't even notice the sun had set or that dark storm clouds loomed on the horizon. Coal, who lay asleep beneath her desk, raised his head to acknowledge the distant rumble of thunder. Seeing no reason for alarm he lowered his head and returned to his nap.

The telephone rang unanswered several times throughout the evening as she focused exclusively on completing the final scenes of the screenplay. With each keystroke she sank deeper and deeper into the climactically concluding story line.

The characters' dialogue flowed freely from her fingertips as she actually visualized the scenery and art direction. The screenplay, as with the book, had basically written itself. A content smile curled her lips. By the time she typed in the direction *fade to black,* and the words *The End,* it was dawn.

She was exhausted yet giddy with anticipated excitement. After a long hot shower to relieve the stiffness she lotioned, dressed, then slid between the coolness of satin sheets. The phone rang. She let it ring until it finally stopped. She closed her eyes satisfied with the completion of her work. Just as she drifted off to sleep the telephone rang again. She picked up. "Good morning, Alex." Lance's tone was disquieted yet composed.

She yawned. "Hello, Lance."

"Did I wake you?"

"No, actually I'm just getting into bed."

"Up all night?" he questioned.

"Umm-hmm," she hummed sweetly.

Trepidation gripped him, tensing his body rigidly. He tightened his hold on the leather-padded circle. "I called you several times last night. You didn't return my calls. I wanted to make sure everything's all right." Silence returned his inquest. "Alex?"

Her thoughts drifted. "Yeah, I'm here. She unsuccessfully stifled another yawn. "Everything's fine. I've just been busy. How were your film interviews?"

"Exhausting. Sitting in a hotel room with assembly-line reporters asking the same question over and over again can be monotonous, but it's all part of the job, right?"

"I remember." He heard the smile in her voice. "Ten minutes for print and fifteen minutes for television reporters."

"So, what kept you up all night?"

"I had to finish something."

Lance tensed immediately. "Did you finish it?" he asked, eagerly anticipating her answer.

"You're full of questions this morning, aren't you?" she responded evasively in a small fatigued whisper.

He changed the subject. "It was good seeing you the

other night. I wish I'd known you were going to be in town, we could have gotten together."

"It was a spur-of-the-moment thing. My mom persuaded me to go with her."

"How is Lillian?" The front gate's doorbell sounded. Alex frowned at the early morning intruder. "Good, she's doing good. I spoke with her the other night." Alex put her robe on and headed for the living room.

"I was really disappointed that she declined to represent me. I intend to change her mind. I think she'd be perfect for my needs."

"Well, good luck, she's usually adamant about her client list." Upon arriving at the panel she put Lance on hold and pressed the speak button. "Yes?"

"Open the gate, Alex."

"Lance? What are you doing here?"

"Open the gate, Alex." She pushed the button.

Hot black coffee spilled into the lap of the tabloid reporter. He lurched forward trying to get a better look at the driver of the approaching car. His mouth gaped open as he set the thermos down on the passenger seat. A smile of recognition covered his face. He immediately pulled out his cellular phone and dialed his boss's home number.

The call was slow to connect. He grabbed his binoculars and grinned happily. This was too good to be true. Just last night his boss had ordered him to drop the Alex Price stakeout and get back to Los Angeles. He brazenly viewed the driver as he disembarked and walked right into the open door. "Got ya," he muttered as his grin widened.

His boss finally answered the phone. "Who the hell is this?" he yelled into the receiver.

"I've got your next headline."

"Do you have any idea what time it is? I thought I told you to get yourself back here."

"You're never going to guess who just drove up to Alex Price's front gate," he said into the small phone.

"Shawn Anderson," he said. "It's about time."

"Nope. Try this, his big brother."

"Who?" his interested superior replied.

A cockeyed smile creased the reporter's thin face as he lowered his binoculars. "Lance Morgan."

"What? Lance Morgan is there?" he bellowed as he turned on the small side lamp and grabbed his glasses and notepad.

"He just drove up and walked inside like he owned the place."

"I knew it," came the booming voice from the other end of the line. He slammed his fist down on the cluttered nightstand. "I knew there was something going on with her. I'm glad I decided to have you parked out there." The reporter shook his head. It was his idea to stake out Alex Price's home in New Jersey, not his boss's. But of course he'd take the credit now that something big was brewing.

"Okay, stay put. Gather whatever information you can from there, we'll lead with this on next week's cover. I want to know how long he stays, who else comes and goes and anything thing else you find that's pertinent. I'll write the intro myself. You write and fax the story. Overnight the photos, I want to see them ASAP."

"No photos."

"What, what do you mean no photos?"

"It happened too fast. The gate was already open," he lied. He'd just made a rookie mistake. He was so stunned to see Lance Morgan that he forgot to grab his camera.

"All right, we'll use stock photos from the vault."

"Fine, remember it's my story. Make sure I get the byline."

"Whatever." The line went dead.

* * *

The second Lance saw Alex, his intense hunger for her begged to be satisfied. The power she held over him was puzzling. All he thought about lately was the next time he'd hear her voice or see her face. His fixation on her was perplexing.

The ravenous kiss was sudden and all-consuming. He devoured her, greedily gorging himself on her sweetness. With lips pulsating again and again he wallowed in the rapture of her essence. She filled him as the delicate hold of his restrain weakened. "God, woman, what you do to me," he confessed. Breathless, unnerved and reeling by her power, Lance staggered back. His resolve weakened as she pulled him close again.

Alex swayed within his embrace. The strength of his hard body so near was overwhelming. She closed her eyes to regain control of her wayward feelings. Her motivations were clouding. She pushed back. "Lance, what are you doing here?" she asked, winded by his passion.

He touched the softness of her face, gently moving his fingers over the smooth corners of her jaw and the tender planes of her cheek. "You sound surprised to see me."

"I am."

"I needed to see you," he murmured, kissing her lightly, "to be with you." Caressing her gently as his eyes roamed down the length of her scantily dressed body. "You look inviting." He bit at his lower lip, resting his hands gently on her shoulders.

Suddenly self-conscious, Alex steadied her quivering hands and pulled the sheer chiffon of the robe together. Lance grasped her hands. The intensity in his cycs unnerved her. "No," he whispered, "don't hide yourself from me."

Aided by Lance, the robe's chiffon material slid from her shoulders, flowed down her arms and pooled at her bare feet. Her long nightgown's sheer gossamer fabric revealed the curvy flow of her body. His arousal was complete. He absently fingered the wispy straps of her gown before lifting her into his arms and going into the bedroom.

Alex savored the sensation of being held in Lance's powerful arms. She laid her head on his shoulder and inhaled the sweet spicy scent of his cologne. *If only this were real,* she wished. If only he wanted her and not just her book. After laying her gently on the bed, Lance removed his shoes and lay beside her. She cuddled in his arms as he stroked the length of her back. Alex closed her eyes and listened to the rhythmic beat of his heart and the slow, steady comforting sound of his breathing.

Her stillness prompted him to look down at the sleeping angel in his arms. She felt so good, so right. Lance closed his eyes and willed this moment to last forever.

Hours later Alex showered and dressed and found Lance in the living room. "Well, hello, sleepyhead," Lance said as he looked up from the script he'd been studying.

"Hi," she replied, still drowsy. She yawned. "How long was I asleep?"

"Not long, a few hours." He tossed the script on the coffee table, stood and walked over to her. "I think you really needed the rest."

She ruffled the loose curls around her face and pulled at the hem of the large white T-shirt. "I think I did too." Lance followed as the blue body-hugging jeans swayed casually toward the kitchen. She would always be the sexist woman alive in his eyes. He stood intimately in back of her nibbling at her ear and neck. "Shouldn't you be at the Cannes Film Festival this week?" she asked, pulling down an empty glass from the cabinet.

He smiled jokingly, his skeptical amusement obvious. "If I didn't know any better, I'd say you were trying to get rid of me."

She smirked shrewdly, raising an eyebrow. "I am." Her expression remained indifferent as she moved to the refrigerator.

"Really?" He smiled smugly, then curiously tilted his head. For the first time in a long time, he was completely confounded by her behavior. He couldn't figure out if she was serious or not. Distracted, he eventually answered. "I have a flight out in a few days. Actually, I just came to say good-bye," He said, very obviously not anticipating the upcoming event. He moved beside her.

"Sounds like you're not really looking forward to going this year," she surmised while filling her glass.

"Hollywood on the Riveria. Daily press conferences, continuous photo sessions, hourly interviews, you know the drill, I can hardly wait," he said sarcastically. "Actually there is one thing I'm looking forward to in Cannes." She looked at him questioningly, then moved away. He continued, "I'm a juror this year for the Camera d'Or and Golden Palm Awards."

"Congratulations, that's a huge honor. Not everyone is asked to judge the competition." She walked over to the counter and sat down on the padded stool.

"Do you ever miss it?" he asked.

"Miss what?"

"Acting."

She smiled genuinely for the first time since he had arrived. "The sound of applause is addictive. A true performer never loses that taste for approval. Live stage is the hardest. The sound of an audience's instant reaction to your performance is like none other. The feeling is truly a high." She looked off in the distance remembering the sound of applause.

He reached out and laid his hand on top of hers. "Are you okay?"

"Yes, of course, I'm fine."

"Are we okay?"

"What do you mean?"

"You seem distant. Have I said or done something

to upset you?" His thoughts immediately went to Jake Marrow and his threats of exposure.

Wide-eyed and innocent, she answered, "Why do you ask? Have you said or done something that would upset me, Lance?" A long uneasy silence stretched out between them. This was his opportunity, he had to tell her now. Their eyes held, neither wanting to turn away. Finally she looked down. "What's this?" She motioned to the small, flat, colorfully wrapped package lying on the marble-top tile.

"A present."

"I gathered that much."

"It's for you."

Alex smiled. "For me?" He nodded. She picked it up and fingered the bright yellow bow and curly ribbons. "What's the occasion?"

"No occasion. Can't a guy bring a present to his ladylove without it being a special day?"

She put the thin box down and eyed him squarely. "Is that what I am, Lance, your ladylove?"

He reached over slowly and took her hand in his. "Every man is but half of a perfect unit; and the divine healing of life's wounds comes only when he has the rare good fortune to meet the other half of himself."

Alex smiled stiffly, unmoved by his words. "That's a very sweet sentiment."

"Go ahead. Open it."

Without need of further coaxing Alex ripped through the package within seconds. She carefully opened the black plastic cover. A gold metallic disk sat protectively in the case. "A disk?"

"It's a DVD disk."

Alex picked up the disk and slid it onto her forefinger. "I can see that. What's on it?" She turned her hand from side to side eyeing the shiny golden ring.

"The final print of my film. I picked it up last night," he said shyly with boyish charm. "I thought maybe you'd like to see it with me."

"Of course. I'd love to see it with you." She immediately slid down from the stool and walked over to the entertainment center in the den. Lance followed her and sat down on the sofa. With the disk still on her finger, she opened the tray and laid the ring in place. The flat platform instantly pulled the disk into the machine. Moments later the screen went dark as the opening credits began to roll. "Have you seen any of the film?"

"Just some of the dailies." He patted the seat beside him. She sat down and tucked her stockinged feet beneath her. "This will be my first time seeing the edited version," he said as the opening credits faded into the first scene. "I'm glad my first time will be with you."

Chapter Twenty-one

Alex hurried to her office and picked up the ringing telephone. "Hello?" she said breathlessly.

"Alex." The slurred voice seemed vaguely familiar.

"Who's calling?"

"Alex, it's me, Shawn." A cold chill ran up her back as her heart beat rapidly. This was the last thing she needed.

"This is a private number, Shawn, how did you get it?"

He laughed pitifully. "You'd be surprised how many doors open after hearing my name mentioned. See, I still got it."

"What do you want, Shawn?"

"Ah, Alex, is that any way to sound?" He quickly threw back the shot of iced vodka. "I just wanted to call to see how you were doing, it's been a long time." She didn't say anything. "I also wanted to . . . to tell you how much I've missed you all these years." Alex's eyes rolled to the ceiling.

"Shawn, what do you want?"

"You, Alex. I want you." He poured another shot into his glass. "I want us to be together again like we were before. All this stuff in the past doesn't matter to me anymore. We could be good together just like before, remember?"

"Shawn, you do realize that there was nothing other

than friendship between us. Everything else was all make-believe. We were actors in character. There never was an us. We were friends, that's all."

He laughed heartily. "I know we were acting. But sometimes, I could see it in your face, in your eyes. You felt it too just like me." He opened a small prescription bottle and poured several white pills onto the side table.

"No, Shawn," she said patiently, "I was doing a job, I was acting. I don't act anymore."

Shawn sniffed another line of white powder. He shivered at the sudden acid assault to his inflamed membranes. "No, no, Alex," he coughed out, "I'm talking about the things we did together off the set." He picked up and popped two pills into his mouth, then gulped vodka from his glass. The strong liquid burned his throat as it washed the pills down. "You remember, the trip to Hawaii at spring break and the six days we got lost in the Nevada desert. You couldn't have forgotten those times."

"Shawn, that was all scripted. It was just a television episode. The whole crew went to Hawaii for location shots. We never went to Hawaii alone together. And the five days in the Nevada desert was actually two weeks on location with the director, actors, camera crews and the local Teamsters union. We weren't lost, we stayed at the Grande Hotel. A limo came every morning and evening to transport us to the desert location. There was never anything but friendship between us."

A dizzying kaleidoscope of flashing memories raced through his mind. Staggering, Shawn collapsed across his oversize bed. The room spun as he reached for the bottle of vodka. He refilled the half-empty glass to the brim spilling the excess onto the glass tabletop. "Don't be like this, Alex. I remember the good times and I know you do too. What about the snow fight we had just a few months ago?"

Alex's mouth dropped open. He couldn't actually believe that it was him in that photo, could he? "Shawn, listen to me. That wasn't you in that photo. Don't you realize that?"

"But, Alex," he began, then broke down. "The picture, I saw the picture. They said it was us." Shawn looked at the large-screen television. Alex's smiling face took up the entire sixty-inch screen.

"Shawn, think!" she commanded pointedly. "You've never even been to my house. How could it possibly be you in that photo?" He stared at the screen. Alex stared back at him. She was beautiful. The camera panned back as he entered the scene. She smiled and reached out and touched his face gently.

"It *was* me," he tried desperately to convince himself as his mind swam in an ocean of vodka and Prozac. "It *had* to be me." His voice faded. "It *has* to be me." He grabbed the remote control and paused the picture as the couple kissed on-screen.

Alex sat down slowly. She'd never heard him sound so pitiful. "Shawn, I remember a long time ago when you and I had a very special relationship, we were friends. Remember?" He nodded and smiled into the receiver as she continued. "We were good friends, best friends. But then you started with the wild parties, the drugs and the alcohol. I don't know, I guess we just drifted apart or maybe I just grew up. But whatever it was, it changed us. You chose your path and I chose mine."

"But we can go back. It can be just like the old days."

"No, Shawn, we can't go back. That time has passed."

"No, you're wrong. We can be like we were before. I'll go to rehab. I'll get off the drugs. I'll do whatever you say. You'll see. I'll get better, no drugs, no booze, you'll see."

"No, Shawn, don't do it for me, do it for yourself." The other end of the line was silent. "Shawn? Shawn, are you there? Did you hear what I said? Shawn? You have to do it for you." The connection was broken. Alex stood looking at the receiver. The upsetting conversation was the first time she'd actually spoken to Shawn in over eight years. Alex shook her head, troubled, hoping he'd heard her.

Shawn rolled to his side and poured another vodka shot, then studied the stilled frame. "It was real," he grumbled angrily. He stood up staggering and looked at himself in the wall of mirrors across the large room. "Me!" he shouted. "She wanted me. I was the one she kissed first, I was the one she stayed with in Hawaii. Me! She was with me in the desert."

He collapsed onto his bed until the spinning room slowed. He vaguely heard the DVD player click off and the regular television programming return. Through his haze he heard the announcer mention Lance's name.

". . . has been romantically linked to reclusive actress Alexandra Price for some time. Although his office has refused comment, sources close to the couple report the two stars are possibly headed down the aisle in the very near future. Lance Morgan's upcoming summer release . . ."

Shawn scowled, rubbing his stinging nose frantically. Confusion clouded his mind again as his body jerked and rocked. "Alex!" he screamed to the empty openness, "Alex, it was me, not him! You'll see, I'll show you." He threw the empty glass across the room, shattering the mirror into a large entangled web of silver scars.

Staggering over to the phone, he punched in the familiar number. The ringing prompted Shawn to pat at his pants pocket and riffle through the items on his dresser. When the phone was finally picked up on the other end he slurred out, "I need something."

"What do you need, Shawn?"

"You know what I need. But you gotta bring it here. I, I don't . . . find keys . . . my car." His voice faded as he collapsed on the bed again continuing to ramble. "I lost my car keys."

"How much money do you have, Shawn?" the impatient voice asked.

"I got money," Shawn bit out nastily, insulted by the man's implication. "Just get it here. And hurry up!" Shawn smiled at his masterful handling of the situation. He was still in control. These ignorant peons needed to learn respect. They needed to give him his propers. No matter what those stupid critics said, he was still *the man*.

An hour and a half later the bell rang repeatedly and then the angry hammering fist finally gave up. Unconscious, Shawn never moved from the bed. He fitfully dreamed of his days on the set with Alex. His Alex. She was right, he couldn't go back.

Troubled, Alex walked back into her bedroom. She looked around the room. Clothes hung from every possible post. From the dressing room door, over the oversize lounge chairs and from the canopy bed frame. Empty shopping bags littered the plush carpeting. Going shopping with Victoria was definitely detrimental to her health. But, if she was going to teach Lance Morgan a lesson in humility she needed the appropriate wardrobe.

She picked up the skimpy two-piece bathing suit with matching wrap and smiled. The suit was practically obscene and the flimsy wrap left less to the imagination than she thought conceivable.

She neatly folded the scant pieces of fabric and laid them on top of the already bulging satchel. "That ought to do it," she said aloud to the empty room. The open suitcases on her bed were filled to capacity. She was ready to go.

Chapter Twenty-two

Alex stepped onto the sunny deck of the opulent yacht. She stood at the bow surveying the abundant wonders of this magical land. The distant horizon offered an unobstructed view of the turquoise-blue French Mediterranean Sea and the white sand beaches of Nice.

The French Riveria was the playground of the rich and famous. But, for two weeks in May, the small coastal town became inundated with the glitz and glamour of the world's finest in the film industry.

She smiled the cockeyed smile of lascivious pleasures. This had been a long time coming. Tired of being manipulated, used and deceived, she was poised and ready for her first major acting role in years.

The stage was set and her audience awaited. She looked down at her chosen costume. The silky emerald halter dress flowed to the top of her matching strappy sandals. The deep thigh-high slits on either side added just the right amount of interest guaranteed to wreak havoc on the unsuspecting male population. In one bold stroke she'd announce her return to civilization.

She watched as the launch pulled up next to the massive floating palace. The crew tied off the ropes and secured the plank's steps. Alex walked over to the open rail and smiled down as the first mate saluted her. "Good afternoon, Ms. Price, the car is ready." She nod-

ded and anxiously stepped down onto the waiting platform.

Aided by the overzealous crew, she settled aboard the
launch as the motor whirled to life and the craft stirred
the crystal waters. The vessel glided across the surface
of the water like smoke on glass. The barest stir gently
rocked her pensive mood.

Moments later the small vessel arrived at the extended
pier. Alex got out and walked the short distance to the
waiting car. "Miss Price?" She turned. A crew member
hurried over to her. "Your sunglasses."

"Thank you," she replied graciously, taking the
offered shades, then continued to the car. The bright
sunshine and excessive heat were the least of her con-
cerns. The chauffeur opened the rear door as she
arrived. He bowed low. "Bonjour, mademoiselle. We
will arrive in less than ten minutes."

"Merci." She nodded her approval and relaxed onto
the comfortable seat. She looked at her gold-chain
watch. She would have plenty of time to arrive before
the hordes of paparazzi descended.

As the car neared the Palais de Festival, Alex felt an
exhilarating excitement surge. This was the elite of the
world's film industry. Only the finest films were
screened, judged and awarded in this building. The
familiar entrance announced to all the magnitude of
this auspicious spectacle. Twice nightly and guarded
heavily, the Parade of Luminaries climbed the red-
carpeted stairs to take their place among the privileged few.

The Bunker, the Fortress, Stonehenge Two, the Pink
Gateau were all nicknames to the monolithic structure
overlooking the old harbor. At five stories high and over
two thousand-plus seats, the Grand Auditorium Lumiere
was the dream of every filmmaker, playwright, actor and
director.

As the Rolls Royce limo rounded the American Pavil-
ion, Alex gathered her small purse. The dark stylish

sunglasses and wide-brim hat obscured her identity perfectly. She wasn't ready to announce her presence to the world, not just yet. She decided to distance herself until the right moment. And this, the second week of the festival, was undoubtedly that right moment.

The car stopped and immediately her door opened. As Alex held her hand out, it was grasped by the waiting attendant. "Bonjour, mademoiselle, welcome to Le Moulin de Mougins," he proclaimed illustriously, "the finest restaurant on the French Riviera." He extended his elbow. She cordially accepted and was ushered through the throngs of reporters, paparazzi and curiosity seekers.

The expected buzz followed her as she entered the lavish restaurant foyer. *"Excusez-moi,"* she said softly to the maître d'hotel, "Monsieur D'Lucchia *s'il vous plait.*" The man escorted her to the majordomo, who then accompanied her to her luncheon companion. Passing magnificently adorned tables, Alex walked confidently through the multitude of curious patrons.

The majordomo led her to a secluded terrace surrounded by age-old palm trees. "Monsieur D'Lucchia." He stood and turned with the brightest, most welcoming smile imaginable. Alex couldn't help but be entranced.

Chase was tall, dark, rich and extremely handsome. His tanned olive complexion bespoke his southern Italian ancestry, and women literally threw themselves at his feet. His body was hard and precisely chiseled, seemingly sculpted by Michelangelo Buonarroti himself. He kept his long, thick black wavy mane free and perched gently on his broad shoulders. His dark piercing eyes and mischievous smile could melt and capture the most resistant fan.

"Belladonna," he cooed slowly, kissed both cheeks, then seductively kissed her open palms. "Alexandra, *mí amour,*" he said, stepping back to admire her appearance. Then he took a deep breath and shook his head.

"You look exquisite." His gracious compliment made her blush.

"*Graci,* Chasano. You look fabulous as usual." She sat in the offered seat and removed her hat. Instantly, two waiters arrived and placed their preordered meals in front of them. Alex inhaled the sweet aroma and delighted in the beautifully presented meal. "I must admit, your invitation to lunch was quite a surprise. I presumed you'd be otherwise engaged." She smiled broadly as he grasped her meaning.

"Ah, *sí,* I've been here for several days." He leaned in closer. "Already I'm bored out of my mind. These witless people are relentless, rules, rules, always rules." He threw his hands up in indifference.

"Chasano, you have to bend the rules without getting caught. You know that."

"*Sí, sí.*" He shrugged his broad shoulders. "It is just unduly time-consuming." She snickered at his honest appraisal.

"That amuses you?" he asked, pouring vin de champagne into her crystal glass.

"No, actually I agree completely." She picked up her glass and held it midair to toast. "To abolishing the rules," she offered.

"*Sí,* to relishing every indulgence," he amended. Their flutes clinked delicately. She took a sip of the effervescent spirit. The sparkling pale liquid bubbled coolly down her throat. It was perfection, as was the rest of the extravagant meal. Chase opened the second bottle of champagne and refilled their glasses. "So, Alexandra," he began, "when do you leave for Chirro?"

"In a few days, as soon as Victoria arrives." The waiter arrived later to remove their empty dishes.

"You won't be staying to the ending festivities?" He beckoned for the waiter.

"No, I don't think so. We're stopping in Nice and Monte Carlo before going on to Italy."

"I've just had the most marvelous idea," he proclaimed as he signed the check.

She skeptically grinned at him. "Really? What is it?"

"Why don't I tag along?" Alex picked up her hat and purse as he stood and helped pull her chair back. He smoothly placed his hand on the small of her bare back to guide her. Now completely unmasked, the glamorous couple turned numerous heads as they strolled regally through the crowded restaurant.

"Is that what you call a most marvelous idea?" she asked jokingly.

"Absolutely," he contended. As soon as they stepped outside, the paparazzi instantly descended on the couple taking hundreds of photos and asking a myriad of personal questions. Chase took her waist protectively, then pulled her closer to the solidness of his body. The two waved and smiled dutifully for the numerous blinding flashing bulbs. The car arrived just as Alex and Chase reiterated their close longtime friendship.

"I've never gotten used to that," Alex admitted as she collapsed against the leather seat.

"I don't think anyone ever does. I think of them as mosquitoes, you give them a little blood and they buzz away." Chase looked over to her longingly. She was so beautiful. "You realize, of course, we'll be the latest gossip," he informed her.

She nodded. "Most likely."

He tilted his head, looking at her questioningly. "That doesn't bother you? You, the reclusive Alexandra Price, unfazed by this? I find that hard to believe."

"How bad can it possibly be?" she queried offhandedly.

Chase roared with laughter. "My innocent Alexandra, after the Eurpoean paparazzi get finished with the story, you will have stolen me away from the Queen of England. And I, scoundrel that I am, would toy with your affections, then leave you for a model I met on L'Cote d'Azur." She laughed, unbelieving. "Don't laugh, you think they're bad in the States, I guarantee you your American tabloids have nothing on their European counterparts." He reached up and stroked her cheek gently. "Alexandra." She looked at him. "Why have we never made love?"

"Because, Chasano." She removed his hand and held on to it. "You and I are old friends and I wouldn't want anything to jeopardize what we already have." Her sincerity was genuine.

Chase lowered his head sadly, then peeked up at her playfully. "Are you sure?" he asked enticingly.

She giggled at his tenacity. "I'm sure. Now, tell me about the film competition this year. Who will go home with the Camera d'Or?" That was the perfect change of subject. Chase could talk endlessly about the film festival. He began with his first day of photo sessions, then talked about his press conferences and interviews. He went on to relay details of the fifty chosen feature and short films entered in the international competition. Then he finished with his responsibilities as a judge.

By the time they arrived back at her yacht, he'd told her about every party, gala and soiree he had attended in the past few days. Alex smiled, nodded and asked the appropriate questions, but her thoughts were on a particular face in the blur of restaurant patrons. His stunned expression registered as priceless.

"Mama mia," Chase remarked as he walked around the upper deck, "this is fabulous. I've heard a lot about this vessel. When the studio arranged to use this ship for the party I had no idea it belonged to you."

"All mine." A uniformed crew member appeared and handed her a small stack of messages as she boarded. She nodded and expressed her gratitude, then sat down on the cushioned seat and riffled through the many envelopes and communications. A galley attendant arrived carrying a tray of tiny edibles, glasses and a bottle of champagne. Alex motioned for him to put it down on the side table. He did, then disappeared below.

For the next hour Alex and Chase talked endlessly, then took an abbreviated tour of the ship. Built in the 1970s, the exorbitant toy stayed at port mainly in the waters of St. Croix. It was often rented out to the pleasure-seeking privileged few lucky enough to afford it. When they returned to the gangplank they stopped as Chase took one last look around the deck. "I see why Victoria didn't want to fly home. Why fly in a stuffy private jet when you can cruise in such luxury? You have an exceptional vessel, Alexandra."

"Grazie." She looked around proudly. This was her refuge just after she left Hollywood years ago. Tahiti, Monaco, the Greek Isles, she had toured them all. She sailed around the world, living onboard for over six months. Seeing the world through circular portholes in her cabin. "I assume everything is set for the party tomorrow night?" she asked.

"Sì, my personal assistant has informed me that everything has been arranged. Your captain will move the ship to port tomorrow morning. The studio has taken care of invitations, transportation, catering, champagne, everything. You will not have to lift a finger. As a matter of fact your crew can even take the night off if you desire. Everything is under control."

"Good, then I'll see you tomorrow afternoon."

"Sì." He took her hand. "Unless of course you desire my company this evening." Alex smiled, shaking her head. Chase was hopeless. He shrugged. "Pity, I am very pleased you decided to come to Cannes."

"I am too." Alex smiled. A party on the yacht was just what she needed.

He kissed her cheeks, then walked down the gangway. When he settled in the launch he kissed and waved, "Arrivederci, Bella."

She returned his wave. "Au revoir."

* * *

At dusk Alex lounged on the top deck enjoying the late evening air. She sipped a chilled glass of champagne while watching the sun slowly descend into the Mediterranean Sea. This was her favorite part of the day. The radiant impressionistic hues of sunset dotting the sky far surpassing any Monet painting she'd ever seen. She was captivated. The picturesque spectacle was awe-inspiring.

In the distance she could see the glittery lights of Cannes. She smiled contentedly, then laid her head back and closed her eyes. The hushed sound of water lapping against the ship's hull soothed her mind and led her thoughts adrift. *How perfect was this day,* she mused wordlessly. Her thoughts were answered with loud applause, startling her to sit up quickly.

"Bravo, excellent performance," Lance contended as he continued applauding while walking toward her. As he neared her chaise, his amorous eyes drifted down the length of her scantily dressed body. He stood over her. His mouth went dry and his body tightened at the alluring sight. "I forgot how truly talented you are, Alex." The skimpy two-piece bathing suit left little to the imagination.

Suddenly feeling uncomfortable looking up at him, Alex stood. "Hello, Lance." Their eyes connected, unwavering; then she turned and walked to the bow's rail.

He stared hypnotically as she moved away. The sexy sway of her hips excited him as he watched the sheer fabric of her cover wrap blow restlessly in the gentle breeze. "Hello, Alexandra."

"No need for formalities," she tossed over her shoulder. "Call me Mason."

He smiled intentionally. "You know?"

She held the glass over the side and slowly poured

the amber liquid into the blue-green water, then turned and glared at him. "Obviously."

"Is that what this is all about?" He waved his arms around the yacht's immediate area.

"All what?" she asked innocently.

"Chasano D'Lucchia in the restaurant this afternoon. Why the games?"

"Games." She began laughing. Her long luscious legs crossed as she leaned back on the wooden barrier. "You of all people question me about playing games." She laughed again. "Tell me, Lance, was getting the book your only objective or was making love to me also part of the plan?"

"Alex, it wasn't like that, I love . . ." he began.

She held her hand up to halt his words. "Don't even say it." She closed her eyes and spat out each word painfully slow. "You used me. I've already spoken to my attorney. Mark Summers will have the contract complete and ready for you to sign by the time you return to the States." After inhaling deeply to regain her composure, she smiled triumphantly. "Congratulations. You should be very pleased with your performance, you got exactly what you wanted. You have your book, consider it payment for services rendered." She stared at him for a few seconds, then sighed. "Good-bye, Lance." She placed her glass down and walked away.

Lance mournfully walked to the side. His powerful hands gripped the handrail unmercifully. The delicate scent of her perfume still lingered in the breeze. He stared out at the glittering lights of Cannes reflecting on the darkening waters. Thousands of lines of dialogue rushed to his lips, but none adequate enough to convey how he felt.

"Sir?" The crewman announced his presence. "The launch is ready for your return to the dock." Lance nodded, turned and left.

* * *

Vivaldi's violin concerto emanated through the cabin's speakers. Alex tossed the tabloid newspaper onto the vanity. The stock picture of Lance and her beamed back at her. The headline and attached article were closer to the truth than they realized.

"Alex?" the familiar voice called out while knocking came lightly on the cracked door.

"Come in," she replied.

The cabin door opened and Victoria stood in the doorway, her mouth open, captivated by the sight. "My God, Alex, you look phenomenal."

Alex smiled happily. "Thank you."

"I have never seen you look so spectacular," Victoria said. "You're stunning."

"Okay, okay, I get the point," Alex said as she returned to the full-length mirror. She studied her face. Her cinnamon complexion was flawless. A light touch of makeup and lipstick added to her already astounding attractiveness. She backed up to appraise herself full length. The seductive gray evening gown she'd chosen hugged every curve to perfection. She attempted to adjust the front's deep-gaping plunge.

Victoria appeared beside her reflection. "Let it be. It's about time you accentuate your endowments. If you have 'em, flaunt 'em, that's my motto."

"Naturally." Alex stepped aside to get a better view of her friend. "Victoria Reese, you look fabulous."

Victoria primped in the mirror. "Of course I do."

"Come on, let's get this party started," Alex announced.

"I'll meet you in a bit, I need to get Ted out of our cabin. He's been on the phone for over half an hour." The two women sashayed through the cabin's wide double doors. Victoria walked to her cabin and Alex climbed the main stairs.

The yacht, now anchored and berthed at the pier, was immaculate. The brilliant luster of polished lacquered wood and the luminous brightness of the bleached hull glistened against the raven sky. The inky water sparkled, reflecting the tiny white lights adorning the ship. Each upper-level compartment in the multilevel vessel was dimly lit for added ambience. Large crystal-clean windows surrounded the main upper chamber bestowing a panoramic view of Cannes's glaring searchlights roaming the heavens.

At the marina, limousines paraded nonstop as party-goers eagerly arrived. The captain, dressed in nautical white, hailed and greeted each boarding guest. The weather was perfect. A warm tranquil breeze stirred the posted American flag at the stern. The subtle tang of salted air mingled with the aromatic scent of the mouth-watering catered cuisine.

The early assembled guests parted down the center as Alex stepped on deck. Both men and woman openly stared as she walked past, her beauty radiant and classic. Alex handled the attention with admirable charisma. If graciousness were a sword, she wielded it masterfully. She greeted each guest personally, immediately putting them at ease with her exceptional beauty. Her smile and poise were unquestionably genuine.

Chase spotted Alex as soon as she crossed the room. She stood out like a diamond among cut glass. "Ah, here is our lovely hostess now." She took his offered hands and held them as he smoothly pecked each cheek. "*Mí amour,* you are a supreme vision of loveliness." She stood next to Chase as he introduced her to his associates.

The gala rivaled the most elegant affair Hollywood could conceive. The glitz and glamour abounded. By midnight, the rich, the famous and the opulent all descended on the adorned yacht. White-jacketed and gloved waiters roamed throughout carrying silver trays of Beluga caviar and magnums of Dom Perignon and Veuve Cliquot champagne.

The guests mingled in fitted tuxedos with tasseled Gucci loafers and elegant gowns in stiletto heels. Balding, backless and strapless they arrived as if on cue, baring tight abs, tiny waists, tanned, taut faces and dark sunglasses. Everyone air-kissed everyone as sparkling-jeweled chokers glittered and boulder-size diamond rings twinkled. Laughter and gaiety were the order onboard.

Adversely, he stood to the side marveling at the radiant celebrity. A villain never looked so devastatingly handsome. Black tuxedo, black silk shirt open at the neck with a black bow tie hanging unbound around his neck. His was the appearance of menacing thoughts.

She noticed him, it was impossible not to. He eventually approached her and held out his hand. "Shall we?" he inquired. As would any exceptional hostess she smiled courteously and yielded her hand, allowed him to lead her to the dance floor.

As a single vision, they moved to the melancholy rhythm of the blues. The slow, measured cadence of the doleful beat seeped into their souls. A distinctive yet intangible aura of sadness surrounded them.

Alex closed her eyes and inhaled deeply. She drifted on the exotic mixed aroma of Acqua di Parma and Lance Morgan. Wistfully, she allowed herself to experience the dense hardness of his physique as their bodies moved in unison. An array of memories unfolded before her.

He held her tightly, pressing the small of her narrow waist against his body. He nudged the side of his face against her mounds of dark curly tresses. This was where she belonged, he decided. The touch, the scent, the sight of her, was branded in his heart forever.

Neither spoke as the song ended. They stood apart. Rendering silent expressions of pain and anguish, their eyes, fixed on each other, spoke volumes. She turned to walk away.

He grasped her upper arm, stepped closer and whispered in her ear, "You had your say earlier, now it's my turn." He led her through the throng of guests and out onto the secluded deck. "You and I are not over, Alex," he emphatically assured her. "We will never be over."

He released his hold, letting his fingers tingle down her bare arm until he grasped her hand. "I'm in your blood and you're in mine. That's just the way it is, and the way it will always be." He closed his eyes and longingly kissed each finger slowly, one at a time. "I love you, Alex. I've loved you since, since forever, since before we even met. I just didn't realize it until now."

She looked up into his dark piercing eyes. "You don't love me," she assured him. The steel in her voice was obvious. "You love three hundred and ninety-eight pages written by Mason Turner. That's what you wanted, that's what you went after and that's what you got."

"You're right, at one time all I wanted was the book, but not now, not anymore." His sincerity overflowed.

"Then I suggest in the future you be careful what you go after, you just might get it."

"I don't care about the book, Alex, I don't even want the book."

"As you like," she stated nonchalantly, then turned to walk away.

"No, not this time, Alex," he warned. "You're going to have to step out of character soon and when you do, I'll be there, waiting." He felt her body stiffen as several joyous guests passed near enough to overhear his words. "We need to talk in private. Expect me tomorrow evening." He turned and strolled down the plank leaving her to gaze after him in the darkness.

She smiled knowingly. "Bon voyage, Lance."

The buffet tables never diminished, the champagne continued a ceaseless flow and the band played until dawn. The event would be talked about for days following. Each recounting relayed the festivity's grandeur, the yacht increasingly spectacular and the hostess more and more omnipotent.

Lance returned to the yacht early evening the following day. The slip was empty, the yacht was gone.

Chapter Twenty-three

"Hmm," Linda moaned as she rolled to the other side of the large bed. She threw her leg over Jake's thigh. He laid his head back on the pillow and closed his eyes, his thoughts whirling. He was almost to his goal. The only uncertainty was Morgan's initial hesitancy to divulge Turner's identity. Remembering the night at the restaurant and their conversation at the penthouse, Jake was skeptical of Lance's conviction. He recognized that Lance had the same whipped expression that Burke had when Lillian left his L.A. office. If Lance backed out of the deal, having Mason Turner would have to be his ticket. He needed a contingency plan.

Picking up his notebook from the nightstand, he flipped back a few pages. There, he detailed a method of obtaining Turner's identity. He had four possibilities, Mark Summers, Lance Morgan and Lillian Turner-Price, all of whom were too powerful to provoke. He picked up his pen and underlined the fourth name scribbled on the page, Alexandra Price. She was long past her value in Hollywood; thus she was expendable. She would have to be the key.

The answer was at Stoneridge, of that he was certain. He reached down and rubbed Linda's bare leg. She murmured incoherently, then rolled away. Writing quick notes, he began to plan. Linda would get the key and security codes from Lillian. He'd go to Jersey, search the house, find the information and contact Mason Turner. Then, in another few weeks he'd have his own agency. Jake smiled, then lay back against the pillow. If things worked out as he planned, he'd be running the negotiations for Turner's film deal by the end of the month.

It was a well-known fact that two studios and numerous others were locked in a bidding war for the project. Tens of millions of dollars could be made within the next few weeks. His commission alone would be immeasurable. He quickly wrote down a few numbers. At fifteen percent commission, at twenty percent commission; then smiling excitedly, he calculated forty percent commission. The sight of so many zeros was arousing.

He reached and pulled Linda to his side. She immediately awoke to his amorous touch. Within moments she lay beneath him, consumed by his sexual aggression. His kisses were hard and domineering. But it excited her. As she readied herself for the onslaught of Jake's lustful passion, his thoughts roamed elsewhere.

A vision of Alexandra Price dressed in the golden-beaded lace bustier came into focus. She slowly walked to him through the crowded restaurant just as she'd done before. This time the outcome was different, she didn't turn her back and walk away as she did with Lance. This time she begged him to take her, right there, on the floor of the restaurant. He did repeatedly.

The next morning Jake made breakfast. Linda came bouncing into the kitchen. He kissed her passionately. "I need a favor," he began. "It's for us, our future."

She smiled dreamily. "Sure, anything."

Troubled and bewildered, Alex stood at the ship's stern and found solace in watching the coast of Cannes disappear into the horizon. The buoyant sound of excited seagulls and the choppy churning sea unsettled

her. There was no way she could face Lance again. Each
time she saw him weakened her resolve.

She closed her eyes, seeing him dressed dark and
dangerous. The enticing gleam in his eye was unbear-
able. She had to touch him.

She knew she was playing with fire but after seeing
him the day before she didn't care. He was correct in
his assessment, he was in her blood. It took every iota
of strength she had not to rip the silk from his body
and bury her face in his chest.

She looked out at the horizon. Cannes had completely
disappeared into the sea. She wished her desire for
Lance were that easily extinguished.

Shopping in Nice was tedious. Gambling in the casi-
nos of Monte Carlo was wearisome. And, the pebble
beaches of St. Tropez had lost their appeal. Thoughts
of Lance intruded on every indulgence she usually
relished.

"Belladonna," Chase sighed, "what do I have to do to
give you pleasure? Your sadness has broken my heart."

Alex smirked at her traveling companion. "Chase,
don't you have a script to memorize?"

"*Sí*, that's why I always use cue cards. You see, I have
a special relationship with every cue card girl in every
one of my films."

"So what happens if the director hires a cue card boy
instead?" She laughed.

"That's not funny, Alex," he said seriously, then
laughed along. "I'll tell you a secret," he whispered
closer, "it is in my contract to have a female, always."

"Figures," she piped out.

"But of course."

Alex shook her head. "What am I going to do with
you, Chasano?" she asked rhetorically.

"I have a number of marvelous ideas. First we remove
your clothing . . ." he began. Alex threw her hands up
and walked away. He pulled her back playfully into his

arms and the two hugged platonically. "Ah, *sí*, there is the smile I longed to see these many days."

Alex brightened more. How could anyone be pensive with Chasano around?

"Ah, look." He pointed to a far speck in the distance. "There she is, Italy."

The following day the yacht came to port in Chirro. A day later a restless Alex left for Stoneridge.

Linda jumped up as soon as Jake entered the outer office. She dashed around her desk and grabbed him. "I missed you so much," she cooed loudly.

Jake, unnerved by the outward show of affection, stepped back. He scanned the empty room nervously. Linda also looked around. Then, understanding his apprehension, she volunteered, "There's nobody here. Mavis and Helen are running errands and Lillian will be out the rest of the afternoon. I'm in charge," she stated proudly.

Jake dropped his notebook and briefcase on the desk. "Did you get the key and codes?" he asked.

Linda swayed her hips closer. "Later. I've got a better idea." She ran her hand down the length of his arm. "Lillian has an extra-wide sofa in her office. Why don't we test the springs?" She ended the statement with a wide grin and wink.

"I don't have time for this right now, Linda, just give me the key and codes," he demanded impatiently.

Pouting, she marched back behind her desk. "I knew it. I knew it. There had to be a reason why you wanted me to spend the night with you. Any other time you'd make me get up and go home. You only wanted me to stay the night with you to get the key, didn't you?"

Jake moved behind her chair. He needed to do damage control. Linda was floundering again. "Linda," he gasped in mock horror, "how can you say that? What I'm doing, I'm doing for us. For our life together, our future. How can we have a future in this town without money?" She sat with her arms folded across her lacking chest. "Linda." He swirled her chair around, then knelt down before her. "This is it, our chance to make every dream come true. For us to be together, you a star and me as your agent."

"But Lillian will know I took the key. I'll get fired," she wailed.

"So what? You're out of here anyway. Do you think I like seeing you work here all day for that woman? Remember, Lillian is the one person who told you that you didn't have the looks or talent to be a star." Linda raised her eyes at his words. Jake smirked, he knew he had her again. "She doesn't believe in you the way I do. She just hired you because she felt bad about shooting off her mouth."

"You're right, I'm sorry." She stroked his face. "I guess I just needed you to reassure me."

"I understand," he lied as he kissed her lips gently. "The only reason I had you leave the other times was" —he lowered his head, stammering—"I . . . I didn't want you to see how much I love you. And the reason I'm so anxious for the key is that I want to get all this over with so that we can be together as soon as possible."

"Oh, Jake," she muttered, smiling brightly. Yet, the look in his eye didn't match the words from his mouth. Still, she opened the top drawer and handed him the key and a slip of paper. He took the items and stood.

"Thank you, I'll call you as soon as I return. We'll celebrate, dinner, dancing, the whole thing. We'll do it up right. Then we'll have a private party. Just the two of us." He sneered seductively. "All night long just the way you like it." He pecked her quickly on the forehead, gabbed his briefcase, then hurried out of the room.

Linda smiled dreamingly. It was just like her horoscope said, *A short trip will alter your life . . . Your true love will be revealed.*

It wasn't until she was gathering her things to leave for the day when she realized Jake had inadvertently left his notebook on her desk. She picked it up and took it home with her.

Chapter Twenty-four

"So how was Cannes?" Franklin asked Lance.

"Don't ask."

"That good, huh?"

"Same as always, yachts, villas, glitz, glamour," Lance responded nonchalantly as he eased back into the office chair. "Oh, there was one interesting occurrence, Alexandra Price was there."

"I presume that explains your less than jovial mood." Franklin tossed a European tabloid newspaper across the desk. The headline read FAMED AMERICAN ACTRESS DUMPS ACTION SUPERSTAR LANCE MORGAN FOR ITALIAN LEADING MAN CHASANO D'LUCCHIA. The article went on to account her leaving Cannes aboard her yacht with Chasano en route to Italy for a quickie wedding. The story was accompanied by photos of the happy couple aboard her yacht, shopping in Nice and walking on a beach in St. Tropez.

Lance scanned the article, then glared at Franklin and tossed the paper back. Franklin stood and walked around to lean back on his desk. "What's this?" Lance picked up the letter Franklin placed in front of him.

"It's what you wanted," Franklin confirmed. "It came registered mail yesterday morning. Seems Ms. Price has accepted your offer pending certain stipulations."

Lance didn't look especially delighted by the news. He read the letter absent of all emotion. It basically stated that his production company was awarded the media publication rights to the book *A Pilgrimage to Heaven.*

"You don't look particularly pleased," Franklin said, seeing Lance's reaction to the positive letter. "This *is* what you wanted, isn't it?"

"Yeah, sure. I'm happy, why wouldn't I be? After all, this was the goal. I got exactly what I wanted."

"Are you sure about that?"

As soon as Linda stepped into the small one-bedroom apartment she felt it. The place was sweltering. She tossed her purse and newspapers down, then marched over to the circular dial. She pushed the lever to the very bottom. The red line said fifty degrees. She waited for the familiar click, then the blast of cool air to pour from the floor vents. Nothing happened. Frustrated, she took her fist and banged on the dial several times. Still nothing. Apparently the central air conditioner was on the blink again. This was the last thing she needed after her day.

Linda grabbed the phone and punched in the superintendent's number. His answering service informed her that he was on an audition and would return her call at his earliest convenience. "That's the trouble with living in L.A.," she surmised for the umpteenth time, "everyone's out on auditions." Continuing to mumble openly, she headed for the kitchen, opening every window along the way.

"Ahh," she cooed as she stood in front of the open refrigerator letting the cool air wash over her sticky body. She stood enjoying her newfound relief for a few moments, then pulled out a beer and a cardboard container. After dispatching the container into the microwave she opened the beer and gulped it down as she made her way to the bedroom.

She took a cool shower and slipped into a tank top

and shorts and padded barefoot back to the kitchen. She grabbed the mail and loose newspapers on the way, then stood by the trash can. Tossing the occupant mail, she began flipping through the remaining bills. The frozen dinner continued to rotate slowly in the microwave so Linda sat at the kitchen table with the last of her beer.

Following a few finishing gulps of ale, she discarded the rest of the mail unopened. Taking another beer, she walked back to the living room and turned on the television to the local news. The perky weathergirl predicted another hot humid evening with temperatures topping the upper eighties. Linda slouched back on the sofa and frowned. "This is L.A., moron," she shouted, annoyed with the woman's cheerful disposition. "Of course it's hot and humid. What else would it be?"

After concluding that she'd be a much better weathergirl, she changed the channel to the entertainment news, picked up her oversize purse and rummaged through for her cigarettes. She found her full pack but was unable to locate her precious gold-plated lighter. The one she had received as a gift from Jake after a particularly unpleasant argument. Frustrated by thoughts of Jake, she dumped the contains of her purse on the coffee table.

A tube of hot-pink lipstick, a diaphragm, several smudged receipts, eighty-three cents in loose change and her wallet went sprawling across the table. She fingered the jumble, no lighter. Digging deeper, she pulled the remaining items from the large bag. Three tabloid newspapers she purchased on the way home, an emergency pair of white lacy panties and six disk-shaped connecting condom packets. The last item was Jake's leather-bound date book. The coveted lighter had worked its way between several of the pages.

She lit a cigarette, sipped the beer, then flipped through her tabloid newspapers. They'd all led with the same basic stories, aliens living in Omaha, skinny people dieting, speculations of years-old murder mysteries and has-been movie stars still vying for attention. She read the articles hungrily, figuring if they all published the same news it had to be true. Four cigarettes later she finished by reading her horoscope from each paper. She considered all three predictions, then went with the most promising excerpts, *Your future will brighten shortly . . . Be prepared to take chances . . . A journey will change your life.*

The beer bottle was empty and she was still hot and sticky. She stared blankly at the small color screen, then picked up and lit another cigarette. Glancing at Jake's open date book, she picked it up lovingly. She couldn't believe he had walked out and left it on her desk. He never went anywhere without this book. This was Jake's entire life. Everything and everyone important to him was in this book. Names, addresses, phone numbers, everything an agent could possibly need or want was now here, in her hands. She looked around the empty room sneakily. One peek wouldn't hurt, she decided.

It was just as she expected. Basic information on his clients and half the people in Hollywood. He'd meticulously outlined everything including likes and dislikes, birthdays, anniversaries, kids' names and dates of birth. What she didn't expect to find listed were their aspirations, fetishes, obsessions and vices. Amazed and astonished she giggled openly at some of the more risqué entries.

Linda's mild amusement soon diminished. She always knew Jake did some unscrupulous dealings, but this was even more than she'd imagined. She had no idea he was so heavily into drugs and prostitution. Names, numbers and specialties, they were all indexed in detail. Under a heading of substance connections, he'd listed several well-known actors, businessmen, government officials and a very prominent assistant D.A. "No wonder they can't get rid of illegal drugs, the big boys are the ones profiting," she mused. Page after page of manipulations and deceptions, blackmail and extortion. She couldn't believe her eyes.

There was little mention of her name until a date two months earlier. After reading the scribbling on the page her mouth went dry as it hung open. She was dumfounded. "That slime," she mouthed. Apparently Jake's devious treachery knew no limitations. The notation regarded a man he'd set her up with a few months ago. Evidently Jake had pimped her out and she didn't even realize it. "That son of a . . ." she muttered.

Lighting her last cigarette in the pack, she continued reading. There were all sorts of future plans and schemes listed, each carefully detailed in specifics. None of which included her.

Eventually she turned to the date when she'd spent the night at his apartment. It began with a few rants and ravings about Lance Morgan's lack of commitment, then ended with double-underlined wording, *note to self, time to remove deadbeat albatross.* Instinctively, she knew he referred to her.

The last notation stopped her cold. He detailed several alternative plans to get Mason Turner as a client. Her shaking hand stamped out the cigarette. Her heart beat rapidly and sweat beaded on her forehead. Surely Jake couldn't be serious. Opening his own agency wasn't that critical. For the first time since she could remember, she was afraid. She couldn't believe what she'd read. Jake was a dangerous man. She closed the book. He had gone too far.

She picked up the phone and dialed her work number. The phone was picked up after the fourth ring. "Mrs. Turner-Price," she stuttered, "this is Linda Beale from work. I'm glad you're still there. I'm on my way back to the office. I need to talk to you. It's important."

Lillian frowned. Linda didn't sound like her usual perky self. "Can it wait until the morning?"

"No. I don't think so." Linda looked down at the

open date book lying on the table. "You need to see something."

"Fine. I'll be here."

Ted lay back on the huge mound of silken pillows. Sweat glistened on the mixed gray hairs on his chest. His breathing was just returning to normal. He smiled to himself thinking, *This woman is going to be the death of me. But what a way to go.*

Victoria came back into the bedroom. She half smiled at the man in her bed and slowly sauntered to his side. Her flimsy lace robe lay open exposing her slender curvaceous body beneath. She smiled seductively, kneeled on the bed, then leaned in closer to Ted. Her firm round breasts gently touched his wide chest. Ted smiled.

"I know that look."

Innocently a wide-eyed Victoria opened her mouth in mock offense. "What look? I have no idea what you're referring to."

"You know perfectly well what look I'm talking about." He reached up and stroked the shiny black hair, then laid the locks over her shoulder. He was hypnotized by the slim beauty of her neck and shoulders. He leaned over to kiss her neck. Victoria threw her head back, giving him ample leeway to indulge his pleasures. "What is it this time?" he moaned while nibbling.

"Well, now that you mention it," she mouthed enticingly, "I do have a teeny-weeny little notion. Actually it's more like a thought, or an idea. That's it, I have a small idea."

Ted grinned adoringly. God, he loved this woman. She was the best thing in his life and he couldn't imagine a single day without hearing her voice. Even now that they were divorced he still couldn't stay away from her. Being a famous movie director and producer, he always had a number of beautiful starlets begging for his attention but it was always Victoria that he came home to. Artistically she was his muse. Romantically she was his heart and ultimately she was his future.

"All right, Victoria, what's this week's stunt, lime jello in the Washington, D.C., Reflecting Pool, take apart and reassemble a tank on the Oval Office or maybe hop on the next shuttle launch and sprinkle candy jimmies and chocolate syrup on the Himalayas?"

Victoria giggled at Ted's outrageous suggestions. "No, silly." She cuddled closer as Ted wrapped his arm around her tightly. "I thought maybe we'd try something a little simpler this time, you know, something not as dramatic as our usual stunts." She quickly sat up. "This will be the pièce de résistance, the pinnacle, the final glimmer in our illustrious career." The telephone rang.

Ted's interest was piqued. He couldn't imagine what Victoria had in mind this time. But whatever it was, he knew he'd be right there beside her every step of the way.

Victoria picked up the receiver and listened as Lillian spoke. After disconnecting she dialed the airport and made arrangements. Ted sat up. "What's going on?" he asked as Victoria quickly threw on some clothes.

"It's Alex, there's trouble. I have to go."

Ted jumped up from the bed and began grabbing his clothing. "Not without me, you don't." A half hour later the two were seated in the private luxury plane taxiing down the runway, destination, United States.

Chapter Twenty-five

"Alex, I just read the screenplay. It's wonderful! I just love the new twist at the end. I like this ending even better than the book's ending. Call me back when you get back from Italy."

The machine was fast-forwarded to the next message. "Alex, it's Mark. I'm having the contracts delivered tomorrow morning. I have a feeling the studios are going to be very disappointed that you went this way. If there are any last-minute changes let me know; otherwise we'll have to wait to see their counteroffer. But with this price tag I hardly think there'll be one. Talk to you later. Oh, by the way, I read the script. Bravo, you've got another winner. I can't see them changing a single thing."

Several more messages played. None as interesting as the first two. They were replayed again and again. Jake stood with his finger on the button. Smiling, he played the messages one last time.

Alex reached up, pushed the button and watched in the rearview mirror as the garage door slowly descended. She sat in the car and just stared hypnotically out of the windshield. Her head pounded from a horrendous headache. In the past few days she'd hardly eaten and gotten even less sleep. Eventually her weary eyes focused on the dashboard clock. It was after five o'clock in the evening. She'd been traveling steadily since she left Cannes a week ago.

Hours after docking in Italy she had caught a flight to Rome with a direct connection to London. There she grabbed the Concord to New York and picked up her car at her mother's apartment garage. After a quick pit stop at Mrs. Fletcher's she was finally home.

And for the last two days she'd chided herself for her behavior every step of the way. She'd been childish and immature. The truth was she was angry and insulted. Lance had used her to get a book deal and she wanted to punish him. So she did. Unfortunately, it didn't make her feel any better.

Coal nudged his way to the front seat. "Come on, boy," she said as she got out of the car. Excitedly he rushed past her barking loudly. Alex went to the trunk of the car and began pulling and sorting the suitcases. She intended to grab a few hours' sleep, then leave for St. Croix as soon as possible. "Coal!" she called out. "Would you please stop all that noise?"

After emptying the trunk Alex grabbed her overnight case and headed for the rear stairs. She stumbled as Coal dashed around her legs eagerly. "What is wrong with you?" She set the bag down and grabbed Coal's collar. "Come on, let's get you outside." She guided him to the side door and waited for him to dash for freedom. Instead, he continued to bark loudly and lingered at her side.

She bent down and rubbed his black fur. "I know you missed me. I missed you too. But I also know that Mrs. Fletcher spoiled you rotten and took very good care of you. So, why don't you be a good boy and make a quick run outside before we go upstairs?" She waited again but he stayed by her side until she closed the door. "All right," she warned, "once I go upstairs you won't be able to run around outside until tomorrow morning."

Alex began walking back to the stairs as Coal jumped around her legs barking loudly. She picked up her bag and continued to the stairs. Coal ran in front and jumped at her again. "Stop it, Coal," she commanded. He barked again. "All right, mister. You'll just have to sleep in your doghouse tonight." She grabbed ahold of his collar again and led him into a small room off the garage.

The cozy room was littered with chew toys, balls and a host of doggie delights. In the far corner was a large built-in miniature house with pillow-padded floor and faux windows. She adjusted the automatic water and food dispenser, pouring a generous amount of each into the large dishes. Satisfied, she turned to go. As she pulled the door closed and latched the lower swinging door Coal began barking and whining. "I'm not going to feel sorry for you, Coal. You be a good boy and I'll come down and let you out later."

She grabbed her bag and headed up the stairs. She frowned. The kitchen was dark. It was unusual since Mrs. Fletcher regularly left the first-floor lights on when she knew Alex would be returning home. Alex dropped her bag in the kitchen and walked to the living room.

She paused. She wasn't alone. Even in the muted dimness of the room she sensed an unfamiliar presence. Scanning the room, she spotted the intruder. A man sat in the soft glow of the aquarium sipping a glass of amber liquid. "Good evening, Alex," he greeted her casually.

"Who the hell are you and how did you get in my house?"

"That doesn't matter right now. We have plenty of time to discuss trifles. First things first, Alex, have a seat." He gestured for her to sit on one of her living room sofas.

"Here, take it." She tossed her purse. "I have about six hundred dollars in travelers' checks plus some credit cards."

"Please, don't insult me."

"I don't know how you got in here, but I suggest you leave now before I call the police."

"Right now I suggest you have a seat, we need to talk about our merger."

"Fine." She turned back to the kitchen. "I'm calling the police now."

He stood and called out, "Not a prudent idea, Mason." She froze midstep. "Or should I refer to you as Ms. Turner?"

She turned around. "Excuse me?"

"Let's not play coy, Alex. Time is of the essence. We have a merger to discuss. And I believe there are a few studios awaiting our decision. Frankly, I prefer to go with the largest offer, but I'm willing to consider your opinion."

She slowly walked back into the darkened room. A plan, she needed a plan. But more than that, she had to remain cool. As long as she was calm she could control the situation and therefore control him. "All right, Mr.?" she asked.

"You may call me Jake. Jake Marrows. After all, I am your new agent."

She squinted at him. "I know you, don't I?"

"I'm flattered that you remembered. We met some time ago. Robert Burke introduced us. I was his associate."

"All right, Mr. Marrows, we'll play it your way." Her sudden unflustered cool surprised him. He expected pleas of silence and threats of resistance. But her acceptance of the inevitable was refreshing. "What's your offer?"

"No." He wiggled his forefinger as if to scold a child. "You don't understand. There is no offer. I am your agent, period."

"I see." She rounded the edge of the sofa. "What's your percentage, Mr. Marrows?" She picked up a remote and pushed a button. The fireplace switched on, adding the soft glowing flames of yellow and red to the aquarium lighting.

He smiled at the new, more intimate setting. "I've decided to be magnanimous, thirty percent total billing on everything, books, films, whatever."

She nodded her understanding and pushed another button. Unnoticed from inside, the outside lights darkened. "That's a little high for an agent's commission, don't you think? After all, I've done all the work already. The name Mason Turner has already gained renown." As she pushed another button, bright lights turned on in the dining room. Jake squinted at the sudden brilliance. Alex casually walked over to the bar and poured herself a tall drink. She turned, gestured, offering to refill his tumbler. He declined.

"On the contrary. I considered forty-five percent."

She leaned her back against the bar. In the exposing of light, she quickly assessed the man before her. He didn't seem to be a complete lunatic or a crazed fanatic. His mannerisms were too calm and controlling. He seemed cagey and very sure of himself, as if each line had been rehearsed endlessly. The man was obviously no fool. He was arrogant and intelligent; that made him dangerous. If she intended to get away from him, and she did, she needed to call upon every acting ability she ever had.

"Then, I suppose I should be grateful," she conceded as she moved back to the living room. He nodded, lulled into a false sense of victory. "So, tell me, Mr. Marrows." She dropped her voice several octaves as she stood before him. "As your client"—she raised the glass to her lips—"what do I get in return?" She licked her lips and continued walking. Before he answered she pushed another button. Lights surrounding the sunken living room turned on along with the full brightness of the recessed ceiling lights.

Jake blinked, adjusting to the bright lighting. He loosened his tie, then slowly, obediently followed her, absorbing every nuance of her body's movements. The slow sway of her hips dried his mouth to sand. His eyes caressed each curve as he inhaled the delicate scent of her lingering perfume. He moved to stand directly behind her. A tortured moan escaped his throat. He could see why men lost themselves in her. She had a certain air that stimulated something deep inside him. He sipped from his glass, then licked his lips of the bitter liquid. He found his thoughts wondering if she tasted as good as she looked.

To his surprise she quickly spun around to face him. In the brilliant lighting he gawked, seeing for the first time how truly exquisite she was. Their eyes met and held. The quick glance he'd had of her in the dim New York restaurant was an injustice to the woman before him now. Slowly his eyes roamed downward to her lips, her neck, her breasts, then down her long legs. After touring her body his eyes returned to hers.

He reached up to touch her face. She tilted her head away playfully. "Answer the question, Mr. Marrows." She smiled seductively. "What do I get in return?"

"My silence. You see, Alex, I know how much you value your privacy. And"—she allowed him to stroke her cheek—"as long as we're in business together I won't reveal your little secret to the public. We can continue to enjoy your anonymity. All you have to do is keep writing your books and screenplays as usual. I'll take care of the paperwork, the press and all the deals."

"That is so very kind of you, Mr. Marrows. I really appreciate your thoughtfulness and consideration on my behalf. But"—she knitted her brows together distressfully—"that's the reason why I came back so early. There'll be a press release issued in a few days. As of last week I've decided to go public with Mason Turner."

"What!" he raged. "You can't." He nervously paced the floor in front of her. This wasn't a contingency. Damn it, he needed his notebook. He stopped pacing.

"Wait, so, fine, you'll go public. You'll still need an agent."

She smirked. "I don't think so, you have nothing to offer me. Do you?"

He reached behind his back and pulled out a nine-millimeter automatic gun. "How about your life?" He stepped closer, aligning his body flush against hers. Stunned, Alex stared into the barrel of the circular hole. "You see, Alex, I'm starting a new agency and you're going to be my first client." He turned her body slightly. "Do you see those papers over there?" He used the gun to motion to the table. She nodded slowly, ever mindful of the weapon. "You're going to sign your name on the bottom line. We'll be legal partners then. I'll broker the book deal and everybody will be happy."

"But," she stammered, closing her eyes tightly, "I've already signed off on the book."

Disappointed but accepting, Jake snarled at her closed eyes and fearful expression. "I hope we made a killing. How much? Two, three million?"

"No," she stammered.

Jake was overjoyed. He smiled greedily. "Four million dollars!"

"One . . ." she stuttered.

"One! One!" he repeated, unbelieving. "You sold out for a lousy one million dollars!" he ranted uncontrollably. "Damn, you fool. I could have gotten at least four times that amount."

She pressed her eyes tighter. "Not one million dollars, Mr. Marrows," she corrected calmly, "one dollar." She tossed her glass's liquid into his face, then pushed a button on the remote and all the lights blackened at once. Instantly, she ran toward the front door.

"No!" The earsplitting shout was that of an enraged man.

Chapter Twenty-six

Lance chalked his cue, bent down and aligned his polished stick with the white ball. The click of marble instantly scattered balls over the plush green surface. "Maybe I should have gone after her."

"Maybe," Charles responded as he circled the large table in preparation for his shot.

"But what was I supposed to say?" Lance asked Charles rhetorically. "That, yes, I was only interested in the book but now I couldn't care less? And that the only thing I want now is to be with her?" The stick tapped the ball, sending another rolling across the table just missing the side pocket. He shook his head hopelessly. "She'd never buy that."

Charles ducked under the low-hanging Tiffany lamp and carefully eyed his shot. "You never know, she might." He hit the white ball, sending two others barreling into opposite pockets.

"I should have just told her everything, starting with Jake's stupid plan," Lance lamented. "I'm not concerned about myself. It's Alex I'm worried about. Her privacy is precious to her. Do you think he'll eventually back off?"

"Jake?" Charles made another shot. Another ball flew across the green felt and disappeared into the net pocket. He looked up from the table, thought for a second, then responded, "I doubt it."

"But there's nothing he can really do now. He has no choice but to drop it."

"Jake's like a piranha on the scent of blood. He'll keep coming until he's permanently discouraged."

"I can't believe I listened to him, of all people."

"I'm sure you had your reasons for doing what you did," Charles assured him. The cue slid gracefully through his fingers, hitting the white ball. It clicked a yellow ball, then rolled, just missing the center pocket.

"No, not really. Nothing justifies using someone."

"Actually, Jake's plan, as wacked as it was, did introduce you to Alex and find Mason Turner in the process."

"Yeah, that was the only good thing about it." Lance leaned down to align a shot with his stick, then paused and stood up. "Damn."

Charles casually leaned back against the game room wall. "Don't beat yourself up about it. Give her time to cool off. She's hurting right now. After a few days give her a call. Explain everything. I'm sure it's not too late. Go to her, talk to her. Alex is a fabulous woman, she'll understand."

"When did you get to be an expert on women?"

The maid walked in before Charles responded. She announced, "Mr. Morgan, there is a Ms. Price to see you."

Both Charles and Lance looked at each other. This was too good to be true, Alex was here. "Send her in," Lance commanded anxiously.

Seconds later Lillian marched into the game room. Lance's face visibly dropped with disappointment. "Lillian? I thought you were, never mind. What can I do for you?"

"I'm looking for my daughter."

Concern registered on both men's faces. "What do you mean, looking for Alex?"

"She seems to be missing."

"Since?" Charles injected. Lillian looked at him questioningly.

"I'm sorry," Lance interjected. "Lillian, this is my head of security, Charles Taylor."

"How do you do?" she said, thrusting her hand forward. Charles stepped forward and shook Lillian's hand. "Greg's brother?" she asked.

He nodded. "Yes, ma'am. How long has Alex been missing?" he asked again.

"Since yesterday."

"Lillian, she's probably still in Italy with Chasano," Lance quipped bitterly.

"No, she flew back as soon as the yacht reached Chirro. I spoke to Victoria at her villa. Alex left two days ago and hasn't been seen since. Victoria and Ted are on their way to New York now."

Charles relaxed slightly. "Ma'am, I beg your pardon but maybe she's just unreachable for the time being."

"No, you don't understand, there's a threat to her life."

"What?" Lance jumped.

"Mr. Morgan." All three turned in the direction of the maid. She jumped back, wide eyed. "Mr. Moore to see you."

"Send him in," Lance said hastily, then turned back to Lillian. "What threat?"

Lillian relayed her conversation with Linda as the three men listened intently. When she finished she pulled the notebook from her bag and handed it to Lance. He read the last notation, then handed the book to Charles and called the airport to ready his private plane. Charles read it and handed it to Franklin.

Franklin scanned the pages and read the final entry aloud, ". . . after she tells me everything she knows about Turner the headlines will read, *Reclusive actress commits suicide after being shunned by Lance Morgan*. His career will be over! Nobody double-crosses me and gets away with it!" He'd scribbled nearly illegibly.

Within an hour Lance, Lillian, Franklin and Charles were miles aboveground on their way to Stoneridge, New Jersey.

Muted golden rays beamed through the large windows; the sun was setting. Alex closed her eyes and tried to calm herself and catch her breath but the dull pain reminded her of her ominous situation. Her headache had increased in intensity and her ankle throbbed painfully. The silken tie bit into her wrists and grew tighter each time she moved her hands in hopes of freeing them. Hopelessly, she lay on her side watching her abductor. She was at his mercy.

Lazily Jake opened his eyes and stared at Alex, then took a gulp from his glass. He shivered. "This stuff is pretty good," he rasped out, then cleared his burning throat. "I usually don't imbibe in such intoxicants, but I figured, why not?"

He stood and walked over to the aquarium and knocked the butt of the gun on the glass. The fish scattered. He smirked, enjoying his power. "Nice fish tank," he said, then turned and moved to the sofa. Looming above her, he reached down to stroke the hair from her face. "I've seen what you can do. What is this power you have over men? First Shawn, then Burke and now Lance. You have them all under some kind of spell." He knelt down to get a better look at her face. "What is it about you, Alexandra Price?"

He stood and swaggered confidently back to the chair and retrieved his glass. "Shawn is pathetic." He paused and stared at her as if for the first time. "You know, he was actually a pretty good actor at one time. But now." He laughed. "Now he's just another drugged-up alcoholic begging for work." He came closer and knelt down to her side again. "All because of you." Alex pressed her body against the back of the sofa, getting as far away from him as possible.

"I used to sit and listen to him rant for hours about the things the two of you did before you walked out on him. That was cold the way you just up and left him like that."

She glared. "Why are you still here? I told you the book is already under contract for one dollar. If you still want your thirty percent agent's commission, there's some loose change in my purse."

He chuckled. "I'm still here because we haven't completed our business transaction." He reached into his pocket and pulled out his cell phone. "You're going to make a phone call." She looked at him, questioning. "Your lawyer. You are going to call your lawyer and have him void the contract, then draft a new one awarding to the highest bidder." He held the phone to her ear. She leaned back defiantly. He picked up the gun and released the safety. "Do it, Alex," he hissed through clenched teeth, "now!" She did, leaving a message on Mark's answering machine.

"Good girl," he cooed as he tossed the phone on the chair. "Now, we wait for him to fax us a copy of the new contract." Smugly Jake plopped down into the opposite chair. Things had turned around for him. He was back in control.

Time dragged slowly as hours passed. Then the telephone rang, jarring them both awake. Alex looked at Jake wide-eyed; he stared back at her. "Don't move," he ordered, then ran into the kitchen and returned with the cordless extension in his hand. He took out the gun and pointed it at her. "Not a word," he warned, then pressed the power button. Jake listened intently to the message being left on the machine. He hung up and smiled conceitedly. "What do you have around here to eat?"

Victoria hung up the phone and looked around the room. Each face expressed a different concern.

"Someone picked up the extension," Charles remarked.

"Yes, I heard that too. Someone is definitely at the house," Lance added.

"I agree," Ted added. "I can't imagine Alex not picking up after hearing Victoria's voice on the machine. And certainly not after that message." Victoria nodded solemnly as she walked back to Lillian's side.

Lance stood decisively. "I'm going in to get her out of there."

Charles stood and walked to his side. "No." Lance turned and glared at him angrily until Charles elaborated. "We're going to get her out of there. But, we can't just charge in without a plan. We need to know if Jake is alone in there with Alex. We need to know if he's armed, and if so, what's he packing. Going in there blind will only make matters worse. He might harm Alex. What we need is a way to slip inside without being noticed. Unfortunately, my surveillance equipment is in New York and L.A."

"Uh . . . actually," Ted injected after clearing his throat loudly, "I do have a few items you might find useful." He ushered the small crew to a small side door in his office. He unlocked and opened the door. Lance and Charles followed him inside.

The room resembled a prop set from a futuristic espionage sci-fi film. Every imaginable surveillance gadget, device and apparatus adorned the walls. All were labeled with the specific function in detail. Ted gathered three black backpacks and began filling them with the necessary gear.

Lance and Charles looked at each other, then at Ted, then back at the wall of extraordinary gadgetry. Lance snickered, shook his head and held his hands up innocently. "I don't even want to know." The two men stood staring as Ted worked silently. He opened a drawer, pulled out three black nylon bodysuits with matching hoods, boots and communication headsets, then handed them to Charles and Lance. "Here, you'll need to put these on."

Charles took the offered clothing and held it up. "What, no Batman or Spiderman emblem?"

Ted smiled. "Sorry, the suits with the emblems are at the dry cleaner's." The three men chuckled, more to relieve the pressure of the next few hours.

Under cover of the moonless night, three dark figures slipped unnoticed over the eight-foot stone wall. Using night-vision goggles and impromptu hand signals they maneuvered through the thickening trees and shrubs until they reached the main structure. Lance took the key given to him by Victoria and let his fellow comrades in through the back door.

A gust of wind followed them until Ted secured the door, silencing the outside. The three looked around the darkened garage. Each removed his eyewear and black knitted hoods and turned on the miniature beams of light connected to the rims of the communication headsets. Brilliant beams of light erratically encircled the cavernous area. A loud thud, then loud barking came from one of the side doors. Charles alertly stepped forward. "What's that noise?"

"Sound's like Coal's been closed in his room," Ted remarked.

"Doesn't sound like he's going to be in there much longer the way he's going after that door," Lance speculated.

"Shouldn't we let him out?" Ted asked.

"Later, he's safer in there for now," Charles answered into the miniature mouthpiece. "Wait until we find out exactly what we're dealing with. Besides, he knows the two of you. Chances are he'll probably come after me." Lance nodded his agreement.

The men snaked through the row of cars. "Do any of these not look familiar?" Charles asked. Both Ted and Lance said no. "Good, that means Jake has other means of transportation in the area." Charles removed his black glove and touched the hood of Alex's car with the back of his hand. "The engine's cold. She's been here awhile." The three figures moved on to the base of the stairs. A row of five or six pieces of luggage were lined neatly at the bottom. "Ted, you and Lance stay here. I'm going up."

"I'm coming too," Lance rebuked and stepped behind Charles as he began ascending the stairs.

"No," Charles said, "it'll be easier for me to move around if I'm alone. He probably has her in the front of the house. That would give him an open view of the front grounds. I'm sure he wants to see who's coming and going. Unfortunately, there's no cover in that area. If he's armed, and he probably is, I don't want any heroics or casualties. Stay here."

Ted grabbed Charles's arm. "Wait, what are you going to do? If there's no cover in the living room you'd be just as exposed as we'd be."

"I'm gonna make sure she's okay and find out if he's got any help up there. I'll be back in ten minutes."

"What if he sees you?" Lance asked.

Charles smiled cockily. "He won't." Then, silently, he eased up the back stairs, then slipped through the kitchen door.

Chapter Twenty-seven

Alex closed her eyes and wished Jake away. Her thoughts faded as she relived the ordeal. If only she hadn't tripped over his briefcase, she'd have gotten away. A split second after pressing the remote's power button, she made a break for the front door. With the room thrust into total blackness she had the perfect cover and opportunity.

Taken completely off guard by the suddenly darkened room, Jake tried desperately to regain his bearings. Then in the darkness he heard her fall. Quickly he ran toward the muffled commotion. When he saw Alex's shadowy figure stand, he lunged for her. They both went down.

With arms and legs flailing wildly she fought valiantly for her freedom. He was too strong, he grabbed her wrists and quickly tied them with his silken tie. Then he removed his belt and bound her legs together. It was then she felt the pain of her twisted ankle. Within seconds he yanked her to her feet, then half carried, half dragged her to the sofa. He dropped her down heavily on the cushions and moved back to his chair across the room.

"In a lot of ways, Alex, you and I are very much alike. We both recognize weakness for what it is, then utilize it to our advantage." He was reminded of his weakness for her just moments earlier. His lustful stupidity let her take control of the situation and she almost got away.

"You and I are nothing alike," she spat out. "I don't exploit and abuse people. That's your job, yours and Burke's."

Ignoring her remark he changed the subject. "I'm curious, what happened between you and Burke? How did he make you quit the business?" Refusing to answer, she just glared at him. He stood and moved menacingly closer. "I asked you a question."

"Burke had nothing to do with it, I quit of my own accord. After twenty years in the business I'd had enough."

"That's right, you started when you were a kid, didn't you?" She didn't reply. "How old were you? Six, eight?"

"I was two."

"Right, I remember." Jake turned and moved toward the aquarium. "You were on that hospital show. You were that doctor's precious little adopted daughter. So, what, you were like seven or eight in that episode when your character was killed by a drunk driver. They say that was the night America mourned. You know, industry people still talk about how that season finale's ratings went through the roof."

"Are we finished strolling down memory lane yet?" she replied wearily, annoyed by his incessant reminiscing. Then she stopped. She heard something. There was a noise but evidently Jake didn't hear it. There it was again, it came from the garage. Suddenly her pulse raced with anticipation. Mark must have gotten the message and come instead of called. Then, just as quickly her heart sank. What could he possibly do against an armed man? Fear gripped her again. Jake was too unpredictable, there was no telling what he'd do if confronted. She had to warn Mark.

Jake continued, ". . . then you did that movie and got your first nomination." He turned to her. "How old were you then?"

"Eight," she said, uselessly twisting her wrist restraints. She had to get Jake out of the room so that she could warn Mark.

Jake plopped down in the chair. "Damn, eight years old and you got an Oscar nomination." He laughed. "That's remarkable. I actually saw you in that film not too long ago. You were an incredible talent. Even at that age it was obvious that you had what it took. You had that natural ability to connect with your audience and make them care about the character. That's a rare gift. It's what acting is really about, making the audience feel what you feel. You were really good at that."

"Thanks. Now, if you're through, why don't you—"

"You know, some actors go their entire life without getting as far as you did. There you were, with a promising career at age twenty making tens of millions of dollars per film, getting a healthy chunk of the box office take, video royalties. On top of that, you were getting residuals from two successful television shows and your modeling career. All that and you just walked away, gave it all up, the money, the fame, the glamour, just like that." He stared at her unbelievingly.

"Just like that," she repeated smugly.

Suddenly, he jerked to his feet, gripping the gun gingerly. "I'd like to thank the members of the academy, my mother and father. The director for his insight, the writer for writing such an incredible script and finally I'd like to thank my manager." Jake shook his head, half smiling to himself. "Why is it that nobody every thanks the agent for getting them the damn part in the first place?" he asked rhetorically. "Never once have I heard someone thank their agent for making it all possible. For all the endless hard work, the repeated calls and lunches, the ass-kissing. Never once are we thanked." Jake shook his head woefully. "So, where is it?"

"Where's what?"

"The Oscar. I've never actually held one before." He

slipped the gun behind his back and walked toward the dining room. "Well, where is it? Come out, come out wherever you are," he chimed playful, singing the chant.

When he was out of her sight she feverishly worked at her wrist and ankle restraints but to no avail. "I didn't win, remember?" she spat out in frustration.

"No, not that time," he answered from above her. "But you did win the second time you were nominated. Another remarkable performance, I might add. You were truly exceptional in that role." His voice trailed off above her as he began to climb the stairs still singing the children's chant.

She listened carefully as his heavy footsteps moved through the upstairs bedrooms. She wiggled, struggling to free herself. Then she heard the kitchen door swung open.

"Alex," a man's hushed voice called out.

Maneuvering to peer above the sofa, she saw Charles emerge from the kitchen. "Charles?" she mouthed in delight, then quickly looked above to the empty stairs.

He eased closer to the living room. "Where?" he silently asked.

She nodded toward the upstairs.

"Alone?"

Tears of relief streamed down her cheeks as she exuberantly nodded yes.

"Armed?"

A look of total dejection shadowed her face as she nodded yes a second time. She lowered her eyes and blinked away the falling tears. Charles moved closer, stepping down into the living room. He placed his hands on her shoulders and sat her comfortably upright. Quickly he loosened the bindings. "Does he know about the rooms behind the fireplace?"

"No, I don't think so," she replied quietly.

"Good." He winked at her and within seconds he'd pressed the office door panel and disappeared behind the wall.

She sat staring at the closed panel when she heard Jake returning still chanting the limerick.

"Come out, come out, wherever you are." He clumped down the steps heavily. I've been over this house a dozen times even before you got here. I don't remember seeing it anywhere. So, where is it?" He walked back into her line of vision. "As a matter of fact, you should have a couple dozen statuettes around here. Where are they?"

"What difference does it make where they are? How long do you intend holding me like this?" Alex protested.

"As long as it takes your lawyer to fax the new contract."

"Then what?"

"Then I'll look over the contract, you'll okay it and we'll collect our money."

"Mark won't buy it, he knows me too well. Once I've made a decision it's final."

Jake rushed threateningly close to Alex's side. "Then let's hope your exceptional acting skills are still keen, my dear. Because if he doesn't redo that contract he'd better start dusting off your will."

"Lance, Ted, can you hear me?" Charles whispered as he knelt down by the fireplace. "I'm in the bedroom."

Both Lance and Ted nodded to each other. "Yeah, we hear you loud and clear," Lance replied. "Where's Alex, is she okay, did you see her, did he hurt her?" Each successive question angered Lance more and more.

"You've got to calm down, Lance, Alex is fine. She's handling this like a pro. She's sitting on the living room sofa facing me. Jake's alone but he's armed. Unfortunately, there's no direct way to get at him. He's too mobile. We need a distraction so I can jump him from this direction. He won't be expecting it."

"I'll come up there and surprise him," Lance suggested. "He'll forget about Alex as soon as he sees me."

"Yeah, for about one second; then he'll have both of

you. We don't want that," Charles retorted. "He seems to be waiting for a phone call. That ought to distract him enough to catch him off guard. All I need is a few seconds to get the gun away from him."

"All right," Ted confirmed, "we'll wait for the phone to ring. I'll have Victoria call."

"Good," the three agreed at the same time.

The loud thud gave way to splinters as the lower door's latch broke free. Instantly, Coal came bounding from the room. His heavy weight took both Lance and Ted by surprise as he knocked them down and hurdled up the back stairs to the kitchen. Lance quickly followed and grabbed at his collar as he reached the top stair.

The booming sound from below startled both Alex and Jake.

"It's the police. They know you're here. That's them breaking in the door. Why don't you give yourself up? They'll be lenient with you. I'll tell them how much you regret what happened here. I'll say that you were just about to let me go when they arrived."

"Shut up! Shut up, I need to think," Jake shouted anxiously as he pulled the gun out.

"What was that?" Charles asked into the tiny microphone.

Lance whispered into the mouthpiece, still struggling, "Coal got out, but we've got him under control." Ted hastily came up behind Lance. Just then the telephone rang. "That'll be Victoria." Barely holding the rambunctious Coal back, Lance handed him off to Ted. "Here, take him, I'm going up."

Jake moved to the front windows. Alex noticed the bedroom door panel recede slowly. She shuddered, dreading the next few minutes, yet relieved that the nightmare would be over soon. She had to distract Jake long enough to give Charles time to enter the room unnoticed.

She loosened the silk tie and the leather belt. The ringing phone drew Jake's attention. Torn, he stared at the phone, then cautiously peered outside expecting to see a mass of red flashing lights and armed officers. But the stark darkness revealed nothing.

"What are you going to do now, Jake?" Alex yelled, drawing his attention again. He turned to her, his back to the bedroom wall. "The police are here and they're going to arrest you for kidnapping, breaking and entering and assault with a deadly weapon."

"Assault!" Jake turned, yelling back at her. "I never assaulted you with any deadly weapon."

The phone continued ringing. Jake hurried down the steps and crossed the living room shifting his attention to the kitchen door. Alex stood up boldly after he passed. "You threatened me with a loaded gun, that's assault, Jake. What are you going to do now? Why don't you answer the phone? You can't run, you can't hide. They'll find you, Jake. You know they will. What are you going to do now? Give yourself up. It's your only chance."

"I said shut up!" he shouted, turning to Alex. Then, from the corner of his eye he saw Charles emerge from the wall opening for the first time. "What the—" He pivoted completely, aiming the gun in Charles's direction.

"No!" Alex screamed and leaped at Jake's arm just as he pulled the trigger. Charles quickly dove back into the bedroom. The gun's exploding sound was deafening as the bullet-shattered window rained tiny fragments of glass shrapnel onto Charles and the surrounding carpet.

The chaos inside intruded on the muted sounds of the night. Jake turned back to Alex. "You set me up!" He pointed the gun's barrel in her direction.

Hearing the gunshot, Lance burst into the room. "Alex!" he yelled, fearful for her safety. Jake spun around, seeing Lance suddenly appear in the room. He turned the gun on him. "Lance, no!" Alex shrieked as she rammed Jake's legs, knocking him down. The gun fired aimlessly, Lance fell.

"Get down, Alex," Charles yelled out. Jake turned and fired wildly, sending Charles diving behind the sofa.

Jake pointed the gun back at Alex. "I'm afraid there's no one left to save you, Mason Turner." He laughed victoriously.

"No, Jake," Lance said calmly while staggering to his feet. "It's me you want, not her. Let her go." He held his side as blood oozed from the wound.

Jake smirked. "Well, well, well, if it isn't the superstar action hero arriving just in time to save the day. Just like in the movies. Unfortunately, there's no stunt double, no cameras and no one to yell cut. This is the real thing."

Lance stepped forward. "Jake, listen to me. It's over. There's nowhere to run. You're right, this is real life. Once you pull that trigger it's over, for all of us."

Jake laughed, then shrugged his shoulders. "I never liked the happily ever after B.S. anyway." He turned the gun back in Alex's direction, then glared at Lance with a sinister grimace. "Say good-bye."

Charles raised his head up again. He saw that Jake's attention was still on Lance and Alex. Quickly he dashed to the nearest cover, then crunched low behind a chair. Jake saw the movement and swung around briefly. "I suggest you stay were you are, Mr. bodyguard, or your friend here won't live long enough to sign your next paycheck."

"No, wait," Lance yelled, drawing Jake's attention again. "Jake, please, I'll do anything you want. I'll sign with you, I'll give you everything I have, money, houses, cars, everything." He looked over to Alex as his insides twisted. "I'll give you my life, take it. Just please don't hurt her," he begged.

Jake smiled arrogantly, finding humor in his words. "How noble, sacrificing yourself for love. Tell me, do you love her that much?"

Lance looked into Alex's teary eyes to answer. "Yes, I love you that much. I'd gladly give my life for you."

Alex felt the truth in his words pierce her heart. Every fiber in her being screamed to hold him. She smiled. At that moment, nothing else mattered, Jake could do whatever he wanted with her life. Because she knew she was truly loved. She mouthed the words "I love you."

Lance nodded his understanding and added inaudibly, "I know."

Jake laughed openly, half applauding yet still holding the gun in his hand. "Bravo, very touching. I almost bought that myself." He chuckled again. "You two are something else. I'll tell you what, I'll do you both a favor and put both of you out of your—" He stopped, seeing a dark blur streak across the room at the last second.

Coal burst forward. Charging at full speed, he lunged his heavy body at Jake. His menacing fangs instantly clamped onto the threatening arm. Snarling growls and agonizing curses surrounded the pair as they wrestled to the floor. Jake fired off several frantic shots. Ted ducked into the room as bullets whizzed wildly, several missing Lance and Charles by inches. "Alex, get down!" the men commanded in unison.

Alex froze. Her mind's eye stepped out of the realm of reality as she watched the horrendous battle unfold around her. Her physical existence dissipated as the laws of the universe became irrelevant. The axis straightened and gravity no longer held as bullets hovered in space, barely in motion.

She screamed. Then screamed again. Yet each time the sound smothered in the constraints of her throat. The pungent stench of gunpowder caused her stomach to twist as it singed her tearful eyes. The fierce battle continued, yet for her, the unbelievable action was barely perceivable and the sounds scarcely audible. Her heart pounded with such vigor it seemed to leap from her chest. With each rasping breath she tried to regain control.

Then she heard it. Loud and long, the scream was finally released.

Jake maneuvered the gun in Coal's direction. "No!" she screamed, then jumped onto his back. They wrestled as Coal sank his fangs into Jake's leg. He yelled out in pain as the gun went off. Two rounds exploded in succession, then silence. Jake pushed the whimpering bodies aside and ran to the open window. Then, sending several more shots in Lance's and Charles's directions, he disappeared into the night.

After dodging the final bullets, Lance, Charles and Ted ran to Alex. Blood seeped through her fingers as she held tight. Lance fell to her side. "Where are you hit?" he demanded. The urgency in his voice was evident. She shook her head, still completely disoriented by her surroundings. Lance repeated his question as he prodded at her limbs. "Alex, where are you hit?" She frowned. His words were foreign. She looked down. Coal lay whimpering in her arms.

The hollowed sound of her breathing grew louder and louder, slower and slower. Her lungs could no longer perform the essential task of expelling oxygen. Lance grabbed her shoulders. From someplace far away she heard his faint pleas as the blackness slowly ascended into silence.

Chapter Twenty-eight

"Alex! Alex, stay with me. Alex!"

"Where is she hit?" Charles demanded.

Ted hurried to the open window and saw Jake's retreating figure run across the front lawn. Charles grabbed Ted back and snarled, "He's mine," then jumped through the broken window after the fleeing figure. Ted turned, looking around stunned, as if seeing for the first time. The room was a disaster. He walked over to the still ringing phone and picked it up. "Call the police. We need an ambulance," he instructed the caller then hung up.

Sobs of anguish drew his attention. He saw Lance holding Alex with Coal cradled in her arms. He knelt down to the heavily panting Coal. "Help's on the way," Ted assured them, having called the emergency number as soon as Coal broke free.

Charles came running back into the room, his arm covered in blood. Out of breath, he stammered, "He got away, but he can't get far. The police will have the area surrounded." Ted handed Charles the tie lying on the floor. "Here, wrap this around your arm and pull it tight, it'll slow the bleeding." Charles wrapped the material around his bleeding arm.

Victoria and Lillian came running into the house. Astonished by the sight, Victoria ran to Ted as Lillian ran to Alex. Moments later the room was swarming with detectives, policemen, firemen and paramedics.

"Here," Lance instructed, "over here." The paramedics immediately ran to him and began administering aid to his bleeding side. "Not me," he bellowed, "her, help her."

Quickly they removed a slow-panting Coal from her lap and eased him to the side. Blood saturated the side of her dress. One of the paramedics placed his hand on her pulse, then nodded affirmatively to his partner. Gently they felt around for a wound.

Firmly, forcibly, Lance was pulled from Alex's side. "Mr. Morgan, sir, you're bleeding. We need to check your side," the young officer said.

"Lance," Charles called out while having his arm and shoulder wrapped for transportation, "you have to let them check your wound."

Irritated, Lance finally relented. He was taken aside, his black jumpsuit cut away and his injury attended to. Lance looked around. The room was in complete chaos. Several detectives had Ted and Victoria in the corner taking statements while another spoke with Charles as the medic bandaged his injury. Lillian had given Jake's date book to an older detective who was flipping through the pages nodding as she spoke. Her eyes never turned from Alex.

The initial statements taken implicated Jake Marrow as the sole perpetrator. The manhunt began. An all points bulletin had been released nationwide for his apprehension and questioning.

"It doesn't seem like she's been hit," the attendant said to his partner as he broke a small vile and waved it under her nose. Slowly Alex regained consciousness. "Miss Price, do you know where you are?" he asked her. Alex looked at him, dazed and confused, then closed her eyes again. "Let's get her out of here."

The two paramedics placed her on a wheeled stretcher, strapped her down and lifted the gurney to waist level.

They passed a detective who was collecting spent shells. He stopped the stretcher. "Ms. Price, I'm going to need a statement from you." She opened her eyes and nodded slowly.

Lance jumped up wincing with pain. "I'm going," he said to the paramedic.

"Mr. Morgan, I have to finish taping your side so that we can safely transport you to the hospital."

"Later," he said firmly, "I'm going with them." He grabbed at his side and walked over to Alex. He took her hand and she opened her eyes and smiled. "I'll be at your side all the way," he assured her. She nodded.

Hours later Alex awoke to see that Lance had camped out at her bedside. "Hey, you," he said, holding her hand.

"Hi." She smiled up at him. "Have you been here the whole time?"

"Where else would I be?"

"How's Coal?"

"He caught a bullet in his hind." Alex frowned and moved her hand to cover her mouth. Lance smiled, delighted he could report good news. "Luckily Jake is a terrible shot. I spoke with your veterinarian earlier. He said that Coal's doing fine. He also said he didn't think the bullet's grazing will hinder his mobility in the future."

"Thank goodness. What about Charles?"

"He got hit in the shoulder and had some glass cuts, but he's doing fine. He's loving the attention from the nurses."

She smiled, then reached up and touched the tiny growing hairs on his face. "You look like hell."

"Thanks a lot." He laughed, then winced from the sharp pain in his side.

She rubbed her temple, remembering. "And how about you? How are you?"

Lance shrugged. "I got hit in the side. Actually it was more like a couple of notches. The bullet went in and came right out. Ten stitches here." He pointed to his front side. "And twelve stitches here."

"Thank you."

"For what?"

"For coming to my rescue. For saving my life." She lowered her head, letting tears fall. "Lance, we need . . ." she began.

"Don't," he eased down on the bed, then put his finger to her lips to quiet her. "I love you, Alex. The alternative of life without you is inconceivable," he whispered, then leaned in and kissed her softly.

"About the book, I need—"

"Alex," he interrupted, "I told you before, I don't care about the book. I just want to be with you for the rest of my life, if you'll have me."

"Did you just propose?"

"Yes."

The turmoil of the past several weeks surged inside her. A simple answer to a simple question was impossible. "Lance, we have so much to talk about." She noted his disappointed expression as silence surrounded them. "So, what happens now?"

He got up and smoothed the covers, then tucked her in. "What happens now is you lie back and get some more rest. I'll be back later to check on you."

"Lance," she called out as he moved to the door. "I love you." His smile warmed her heart.

Chapter Twenty-nine

The clinic still buzzed with excitement. Guests at the prestigious Van Ives Rehabilitation Center seldom received visitors or news from the outside. But this wasn't just any news to any guest by just any visitor.

"I'm very proud of you, Shawn. It took a lot of courage to do what you did." Shawn looked up at the stately man in front of him. The trace of a British accent was still prominent. He nodded at the compliment and continued packing his belongings.

"It's not going to be easy," the man cautioned as he walked over to the small window and looked out on the pristine lawn. "The next few months are crucial. But I know you can do it. Just take it one step at a time. And I'll be here for you whenever you need me."

Shawn picked up his leather bag and tossed it over his shoulder. "I'm ready."

The man laid his hand on Shawn's shoulder. "Shawn, I know I haven't been much of a father to you or to Lance for that matter. But I want to make things right. After hearing about him in the gun shoot-out and you, so close to overdosing . . ." He paused and shut his eyes in genuine anguish. "I guess what I'm trying to say is that I love you." Patrick nodded his head. He'd finally said it. After years of not knowing what to say or do with Shawn it was suddenly so clear. And all it took was for both sons to face death.

The realization of Patrick's words and the ardent expression on his face was poignant. Slowly Shawn turned to his father. He felt the words penetrate his heart, finally setting his spirit free. The man who stood before him was no longer a performing actor in the role of father. He was Dad.

Too filled with emotion, Shawn remained speechless. "I know I've got a lot of making up to do with you, son," Patrick continued. "And I'm sorry I wasn't the father you needed and deserved. Maybe if I had been"—Patrick waved his hand around the tiny hospital room—"none of this would have happened. I can't change the past. But I can start from this point forward and begin by showing you that I love you."

Shawn smiled tearfully as a euphoric sensation came over him. It was the most perfect high he'd ever experienced. Drugs, alcohol, nothing compared to those three little words. Patrick returned his smile, then in one swift motion took Shawn in his arms, welcoming him into his heart after long last.

"Come on, let's get out of here," he said, "we've got a lot of catching up to do."

Lance looked down at Alex as the elevator doors slid opened. "You still look a little peaked to me. Maybe you should stay in the hospital for another few nights for observation."

"Lance," Alex said sharply as he rolled her down the corridor, "you're driving me nuts. I've told you twenty times already, I feel fine. I just want to go home."

"But you've only been here overnight. I think you need to take more time to rest. You've been through a major trauma in the last twenty-four hours. And what about your ankle?"

Alex looked down at her bandaged foot. "My ankle was barely sprained. I'll be fine."

"But what about—"

"Lance Morgan, I'm warning you."

"Lillian." Lance turned, imploring for support. "Can't you do something with her?"

She chuckled. "I've never been able to before. No sense wasting my time now."

"Fine, I give up," Lance said, completely exasperated. "Are you sure you're ready for this?" he asked as they neared the hospital exit. He held his hand out to help her from the wheelchair.

"As ready as I'll ever be." She turned around to her mother and smiled. Lillian nodded and winked back. "Let's do it."

The onslaught began as soon as the glass doors slid apart. Questions rang out nonstop as Alex, Lance and Lillian walked over to the small podium. Lillian stepped forward, adjusted the microphone and smiled patiently at the mass of reporters. When they calmed down she began. "Thank you for coming. I have a prepared statement; afterward Mr. Morgan and Ms. Price have consented to answer a few of your questions."

She recited the standard statement thanking and acknowledging the paramedics, police force and hospital medical staff. She briefly mentioned the events of the previous evening without elaborating, because of legal ramifications. She concluded, for the benefit of the numerous fans, that both Alex and Lance were well and in obvious good spirits. Lance smiled and pulled Alex closer to his side.

Afterward, the couple stepped up to the microphone. Immediately a rapid succession of questions were fired at them. Lance raised his hand to silence the assembly. "Ladies, gentlemen," he pleaded, "one at a time, please."

"I need your help," the panicky voice whispered as the man remained in the shadows.

Recognizing the distressed voice, Burke smirked,

closed the door and continued walking to his desk. He tossed his briefcase in the chair and turned to face the intruder. "Help? You need my help." He began laughing. "I can't believe you actually showed up in this office," Burke sneered angrily. "Your stupid face is plastered all over the news. You've got every cop and every Morgan and Price fan after your sorry butt."

"Burke, I need help getting out of town," Jake insisted. "I can't hang around here all day. As you said, I've got people looking for me. I have a proposition for you and I think you'll be very interested to hear what I have to say."

Burke picked up and tossed his case on the desk, then sat down in the chair. "What the hell were you thinking? Shooting at Lance and Alexandra, are you nuts? Do you have any idea of the public relations nightmare you've caused this agency? The phone's been ringing off the hook. Threats and accusations of compliance, that's all I've been hearing. The cops have been here for days looking for you. Today's the first day I didn't see them in the lobby."

Jake stared blankly. "Do you want to hear this or not?"

"Not," Burke said. Jake moved toward the door to leave. Burke spun his chair around to face the side wall. "Wait, what do you want?"

Jake smiled. He knew he could count on Burke. After all, they were just alike, power-hungry businessmen. Jake reasoned that Burke was just upset because he didn't come up with the idea first. "I need some cash. I'm starting a talent agency in Mexico. I've already talked to some friends down there, they're hooking me up with an office setup. I'll stay there for a few years until this blows over." He talked as if he were just taking an extended vacation.

Burke threaded his fingers together as he thought to himself. His reputation in this town was at stake. The wrong move could end any future endeavors he had planned. There was one way to come out of all this on top. And Jake had just handed him the opportunity.

"How much do you need?"

"Ten or fifteen thousand to start with. I was thinking, we can be like partners. I'll handle everything down there and once the talent is ready, I'll send them up here to you. We'll split the commissions fifty-fifty. There are a lot of people just dying to get into the business. It's the perfect setup. I figure fifteen thousand ought to get things started nicely. I'll contact you later when I need more."

"All right," Burke agreed quickly. "But I don't have that much with me right now. Meet me back here tonight around eleven o'clock. I'll take care of you then."

Jake nodded and turned to leave. This was better than he hoped. He thought he might have to get nasty and persuade Burke to help him. But it turned out perfectly. He just needed to find Shawn. "By the way, I've been looking for Shawn Anderson, have any idea where he is?"

"Shawn is no longer represented by this agency."

"What?"

"He's sober and he's gone," Burke said as he picked up the phone and spun around so that the back of the chair faced Jake.

Scowling, Jake slipped out the door into the dark empty office. He was surprised by the news about Shawn. He hadn't seen him in a while and just assumed he was still drugged up. The news was very disappointing. He was counting on Shawn to get him over the border. Now he had to fall back on plan B, Linda.

The key wouldn't turn. "Damn her, she changed the lock," Jake mumbled angrily. He rang the doorbell and waited. He looked around the empty hall. Fortunately it was midday and no one was around. He rang the bell again, then rapped heavily on the wooden door. There was still no answer. Frustrated, he turned and stomped away. He needed a place to lay low until he was able to get in touch with Linda. A crooked smile eased across his thin lips. He had the perfect place in mind.

Huddled low, Jake sat in the dark theater watching another preview of Lance's upcoming movie. He'd been hiding out in the multiplex movie house all day. Going from one theater to another, he'd seen four different movies so far. After each film he attempted to call Linda. Finally she picked up. "Linda?"

"You've got some nerve calling me after what you put me through," she raged. "Have you any idea what I've been through the past few days? The police have been on my case and Lillian fired me. Luckily she didn't press charges for theft. Now what am I supposed to do for money? I have no job, no career, no nothing."

He smiled, then softened his voice into a charming coo. "You still have me and I would be honored if you'd consent to be my bride," he purred.

"You've got to be kidding."

"I don't joke about the way I feel about you. I want to marry you, I always did, you know that. Nothing's changed. I'm just pushing the time table up a little. I was going to ask you once we started our agency here but now, I've found that I want to marry you more than ever."

"The police are looking for you," she replied.

"I know. Don't worry about that. It's already taken care of."

"Really?"

"Yeah, don't you believe me?" he asked accusingly.

"What happened?"

"Nothing really, things got a little out of hand, that's all. But everything's fine now."

"That's not what my newspapers say."

"You need to stop reading that tabloid trash," he spat out bitterly.

"That's funny. You used to say that the tabloids were the only papers I should read. You said that they'd prepare me for future roles as a dramatic actress. Now you tell me to stop reading them? Is it because they say you tried to kill Lance Morgan and Alex Price?"

"Don't believe everything you read. It didn't happen like that. You should know me better, I'd never try to take somebody's life. Lance is blowing it all out of proportion to hype up his new movie and Alex is just using me to get publicity."

"So they're all lying."

"Of course," he said as the theater emptied out. Ushers standing by to clear the floors eyed him suspiciously, knowing that he'd been there all day. "Listen," he said in whispered tones, "I need to borrow your car. I have to meet Burke tonight. The police are still all over my place and they towed away my BMW." He turned his back to the curious young usher as Linda reluctantly agreed. "I won't be long at the office. Afterward I'll tell you all about what happened in New Jersey."

"Did you see Mason Turner?" she asked excitedly.

Jake chuckled. "Yeah, I saw Mason. But I'll tell you about that later. Get packed, we need to hit the road as soon as I get back tonight."

"And just where are we supposed to be going?"

"Mexico," he said brightly. "Remember all the fun we had the last time we were there? I thought it would be a great place to have our honeymoon. I have it all figured out. We'll drive down tonight and get married first thing in the morning. It'll be wonderful, you'll see, and while we're down there it might be a good idea to check out office space. I'm considering opening an agency there."

"What about money? We need money, don't we?"

"You are so smart. I'm glad you thought of that." He looked at his watch, it was getting late and he had to get back to the Burke's office. "I'll talk to Burke. He's always been hounding me about helping me start an agency. Besides, he owes me a few thousand dollars."

"I don't know," Linda waffled.

"It'll be fabulous. You and me together finally. You can even be our first client. There are so many jobs in Mexico that will be perfect for you."

Linda looked down at last week's papers scattered across her coffee table. "I don't know, Jake, this is happening too fast." The horoscope caught her eye . . . *A journey changes your life* . . .

"Fine, I just thought you wanted to be a serious actress. To be a star you have to always be ready," he warned as she read another line from the horoscope . . . *Be prepared to take chances* . . . *Your future will brighten shortly*. Right then she knew what she was going to do.

Confidently, Jake used his keys and strolled into Burke's outer office. The place was unusually empty and quiet. Burke must have gotten rid of everybody early. That way nobody would be around when he showed up. Jake smiled happily. Things were certainly beginning to look up for him again. He had a way to get to Mexico and in a few minutes he'd have the money. He rapped on the door, then walked right in.

Linda waited until late. Her bags were packed and she was ready to begin her new life as Mrs. Jake Marrows. She flipped through the newspapers she had impulsively bought earlier. She read the week's horoscopes. . . *Careful of loved ones* . . . *Disappointment is on the horizon* . . . *Caution, a change is coming soon* . . . none of them were particularly reassuring. So, she decided that Jake was right. You can't believe everything you read.

Looking forward to a bright future with Jake she began scribbling notes on the papers. Within minutes she'd autographed the page numerous times. *Mrs. Jake Marrows, Mrs. Linda Marrows, Mrs. Linda Beale-Marrows.* Satisfied with her new title she circled the signature with a huge heart. "Mrs. Jake Marrows," she proclaimed happily as she waited some more.

Charles walked into the room and stood scowling for a moment. He sighed heavily, then moved to lean against the mirrored wall opposite his friend. "Have you been in here all morning?" he asked after taking a sip of his orange juice.

"Yeah," Lance rasped breathlessly as he heaved the seventy-pound weight into the air, then slowly bent his muscular arms and lowered it to his chest. Sweat beaded on his forehead as he fought to remain focused and concentrate.

"Have you spoken to Alex today?"

"Not yet. I'm headed there later this evening. I talked to her last night. Victora and Ted called her from Italy. Apparently they're still wrapped in wedded bliss," he said, huffing in short puffs of air. Lance pushed the weight from his moistened T-shirt and gently placed it in the brackets. He sat up and Charles tossed him a towel.

Charles chuckled. "I can't believe those two actually remarried." He finished his juice while laughing harder. "But, now that I think about it, nothing those two do will ever surprise me."

Lance laughed along. "I know what you mean. I still can't believe they did all those stunts as the night prowler." They laughed harder, remembering the small room filled with high-tech equipment. "Looks like Victoria told the truth when she confessed to Alex when Jake was holding her."

"I thought she was just making it up when she left the message on Alex's machine. But, I guess not." The two looked at each other and shook their heads in amazement. Lance picked up a smaller weight and began curling it with his forearm.

Charles moved closer to Lance and lowered his voice. "Speaking of Jake, my friend on the force in L.A. just called."

Lance grimaced as he exhaled and released the weight. "Anything new with the search for Jake?"

"Plenty. It looks like Jake tried to break into Burke's office late last night. They suspect he was looking for money. The police cornered him and he made a run for it."

"That was stupid."

Charles nodded in agreement. "No one ever said Jake was the brightest person. Anyway, apparently he was bright enough, he slipped through and got away." Lance stopped wiping his face and looked at Charles and started laughing in disbelief. Charles threw up his hands. "Hey, talk to the L.A.P.D."

"So what happens now? Are they still looking for him?"

"Here's where the tale gets really strange. Early this morning Jake was spotted by the California Highway Patrol a few miles north of the Mexican border. There was a car chase, he eventually lost control. The car rolled over an embankment and burst into flames." Charles continued stoically. "He didn't survive." Lance remained silent and just shook his head in pity. "Yeah, I know," Charles added, "hell of a way to go out. Anyway, my friend isn't going to release the information until later this morning. The press will have the story sometime this afternoon."

Lance nodded his understanding as Charles turned to leave the room. "Charles." He stopped and turned. "Please thank your friend for me."

"You'd better get dressed, you've got some visitors waiting in the living room and a meeting with Mark Summers at ten o'clock."

Lance frowned and looked up at the wall clock. It was 7:30. "Who'd be out this early?"

Charles smiled, shaking his head. "I think you'd want to see this for yourself."

Interested, Lance picked up a fresh towel, draped it around his neck, then headed for the living room. As he approached he heard muffled voices. He peered into the room. "Dad?" he said, surprised. "What are you doing here?"

Patrick walked over to Lance and hugged him. "Good morning, son. I brought you a surprise." Patrick looked toward the drapes. For the first time Lance noticed the man standing by the window.

Chapter Thirty

"I don't think this is such a good idea anymore," Shawn said as he peered through the blackened privacy windows.

"Nonsense, it's a great idea. One of my better ones, I might venture to add," Patrick said joyfully.

The limousine drove up to the iron gate. Cameras flashed and reporters swarmed as the driver lowered his window and leaned his head out. He picked up the microphone and pulled it into the car. Speaking softly, he announced his employer's presence, then waited.

"What if she doesn't—" Shawn began. Before he was able to finish, the massive iron gates eased back into the stone housing. The chauffeur returned the microphone, then continued up the driveway.

"I've never met her, but I've always enjoyed her work. She seems like a class act."

"She is," Shawn acknowledged without hesitation. Then, nervously, he rubbed his moist palms over his pants. The warm friction steadied him. "I'm just not sure how she's going to react at seeing me after all these years. I haven't exactly been cordial to her."

"As you said, she's a class act."

Telephoto-lensed cameras clicked away and cellular phones buzzed endlessly when the horde of reporters spotted the limo's occupants for the first time.

Lillian opened the door, smiling warmly. "Good afternoon, gentlemen." She stepped aside. "Please come in."

The two men walked in and stepped down into the living room. Patrick turned, held out his hand and in his most extreme British accent returned her greeting. "Mrs. Turner-Price, a pleasure to finally meet you. I've heard so many wonderful things about you for such a long time, I feel as though we're already acquainted."

"How kind, but please, call me Lillian." They shook and Patrick held on to her hand.

"It would be my pleasure, Lillian." He bowed slightly and kissed the top of her hand. "If you will call me Patrick, naturally." She nodded. "I believe you already know my youngest son, Shawn Anderson."

"Yes, of course. Shawn, I understand you've put some things behind you. I'm very glad to hear it. How are you doing?"

He nodded his understanding. "Hello, Lillian." He smiled brightly. Lillian was never one to mince words. She was honest and direct, he always appreciated that. "Yes, I have put some things behind me and I'm doing pretty good."

She reached out to hug him warmly. "I'm glad to hear that." She smiled softly. "I just made a pitcher of lemonade. May I offer you a cold glass?"

"That would be delightful, Lillian. May I be of assistance?"

"Heavens no. Have a seat, I'll be right back." She turned to walk away. "By the way, Alex is on the telephone, she'll be in shortly."

"This is marvelous," Patrick proclaimed as he stepped up closer to the enormous tank. "I've never seen anything like it." Patrick gently ran his finger along the protruding bend of the enormous tank. The semicircular ballooning effect fascinated him. "I must find out where she had it made."

Shawn stepped up behind his father. "Alex always loved her fish."

"I still do." The soft-spoken voice prompted both men to spin around. Alex stepped into the room with Coal close behind. He hadn't left her side since he returned from the veterinarian. His bandaged rump did little to deter his movement.

Patrick stepped forward, meeting her halfway. He took her hand in his and kissed it. "My dear, your aquarium is truly extraordinary. The design, simply stunning. Your choice of coral, sponges, sea fans and mantles is remarkable."

"Thank you, Sir Anderson. I presume you are an aquarist?"

"We'll have none of that Sir Anderson drivel, the name is Patrick. I must say you are even more lovely than I've heard, Alexandra. I see my sons have their father's eye when it comes to exquisite women."

She blushed. "Thank you, Patrick." She turned her attention. "Hello, Shawn."

Shawn walked over. "Alex ... I ..." he began but had no idea what to say. She moved closer and embraced him and he reveled in her kindness. "I'm sorry," he mumbled in her ear, "for everything."

"I know." Tears welled up. "It's over and done with. That's all that matters." When the embrace ended they stood back from each other. Each feeling the beginning of a friendship rekindling.

By the time Lillian returned with the lemonade, Patrick and Alex were deep into a conversation regarding reef tank alga and photosynthesis. Shawn listened, amazed by Alex's extensive knowledge on the subject. She hadn't changed a bit. She was exactly as he remembered, vivacious and passionate. Whatever she did, she did to the best of her ability.

An hour later the pitcher was empty. Alex excused herself and went into the kitchen. "Alex," Shawn said as he peered around the swinging door.

She turned from the refrigerator with her hands filled with lemons and limes. "Yes?" she answered, dropping a lime on the tile floor. Shawn bent down to retrieve the rolling fruit. As he stood up he noticed Coal stealthily moving across the room toward him.

"He's beautiful," Shawn said, nodding to the approaching canine.

"His name is Coal," she said, smiling proudly. Coal circled Shawn, sniffing mistrustfully, then followed Alex to the counter and reclined beneath her feet.

Shawn placed the lime on the counter. "I need to apologize. There is no excuse for what I did. I just hope you can forgive me."

Alex looked at him curiously, set the fruit down and took out a long, thick cutting knife. "What are you talking about, Shawn?"

He took a deep breath, then lowered his head. "I was the one who told Jake Marrows how to find you." He looked up at her. "I'm sorry, I was high and drunk one night. We were talking. I started rambling about how you bought this place years ago. I guess he was paying attention. I never thought he'd do anything this dangerous. If anything, I thought he was going to talk to you about returning to the business."

"Don't worry about it, Shawn. It's over." She began cutting the lemons and limes in thin slices. "The whole episode will be forgotten in a few days."

"I also insinuated a relationship between you and me to my ex-wife. I understand she's suing you."

"Yes, she is."

"I'll make it right."

Still cutting, she nodded her head. "I'd appreciate that."

"One more thing," he added, "it's about you and Lance—"

Alex stopped cutting and looked up. "What about me and Lance?" she interrupted before he continued.

"I just wanted to say that I think you two make a great couple and that I'm happy for both of you."

She began cutting the fruit again. "Thank you."

"I spoke to him earlier. He told me he proposed."

"You spoke to Lance?" she asked in disbelief.

"Yeah, he seems really happy. Are you going to accept?"

"I have no idea what you're talking about."

"His proposal, are you going to say yes?"

"We still have a few things to work out."

"Alex, don't blame Lance for what happened, it's not his fault. It's mine. The whole thing was my idea, everything, from the very beginning."

Shawn sat down heavily on the stool, cupped his forehead in his hand, then leaned on the counter with his head lowered. "Jake wanted Lance with him when he opened his talent agency. But he knew Lance wouldn't sign. He also knew how desperate Lance was for the Mason Turner book rights. I suggested he make a deal with Lance." Shawn paused and looked up.

Slowly Alex slid onto the opposite stool. "Go on."

"I told Jake that if Mark and Lillian knew who Mason Turner was, then chances were you did too. That's when I told him when and how to find you. I knew you'd be back for Victoria's party. Jake told Lance. And that's how it started."

"You sent the roses, didn't you?" she asked.

He nodded. "Yes. I'll always be your greatest fan."

"Why, Shawn?"

Shawn looked away. "I was jealous. No one knew who this phantom writer was. I was afraid you and Mason Turner were together and Lillian and Mark were covering for you. I figured that Lance could break you two up; then I'd step in and rescue you from him. I'd tell you the whole story, minus my part of course, and you'd be so grateful . . ." Shawn looked into Alex's eyes. ". . . After all these years you were still the one person I wanted to be with. You were the only person who really understood me."

Alex reached over and took his hand. "Why are you telling me all this now?"

Shawn smiled his boyish grin. "Because I'm clean and sober for the first time in ten years." He squeezed her hand. "I was wrong to manipulate people. Because of me, you and Lance were nearly killed. I'll never forgive myself for that."

"I'm glad you told me, thank you."

"No, thank you, Alex. Because of you I went into rehab and I'm getting my life back together."

"Me?" She dropped the sliced lemons and limes into the glass pitcher.

"You."

"I don't think so. I haven't seen you in years." Alex added two scoops of sugar and ice-cold water. She motioned for Shawn to add the ice.

"You told me to do it for me, so I did." He twisted the tray, sending the cubes into the cold liquid.

She smiled as she stirred the drink. "I'm truly happy for you and I wish you the best."

They smiled. "So, are you going to answer my question? Are you going to accept?"

Alex looked to the ceiling, then back down at Shawn, refusing to answer. "I see you haven't changed much, you're still as persistent as ever."

"Nor have you. You're still as evasive as ever. Fortunately, I can still read you like a book." He smiled knowingly. "I guess I'd better start looking around for a wedding gift."

"Tell me about your new television series. I hear it's a medical drama and it's already gotten the networks drooling."

Shawn smiled at Alex's change of subject. "Actually it's not half bad. The preseason reviews have been very promising."

"Trying to take my girl, little brother?" Alex and Shawn turned around. Lance stood holding the door open.

"I don't think I could," he said honestly, "even if I

wanted to." The brothers shook hands. Then Lance strolled over to Alex as Shawn slipped out of the kitchen.

Lance held Alex firmly. "You're early," she mumbled as she snuggled closer.

"I know. I have some news about Jake." Alex pulled back to see his face. "There was a car chase in L.A. Jake was killed when his car went out of control."

Alex's expression saddened as she lowered her head. Lance tipped her chin upward and ran his fingers down her slender neck until he reached the diamond and ruby pendant. He fingered the sparkling necklace. "I love you, Alex."

She smiled warmly. "I love you, too." Instinctively she snaked her arms around his waist. "How's your side?" She looked up at him. Her expression was angelic.

"Much better." He kissed her passionately, then kissed her forehead, her cheek, her neck and her shoulders. "Now that I'm here with you." Alex beamed inside. She couldn't be happier. "I had an appointment with Mark earlier," Lance began. "I made a counteroffer to the *Pilgrimage to Heaven* contract." Alex pulled back to look at Lance as he continued, "I'd like Mason Turner and Lance Morgan to produce the film together." He smiled down at her.

"I think that could be arranged," she said with delight.

"Good, I'm looking forward to working very closely with Mason Turner in the future. I think we'd make an incredible team." He began gently kissing her neck and shoulders again.

Alex moaned lovingly. "Lance, about what you asked me earlier . . ."

He stopped kissing her. "Take as much time as you need, Alex, I'll wait." He hugged her close to his body.

"Yes," she whispered quietly. He leaned back far enough to see her face; then he looked into her eyes hopefully. "Yes, Lance, I want to be with you for the rest of my life, if you still want me."

Lance laughed joyously at the absurdity of her remark. He nodded, she nodded, he smiled, she smiled. Then, together they laughed at nothing in particular. Coal lifted his head from his short nap. He tilted it curiously from side to side, then lay back down as the couple walked hand in hand into the next room.

Dear Reader,

I hope you enjoyed reading the exciting romance of Alex Price and Lance Morgan. They are a great couple and I had a fabulous time writing about them. The glamorous, privileged, and often-times fishbowl world of Hollywood stardom has always fascinated me. I would love to hear what you thought about this novel. Please feel free to contact me at my web site http://www.celesteonorfleet.com. Or, if you would like a **Since Forever** bookmark, other promotional material, and to be placed on my mailing list send a #10 SASE to: Celeste O. Norfleet, P. O. Box 7346, Woodbridge, VA 22195-7346.

I'd like to take this opportunity to thank all of you for your continued support and well wishes. It's truly heartening to open mail and E-mail and read your wonderfully touching remarks. Thanks to you, my previous novels, **Priceless Gift** and **A Christmas Wish** have been extremely well received and I am genuinely touched by your encouragement.

With so many distractions, I consider it an honor to write these stories and hopefully bring a few moments of entertainment to your busy days. With this in mind, I look forward to bringing you my next exciting romance entitled, **One Sure Thing**. For those of who repeatedly asked for a sequel to the **Priceless Gift** story, here it is. It begins almost exactly where **Priceless Gift** ends. Talk about a continuation. **One Sure Thing** is due to be released in September 2003.

My most sincere best wishes,
Celeste O. Norfleet

ABOUT THE AUTHOR

Celeste O. Norfleet, born and raised in Philadelphia, Pennsylvania, is a graduate of Moore College of Art & Design, with a B.F.A in Fashion Illustration. She has worked as an Art Director for several advertising agencies and now does freelance design for area businesses.

An avid reader and writer, Celeste has sold several more novels to BET/Books. She is an active member of Washington Romance Writers and Romance Writers of America, and lives in Virginia with her husband and two children. She is blessed to have the endless support of caring family and friends.